ORBITAL
CLOUD

TAIYO FUJII

ORBITAL CLOUD

TAIYO FUJII

WITHDRAWN

TRANSLATED BY
TIMOTHY SILVER

HAIKA
SORU

SAN FRANCISCO

Orbital Cloud
© 2014 Taiyo Fujii
Originally published in Japan by Hayakawa Publishing, Inc.

English translation © 2017 VIZ Media, LLC
All rights reserved.

Cover and interior design by Sam Elzway

HAIKASORU
Published by VIZ Media, LLC
P.O. Box 77010
San Francisco, CA 94107

www.haikasoru.com

Library of Congress Cataloging-in-Publication Data

Names: Fujii, Taiyo, 1971- author. | Silver, Timothy, translator.
Title: Orbital cloud / Taiyo Fujii ; translated by Timothy Silver.
Other titles: Obitaru kuraudo. English
Description: San Francisco : Haikasoru, 2017.
Identifiers: LCCN 2016052856 | ISBN 9781421592138 (paperback)
Subjects: LCSH: Science fiction. | BISAC: FICTION / Science Fiction /
  General. | FICTION / Technological. | FICTION / Science Fiction / High
  Tech.
Classification: LCC PL870.J54 O7313 2017 | DDC 895.63/6--dc23
LC record available at https://lccn.loc.gov/2016052856

Printed in the U.S.A.
First printing, March 2017

CHARACTERS

Kazumi Kimura: Freelance web designer.
Akari Numata: Freelance IT engineer.

Daiki Kurosaki: JAXA official.
Makoto Sekiguchi: JAXA official.

Jamshed Jahanshah:
Professor of astronautical engineering
at Tehran Institute of Technology.
Alef Kadiba:
Jamshed's friend. Assistant professor of law
at Tehran Institute of Technology.

Ageha Shiraishi: Ex-JAXA official.
Chance Park: Contractor for North Korea.

Ronnie Smark: Investor. Head of Project Wyvern.
Judy Smark: Journalist. Ronnie's daughter.

Ozzy Cunningham: Amateur space photographer.
Friday: Ozzy's assistant.

Claude Lintz:
Chief of Orbital Surveillance at NORAD. Colonel.
Sylvester Fernandez:
Member of Orbital Surveillance team at NORAD. Major.
Daryl Freeman:
Member of Orbital Surveillance team at NORAD. Staff sergeant.
Jasmine Harrison: Aide to Colonel Lintz. Captain.

Chris Ferguson: CIA official.
Bruce Carpenter: CIA official.

Ricky McGillis: US Air Force pilot. Captain.
Madu Abbot: US Air Force pilot. Second lieutenant.

TABLE OF CONTENTS

PROLOGUE

August 15, 2015

A Suburb of Tehran

A red van turned off the highway into a scrubby, rock-strewn field and came to a stop. The white "〒" symbol of Japan's postal service visible on the door told of the repurposed vehicle's origin. Its faded frame was riddled with patches of rust and large holes sealed with silver duct tape.

The figure in the driver's seat coughed lightly several times as a cloud of sand swirled in through the crack between the window and the door. His face was hidden behind sunglasses and a baseball cap was pulled low over his eyes, but his smooth cheeks and thin mustache revealed that he was not yet thirty years old.

The young man pulled the scarf wrapped around his neck up to his nose, turned on the military radio in the driver's seat, and held the receiver to his ear. After listening intently for a while, he tossed the receiver aside and began to murmur in a silly voice: "*As-salamu alay-kum*. Peace be upon you, my brethren. It is now time for the weather report. The detestable Anjian unit is heading west from Tehran. All those living in its path, please be mindful of twenty-millimeter cannons and rockets overhead." From beneath his scarf, the young man gave out a muffled laugh.

He had been listening to an unofficial program broadcast by an antigovernmental organization. Ever since the government had announced the date of the presidential election, it had been using the Anjian drones it had just purchased from China to eliminate suspected rebel groups. Their so-called triumphs in this campaign were reported almost daily, but the rumors that a certain percentage of those who lost their lives were regular people with no connection to the movement had not escaped the young man's ears.

The young man knew just how he would appear through the shoddy lens of a drone's camera, out here in the middle of this desolate field thirty miles west of Tehran, manipulating an all-too-suspicious device that emitted radio waves. The drone's operator, sitting in some underground bunker in the city with bloodshot eyes eager for more "triumphs," would surely fire a rocket at him without hesitation.

"I hope I've got the right timing," the young man said, shifting the scarf he had just raised back down to the base of his neck and stroking his mustache. There was no way they'd be able to recognize his face through a drone's camera, but they would be able to tell if he was trying to hide it. Taking off his glasses, he directed his dark-brown eyes to the smog drifting over the streets of Tehran and then to the cloudless blue sky spread out above it. He saw no glittering dots there and heard no engine sounds approaching. Hardly enough information to cure his uneasiness. "Inshallah. Come on. Tell me they won't be coming. Just for one hour."

The young man stepped slowly out of the van and went straight around to the rear. Flinging open the trunk, he took out a large, rolled-up canvas tarp and dropped it onto the ground. He grimaced as a puff of sand danced up into his face and pulled the scarf he had just lowered back up to his nose. The young man then began to unroll the tarp behind the van but immediately found a small piece of wood caught inside and plucked it out. It was the twig of an olive tree.

"Oh, Alef . . . How could you use this for the harvest?" Spreading the tarp out on the ground, the young man slumped his shoulders in disappointment when he saw the appalling state it was in. Twigs and leaves were scattered all over its five-square-meter surface, and it was smeared with the crushed remains of olives. He had lent the tarp to his friend, Alef Kadiba, whose father owned a wealthy estate, after Alef had said he was going for a picnic. But the young man had never suspected for a moment that he was borrowing it to collect olives.

The young man knelt and began to pick away the mess bit by bit. Every time he moved, sweat dripped off him, making spots on the tarp that immediately evaporated under the searing sunlight and dry wind. Working in silence, he cast aside all the scraps he removed. "If my balloon pops because of this, you'll be paying me back, Alef."

When he had finished cleaning up, the young man took a bag of lime out of the trunk and sprinkled the white powder on top of the tarp with a shovel before evening it all out with his hands. This was to prevent the balloon from sticking to the tarp. His movements became increasingly fluid as he continued this task, the lime that misted upwards turning his arms and clothing all white.

Next, he carefully unfolded a big plastic sheet atop the tarp. This was a balloon designed to carry equipment for high-altitude weather observation. A tube extending from the trunk of the van was attached to the balloon's base. The young man now sprinkled lime over the unfolded balloon as well.

"Please! Let there be no holes!" Putting together his sweaty, lime-dusted hands, he bowed his head to the heavens and raised his voice in prayer. What God would think of the challenge to his supremacy this experiment represented, he had no idea, but he had nothing to lose by praying. He then opened the valve of the helium tank laid on its side in the trunk, and first the tube, then the balloon, began to wriggle. Lime slid off the surface of the balloon. The young man bent down and cocked his ear toward the balloon, listening for any major leaks. Then, standing up straight again, he took out a scratched-up smartphone from a pocket in his cargo pants, held down the home button for a few seconds, and set it by voice with the command, "Tell me when twenty minutes has passed."

"The alarm has been set for twenty minutes," his phone replied in excellent Persian.

"Now if I could just make calls with this . . ." The young man had acquired this smartphone, usually reserved for foreign business-men, through his friend Alef, but his contract only allowed him to use it for data transfer, and even that had to be with government-approved service providers. He supposed he should feel grateful that he at least had permission to use a server that processed voice input.

Reaching deep into the trunk, he dragged out a tool kit and a boom box. "All right. You better keep working for me today," he said. "I paid three hundred whole euros for you."

Inside the tool kit was a roll of wire and two Tupperware con-tainers. "Test device #42" was written on the lid of the tool kit in permanent marker. The young man carefully removed the containers and wire and placed them beside the balloon, which was beginning to expand. He then immediately began to untangle the wire, both ends of which were threaded through jagged holes that he had opened himself in the containers.

Picking up one of the containers, the young man opened the lid. Inside a vinyl chloride case, a homemade electronic circuit had been taped with red and blue wires connected point to point. With a power supply, radio, and gyro sensor inside, this was the controller. Installed in the other container was an electron gun, which he had scrounged up the last of his money to purchase. He inserted some AA batteries into one side of the circuit and turned on the boom box, which had been tuned to a specific frequency in advance. It began to emit a clear electronic beeping sound. "It works," he muttered, as he sat on the edge of the trunk and took a bag of rolling tobacco from his thigh pocket.

"I guess for number 43 I could try attaching a switch . . ." He began to consider the design of his next experiment while rolling a pinch of tobacco in crinkled paper. He had spent the entire research budget that allowed him to work on his own projects months ago. To conduct this launch, he had saved up by cutting down on his expenses, even food. If he had had the option, he would have preferred to use a rubber balloon like the ones people in developed countries used, not this heavy plastic one that was a nuisance to fold up. With a lightweight rubber balloon, he would have been able to carry the experimental craft up to an altitude of twenty-five, no, thirty miles.

The young man turned over his smartphone, still displaying the alarm countdown, and stroked the diamond-cut edge of its case. Apparently, one hundred million of these smartphone cases had been produced, and each one had been chiseled from a solid lump of aluminum with a laser. The fact that such a design not easily suited to mass production had been realized showed just how much the engineers involved were respected. If only he lived in a country that had technology like this, someone like him who worked exclusively on spacecraft propulsion systems would be sure to find investors. That wasn't going to happen in this country, though. To get funding here, he had to conduct applied experiments that were practical enough for his advisor, Professor Hamed, to understand. A surveillance satellite?

Nope. That would be impossible. With its current design, his craft couldn't carry a camera. And he had no access to atomic clock units like those used in GPS satellites. What else was there? What could you do with a small satellite able to move freely in orbit and—

The smartphone vibrated in his hand, and the alarm went off. He looked up. The balloon had expanded to about twice the size of his van and was swaying in the wind. At the moment, it appeared as though it wasn't even filled halfway with helium, but it would swell almost to the point of bursting in the low pressure of the skies. There were no holes in it. "All right," he said. "You were lucky this time, Alef."

The young man reached out to the tank in the trunk and closed the valve. "Verification test launch number 42. Counting down: ten, nine, eight . . ."

As he counted down, the young man took one of the containers he'd placed on the tarp and hung it from the base of the balloon. He then unrolled its wire all across the surface of the tarp and put the sole of his shoe down on the other container. "Four, three, two—"

When he removed the tube from the base of the balloon, it wavered once like a bubble and then floated up into the sky. The attached wire began to reel out rapidly from the container.

"One—"

The wire was now stretched taut from underneath the man's foot to the base of the balloon twenty yards above. From beneath the sole of his shoe he could feel the force of the container trying to rise into the air. The balloon, tethered by the wire, swayed like a jellyfish.

"Zero. Release."

The young man lifted his foot. The container he had been holding to the ground leaped up with suppressed energy and flew past his face. Floating now in the clear blue sky, the balloon made one last wild jiggle before shooting up even higher.

The pitch of the beep from the boom box in the backseat changed. After checking that his cassette had been rewound, he pressed down the record button. Then he opened his hands wide and used his fingers to count the number of beeps, which had been encoded into 8 bits.

"Altitude one hundred . . . one hundred and fifty-eight meters. Acceleration three meters per second. This launch is a success!"

The balloon was sucked into the sky. One hour later, it reached an altitude of twenty miles. Looking upwards from its location, the sky would likely be dark even during the day, and the warped outline of the Earth wrapped in a thin, blue-hazed layer of atmosphere would be visible. There the balloon popped and dropped the two containers back to the ground.

This was where the experiment began. The timer went off, and the electron gun in the lower Tupperware began to fire electrons into the space. When the current passed through the wire, it bent slightly under the influence of geomagnetism and shifted the two containers off course from freefall a very small distance, approximately two hundred meters over the whole fall. The effect was very slight. Even so, this marked a major advance for the young man's research, providing evidence that a revolutionary propulsion system no one else had ever put into practice, one that could move objects in orbit without the use of propellants, was actually in action.

The man's limply hanging fingers moved in time to the beeps he was recording. His only equipment for documenting the experiment was a cassette tape, and even those were difficult to acquire of late. His only equipment for analyzing it was his brain and fingers decoding the 8-bit signal, pencil and paper, and a scientific calculator he had purchased with a loan from his relatives. He had no friends to help him with this painstaking, hopeless work. If he had just had a bit of money, he could have increased the altitude of the balloon by another twelve miles, run some computer simulations. Perhaps he might have upgraded the precision of his experimental devices too.

The young man lay down in the shadow cast by the raised door of the trunk. "What I wouldn't give to go to America," he mused, gazing up at the sky.

Here he was, spending the earnings of his part-time job, making his gear himself, all to take these tiny hops toward the cosmos. Little did he know that in a few short years his research would shake the whole world.

PART ONE
Safir 3 R/B

1 Erratic Debris

Fri, 11 Dec 2020, 08:30 +0900 (2020-12-10T23:30 GMT)
Fool's Launchpad, Shibuya

A length of sewing thread with one end tied off in a two-centimeter loop, and an eraser.

Kazumi Kimura fished the two objects out of his pencil case and placed them on his desk before brushing his bangs back from his forehead. Beside the thread and eraser, a laptop sat open, its screen covered with numeric data.

It was 8:30 in the morning. The sun shone horizontally through the blinds into Fool's Launchpad, a shared office space on the fourteenth floor of a building connected to Shibuya Station, casting stripes of shadow on the desks by the windows.

Kazumi swept his gaze across the chilly, deserted office. He was first in again today. After a brief internal debate, he removed his quilted down vest and hung it over the back of his chair. His "coworkers" would start arriving in about half an hour, and the heating had probably already come on. Better to begin *the ritual* while he had the chance.

After tying the loose end of the sewing thread around the eraser, he slipped the loop at the other end over his right index finger. Then, rolling back his cuff and straightening his arm, he let the eraser hang there suspended by the thread, swinging gently like a pendulum.

"Hmm, 9.8 meters per second squared." Kazumi recited his first incantation: the gravitational acceleration of a free-falling object. With a flick of his wrist, he set the eraser swinging to the right. It arced smoothly through the air, circling Kazumi's index finger counter-clockwise at the end of its thread.

Spinning the eraser faster and faster, Kazumi used a finger on his left hand to keep his place on the laptop's screen.

"SAFIR 3's rocket body should be . . ."

Kazumi closed his eyes, feeling the weight of the spinning eraser as he sorted through the information he had in his head. SAFIR 3 had been launched from northern Iran's Imam Khomeini Space Center on December 1, ten days ago. The first-stage rocket booster that had gotten it off the ground had fallen back into the ocean that same day. Its third-stage apogee motor had successfully completed the launch's primary mission of inserting two satellites into orbit at 500 km before settling into orbit itself at the same altitude. It would most likely stay there for a few decades, circling the Earth as space debris. What interested Kazumi was the second stage: the rocket body that had allowed SAFIR 3 to climb into an initial parking orbit 250 km up. US Strategic Command had named it "SAFIR 3 R/B."

When would *it* fall back to Earth?

Satellites, rocket shells, and other debris orbiting lower than 500 km slowly but surely lost velocity and altitude as they collided with atmospheric particles, scarce but not absent at those heights. Once a piece of debris dropped below 170 km or so, things started to change. Atmospheric molecules bounced off the object, now moving at eight kilometers a second, which began to glow with the energy of the collisions. It also developed a tail, albeit one too faint to be seen from the Earth's surface.

Under 80 km, the atmosphere became so dense with molecules attracted by the gravity of the Earth that it became like a thick soup enveloping the debris. No longer able to bounce freely off the moving object, molecules were pressed against each other. This compression resulted in temperatures of thousands of degrees Celsius, which in turn melted the front of the object and caused a long tail of plasma to flare up behind it.

The birth of a shooting star.

Kazumi's web service, Meteor News, was in the business of predicting the appearance of shooting stars for its subscribers. And SAFIR 3 was a much-anticipated bit of debris, set to make its glittering debut in the sky that very weekend.

Unlike satellite fragments or similar miscellaneous debris, the several-meters-long metal cylinder of a rocket body still contained some liquid fuel and was highly likely to turn into a brilliantly shining kind of shooting star called a "fireball." In fact, rocket bodies were often long and fragile enough to break in half, creating twin shooting stars. If Meteor News could predict when and where a shooting star like that would fall, its reputation among space enthusiasts and photographers interested in celestial bodies would receive a significant boost. In fact, this might be the best chance they ever got to increase their paid subscriber count, which was currently languishing in the low two hundreds.

Kazumi looked down at the laptop's screen. It was filled with two-line elements, or "TLEs," a data format for describing objects in orbit that packed orbital angle, motion, and other useful information into just two lines of text.

These TLEs were only a couple of hours old, fresh from USSTRATCOM. Every day, TLEs for thousands of objects orbiting the Earth were updated by the Joint Space Operations Center run by the Joint Functional Component Command for Space within STRATCOM. The primary intended beneficiaries were companies operating communications and other satellites, but the information was a treasure trove for space fans too. They used it to identify the lines of light they saw arc across the sky, to check when the ISS would be visible overhead, to plot satellites on maps, and more. Kazumi used it to forecast shooting stars at Meteor News.

"Parked at 250 km. How far has it slipped, I wonder?"

Kazumi opened the TLE from yesterday and placed his left index finger against the eighth field of its second line: Mean motion, 16.1. That was fast enough to go around the Earth just over sixteen times in a day. A higher mean motion generally meant a lower orbit. The ISS at its 420 km altitude had a mean motion of 15.5, while the Chinese space station Tiangong-2 at 350 km had a mean motion of 15.7. You could estimate an object's altitude fairly well by comparing its mean motion to representative examples like this. This sort of calculation was second nature to Kazumi, who spent every day staring at TLEs for orbital debris.

Kazumi opened the TLE for today.

"Huh? 15.8 . . . ?"

A mean motion of 15.8 implied an altitude over 300 km—which would mean that the object's altitude had increased.

"Must be some kind of mistake," Kazumi muttered. Still swinging the eraser with his right hand, he used his left to place the two TLEs side by side so that he could compare their other orbital elements.

"Eccentricity holding stable near zero. Yesterday's inclination eighty-five degrees . . ."

Kazumi held his right arm out horizontally in front of him, eraser still orbiting his finger, then raised it half a fist higher. He had memorized some of the angles different parts of his body made. At the end of an outstretched arm, his fist covered around ten degrees of arc. His thumb at the same distance was about two degrees across.

Kazumi imagined a sphere with a 6,400-kilometer radius—Earth—superimposed over his right finger. The eraser became the duralumin rocket body that was SAFIR 3's second stage. The thread connecting the two was gravity.

"December, so the sun's declination is minus twenty degrees or so . . ."

He spun the Earth superimposed over his finger away from himself. The sun was about two kilometers behind him, near Komaba-todaimae Station, two stops from Shibuya. As he added the alternation of day and night to the Earth in his mind's eye, Kazumi followed the same orbit around it as the one given for SAFIR 3 by the TLEs. He looked down and saw the surface of the planet passing by 300 km beneath his feet.

He was in.

He soared north past the reddish-brown expanse of Australia and saw the Hawaiian Islands appear up ahead. This was yesterday's inclination. Kazumi tried to shift his orbit exactly ten degrees, to match the TLE from today. The pull against his index finger was surprisingly strong. This was SAFIR 3's moment.

Strange. Had SAFIR 3 really made an orbital adjustment requiring this much power? And if so—

"The last big deal of the year has arrived!"

The voice came from diagonally in front of him, bringing Kazumi back to his surroundings. The Earth floating at his fingertip vanished. The whitewashed duralumin tube that was SAFIR 3's second stage was just an eraser once more.

Ten or so of Kazumi's "coworkers" were gathered at the round table in the middle of his working space. Watanabe, the most senior among them, held court at the center of the group, holding up a tablet displaying an article on a news website.

The row for TOKYO on the world clock hanging on the wall had just hit 9:30. This was when the morning information exchange, known as the "AM exchange" or "AMX" for short, began. The AMX was an institution at Fool's Launchpad, designed to help prevent chronically unpunctual freelancers from drifting away from regular working rhythms.

"Let's go with this for today's AMX," Watanabe said, showing his tablet to the assembled attendees. "A pure software service, sold for forty billion. That's a first. Let me open up the VisGen release and Pat's blog and see what we can learn from them."

VisGen had been founded by Pat Feuer, an IT entrepreneur who'd only just turned twenty. That made him eight years younger than Kazumi and twelve younger than Watanabe. Watanabe called him by his first name in an attempt to communicate to the other Fool's Launchpad tenants—Watanabe preferred to call them "coworkers"— that such success was attainable even for someone in their generation.

"First, let's have a big round of applause. Pat, congratulations on your exit!"

There weren't many sitting at the table, but they were passionate and applauded vigorously. Even Kazumi lightly tapped the fist in which he held the eraser against his left hand. In the wake of the touch screen revolution, inaugurated by the smartphone and then the tablet, attracting as much capital as Pat had for software alone wasn't easy. A sale like this was the ideal exit for VisGen.

A hand went up at the table. It was Hamada, who'd just joined Fool's Launchpad that week.

"Forty billion dollars—that's four hundred *oku* yen, right?"

"Hamada-kun," said the woman sitting next to him, using a slightly patronizing form of address. She was the only person at the table wearing a suit. "You've got to stop converting everything to yen in Japanese numbers. You won't even get a start-up off the ground if you don't get used to thinking in dollars."

This was Mary, the resident English expert. She was Japanese—her real name was Hitomi or something similar, as Kazumi recalled—but she used an English name for business like they did in Singapore or Taiwan.

"Come on, Mary. That's a bit harsh," said Watanabe, noticing Hamada's wounded expression. "You really should get used to thousands and billions though, Hamada," he added. "If you ever end up working on a job where these figures come up a lot, just ask someone for help. Like this. Hey, Kazumi! What's $40 billion in yen?"

Kazumi raised his hand to acknowledge the address. "Forty billion dollars at today's rates? Four point five *cho* yen."

The table nodded in approval. Kazumi forced a smile, then turned back to his laptop. Mental arithmetic was no big deal. He just happened to run a site that took payment in foreign currencies and occasionally made orbital calculations with figures representing distances of hundreds of kilometers but written out to the millimeter.

"Cheers," Watanabe said, and turned back to the group. "You see? If you need help, just ask for it. That's how VisGen got so big. Oh, that reminds me—when I was at my publisher's yesterday about Pocket Folder, I presented my one-click purchase proposal, and . . ."

Watanabe had entered his Sales Tales phase. This was his way of reminding the other tenants of Fool's Launchpad how important it was to develop services beyond straight contract work.

Watanabe's insistence on always keeping your eyes on the prize could be tiresome, but Kazumi liked the atmosphere here. He doubted he could maintain the motivation to keep Meteor News going if he switched to an office full of unambitious web designers for hire, even if the rent were cheaper there. Being able to work alongside people who wanted something more was one of the reasons he was willing to pay the ¥40,000 a month that Fool's Launchpad charged, despite the impact on his budget.

A mass of orange moved at the corner of his vision. "Good morning, Kimura-san," it said.

A gigantic MacBook slid onto the desk opposite him. Here was the other reason he was at Fool's Launchpad: Akari Numata, whose trademark was a fluorescent orange Afro more than twice the size of her head.

Akari unloaded an assortment of devices and cable bundles, piling them up on either side of her MacBook. Three smartphones, two tablets, one sixteen-port USB hub, a portable Wi-Fi hotspot, and a large mobile battery. It must have weighed twenty pounds or more altogether.

One thing Kazumi hadn't seen before was the two-inch-square circuit board wrapped in clear film. Noticing that it had both a USB and an Ethernet port, he craned his neck to get a closer look, but Akari's voice interrupted him before he could.

"Is today's news ready?" she asked.

"Not yet, sorry," Kazumi replied. "I was planning to write about SAFIR 3, but something's off about the data."

"The top story's not the meteor shower? The pageviews for that are going crazy."

"Yeah, but the people coming for that one aren't going to become paying subscribers."

Kazumi had written a blog post about the current Geminid meteor shower containing a brief overview of the Geminids and some observational data. The post had become much more popular than he'd expected after a web-development site praised the intricate 3-D graphics of the Earth he'd included, bringing a flood of engineers to Meteor News in addition to their usual customers.

"Oh," said Akari. "Well, I'll increase the server count anyway. Otherwise, the subscriber pages will slow down every time visitor numbers double. Is it okay if I just set it to add servers automatically as the pageviews go up? I could do it manually, but then there'd be long times when the servers would just be idling."

"Adding servers automatically sounds a bit risky to me," said Kazumi.

Meteor News was hosted on virtual server space rented from a cloud service run by the world's biggest retail site. The service let you specify how many servers to use and for how long, down to the second, but the servers weren't free. Renting a middle-spec server cost ¥150 per night, so if a hundred were added due to an unexpected wave of visitors, the bill could go up ¥15,000 overnight. That would hurt.

"Trust me, it beats managing the servers manually," said Akari. "How about if I set up the dashboard so you can cap the number of servers from there? It's all ready to go, just waiting for deployment."

Kazumi knew she was right. He should be spending his time on writing, trying to draw in more subscribers, not micromanaging the server count week after week. And if they could just get up to a thousand subscribers or so, he'd be able to devote half of each week to the site.

"All right," he said at last. "Go for it."

"Thanks," Akari said. She turned her attention to her MacBook and began tapping rhythmically away at the keyboard. Having an engineer as skilled as her on his side—and for so little that she practically worked for free—gave Kazumi the time he needed to write his news posts. If giving her free rein was what it took to keep her motivated, it wouldn't do any harm.

With a final flourish from Akari, the sound of the keyboard stopped. "Deployment complete," she said.

"Already?"

"Just let me test it. Ten thousand pageviews per second on the 3-D view. You watch the analytics."

Kazumi scrambled to open his view. Ten thousand pageviews per second? That was worse than a denial-of-service attack. His server setup couldn't handle ten thousand requests per second for plain HTML, let alone 3-D image data.

"Ready?" said Akari. "Here we go."

Without waiting for Kazumi to nod, Akari began typing furiously again. As Kazumi watched, the figure "10,000" appeared on the real-time hit counter and a new bar appeared at the edge of the hit graph, so much larger than the others that the graph was forced to rescale. The previous rises and falls of a dozen pageviews here, a dozen there were too small to see at the new scale. Page requests were flooding in from Seattle, Singapore, Hong Kong, Brazil.

"Ten seconds, one hundred thousand pageviews in total," said Akari. "All distributed among the servers so only the 3-D pages should have slowed down."

Just as Akari said, the real-time hit count held steady at 13,400.

Kazumi opened Meteor News, dreading the worst, but the 3-D-free top page loaded just as smoothly as ever.

"The virtual server count went up by 120 to deal with the activity, just as planned," Akari continued. "Okay, I'll pull the plug now. Cost for this test . . . let me see, ¥122. Can I send you the bill?"

Kazumi was speechless for a moment. "Sure," he said at last. "Of course. But, wow, that's amazing. I've never seen the pageviews move like that before."

Thanks to Akari, the virtual server control panel now included round-robin and test functionality. Which was ridiculous—things like that were used by services with user counts in the millions, like VisGen. A site like Meteor News, which saw a few thousand hits per day at most, didn't need that sort of power, and neither did the ones run by the web designers that Akari did most of her day-to-day contracting for.

"By the way, aren't you going to post about this?" Akari said, holding up one of her tablets. "The launch is coming up soon."

The tablet displayed a news story about what promised to be not only the last but also the biggest space event of the year: Ronnie Smark's Wyvern Orbital Hotel.

Smark was a legend in the IT industry. In the late nineties, he'd made his fortune founding a service for transferring money over the Internet, allowing anyone to set up shop online. Today he was at the cutting edge of space development. Having started Project Wyvern with the goal of making consumer space tourism a reality, he'd developed one rocket after another in his Loki series, and now even did contract work for NASA. The International Space Station, whose rising maintenance costs had gradually eroded the international assistance it had once enjoyed, already received 20 percent of its supplies via the Loki 8 rocket and Wyvern spacecraft, both Ronnie's.

Loki 9 was set to launch from Cape Canaveral this week with both Ronnie and his journalist daughter Judy on board. The two of them would then spend a week in space, staying at an orbital hotel that Wyvern was to spit out, and then transfer to the ISS. It would be the most sensational twenty-day vacation in history.

"Loki 9's planned orbit is available on the Wyvern site," Kazumi said. "But maybe I'll do a write-up."

"You should," said Akari. "Some readers might be interested if you have any kind of scoop on it, even if it's mostly just a bunch of numbers. But enough about that—when will the news going out today be finished?"

"I'll start work on it this evening. Some last-minute design work came in. I could use some help, actually. "

"Sounds like you're pretty busy." Akari closed her MacBook instantly, signaling her utter lack of interest in web design work. She didn't seem to have much interest in space either, but for some reason she worked hard to make Meteor News look good.

It had been Akari's help that had taken Meteor News from an unremarkable email magazine to a rich online service accessible from PCs, tablets, smartphones, and even those smart glasses that were just starting to catch on. The content came from Kazumi, but the app and the server programs supporting the service were all Akari's work. The site could accept payment in currencies from around the world, not to mention mobile credit. It even had support systems to help Kazumi write articles in English, one of his weak spots. It would have cost millions of yen to outsource the entire tech infrastructure for Meteor News, but Akari had taken care of everything herself. What's more, she'd done all this for a mere 20 percent of revenue. Given that monthly revenue was currently twenty or thirty thousand yen, her share was practically nothing.

"I'll be working on advertising until the evening," she said. "I think we should be able to increase AdSense purchases by at least 2 percent."

"Thanks. For everything. I'll get the article up this evening. Will you be at Fool's Launchpad all day?"

"Until nightfall." Akari swept the gadgets on her desk into her backpack and stood up. "All right, talk to you again this evening. Let me know when you're ready."

She turned toward the round table, Afro swaying. The AMX was still in progress.

"Watanabe-san," she called. Her voice cut through the conversation at the table, bringing it sharply to a halt. "That job from yesterday, fixing the payment code for Pocket Folder? I took a look, but what you've got so far is no good. Credit card security codes are being stored in the database."

"You mean you're not supposed to do that?" said Watanabe. "I thought that's what VisGen did."

Akari sighed and shook her head. "Those big companies put hundreds of millions into settlement compliance. Do you have any idea how much it costs to reach PCI Level 1? Same goes for VisGen. Do you read Pat's blog? That's where the two hundred million they raised in their first stage went—all of it."

Mary stared at Akari, face stiffly composed. So did the other members. Akari continued, showing no sign of noticing the subzero atmosphere in the room. "I rewrote it to require that the codes be entered for each settlement event. If that's okay with you, I can deliver it right away."

"Okay," said Watanabe after a brief pause. "Can I have your invoice?"

"Payment at month's end, right?" Akari said. "I'll send it over." To the rest of the group, she added, "Let me know if you need any coding help, everyone. I still have plenty of free time this month."

None of the web designers at Fool's Launchpad were any good at IT engineering, and Akari made her money by compensating for this weakness. Kazumi had no idea why she bothered with Meteor News, which turned no profit at all.

No use worrying about that now, though—it was time to get to work on today's news. As for SAFIR 3's predicted location . . . maybe he'd just put up the TLEs from STRATCOM as they were.

Thu, 10 Dec 2020, 17:50 -0700 (2020-12-11T00:50 GMT)
Peterson Air Force Base, Colorado Springs

Colonel Claude Lintz, chief of Orbital Surveillance at NORAD, had been toying with the object for some time before he finally put it on his head. A conical red cap with white fur trim and a pom-pom at the tip. A Santa hat, in other words.

Lintz peered at his reflection in one of the jet-black displays. The cheap novelty item went oddly well with his somewhat too ruddy complexion. It had been his second in command, Major Sylvester Fernandez, who had brought him the hat, and he could see now why Sylvester had been delighted enough by the sight of him wearing it to applaud. Fifty-nine years old and overweight, Lintz was one snowy white beard away from being the spitting image of Santa Claus himself.

Scowling, Lintz pulled off the hat and tossed it into the cardboard box beside his desk. The hat been issued to Orbital Surveillance as the "equipment" they would need for NORAD's best-known annual event, only days away now: NORAD Tracks Santa. There, this military organization would "track" Santa's flight path across the

North American continent for the benefit of any children who cared to follow along.

Begun in 1955, NORAD Tracks Santa had grown more extravagant each year and was now seen as one of their most important annual events. There was a website, of course, and also apps for smartphones and tablets that received tracking information in real time. A thousand volunteers were allowed into the base to help manage groups of visiting children. For NORAD, the exercise was an excellent opportunity to showcase to the world their seamless surveillance net that covered all of North America. Lintz had been tracking Santa for forty years now, never taking a single Christmas vacation, and knew the rationale behind it all—but this new policy requiring personnel to wear the hats during their video calls was, he felt, a bit much.

True, it was precisely the spectacle of stony-faced men saying things like "Information from Oregon site places Santa over Vancouver moving at Mach 2, over" that convinced children Santa was real. But did the public also recognize that under their funny hats the personnel involved were professional members of the armed forces?

Pushing the issue of the hat out of his mind, Lintz turned to the task at hand. His office had received twelve videos to play on Christmas Eve from Larry Russell, their CG producer in Portland, and it was Lintz's job to review them.

The quality of the videos was exceptional. There was Santa on his sleigh, riding in to the sound of jingle bells from the east. The NORAD F-22 squadron's scramble to intercept this "airspace incursion" had been filmed right at Peterson Base. This real footage had then been masterfully combined with computer graphics.

Lintz watched as the F-22 pilot who had made visual confirmation of Santa performed a low-speed barrel roll around his sleigh and reported that the jolly old elf's mission was now a Santa-NORAD joint operation. Lintz whistled in approval at the relatively slow aerial acrobatics, difficult to pull off in previous-generation aircraft without stalling. Sylvester had selected the pilot personally: Second Lieutenant Madu Abbot, a promising young woman of Indian extraction. Despite her youth, there was no better F-22 pilot in the whole of US Northern Command.

On the screen, Santa paused in his work of distributing presents to snowy US and Canadian cities and looked up at the night sky. Then he reached under his seat and took out a helmet with two hoses attached.

Lintz's chair creaked as he leaned in closer and muttered to himself, "You're up, old man."

Lintz would have his staff check Santa's exploits within the atmosphere. The F-22 acrobatics in particular were sure to receive close attention from Sylvester, an ex-pilot himself. But he wasn't delegating space to anyone. He had been involved in space surveillance at NORAD since joining the air force at the height of the Cold War in 1980. This part of his job he yielded to nobody.

The reindeer, now snorting inside airtight helmets that Santa had put over their heads, waved farewell to their air force escort with their front hooves, then kicked off into outer space. Lintz watched the map and velocity data displayed beside the animation closely.

The sleigh's velocity increased with each kick of the reindeers' legs. One kilometer per second, two, three . . . The once-flat horizon gradually curved down at the edges, and more stars appeared in the sky above. Lintz was gratified to see that the twinkling of the stars had subsided too. His repeated warnings at the storyboard phase had had their desired effect. Even in a video starring Santa Claus, there were some things he insisted on getting right.

Just as Santa's sleigh reached 7.6 kilometers per second, its target came into view—the International Space Station—looking like a giant dragonfly with its great solar panels spread wide.

The sleigh performed a series of minor course corrections to get the ISS lined up directly in front of it, then gracefully swung forward and over it.

Lintz grunted with approval. "I see you did your homework, Larry."

Santa's sleigh had just performed the same maneuver the Russian spacecraft Soyuz used to dock with the ISS. It was the sort of unnatural-looking move that only made sense in orbit, but the video made it entertaining. Even the most demanding space fans would surely be satisfied.

The ISS scene would be the highlight of NORAD Tracks Santa in 2020. Santa was stopping off there for the benefit of one Judy Smark, whose father Ronnie had made them the first tourists in space. In the video, Judy was a little girl with both palms pressed to the cupola window as she watched the sleigh dock. Her father, fierce eyed and goateed, stood beside her with one hand on her shoulder.

"A bit overdone there," Lintz murmured to himself.

The girl on the screen looked ten at most, but Judy Smark was twenty-eight. Lintz was still wondering whether it would be out of line to suggest a change there when he heard someone speak to him.

"Colonel Lintz, sir, may I have a moment of your time?"

Lintz turned his head to see a dark-complexioned serviceman standing just outside his office. "Sorry," he said. "I didn't see you there. You should have just come in. I have an open-door policy."

Lintz glanced down at his visitor's name tag: D. FREEMAN, STAFF SERGEANT. What was Freeman's first name again?

He noticed a message blinking at the corner of his display. His aide, Captain Jasmine Harrison, had sent him a précis of his visitor's organizational affiliation and background. Orbital Surveillance wasn't as big as it had once been, but it was still home to over two hundred personnel. Back when they had been watching Soviet missiles and bombers from under Cheyenne Mountain, Lintz had known all of his coworkers, but with all the reassignments and restructuring these days, that was no longer possible. His advancing age didn't help either. Jasmine's assistance was invaluable.

His visitor, he read, was one Daryl Freeman, staff sergeant. Indonesian born, Catholic, entered the country five years ago on a student visa. An engineer who'd signed up hoping to earn citizenship and this year had finally been assigned to a long-requested post at NORAD.

"Just the man I wanted to see, in fact," said Lintz, motioning Freeman in. Noting with satisfaction his visitor's consternation, Lintz clicked the link in Jasmine's message to display Freeman's current orders. It seemed he was working under Sylvester, putting together a report on the ASM-140, an experimental antisatellite weapon currently being developed. "How's that ASM-140 coming along? Bring me up to speed, um . . . Daryl."

Daryl straightened his back hurriedly and saluted. Lintz smiled to himself. These were all techniques he'd learned in a seminar the air force had held for administrators nearing the end of their careers. They were what allowed him to maintain an open-door policy despite being bad with names.

First, always call people by their first names. It inspired loyalty and caught people used to a more formal organizational structure off guard. Second, be the first to ask a question. This was a way of seizing the initiative.

"The project is proceeding as planned, sir," Freeman said. "We have received a delivery of three ASM-140s from Lockheed and successfully installed a fire control system obtained from the Smith-sonian into that F-15C you claimed for us just before it was due to be scrapped. The firing test should take place as scheduled on week 50."

As he listened, Lintz recalled the details of the project. The Chi-nese space station Tiangong-2, operational since 2017, and the stream of low-cost miniature satellites launched every time a taikonaut stayed there were a serious headache for the United States. Equipped with high-definition cameras so cheap they were practically disposable, the satellites were an attempt to surpass the surveillance net the Ameri-cans had already built in quantity if not quality.

The US had decided it needed to demonstrate its ability to respond meaningfully to this provocation. Asked to come up with a proposal, Lintz had unearthed an old idea from the days of the Stra-tegic Defense Initiative: "the flying tomato can."

The design was simple. A missile with homing capabilities was attached to the outside of an F-15 fighter and carried high enough to render atmospheric effects negligible. Once launched, it flew toward the satellite that had been designated as its target for a direct hit. Much cheaper than ground-based ASAT weaponry, unaffected by weather conditions, and with a very rapid launch process, the idea had many advantages. It had been shelved for a range of reasons, but now that it had been recognized as a possible solution to the problem with China, NORAD's proposal to revive it had been taken up, and development was under way. Destroying objects in orbit was forbid-den by the guidelines of the UN's Committee on the Peaceful Uses of Outer Space, but it would be useful as a deterrent.

Lintz had thrown himself wholeheartedly into the planning and development of this new weapon and was now facing the problem of securing personnel. The F-15C was already being phased out, so no young pilots held a license for it, and none seemed interested in obtaining one either. Whether his superiors were aware of these issues or not Lintz didn't know, but either way, they seemed to have even higher hopes for the ASM than Lintz did. Wherever the plans for the antisatellite exercise known as "Seed Pod" had come from, it had been made clear to him that he was to implement them as soon as possible.

"Major Fernandez brought me that reassignment petition for your project," said Lintz. "What came of that? I recall signing it."

"Thanks to you, sir, USNORTHCOM has approved Captain Ricky McGillis's transfer to NORAD as requested. I understand that the captain is looking forward to flying an F-15C again."

Satisfied that the report matched what he remembered, Lintz folded his hands over his stomach. "Excellent," he said. "Now, how can I help you today, Sergeant?" Glancing at the monitor again, he realized that he'd missed the final part of Jasmine's message: *SAFIR orbit surveillance request.* So Freeman wasn't here about the ASM-140 at all.

"As it happens, sir, I am not here concerning the ASM-140. I came to request your assistance with SAFIR 3."

Lintz smiled broadly. He was always ready to talk about objects in orbit.

"At ease, Sergeant," he said. "Take a seat if you like."

Freeman refrained from sitting on the sofa, but he did shift his center of gravity and settle into a more relaxed posture.

"I want to use NORAD facilities to keep tabs on the second stage of the SAFIR 3 rocket launched from Iran last week, sir," he said. "I'm sure you remember the launch."

"Indeed, I do," said Lintz. "Licensed production of the DPRK's Taepodong. Parked in orbit at 250 km, as I recall. Not a bad design at all. What about it?"

"I discovered today that its orbit is gradually flattening out, sir," Freeman said, making a sideways *C* with the thumb and index finger of his left hand and letting it grow longer and narrower.

"Atmospheric effects? No, that wouldn't make sense . . ."

"No, sir. I ruled out the effects of the upper atmosphere. And there's another strange thing about it. According to the TLEs from STRATCOM, SAFIR 3's second stage—designation 'SAFIR 3 R/B'— is actually gaining altitude."

"That's impossible. An error in the TLEs?"

Freeman nodded. "Possibly, sir," he said. A rocket shell that had spent all its fuel simply did not gain altitude. "But this is STRAT-COM data, so I don't think it could be a simple mistake. I would like to ask for your permission to use NORAD's radar for further observation."

Lintz glanced at the calendar on his office wall. A thick line ran from the sixteenth of December—next Wednesday—through to Christmas. Santa-tracking season wasn't the best timing for an unscheduled surveillance operation.

"How long do you plan to observe SAFIR's stage 2 for? And on what timetable?"

Freeman shifted his gaze elsewhere and moved his lips soundlessly for a few moments before responding, "For one week, sir."

Lintz was satisfied by the pause. Freeman had obviously been calculating when SAFIR 3's second stage orbit would take it over North American airspace. The next thing he said confirmed it.

"SAFIR 3 R/B's orbital angle is currently seventy-five degrees. We could track it with radar during the day, but I was hoping to use the Oregon site by night to minimize the disruption."

Lintz was about to grant him permission but stopped himself

just in time. He'd delegated the right to decide on surveillance targets to Freeman's superior, Sylvester. It would be bad form not to at least involve him in this decision. "Has the major approved your proposal?" he asked instead.

"I requested permission, sir," said Freeman, looking uncomfortable, "but as I did not receive a reply from the major, I took the liberty of escalating the matter to you directly."

That explained it. Sylvester was a superb administrator, but as an ex-pilot, space wasn't his field of expertise. He probably didn't realize how unusual it was for a rocket body to gain altitude. In that respect he was an excellent fit for the NORAD of today, which had become far more concerned with airborne terrorism than ICBMs since the events of 9/11.

"I see," Lintz said finally. "I imagine it failed to, ahem, capture his interest."

As the two men shared a conspiratorial smile, a long arm reached into Lintz's office to rap on the open door. Speak of the devil.

Sylvester strode in briskly, registered Freeman's presence, and smiled. "Sergeant Freeman," he said. "Just the man I wanted to see. I need you in Hanger 5. The high-altitude pressure suits have arrived. McGillis's fitting can wait until tomorrow, but I want you to ask the maintenance team to get working on the alignment with the ejection seat today."

"Yes, sir."

Sylvester turned to Lintz with a rueful smile, knowing that the colonel would still be stuck on the mention of high-pressure suits. "Hadn't you heard, Colonel?" he asked. "They're making us put the F-15 pilot in a pressure suit to carry the ASM-140 up there. It's all in Sergeant Freeman's report."

"What do they need a thing like that for? A regular pilot's suit was enough in '85. Did the stratosphere depressurize at some point in the past thirty years?"

Sylvester sighed. "Sergeant," he said. "Explain it to the colonel."

"Yes, sir," Freeman replied, and turned to face Lintz. "Sir, as you observe, the pressure in the stratosphere has not changed in the past thirty years. Neither has the aircraft lost integrity nor the human body grown weaker. What has changed is air force regulations."

The operational regulations for pilot environments, Freeman explained, had been tightened in 2010. The air pressure and temperature in the cockpit now had to be slightly more comfortable than before. New aircraft like the F-22 met the new requirements, but the F-15 was a product of the seventies. Going high enough to launch the ASM-140 would cause conditions in the cockpit to fall below the new acceptable minimum level.

Sylvester threw up his arms: *What are you going to do?* "I argued against it. The pilot will barely be able to move bundled up in that space suit, and they can't wear a regulation helmet. We even have to modify the ejection seat. Oh, that reminds me—we removed the standard-issue AC."

"Fine, fine," Lintz said, waving a hand dismissively. How had a project designed to reuse existing technology gotten so bloated? "Did you read Freeman's report about SAFIR 3's second stage yet, Major?" he asked, changing the subject.

"I believe so," Sylvester replied. "Request for permission to observe a rocket shell gaining altitude or something? No argument from me as long as his regular duties aren't affected."

"Thank you, sir," said Freeman.

"But first get to Hangar 5," Sylvester continued. "Make sure those pressure suits come in okay."

"Yes, sir. I'm on my way."

Sylvester sat down in a chair and watched Freeman leave. "Unusual orbit, I think he said? Amazing that he noticed. I've never been able to get my head around all that business myself."

"There are amateurs out there these days who make a hobby of tracking objects in low orbit," said Lintz. "Someone would have noticed sooner or later." More importantly, he explained further, if NORAD could find out what was causing the irregularity, STRAT-COM would owe them a favor.

At this, Sylvester nodded, apparently in agreement.

"Enough about that, though," Lintz said. "This hat. Can't we send it somewhere else?"

"Anywhere else it would just get in the way," grinned Sylvester. "It's just two weeks, Colonel. I'm sure you can manage."

Fri, 11 Dec 2020, 05:55 +0400 (2020-12-11T01:55 GMT)
Desnoeufs Island

In a room lit only by the stars and a monitor on its dimmest setting, a tuneless voice broke into song, "Ozzy in Seychelles, telescope to the sky . . ."

The room was so large that the starlight couldn't dispel the gloom of its farthest corners. In its center stood a gigantic desk, and sitting at this desk in a tank top and shorts was Ozzy Cunningham, owner of the tuneless voice. Every time Ozzy moved, his Aeron chair groaned in protest; he was at least 25 percent over the three hundred–pound weight limit of the famous chair, used in offices worldwide, and the sides of his thighs were well beyond the edges of the seat.

Ozzy's desk faced a curved window twenty meters wide and four meters high that took up one entire side of the room, offering him an uninterrupted 180-degree ocean view.

Through the window, he could see the Milky Way sprayed across the eastern sky like vapor from a whale's blowhole that had frozen in midair. The sea was still; no fishermen were out chasing sardines tonight. Desnoeufs—thirty miles southwest of Mahe Island, home of Victoria, the capital of Seychelles, and not far from Madagascar—was owned outright by Ozzy. Living with his "man Friday" in a UFO-shaped building jutting out from a cliff overlooking the Indian Ocean to the east, he devoted himself to his hobby: observing the skies through the three-meter reflective telescope and low-orbit radar of his private observatory, the Seychelles Eye.

The ocean view was astonishing, without a single artificial light in view, but right now Ozzy was ignoring it. Instead, he was squinting at a two-by-two bank of monitors, like something you might see on a trader's desk, while his fingers worked a trackball. He didn't like to use a mouse; moving his arm was a chore.

Ozzy checked the radar in the upper-right quadrant of his setup. No rain clouds to the east. The weather forecast for remote islands like his was useless; you needed high-quality radar if you wanted to observe the skies. All the more so when your target was Mercury, whose visibility was notoriously susceptible to atmospheric effects.

Photographing Mercury was no easy task to begin with. Much closer to the sun than Venus, this tiny planet was completely blotted out by the blue-tinged atmosphere of Earth when the sun was shining. You had to catch it just before sunrise or just after sunset.

Ozzy spun the trackball, selecting "Mercury" from a list of celestial bodies on the screen. He had spent a lot of money streamlining his setup so that no finicky adjustments were required. His lower-right monitor sprang to life, displaying a close-up of the planet lit by the sun directly below it.

Nodding with satisfaction, Ozzy set the lower-left monitor to display the feed from the support camera. It was pointed in the same direction as the telescope but took in a much wider area. The part of the screen that would be photographed by the telescope was indicated by a small white frame at the center of the monitor. Overlaid on the image was information about the celestial bodies currently visible. Right now it was showing the predicted orbit of Tiangong-2, which was currently just above Mercury. Ozzy put one finger to the monitor and confirmed that the line gently curving away from Tiangong-2 would pass through the shooting area, before zooming the camera in. In ten seconds or so, space station and planet would be in alignment.

"Counting down! Eight, seven, six . . ." Ozzy raised his right arm from the desk and aimed at the trackball button with his right index finger. "Four, three, two . . . Ah, crap, not quite."

Peering at the live view, Ozzy waited for the right moment to shoot. He was recording the video feed in full HD, but a still from an HD video wasn't worth much these days, when even television was broadcast in 4K or 8K. A photograph had to get above the gigapixel level to be worth anything at all. And the raw data of an image stitched together from twelve high-sensitivity CCDs could easily pass the gigabyte mark. Burst shooting was impossible. You had to take one shot at just the right time.

The dot for Tiangong-2 entered the white frame in the live view as a shining point appeared in the view through the telescope.

"Zero!" Ozzy cried, letting his fat finger fall onto the button.

The trackball made an ominous sound. Ozzy's chair began to spin clockwise from the force of Ozzy's button press, but it groaned to a halt only a quarter of the way around. Cursing, Ozzy grabbed the desk and pulled himself back around to face front again. The trackball button had gotten stuck pressed down.

"This chair cost a thousand bucks, and it already needs replacing," he complained, prying the trackball button free with one fingernail. "They don't make anything like they used to."

When he looked up and checked the photograph he had taken, Ozzy stroked his chin in satisfaction. "Not bad. Not bad at all! Never seen this combination in a resolution this high before."

The Tiangong-2 was visible in silhouette, its two pairs of solar panels extended. Below it hung Mercury, visibly spherical rather than the indistinct disc it appeared as in most photographs. The contrast was too high to see any craters, but the heat haze rising from the Indian Ocean had been neatly removed by the image-processing engine. A superb result, all in all.

Ozzy tagged the image *Tiangong-2* and *Mercury*, then uploaded it to Wikimedia under his pseudonym, "X-Man." Wikimedia's voluminous archives already included thousands of high-res photographs from X-Man, consistently an order of magnitude better than what others had to offer, and this mysterious user from Seychelles was starting to attract attention among the amateur-astronomer community—even if part of his reputation was as an unreliable purveyor of disinformation and half-truths.

"Nothing beats being here all by myself," Ozzy said to no one in particular. The Seychelles Eye's location suited him just fine. Being alone on an island in the middle of the Indian Ocean had plenty of advantages. No light pollution, for one, but best of all, no competition. North and South America were full of hobbyists and professionals alike turning their telescopes to the night sky. The South Pacific was too close to Australia and New Zealand and their nature-loving populations. Ozzy's formal knowledge of astronomy was limited, so it was important not to have to compete with people who specialized in it. All he wanted was to fire up an interest in space, even if only a spark, among people who never usually looked at the stars. That was what he sought with his beautiful photography and startling writing. He didn't want people getting in his face and telling him to stop writing nonsense.

Ozzy's young friends had often extolled the virtues of getting out on your own. "You don't find opportunities staying with the herd," was how Ronnie Smark had put it—and he was a billionaire now.

Ozzy would never forget that night in the summer of 1998, when Ronnie came to visit him at his penthouse apartment carrying nothing but a single scrap of paper.

"We're going to open a bank on the Internet," he had said.

This was back when Ozzy himself had barely even started doing his taxes on a computer. The Windows operating system was spreading in the consumer market, but communicating with others using computers was still just a hobby for geeks. Ronnie had still been a tenant of Ozzy's then, a young man in an ill-fitting suit and dirty Converse sneakers speaking passionately about his plans for the future.

"It won't be long before the whole world's connected to the Internet," he said. "I'm going to create a way for anyone to open up shop there. We're already in negotiations with our first bank. One success, and the rest is repetition and refinement."

Ozzy looked down at Ronnie's dirty shoes. The poky offices he rented on the second floor for $400 a month weren't even air-conditioned. Security deposit was $1,000, if he recalled correctly.

"I'm not sure I understand that part," said Ozzy, "but what you're saying is, you want me to let you have the office rent-free until you get into the black?"

"That's not it at all, Mr. Cunningham," Ronnie said, brows knit in a wounded expression. He held the scrap of paper up to Ozzy's face. "We want you to *invest* in us. We'll give you ten thousand dollars' worth of nonvoting shares. That's 20 percent of our total capital. In return, all we want is use of the office for three years."

"Right. You want me to let you stay there without paying rent."

"No, no. It's an *investment*."

"Don't give an inch, do you? You can't even get a ten-grand loan?"

But even as he complained, Ozzy was mulling the proposal over. It wasn't as if people were clamoring for an office in his partially converted warehouse outside San Francisco. Better to have young people coming and going than to let it stand empty. If there were enough of them to entice a coffee cart to set up shop out front, it would be easier to fill the rest of the space too.

"All right," he said. "Give me that note. You're going to expand, right? Go ahead and use the warehouse space on the first floor too. The office there has AC."

"Thank you kindly, Mr. Cunningham. Welcome to our stakeholder roster. I assume I can leave the power bill to you as well."

Ozzy couldn't remember the expression on Ronnie's face at that moment. But that had been the beginning. Ronnie and his friends had gotten to work, briskly encircling the torpid credit card companies and building out a settlement network that soon became an indispensable piece of online infrastructure. They were out of the warehouse within three years, and when their Internet bank was bought out by an online auction company, the scrap of paper in Ozzy's desk was worth well over a billion dollars.

But Ronnie's success did more for Ozzy than just make him a billionaire. As young entrepreneurs began flocking to Ozzy's building in their own suits and scuffed Converse shoes, Ozzy offered access to what they needed: lawyers, accountants, free high-speed Internet connections. Then he bought another building. The entrepreneurs were a superstitious group, so Ozzy bought them what they wanted—another converted warehouse. Rent was payable in nonvoting stock. Ozzy's hands-off approach was a success, ensuring that every time a tenant moved out they left behind a substantial chunk of capital. But none had ever made as much for Ozzy as Ronnie had, and none were ever as successful as Ronnie himself.

After ten feverish years, a new age dawned, this one dominated by the megaplatforms: Google, Amazon, Facebook.

Many successful entrepreneurs from the early days of the boom pivoted from IT to so-called commodity industries like automobiles and infrastructure. No small number of them became photographers as well. Ozzy was fascinated by the photos they took now that their success had freed them from financial concerns and made it possible for them to travel the world focusing on their art. So fascinated, in fact, that he decided to reinvent himself in Seychelles too. Since he couldn't walk a mile without getting out of breath, he decided to take up astrophotography. As long as you had the facilities, you could do that right from your chair.

The most successful entrepreneur of all, though, had taken a different route entirely. Ronnie had invented the industry of commercial space development, and now he was two days away from leaving Earth with his daughter, on a rocket he had built himself, and checking in to accommodations to be injected into orbit by his tested and true Wyvern spacecraft.

"Talk about friends in high places," Ozzy muttered. He briefly toyed with the idea of applying to go on one of Ronnie's space tours himself, but a creak from his chair brought him back to earth. The additional fees required to carry his massive 190-kilogram frame into orbit would be in the hundreds of thousands of dollars. And there was still plenty for him to do here, away from the herd.

Today he had to run checks on more than a dozen satellites. Busy didn't begin to cover it. The second stage of SAFIR 3 was particularly intriguing. Ozzy scanned the latest newsletter from Meteor News in Japan again. Could SAFIR 3 R/B really be gaining altitude?

If you had a story no one else did, that was valuable. Pair it with a shiny image, and Internet tabloids like Geeple would be sure to pick it up. As the source of the story, Ozzy's blog would see pageviews well into five-figure territory, and that in turn meant more incoming payments for advertising via good old Ronnie's Internet bank.

In fact, Ozzy could make money without putting much thought or effort into it at all. Some of the stock he'd accepted in lieu of rent back in his landlord days was starting to pay serious dividends as the issuing companies moved into their growth phases. But the money he made from his photographs and writing—and of course advertising payments—that was different. That was money he'd earned with his own hard work.

Ozzy highlighted the TLE for SAFIR 3 R/B in the Meteor News newsletter and selected Copy.

"Into the moon with me . . . My heart's in its orbit . . ."

Singing a half-remembered song, Ozzy pasted the TLE into his orbital-forecast software. "SAFIR 3 R/B" appeared in his telescope's list of tracking targets. A quick spin of the protesting trackball and a line appeared across the wide-view monitor. Perfect—the object's orbit would take it directly over Ozzy's island.

Satellite rise was in ten minutes. Better prep the radar. SAFIR 3 would be lit up by the sun about two minutes after it rose above the horizon and reached thirty degrees or so of elevation. It would then pass directly overhead before sinking again in the east. This was the perfect path, allowing him to see it lit from both front and back.

Ozzy watched the dot on his monitor representing SAFIR 3.

Its orbit was so low that its motion would be visible to the naked eye while it was overhead, but while it was over the horizon the dot moved slowly enough that he couldn't tell whether it was moving or not. The dot approached the horizon, touched it, rose above it . . .

"Strange. Should be out by now."

The predicted location for SAFIR 3 superimposed over the low-zoom field view to the west was well clear of the horizon, but Ozzy couldn't see anything through the telescope except stars streaming slowly through the frame with the rotation of the Earth. He watched SAFIR 3's expected location rise until it was high enough that the sun's rays should have been reaching it. But not a hint of sparkle appeared.

Just as Ozzy was wondering if he'd missed it altogether, a point of red light appeared in the field view—an object in orbit lit up by the morning sun. The redness was due to the light's long passage through the atmosphere, the same effect that gave you red sunlight at dawn and sunset. The red dot was moving roughly parallel to the predicted path of SAFIR 3, just below the area framed by the telescope.

"Off the rails a bit there," muttered Ozzy. The TLE in Meteor News must have been inaccurate. He'd almost missed the object entirely.

Ozzy switched off automatic tracking based on the bad TLE data and activated visual tracking instead. One click on the red dot in the wide view and the telescope was on its way. The telescope image panned swiftly across the sky until a cylindrical object appeared clearly on the screen, slowly stabilizing at the center. It certainly looked like a rocket body.

As he watched, there was a flash of light from the cylinder. The image blurred for a moment.

"What was that?" Ozzy leaned close to the monitor. The cross in the center of the image was still directly over the rocket, the tracking operating as expected. "Shit! Should have been watching more closely."

He could look back over the video and the logs to see what the telescope had captured and how the object had moved. But if the same thing happened again in the meantime, he'd miss it.

"Come on, once more . . . Aha!" There was another flash, and the telescope's angle began to move, slowly but surely. "A flash from behind, then it moves forward . . . That settles it—those lights are thrusters. That piece of space junk is accelerating!"

Ozzy stared at his monitors, transfixed.

"This is big, Ronnie . . ."

Three minutes later, SAFIR 3's second stage disappeared beneath the eastern horizon, and the brief show came to an end.

Reviewing the video, Ozzy found that the light had flashed five times in total, including a couple of flashes he hadn't noticed.

Now things were getting interesting. What was the most sensational way to report his findings? A weapon, he decided—that would be the most suitable for X-Man, who was well known as a kook. NASA and the professional astronomers would be sure to ignore his outlandish claims, and the stuffy astronomy community was starting to catch on as well. "There he goes again with his crazy theories," they'd say. Fine—let them talk. All Ozzy wanted was for people to look up at the sky. Geeple would run the story. Their geeky audience would love it.

"Nuclear weapons are old hat. Aliens and Area 51? Naw! But a killer satellite . . . ?"

It couldn't be some obscure idea that only specialists knew about. On the other hand, it didn't have to be original either. Most of the failed start-ups from Ozzy's time at the converted warehouse had been trying to come up with something new and original, but the key to Ronnie's success had been founding something that actually *was* original but insisting on calling it a bank, one of the least original business models people could think of. Ozzy couldn't just call it "a man-made object propelled by bursts of light," obviously. That would go over like a lead balloon. He needed a name that would astound the gods themselves . . .

"That's it! *Rod from God!*"

That B movie about a superweapon that rains giant tungsten warheads on Earth from orbit! Awful film, of course, rumored to have wasted half its budget on the lead actor. The critics hadn't thought much of it, but any self-respecting geek would remember it.

Okay, so this object was a Rod from God. What was its target? Since the rocket was Iranian, probably Israel or the United States, but a Rod from God aimed at the Earth wasn't very original. Better to twist the narrative and say it was headed for . . . the ISS. Now *that* would be out there. Best of all, the average reader would have no idea how unlikely it was.

" 'Rod from God attacks ISS!' Perfect. I'll need an illustration at some point too."

Ozzy quickly sketched a cylinder with a few thrusters sticking out, then took a photograph with his cell phone and uploaded it to MegaHands, a job-matching site with a thousand-dollar reward for the best image. Freelance illustrators with Hollywood aspirations would be all over it.

He hadn't been able to take a gigapixel photo, but stills captured from the video would be enough for Geeple. He'd put the original images and the radar observation data up on his blog, the Seychelles

Eye. The professional-looking data would be enough in itself to make the story seem reliable. He accumulated more data every day than he knew what to do with—might as well make some use of it, even if only as decoration.

Oh, and one more thing—a complaint to Meteor News. They'd almost made him miss his chance to photograph SAFIR 3 accelerating.

"Fuckin' shitty TLE data . . ."

Thu, 10 Dec 2020, 19:58 -0800 (2020-12-11T03:58 GMT)
80 Pike Street, Seattle

Seated outside at a café on the edge of Pike Place Market, Chance glanced at their reflection in the window to check how the rendezvous would look to passersby. Her hair was blond, dyed black at the roots, and she wore oversized sunglasses and fashionably vibrant rouge. A black pantsuit and long coat concealed her toned body, while the battered editor's bag she carried suggested a career in advertising without offering any specifics.

The man sitting across from her was dressed in a turtleneck knit and designer jeans. Over these he wore a black coat much like Chance's. His name was Ageha Shiraishi. He could have been an artist, with that long black hair of his. Chance wished he'd ditch those old-fashioned metal-framed glasses for a newer pair, but they weren't bad enough to actually attract attention.

Sitting across from each other with a tablet between them, the two could have been a media salesperson and a designer. No one in an IT industry hub like Seattle would look twice at a meeting like that.

Pretending to brush back her hair, Chance checked the external security cameras. Two at the intersection, one at the entrance to

Starbucks where the tourists milled about, and one over their heads. None had been added since she'd checked last week. All four cameras had been taken care of for the duration of the meeting.

Chance tucked her hair behind one ear and picked up a leather portfolio. Brushing off the powder snow that had fallen on it, she extracted a sheet of paper and offered it across the table to Shiraishi.

"Email from Koyanagi at Sound Technica about the D-Fi cable," she said in Japanese. "You haven't read it yet, I assume?"

Shiraishi looked at the paper, his glasses steamed up from the caffe latte he was holding. "Ugh, Japanese people, right? Even in English, they can't help themselves from starting with small talk about the weather . . . What, so it's just a thank-you?"

"It turned out to be a good deal for both sides."

Chance took the printout back and reread it herself before slipping it back into the portfolio. Sound Technica, a Japanese audio-equipment maker, had been the official distributor of D-Fi, a line of USB cables for audiophiles "invented" by a dummy company that Shiraishi had set up in Portland. Manufactured in Singapore, more than a million of the two-foot cables had been sold worldwide, despite costing $300 each. Koyanagi, their contact at Sound Technica, had responded to Shiraishi's curt message announcing that the line would be discontinued with a polite letter of thanks.

Shiraishi put his mug down and wiped the condensation from his glasses. "How much did we make?"

"Around 2.2 million net, I think. They were practically free to manufacture, after all."

"Not bad at all. That's more than we made selling poison gas to the Iranians. Make sure you report the good news to El Leaderino in the North."

"Don't call him that."

"Who cares what I call him? No one here understands Japanese anyway."

"I said stop it." Chance lowered her sunglasses to glower at Shiraishi. "And start thinking of how you're going to clean up the mess you made this week. There's talk of canceling the whole project. "

"What are you talking about?"

Chance extracted a second printout from her portfolio: an article from the online tabloid Geeple. Under the headline "ROD from GOD attacks ISS!" was a series of photographs apparently taken through an astronomical telescope. "Your work, I presume," began Chance, but Shiraishi snatched the printout from her hand before she could continue.

"Wow," he said. "Wow. I never thought anyone would get a photograph of that. Who's the shutterbug? Must have a pretty good telescope."

Shiraishi reached for the tablet on the table and followed the links from Geeple to its original source: the Seychelles Eye.

"X-Man, huh? Who's that supposed to be? Oh, I see. A kook."

"This isn't something to celebrate."

"Are you kidding? Of course it is. Now you can tell those idiot generals who never believed in my project that it's already in motion."

"But targeting a rocket belonging to an ally—"

"Shut up," Shiraishi said, cutting her off with an open palm. "We can *use* this." He made an odd gesture, as if grasping something in midair.

In her mind's eye, Chance visualized a blank sheet of paper. Shiraishi was about to get to work. She would have to memorize his planning word for word. There could be no notes, handwritten or electronic.

"Can you get moving right away?" Shiraishi asked.

"Yes," Chance replied.

"The Supreme Leader should have a speech scheduled for this weekend. Probably just the usual whining. I want you to switch the script."

"Document number?"

"It's 034524," Shiraishi said. "The one I wrote. Remember it?"

Chance nodded. The script bearing the six-digit number he'd just given was a criticism of the great powers for their irresponsible development of space, most notable for its harsh criticism of the US's support for commercial space development.

"Next," Shiraishi continued. "The Cyber Front."

Chance wrote the name of North Korea's cyberwar squadron on her internal notepad. They hadn't achieved much in the way of terrorism so far beyond bringing a few websites down with denial-of-service attacks, but over the past few years Shiraishi had trained them into a formidable team capable of implementing sophisticated tactics.

"Get them to corrupt Google's translation engine."

"Translation engine? What are you planning?"

"Is your brain blond too?" Shiraishi snapped, rapping on one temple. "We're going to bring this crazy story of X-Man's to the attention of the intelligentsia. People can never resist if they think they know something someone else doesn't. Anyway, it doesn't matter whether you understand or not—just do as I say."

Chance nodded. Shiraishi's arrogance reached intolerable levels when he was concentrating.

"Next—ready?—pull out those plans for a low-orbit ASAT weapon from the North's archives. There should be some negatives they got from the CIA." Shiraishi then explained how the plans were to be used.

"All right," Chance said. "But is this Geeple story really that important?"

"No," Shiraishi said. "It's bullshit. I doubt X-Man believes it himself. No one with a professional interest in space believes in this 'Rod from God' orbital weapon business."

"So NASA will clue in that it's a lie right away, then?"

"Exactly." With a crooked smile, Shiraishi used his middle finger to push his glasses back into place. "That's what's so great about it. The experts will tell the truth, and everyone who ignores them is going to get taught a lesson."

The smarter you were, the easier it was to fall into that trap, Shiraishi explained. Then he pointed at the advertisement to the right of the article on the tablet.

"Also, web advertising. Get a few accounts ready. The Cyber Front should have plenty to spare. Got it?" Shiraishi blew his hair back from his forehead and leaned back in his chair.

"That's everything?" Chance asked.

Shiraishi nodded.

Chance went over Shiraishi's orders in her head. Replace the script for the speech. Corrupt the translation engine. Find the plans for the real low-orbit ASAT weapon. Prepare an advertising account. The goal was to muddy Shiraishi's intentions and conceal what had actually happened to SAFIR 3. The world's intelligence agencies, not least the CIA, would be beside themselves trying to figure out where the ASAT information that only North Korea was supposed to have had come from.

"All right, my turn," Chance said. "First, the replacement SIMs." She pulled her editor's bag toward her and felt inside the lining at the edge. There was the sound of Velcro, and then she produced two plastic cards from the secret compartment inside. The markings around the square cutout in the middle of the cards identified them as international roaming SIM cards from China Mobility.

"Hey, what did you do to that bag? That's a genuine Balenciaga. Cost me twelve hundred dollars."

Lowering her sunglasses again, Chance fixed Shiraishi with her coldest stare.

"I found a transmitter while I was making this pocket," she said. "I suppose Hedi Slimane put it there?"

Shiraishi laughed. "Should have known better than to mess with a pro," he said, taking the cards from her.

"Don't think you can work around me," Chance said. "I don't know how the last Chance ran things, but until this project is over you're under my supervision."

"All right, all right," Shiraishi said. He was already removing the SIMs from his cell phone and tablet to replace them with the ones he'd just received from Chance. The two of them changed the IC chips and SIMs they used for their mobile contracts weekly. All communications in America were hoovered up by the CIA or the NSA. Even if you used a roaming SIM, your messages and calls were still eavesdropped on via AT&T. Only constantly changing your number could reduce the risks.

Each week, their old SIMs were sold on to cell phone stores in Chinatown. When some Chinese tourist in Seattle bought one and used it to phone home, this helped cover Chance's and Shiraishi's tracks. And, when necessary, they could activate the virus they were careful to install before selling each card and use that tourist's phone as they pleased. This had been Shiraishi's idea.

Shiraishi looked up from entering the SIM activation code into his phone. "By the way, what hotel should I go to tomorrow?"

Chance slept with Shiraishi exactly once a week, to keep sexual frustration from endangering the mission. It would be far too dangerous to have him find a prostitute in the US.

"I'll let you know later," Chance said.

"You're so standoffish," Shiraishi said. "The last Chance was much nicer to me."

"That's why she was recalled."

"Oh, so she really was in love?" Shiraishi adopted a look of regret. "I should have been nicer to her."

Up until two months ago, Shiraishi's handler had been a young Korean American woman. But that Chance—the fourth one—had been so smitten by his boldness and genius that she had stopped sending accurate information to the North. The current Chance had been contracted to replace her.

"That reminds me," Chance said. "I got distracted, but let me emphasize this. SAFIR 3 can't be helped, but make sure you do everything according to plan from now on. Do not touch that billionaire's rocket."

"Aw, and I was looking forward to messing around with it," Shiraishi said. "Fine. Whatever. I'll satisfy myself with SAFIR 3."

"So SAFIR 3 was intentional."

"Pure coincidence. I swear it. Want me to make an affidavit right here? Got a Bible? If we need a witness, that barista—"

"I'll leave this out of my report," Chance said curtly, rising to her feet. She'd only been working with Shiraishi for two months, but she could already see the appeal he had for certain people. His mind, his background . . . He had a mysterious magnetism that some just couldn't resist. It wasn't surprising to learn that a young woman without much life experience had gotten in over her head with him.

Knowing that Shiraishi would be eating dinner at the Pike Street

Market, Chance turned her back to him and began climbing the hill in the opposite direction. Once she'd confirmed that Shiraishi had left the table, she'd have to return the security cameras around it to normal operation.

Sound Technica would send back the unsold D-Fi stock. She would have to think of a way to dispose of it before it arrived next week. Shiraishi would have to move out of his warehouse by the docks and into a safe house in the business district. There was a lot to get done. The sloppy tradecraft of the previous Chances would not have sufficed.

In a country where every communication, every street corner was under surveillance, there was no sure way to get away with illegal activity for long. The only reason Shiraishi had been safe these five years was because he hadn't actually done anything yet.

Things were about to change.

The Cloud was coming online.

Thu, 10 Dec 2020, 23:40 -0500 (2020-12-11T04:40 GMT)
Project Wyvern

Judy Smark here. Luckiest journalist in the world—
but I'm getting ahead of myself.

As many of you already know, the day after tomorrow I'll be accompanying that respected vision-
ary, supremely influential entrepreneur, liberator
of space itself—am I overdoing it? Yes, I'll be
accompanying my father, Ronnie Smark, as he sails
his twenty billion-dollar luxury yacht, the Wyvern,
into space. That's right, space.

Outer. Space.

We'll be blasting off from Launchpad 36 at Cape
Canaveral, just like the Space Shuttle, on top of
the reusable and eco-friendly rocket Loki 9. Once
the Wyvern reaches orbit, it'll go around the Earth
for an entire day on autopilot. Then we'll spend
five days in a zero gravity, one-room orbital hotel.
I hear it's a suite room, at least.

Then comes the part I'm looking forward to most of
all: docking with the International Space Station,
where we'll be staying with the astronauts through
Christmas before returning to Earth. Don't miss the
livestream of the docking! It'll be history in the
making, that much I can promise.

The hardest part will be spending all that time
alone in a single room with that irascible old
mule Ronnie. I'll just have to try to remember the
time when we used to get along . . . You know, back
before I started elementary school. I wonder if
he'll be okay. Did you notice him peeking at that
phone he was hiding behind the mic stand at the
press conference? I can hear him yelling at someone
on the phone right now! Is this a man ready to spend
two weeks in orbit?

P.S. I've decided to update my blog with my thoughts
in real time. Don't worry, though, I'll write it all

up professionally for the book afterwards. (See,
K.? I wouldn't leave my favorite agent out in the
cold.)

Judy Smark
Florida

2 A Proclamation

Fri, 11 Dec 2020, 03:23 -0800 (2020-12-11T11:23 GMT)
Pier 37 Warehouse, Seattle

Beneath the Alaskan Way Viaduct cutting north-south along Seattle's coastline, Chance parked her Porsche Cayenne, checked to make sure that no one was around, and then headed for the warehouse at Pier 37 where Shiraishi was lying low. The very location revealed how incompetent the previous Chances had been. An East Asian person walking around in such a sparsely populated warehouse district was bound to stand out. To make matters worse, just past the warehouse was an office of the United States Coast Guard. A pier crawling with guardsmen 24/7 was simply the worst spot imaginable for a hideout.

As she climbed the warehouse's exterior stairs, Chance's thoughts turned to the progress being made on the construction of their new hideout downtown. They had secured the second floor of an office building right in the center of the city, and its "sterilization" would be finished within the week. Replacement of the wallpaper with material that blocked electromagnetic waves was still under way, but they could probably move in next week, though perhaps not start working there just yet. Chance raised her left hand, implanted with an RFID chip, to open the electronic lock beside the door. From inside the room, she heard Shiraishi's fluent but strongly Russian-accented English. Chance opened the door a crack. In a room lit only by a single bare bulb, Shiraishi was seated on a bed facing a television, in the middle of a videoconference. Under the wavering light, she could see Shiraishi exhale white breath with every word he spoke. In this season, the unheated warehouse control room they used could drop below freezing. Thinking of Shiraishi holed up in these atrocious conditions for five long years, Chance felt renewed admiration for his devotion.

"That is right, Jose," said Shiraishi. "X-Man prefers them Syd Mead–style. I have no doubt that he will choose the illustration you made based on my sketch. So let us get that thousand dollars, yes."

"Thanks so much for your help, Kirilo," said the man on the television screen. "But this satellite plan . . . Where did you get it? It's uncannily realistic."

"My father drew up the plan himself. He used to design Soviet communication satellites. I just added a little touch of my own to make it more like the Rod from God."

Chance confirmed with some relief that Kirilo, the name Shiraishi was using, was from a zombie profile prepared by the Cyber Front. The real Kirilo Panchenko, a Ukrainian design drafter born in 1979, was already dead. It was no longer wise to use a made-up identity for illegal activities in the present age, when people could perform background checks online.

Chance went behind the television so as not to enter the frame of the camera. Shiraishi continued his conversation with the man he had called Jose without even glancing at her. His lengthy time spent in hiding had taught him to dissemble flawlessly in this way. It amazed Chance that he had learned so much under the wing of such incompetent handlers.

Shiraishi smiled brightly with his whole face as he spoke facing the camera. He had never smiled for Chance in that way. He seemed to be having a great time pretending to be someone else.

"We have little time, Jose. Now is the time to get moving, is it not?"

"You're absolutely right. Speak to you soon then."

The television went dark, and the bare bulb overhead shaded Shiraishi's face with thick shadows. "Thanks for the drawing, Chance," he said. "I just took the liberty of using it. Well, aren't you looking pissed? Is something wrong?"

Chance came around to the front of the television and checked the videoconference log still displayed on the screen. Shiraishi had been talking with a man named Jose Juarez in East LA. His profile listed his job as "conceptual artist." Probably working around Hollywood, she supposed.

The source of the communication was listed as "University of Ukraine." It was one of the many computers that had been seized by the Cyber Front, which were collectively referred to as "Sleeping Gun." There was no shortage of computers in the world with laxly managed security. The Cyber Front's particular target was devices in poor countries unable to update to the latest version of Windows. Shiraishi used these sitting ducks to route his conference calls.

"You seem to have concealed the communication properly," said Chance. "But exposing your face was a mistake."

"Relax. I took care of that."

"How exactly? Don't underestimate the CIA and NSA. They can't follow each and every transmission, but everything gets recorded."

Though nearly every communication over a network, including videoconferences, was encrypted, government organizations also held the encryption/decryption key for major services. Shiraishi's connection to Ukraine would therefore remain encrypted (though even this could likely be cracked within eight hours or so), but the video signal received by the illustrator in Hollywood would be saved in CIA servers as nonencrypted video.

"I know. That's why I altered my face," said Shiraishi, pointing to his eyes. He explained that he had used an intermediary program that randomly changed the angle and position of his mouth and eyes, which were used as recognition criteria by the facial-recognition engines of the software companies that supplied the CIA. He had also run his voice through a program that simulated the mouth and voice box to throw off voiceprint recognition as well. "The machines won't even recognize it as a person's face. The CIA's continuously recording hundreds of terabytes every day. There's no way they'd check video-conferences where no humans even appear."

"But that guy saw your face."

"True, I guess," said Shiraishi with a shrug.

"Never do that again. If you ever need to do another videoconference I can sit in for you."

"Okay. I'll ask you next time."

Chance sighed. It wasn't as if Shiraishi would ever keep such promises.

Chance passed him two thermoses full of coffee. Shiraishi thanked her and poured some coffee into his cup.

"So how's the script for the Supreme Leader and the advertising account coming along?" asked Shiraishi.

"I merged your account with the advertising sponsor. The cat food manufacturer Kitten Master. Payments come from the president's Amex."

Chance forwarded information about Kitten Master from her smartphone to the television. It was a rapidly expanding manufacturer of cat food made from organic ingredients specifically for kittens. The Cyber Front had got their hands on the president's lost smartphone and had stolen all the passwords for his accounts, including email, social networks, and advertising.

"What's the limit?" asked Shiraishi.

"It doesn't seem to have one. You could probably use it up to around $1 million."

Shiraishi whistled. "Poor guy. And all because of you, Chance."

"His fault for not looking after it," she said, curtly ending their discussion of the advertisement before explaining that she'd already received permission to switch the Supreme Leader's speech. The rehearsal and recording were to be conducted in Pyongyang at 9:00 p.m.

"At 9:00 p.m. today?" Shiraishi said, half-closing his eyes and lowering his head slightly for a moment, as though thinking hard about something. "That means it'll be starting soon."

"What?"

"The rehearsal."

"Did you memorize all the time zones?"

"You think I'd waste my time doing that? I just shine a light on a globe I imagine in my head and correct for economic blocs, that's all. I'd never do something so stupid as memorize each and every one." Shiraishi patted the sleeping bag he'd laid out on top of the bed. "Take a seat, why don't you? Let's have a gander at the princeling's speech."

Fri, 11 Dec 2020, 12:15 -0700 (2020-12-11T19:15 GMT)
Peterson Air Force Base

"Come in."

Hearing the knock on his open door, Colonel Claude Lintz rolled up the mouth of the paper bag he'd had his nose in and put it behind his computer display. He'd never live it down if rumors spread that the reason he'd been late for work was that he'd gone to buy one of the organic wheat Danishes that Starbucks had started selling this year.

Looking up at the door, he saw Staff Sergeant Daryl Freeman standing there holding a tablet.

"Colonel Lintz. I've come to report on SAFIR 3," said Freeman.

"Ah yes. The incident from yesterday," said Lintz. "Shouldn't you be reporting that to Major Fernandez?"

"I was told to report directly to you, sir. Let's leave the 'space stuff,' as they put it, up to the colonel."

"First I've heard of that. But he made the right call." Lintz urged Freeman to take a seat. Someone like Sylvester who had started out as a pilot would be in over their head when it came to orbital objects. There was also something he wanted to ask Freeman. "I hate to do this when you're the one who came to see me, but let me ask you something first. This story is about SAFIR 3, correct?"

Lintz took a three-page document from his "undecided" tray and put it on the table. It was an article from Geeple with the headline "ROD from GOD attacks ISS!" The article had been contributed by X-Man, and the banner featured an illustration credited to Jose Juarez.

"What do you think?" asked Lintz.

Dragging his chair over, Freeman took one glance at the headline and frowned doubtfully with his thick eyebrows. "That's the article from yesterday, isn't it? I read it earlier, but this is my first time seeing the illustration. Do you mind?" he asked, picking up the printout and briefly looking it over. "This is very well done. There's a swiveling solar array wing, and to prevent that from throwing off the center of gravity there's a projectile serving as a counterweight. You can also tell that the containment truss has been duralumin welded. Every individual element is outdated, but it's well thought out overall. Like a design from the nineties . . . no, I'd say late eighties."

"And what about the author of the article?"

Freeman flipped through the papers and then put them back on the desk. "It's just some geek's wild speculation, sir. I'm pretty sure there was a B movie with the same title. He just stole that and put it together with some stuff he picked off Wikipedia. It's amazing that someone could draw such a realistic rendering of the Rod from God with only an article like this as their guide. This Jose really knows his stuff. He might have gotten advice from someone in the industry."

In an age when private citizens were visiting the ISS on their own rockets, it wasn't out of the question that a space-development professional might work on the illustration for a tabloid article.

"I completely agree. Let's report it just like that. Can I add your name to say you verified the report, Sergeant?"

"That would be fine, but did you get a request for a report from somewhere?" Freeman crooked his neck quizzically.

"Yup. And guess where from? Our friends next door at USNORTHCOM. From what I hear, the aeronautics people and political people are fretting like mad over this issue. They're even asking if we can deploy the ASM-140, experimental stage or not. Space experts like us have got to keep our cool when we deal with this. So tell me about SAFIR 3."

Lintz wrote "checked by Sgt. Freeman" on a Post-it note and stuck it on the document before tossing it back into the tray.

"Thank you, sir. I'm here to report the results of last night's observations." Freeman woke up his tablet and looked down at it. Lintz caught a sparkle of stubble on his chin that hadn't been there yesterday.

"You're fast, Sergeant. Did you stay there overnight?"

"Yes, sir. SAFIR 3 made an overhead pass just last night, so I watched it on the monitor at the Oregon site. I wanted to avoid the heavy daytime air traffic around there by going late and . . ."

Stopping his words short, Freeman looked down at the tablet again, as though he was searching for some kind of error.

"What's the matter?"

At Lintz's question, Freeman straightened up and looked him in the eye. "The second stage of SAFIR 3 is accelerating," he said.

"Are you sure?"

Freeman swept the tablet to the side and put his hands together on top of the table. "There's no mistake. I double-checked. With an optical telescope, I could even see the light that X-Man claims is the thruster."

Lintz took out the printout that he'd returned to the paper tray. He turned over the first page with the illustration on it and looked carefully at the sequential photographs with the caption "Moment of acceleration" for the Rod from God.

Freeman slid the tablet across the table. "This is a high-resolution image from X-Man's site."

On the screen was a photograph of a cylindrical object tilted diagonally. Its three-dimensional contours appeared in sharp relief against the blackish-blue sky.

"Where was this taken?"

"At 7.67 degrees south, 52.68 degrees east. That's where X-Man runs his Seychelles Eye, an observatory located on the Indian Ocean."

"It's been asleep for quite a while . . . It can't actually still be rotating?" said Lintz, pointing at the photograph.

The rocket had been launched December 1. The idea that the cylinder might still be angled on its side after ten days was crazy. A long, thin object with a heavy engine on one end should've been standing up by now under the influence of tidal-rising power.

"That's one problem," said Freeman, "but the more important issue is its acceleration."

Lintz couldn't have agreed more and urged Freeman to continue.

"On its two accelerations, SAFIR 3 increased its orbital velocity by 2.4 and 3.2 meters per second respectively."

"So it still had some gas left?"

Freeman shook his head. "The acceleration occurred within one hundredth of a second."

"What's that?" Lintz's gut told him this was impossible. In his head, he made a simple formula. For a four thousand–kilogram object to increase its velocity by 3.2 meters a second in one hundredth of a second would require 1,280,000 newtons of thrust. Only a few rockets had that kind of power, such as—

"You're telling me it's on par with the Space Shuttle? The *Energia*?"

"Well, we've only made two observations so far, sir, but . . ." Freeman nodded.

As Lintz stared at him, he felt a certain heat deep in his sinuses that he hadn't felt in ages—not since the bunker beneath Cheyenne Mountain. In a shelter four hundred meters below ground, through 1.6 kilometers of tunnel, protected by two twenty-five-ton explosive resistant doors, he'd sat wondering whether an unidentified blip floating in Russian airspace was a passenger plane or a bomber or maybe an ICBM, nervously watching for indications of all-out nuclear war.

"Sergeant, that's . . ." Lintz stopped himself. He wanted to work with Freeman to solve the mystery of this object. But, unfortunately, the job was outside his domain of authority. NORAD was no longer the main player in orbital monitoring. If SAFIR 3's second stage was an orbital weapon as X-Man claimed, Lintz was supposed to report it to USNORTHCOM, and if it was debris, to the Inter-Agency Space Debris Coordination Committee established in 1993. Both of these organizations were surely following the Rod from God story, which had even been taken up by the popular media site Geeple. They would probably be grateful for observational data from NORAD, but, Lintz realized, offering a hypothesis that was largely subjective would not be a wise move. "Sorry, but I'm going to handle this myself."

Freeman's lips tensed ever so slightly. Lintz wondered if he'd crushed the young man's hopes. A spent rocket was displaying obviously erratic behavior, and here was some incompetent commander trying to shelve the whole thing. If that was how he took it, well, too bad. Though it might be best to have Freeman continue his observations and—

"Colonel! Your hotline isn't connecting." A deep voice overlapped with Lintz's thoughts. Captain Jasmine Harrison was standing in the doorway with her hands on her hips. "Your BlackBerry's out of batteries, isn't it? Maybe you would have remembered if you hadn't been fooling around at Starbucks!"

Jasmine's round black finger pointed below Lintz's belly. Tucked somewhere down there was his BlackBerry, which he used for important official communications. The cell phone was ancient, having been issued to Lintz fifteen years ago, and its battery had to be replaced twice daily, as Jasmine had implied.

"Sorry." Noting his hefty flab, Lintz inserted his hand beneath his belly and withdrew his BlackBerry from his belt case. The battery still had 30 percent left, but as he watched, the signal indicator switched from OUT OF SERVICE to SEARCHING.

"I've heard that fat blocks reception, you know," said Jasmine. "Since you refuse to diet, please strap it to your arm or somewhere more appropriate. Major Fernandez got in touch while he was on lunch."

"I'm really sorry. I'll be more careful. So what was the major contacting us about?"

"This is a matter for field officers and above. If you'll excuse us, Sergeant Freeman." Jasmine pointed to the doorway and gave Freeman a wink. At this polite dismissal, Freeman stood up.

"Hold on there, Sergeant," said Lintz. "You have my permission to continue with your observations. If you learn anything, report directly to me. Understood?"

"Yes, sir. Thank you, sir."

After watching Freeman leave, Jasmine approached Lintz's desk and pointed to a message that had been blinking in the corner of his display.

"The major requested that you watch a video. It's a speech from the Supreme Leader of North Korea set to be broadcast in twelve hours. Since it's critical of American space development, the video has been passed on to us for verification. The CIA found it uploaded to a YouTube account and sent it here."

"Thank you for coming to let me know."

"You're welcome. There's anything you need, just let me know." Promptly turning her plump body around, Jasmine was about to step out the doorway when she looked back over her shoulder. "What sort of mission are you going to say you were on when you went to

Starbucks for that Danish? I'll leave the pleasure of that little secret all to you. Your office just reeks of pastries."

The door closed with a bang.

Sat, 12 Dec 2020, 10:15 +0900 (2020-12-12T01:15 GMT)
Japan Aerospace Exploration Agency's Tokyo Office,
Solar City, Ochanomizu

Surrender space, America!

A man in an olive-colored outfit that wasn't quite a military uniform and wasn't quite a work suit raised his fist into the air and smashed it down on a press conference–style table.

Daiki Kurosaki was watching the man give a speech in a thirty-person capacity room on a one hundred–inch display used for meetings. With him was a coworker under his supervision, Makoto Sekiguchi. They were both taking notes while nibbling on junky snack foods.

A report that North Korea would be giving an "important" speech on space development had reached Kurosaki at six o'clock that morning. The JAXA International Relations Department, to which Kurosaki belonged, had to provide their "space experts' opinion" to the minister of science and education and the minister of space policy. A Japanese space-development official had brought him on board and gotten him up to speed, but apparently the original intelligence had come from America. A country that listened in on all communications was on a whole different playing field.

As he was thinking all this, Kurosaki followed the machine-translated English subtitles superimposed over the chest of North Korea's leader, without which he would have been unable to follow the speech.

The steady march of our space program has been impeded again and again by the superpowers. The test launches of our rockets intended for peaceful use are called missiles, and mere observational satellites are seen as orbital weapons. Why are such iniquities allowed to prevail?

Kurosaki couldn't understand the audio at all, but YouTube's machine translation was smooth, if a bit wordy. And the same sentences kept looping over and over.

"That's the third time he said that," muttered Sekiguchi in the seat across from Kurosaki.

Looking over, Kurosaki saw him poking at his tablet with his elbow on the table. "You look really bored," he said.

"Yeah, because he just keeps repeating the same thing."

"Hmm. So he does." Following Sekiguchi, Kurosaki pushed his pen and pad to the side and reached into a bag of potato chips. The speech was the usual vitriol dressed up in courageous language. "We'll be watching this recording a few times more anyways. So let's try to enjoy it as regular viewers this time around. Like, just look at the kid. He's completely transformed."

In the eight years since the Supreme Leader had been inaugurated, his eerily glossy skin and frequently trembling voice had begun to settle into maturity, and he was giving speeches to the people more frequently. The careful choreography of following in the footsteps of his grandfather rather than those of his more reticent father had probably forced him to grow up, thought Kurosaki.

"Is there something different about him?" asked Sekiguchi.

"Sure. He's a big boy now. Before he was so obviously a child."

Give back space! The leader's voice and the sound of him punching the table rang out together.

"No way, Kurosaki-san. That's a little kid right there if I ever saw one." Sekiguchi pointed to the screen with his straw and laughed, showing a flash of white teeth. Being in his midtwenties, Sekiguchi probably didn't know how bumbling and green the Supreme Leader had been at the time of his inauguration. That would've been when Sekiguchi was in high school.

"I'd watch what you say there. Child or not, this is the ruler of a nation we're talking about. But, man, is this long. The guys making the official Japanese translation must be in tears. Poor suckers."

"If all we needed was English, this machine translation looks like it would do the trick. It's just scary how smooth it is . . . Huh?"

Sekiguchi cocked his head to the side quizzically and looked at the English subtitles on the screen in bewilderment.

At this juncture, we of the Democratic People's Republic of Korea have decided to strike the iron hammer of justice upon those symbols of American supremacy and imperialism—space stations.

"What's up?" asked Kurosaki.

"The speech and the subtitles don't match."

"You can speak Korean too?"

"Just a touch. It's not as good as my Chinese."

Sekiguchi gave Kurosaki a wink through a thin slit he created between his index finger and thumb. A career bureaucrat on temporary assignment from the Ministry of Science and Education, Sekiguchi's language abilities had been recognized by JAXA, who'd assigned him to the Department of International Affairs. He'd told Kurosaki he only had "a smattering" of foreign languages, but as it had turned out, he was proficient in English, French, German, and Chinese, and now a fifth language had been added. If he suddenly starting speaking Arabic next, Kurosaki wouldn't have been surprised at all.

"There it is again." Sekiguchi pointed at the screen.

"You mean the bit where he says 'iron hammer' or whatever?"

"Yeah. You hear where he says *cheolgwon*. That means 'clenched fist,' but the English subtitles say 'strike the iron hammer.' He's not saying anything about any space station at all. If you put it together in context and translate it roughly into Japanese, it's something like 'American space development will come up against our powerful fist-like will.' The fact that YouTube's machine translation has been this smooth is just weird to begin with."

"I don't really get it, but . . . This is no good."

"What isn't?"

"It's the minister." Kurosaki turned over the paper on which he'd been taking notes and handed it to Sekiguchi. Printed on the back were the schedules of the minister of science and education and the minister of space policy. The former could be set aside because he was currently traveling abroad, but the problem was the space minister, who was known for frequent gaffes. "He loves English—actually, that's about all he has going for him—so he should be able to read these subtitles himself. Then he'll jump to mad conclusions about the speech."

The minister of space policy was set to have an interview that evening and then make an appearance later that night on the online media site Piyo Live. It was up to them to make sure he didn't say anything stupid.

"Oh boy. Piyo Live, is it?" said Sekiguchi. "Journalists doing the Japanese version of Geeple will be there too. Did you hear the news? The headline in English was 'ROD from GOD attacks ISS!' I'm pretty sure there was a Japanese—ah, here it is."

Sekiguchi turned his tablet to show the screen to Kurosaki. Above what could only be called random nonsense about orbital weapons was an all-too-well-realized illustration. Annoyingly, a kitten leaped out of an advertisement for cat food and ran across the article.

"Take a look at the comments. Someone is posting from their Facebook account that North Korea's 'iron hammer' from the speech is the Rod from God."

"Who? What idiot would write something as irresponsible—"

"An ex-NASA engineer, apparently." When Sekiguchi opened the link for the comment, a Facebook account appeared. After staring at it for a while, he said, "This is weird."

"What's wrong?"

"If this is a real ex-NASA engineer's profile, I'm Neil Armstrong."

"A prank, huh? Oh boy."

Kurosaki pressed the sides of his eyes. If the minister improperly understood the subtitles of the leader's speech and then heard from a journalist that a NASA engineer had stated that the 'iron hammer' was the Rod from God, he'd probably be seized by the idea that North Korea was using orbital weaponry to keep America in check. Kurosaki was reminded of what an old friend had once told him: "People are most certain about the things they discover for themselves." The minister simply lacked the familiarity with space-development technology to tell how preposterous the Rod from God theory was.

Sekiguchi was tapping on his tablet like crazy.

"What are you doing?" Kurosaki asked.

"Translating the North Korean speech into Japanese. Ugh, this sucks. And I thought I'd be home by evening." Sekiguchi was smiling. By nature, he liked to be the one to resolve a crisis.

"I see. Well, I'll send in a report that says the so-called Rod from God is not a plausible weapon. If we can get the minister some information that'll make him feel more in the know than the journalists, that should stop him from loosing his lips."

Kurosaki remembered his friend. If he'd been here in this situation, what kind of report would he write? Just like Sekiguchi smiling

there before him as he rushed in to put out the fire, he'd surely
have . . .

Shambe, 22 Azar 1399, 09:02 +0430 (2020-12-12T05:32 GMT)
Tehran Institute of Technology, Aviation Research Building

A spider descended from the ceiling on a thread and landed on
a drafting table that stood on the edge of a grubby desk. Jamshed
Jahanshah swept the cuff of his loose work suit over the paper resting
on the drafting table and tried to knock the eight-legged intruder that
had interrupted his calculations onto the floor. The dangling thread's
movements defied Jamshed's predictions, and with a soft flutter, it
tangled itself into his mustache. The cause of this little incident was
that someone had opened the door.

Wiping off the thread, Jamshed turned around in his chair.
There, in the dim laboratory doorway, stood Alef Kadiba, a friend of
his enrolled in the Department of Law.

"*Here* you are," said Alef. Wearing brand-new jeans, a warm-
looking sweater, and a North Pole mountain parka, he carried a tablet
in a yellow case under his arm. An American model owned only by
a select few at Tehran IT, it was even fitted with a SIM that let him
access the websites of America and the EU. Such service contracts
were usually reserved for foreigners, but he was able to acquire the
privilege because his father ran a trading company.

The cuff of Jamshed's cotton work suit was all black now, so he
stripped down to his regular clothes underneath and slung the suit
over the back of his chair. Another draft came in, and the threads
hanging from the ceiling began to sway about erratically.

"I'm surprised to see you too. What are you doing up so early in
the morning, Alef, and all the way out here?"

Alef frowned with his shapely eyebrows, brushed off the thread that had made contact with his nose, and looked up at the web-covered ceiling. "This room is just incredible."

"I've got no funding. No tea to offer you. No students even." Jamshed beckoned his friend over.

The exterior of the Department of Astronautical Engineering research building looked impressive, but everything else about it was sorely lacking. The electricity was insufficient, to say nothing of the computer network. The walls were uninsulated and the ceiling bare of panels. Power cables and the absolute minimum number of Ethernet cables ran along the rungs of wiring racks that spanned exposed beams down to an array of computers directly below them, and countless spiders had made nests in the cracks. The computers, too, left much to be desired, all of them outdated models connected to bulbous cathode-ray tube displays. Even Jamshed, the head of the research center, had been reduced to applying a Chinese-made update to a pirated version of Windows XP and was nursing that along carefully.

"I found an interesting news clip," said Alef. "It has to do with Korea."

"You mean Professor Ryu?"

In the Department of Astronautical Engineering, if you said "Korea," it meant "Professor Ryu," sent there from North Korea on a technological exchange program. He'd been sold as an engineer involved in the important task of constructing the Taepodong-2 missile, but the professor was not exactly pleasing to the eye and had garnered little respect. Rumor had it that he had been demoted for failing at some project or perhaps inciting the displeasure of the upper echelons. Saying they were exchanging personnel and technology made great PR, but the program was also being used by both countries to foist incompetent rejects on each other.

"No, I mean North Korea. The professor's home country. Those guys are really going for it. You should take a look for yourself, Jamshed."

"I couldn't care less what North Korea is doing. Underdeveloped countries have no bearing on my research."

"You mean like those balloons you sent up? How did that go, by the way? You don't seem to be working on it much these days."

"Oh, I'm working on it," said Jamshed, glowering at Alef. He had finished a paper summarizing his experiments dropping homemade devices from a balloon, but Hamed, his advisor, had been demoted to a post in North Korea without ever understanding its real significance. His demotion had come about because the SAFIR 2 he had helped to design had failed to release its satellite. "There's no way I'd stop this research. The experimentation stage is over. All that's left is to do calculations on paper."

"Well, keep on it, then," said Alef, pulling a sheaf of papers piled on the desk toward him and propping up his tablet against it before pressing play on a video. "This is a speech given by the leader of North Korea that was broadcast earlier today, but did you hear that thing he just said, 'iron hammer'? I thought you might be interested in seeing the real thing."

Looking proud of himself, Alef stroked the screen and brought up an English article entitled "ROD from GOD attacks ISS!"

"This is from Geeple, right?" Even Jamshed, who was unable to connect to America and the EU through the Internet, had heard of the online tabloid Geeple. That was because the Japanese service Meteor News occasionally pointed out Geeple's mistakes in their paid newsletter. The subscription fee of two euros a month was a lot for Jamshed, but he was grateful to have access to the service, as it provided glimpses of the outside world.

"I know this site is full of hoaxes, but it all depends on the article. This one seems legit. There's even an illustration to go with it. Have you heard of the Rod from God? It's an orbital weapon that uses *connected* energy to smash a *token project* into the Earth."

Jamshed skimmed through. The article was filled with hyperbole and text in all caps, so he could kind of understand Alef's mistakes, but still . . . "Hey, Alef. I know this article might be a tough read, but it says the weapon drops *tungsten projectiles* on the Earth with *kinetic energy*."

"Oh. What does that mean?"

Jamshed sighed. "To put it plainly, all it says is 'drop a metal rod from orbit onto the Earth using gravity.'"

"Wow, that's amaz—"

"Sure, but hold on," Jamshed interrupted, trying to think how he was going to explain this to his friend, whose major was law, so that he would actually understand.

"Smacking an orbital object into the Earth is much harder than you'd imagine." Jamshed flipped to a fresh page on the drafting board and drew two concentric circles. On the outer circle he also drew an arrow.

"The inner circle is Earth, and the outer circle is the orbit followed by satellites. Got it?"

Alef, hand to his chin, nodded.

"Satellites with the altitude, for example, of the International Space Station fly at a velocity of 7.7 kilometers per second." Jamshed added an X to the outer circle and wrote *7.7 km/s*. "Now imagine we were to release a metal rod here. What do you think would happen?"

"It would fall to Earth."

"Nope. The inertial motion of 7.7 km/s isn't going to just disappear. It would keep flying along the same orbit." Jamshed drew a curving line from the X along the outside of the outer circle and added another arrow.

"The only way to make it fall to Earth is to whack it in the opposite direction." Jamshed added a short arrow above the X going in the opposite direction of the previous one.

"When disposing of satellites, reverse thrust is used in this way to bring them down to a lower orbit, where they come in contact with the atmosphere and burn up." Jamshed drew a straight line from the X toward the perimeter of the inner circle, the surface of the Earth. "To do something like what's described in that article, you would have to eliminate the weapon's orbital velocity all at once. But you've got no brakes or anything like that to work with. The only way is to accelerate against the direction of motion."

"So you'd need something like a rocket engine, I guess."

"Exactly. And there would have to be fuel in the engine. So say we wanted to knock ten tons of metal from the altitude of the ISS on a course directly perpendicular to the ground. Well, the gravitational acceleration is a bit small, but if we were the SAFIR's engine . . ." Jamshed wrote *10exp(7700/350/8.7)* on the margin of a piece of paper. He was using the Tsiolkovsky rocket equation. Formulated more than one hundred years ago in 1898, the equation remained valid even today, obeyed by all rockets that flew by expulsion of propellants. Jamshed tapped on a scientific calculator with the numbers worn off and completed his calculation.

"It looks like one hundred . . . and twenty-five tons of fuel would be required. Keep in mind this is an extreme example."

"One hundred twenty-five tons to drop ten tons . . ."

"And to get that up into orbit, you would need an immense amount of fuel as well. Just to put it in perspective, the object we used SAFIR 3 to send up only weighed 100 kg."

Alef looked back and forth between Jamshed's face and the numbers at his fingertips, his mouth agape.

"You didn't get your PhD with only pencil and paper for nothing."

"Are you being sarcastic?"

Alef opened his eyes wide, looked up at the ceiling, and clicked his tongue. A gesture that meant "no."

"Fine, whatever. You're right that no one does calculations like these in their head these days. But paper and a calculator"—Jamshed crumpled up the piece of paper with the circles on it and threw it in the garbage bin—"are the only tools I've got. Only the students working on the SAFIR get computers."

"Sorry, Jamshed. I was out of line. So anyways, this 'iron hammer' . . ."

"It has to be North Korea. Just another one of their bluffs probably. Putting weapons in orbit and attacking orbital objects are prohibited by international treaties to begin with. And America isn't going to stay quiet about this. I'm guessing China will make the first move. If North Koreans start playing with fire in orbit where their inhabited space station, Tiangong-2, is, China will bring down the 'iron hammer' of a food embargo."

"But they could just hide it, couldn't they? Like, they could break it down into small parts, launch them one by one, and assemble the whole thing in orbit or—"

"Not going to happen. A debris defense system has been constructed up there. There's no chance it would miss a weapon that large. Even private services can tell you the location of debris only a few centimeters in length."

Jamshed spun his chair so he was facing the computer on his desk and opened Meteor News's "Debris Corner" to show Alef. Some hundreds of thousands of pieces of debris were indicated with small green dots, and the ones with some likelihood of falling into the atmosphere were highlighted red.

"This is an online service from Japan. See how much you can learn even with just the information that's been made public? There's just no way an object big enough to smash into the Earth would go undetected."

"Wow, that's incredible. I can't believe this is all done by a private company . . ."

Jamshed was about to point out that it was, in fact, done by an individual, but then he noticed how intensely Alef was staring at the 3-D display on Meteor News and was reminded of how remarkable it was. With every single piece of debris and satellite on one screen, the amount of information was surely immense, but it was never tiring to look at, and following a particular orbital object that interested you was almost effortless. The service was so well designed it wasn't surprising that Alef would assume it was a much bigger operation than it actually was.

"This service depends a lot on the Internet too, doesn't it?"

"It must," Jamshed replied, an instant before realizing the direction in which Alef wanted to steer the conversation. He braced himself.

"You need Internet too, Jamshed. Why don't you come to the rally next week? We—"

"It's got nothing to do with me."

"Don't just brush me off like that. Having no access to American sites is just as big a problem for you as the rest of us. Not even the guys in the architecture department are using calculators and paper anymore. I'm sure there are countless free tools online for you space people too."

"We can't connect, and that's just the way it is. I'll find a way to work around it. There were no computers a hundred years ago, and space hasn't changed a bit since then. You're the one who should be concerned. You must've heard that some tricky characters are going to be there."

Jamshed had heard that several antigovernmental organizations were planning to co-opt the demonstration that Alef was promoting, "*Azadi Interanet.* Internet Freedom." It was unlikely that such rumors had failed to reach Alef's ears, but it was difficult for someone with the sort of privileged upbringing Alef had enjoyed to wrap his head around the possibility of such malignant intentions.

Whether he had grasped Jamshed's concerns or not, Alef stroked his neat mustache and smiled. "It'll be fine. What we're after isn't so outrageous. Just free Internet access of the kind already enjoyed by foreign companies expanding their business in Iran. Democracy and Islam are highly compatible in essence. If our imams were to see the Internet too—"

Jamshed waved his hand dismissively with a fed-up smile to show he was tired of hearing this.

"I want you to be there, Jamshed. You may not realize this, but the students really respect you."

"Yeah, right."

"They say you have a backbone. They say if you joined us, then even a few of the guys from the astronautical engineering department, who think about nothing but 'the jump' or 'the leap,' or whatever it is, might join us too."

"A few? If it's just a few, then what's the point? And it's like I told you earlier. My research is coming along. So you take care of your business and I'll take care of mine."

"How disappointing to hear you say that, Jamshed. We'll be at the student center if you change your mind."

Jamshed watched Alef brush aside threads of spiderweb as he made his way toward the exit and then shifted his gaze to the drafting board. To the blueprint and formula. The laws that govern the universe might not have changed, but if only he had free rein to use computers, this calculation would be done in an instant. If only he could read the latest academic articles . . . The manager of Meteor News mentioned again and again in various articles that he wasn't a specialist. Jamshed guessed he was just being modest but was still amazed that an individual could create a service of such quality. Without a doubt, the total quantity of knowledge buried in the Internet was just incredible.

Jamshed sighed deeply and added a new line to his drawing. Just how far advanced were the people on the outside?

Sat, 12 Dec 2020, 15:00 +0900 (2020-12-12T06:00 GMT)
Shibuya, Fool's Launchpad

. . . In closing, thanks for your honest words.
Regards,
Kazumi Kimura
Meteor News

Kazumi hesitated for a moment, wondering if his English was okay, and then pressed Send. The English specialist at Fool's Launchpad, Mary, to whom everyone outsourced their language queries, had messed up a translation. Her bottom-of-the-barrel prices were attractive—¥30,000 monthly retainer and ¥3,000 per translation into Japanese—but her translations frequently caused problems because she knew little about IT.

Akari was spreading out her equipment beside Kazumi when she heard him sigh and asked, "What's wrong?"

"Our English whiz screwed me over. Want to a have a look? It's pretty long."

Kazumi chat messaged Akari an email sent to him by someone named Ozzy Cunningham along with Mary's translation of it. The message's subject, "Fuckin TLE!" had been rendered as "Splendid telephone!" and three full screens of biting sarcasm had transformed into a fan letter. Ozzy's mail wasn't just long, it was crammed with technical words related to astronomy and IT jargon. So hardly an easy read, but Kazumi wished Mary would lay off on her stream-of-consciousness translations informed by limited understanding.

By the time she had finished reading the message, Akari's shoulders were shaking with laughter. "Kimura-san. You should take care of English yourself. Mary's is junior high level at best."

Without thinking, Kazumi swept his gaze around the room. Many of his office mates at Fool's Launchpad trusted the services provided by Mary. Akari, with her bizarre style and spectacular skills, had developed enough of a reputation in the office for her strong sense of individuality that she could get away with saying such things, probably even to Mary herself. But Kazumi didn't like the idea of being made her accomplice. Kazumi sighed. Aside from him and Akari, only a handful of their colleagues were present, racing the clock to finish a web creation project. All of them wore headphones and were fully absorbed in their tasks. Luckily, it seemed, there was little chance anyone had overheard the conversation.

"What's the mistake this Cunningham guy's on about?" asked Akari.

"That the TLEs on Meteor News are wrong. According to him, there's something fishy about the ones for SAFIR 3." Kazumi clicked the link in the signature at the bottom of Ozzy's email and the home page for Seychelles Eye appeared on the screen. "Oh. I know this guy. He's famous." Kazumi realized this as soon as he saw the orbital-weapon illustration at the top. The Ozzy Cunningham who was complaining to Meteor News was X-Man, the guy who had contributed the Rod from God article to Geeple that was making a stir. Kazumi had had no idea he was a paying subscriber to Meteor News.

"Wow. Can I have a look too?" said Akari.

"Of course," Kazumi replied, messaging her the URL for Seychelles Eye and then taking a close look at the article. *If Meteor News is being slandered here, we'll have to make a complaint of our own*, Kazumi thought as he began to read the article, but he soon found himself enthralled by the many beautiful photographs. Their resolution was phenomenal. Definitely taken with an optical telescope in the meter class. Their metadata said that they had been taken at Seychelles Eye, surely the eponymous location used as the blog's title. This meant that X-Man no doubt personally owned observatory-quality astronomical devices.

As Kazumi was concentrating on reading the article, orange fingernails leaped in front of the screen. Without his noticing, Akari had come around behind him.

"Kimura-san. Are you listening to me? What's this about 'observational data'?"

Her fingernail, painted to match her hair, was pointing at a bunch of numbers near the end of the article. Kazumi immediately clicked the link without thinking, and the browser window filled with numerals broken up by commas.

"If you don't close the tab, your browser's going to crash. I'm downloading it by cURL, but there has to be 150 gigs there—about three hundred million lines."

Kazumi hurriedly closed the browser.

"Here's the data I have so far," said Akari, and put her tablet beside Kazumi. The screen was completely filled with text, each line containing five pieces of data broken up by commas:

00001, 01:55:02.0201 GMT Friday 11 Dec,
     2103020.135308, 4.782202, 0.003021
00002, 01:55:02.0201 GMT Friday 11 Dec,
     2106932.396025, 4.782674, 0.014942
00003, 01:55:02.0201 GMT Friday 11 Dec,
     2101959.492682, 4.784925, 0.023065
00004, 01:55:02.0201 GMT Friday 11 Dec, . . .

"Hmm. What could this be?" Kazumi wondered. "The number at the beginning definitely indicates the sequence, and the next is the time."

"I got that much. But what about the three pieces of data after that?"

"I have no idea. Hold on a second. I think there's a guide to reading X-Man's data somewhere."

Kazumi tried searching within the Seychelles Eye blog. In an entry submitted by an account called "Friday," he found something that said "radar observation data," but technical words were used in an amateurish way throughout the site, so he knew better than to take this description at face value. "I think this data is from observations made with a radio telescope. But there doesn't seem to be a guide to interpreting it. If he's going to put this up online, he should at least tell us how to—"

"Data from a telescope, you say? Sounds like fun. Do you think it's okay to read this however we like?" Akari's eyes were positively sparkling. Apparently there were some things in this world that even she found exciting. Kazumi was amazed.

"It's posted on his blog for everyone to see, so I'm sure it's fine, but what are you thinking?"

"Pattern analysis. The parameter that you said is the sequence number goes up to 1,024 before repeating. It's a 10-bit number. And the time moves forward by one thousandth of a second every time the sequence repeats. That tells me this data has to represent successive changes in a set of values. I want to feed the rest of the data through this little guy."

Akari took a palm-sized electronic substrate from her pocket and dangled it from her fingertips. Kazumi could see USB and Ethernet connectors on a chip wrapped in clear plastic. It was the mysterious device that she had tossed on the table the day before.

"This is the latest Raspberry. It's a miniature Linux machine with a built-in programmable chip. I want to try out parallel computing with him. I won't understand what the data means even after the analysis is finished, so I'd appreciate if you could help me out at that point."

In other words, she had acquired a new toy and wanted to play with it. Kazumi supposed that this was how Akari had cultivated her matchless skills.

"Okay. Just let me know when the analysis is finished. This site has tons of data just like this. We might find something to write about for Meteor News in here," Kazumi said, pointing at the Seychelles Eye page. Suddenly an animated kitten appeared on top of the illustration for the Rod from God. It was an overlay advertisement of the kind growing popular of late.

Akari shrugged. "I see the Kitten Master is here too. It's been on our site ever since yesterday."

"Wha-what? Are you . . . sure?"

"Kimura-san. Don't tell me you only ever look at the site in administrator mode with the advertisements off. There should be a good amount of money coming in from those ads for the past few days."

"Sorry. I'll check right now."

Kazumi clicked on his bookmark for the ad management page. On the control panel was a number higher than he'd ever seen there: ¥300,000.

"See," said Akari. "It's already over ¥300,000 just from yesterday."

"Huh?"

"It looks like Kitten Master has hijacked the pay-per-click advertisements on sites related to the Rod from God. I'll try clicking once, so just tell me how the ad revenue changes."

When Akari brought Meteor News up on her tablet and tapped on the kitten banner, a cat food retail site appeared. It sold a new product marketed as non-GMO and organic. The price was thirty dollars for one hundred ounces, about 3 kg. Not having a cat, Kazumi had no idea if this was a good deal or not. When he saw the number added to the ad revenue, he gasped.

"Five thousand . . . yen?"

This made no sense to him at all. An advertisement that offered ¥5,000 for every click in order to sell cat food for ¥3,000 a pop was inconceivable. The issue of how to post an ad on the web often came up during the AMX hosted by Watanabe, and according to him, a rough target for the conversion rate, representing the ratio of the number of people who clicked on the advertisement to the portion of those people who bought the product, was 3 percent. This meant that to recoup on an advertisement paying ¥5,000, the product should cost approximately ¥1,700,000.

Moreover, this cat had been appearing on Geeple too, which was supposed to get something like 1,500,000 pageviews daily. If 1 percent of the visitors clicked the banner by mistake, the advertiser would have to pay out ¥75 million per day.

"Someone must have made a mistake with the advertisement settings," said Kazumi, "but if you add in the amount for Geeple, it has to run to . . . 100 million—what's wrong?"

Akari was frowning and glowering at the advertisement account displayed on Kazumi's screen, lightly biting her lip. Only then did Kazumi realize she was wearing lipstick of the same orange as her manicure and Afro.

"Numata-san," Kazumi addressed Akari. "Do you know anything about this?"

". . . No, it's nothing. Nice to get an unexpected bonus." Akari shook her head and smiled at Kazumi. He could now see that she was absolutely right. The ¥300,000 was income for Meteor News, of which Akari would take 20 percent.

"It looks like that data is finished downloading," she said. "I'm going to start the analysis."

Returning to the seat across from Kazumi, Akari picked up a monocular display from among the gadgets on her desk, mounted it on her head, and twisted earphones into her ears. With gadgets growing out from her orange Afro and all sorts of devices like the bare substrate in front of her, she looked like a character from an old science fiction movie.

"While you're dealing with that, I'm going to ask if anyone on the Meteor News blog knows how to read this," said Kazumi. "We can't count on Cunningham-san and . . . Are you coming in tomorrow too? It's Sunday, you know."

"Of course. The only time I can lay out all my devices like this is when no one's here, you know." Akari put a small keyboard on her left upper arm and strapped it on. "Also, getting fully decked out like this is way over the top. I can't let anyone see me like this."

Fri, 11 Dec 2020, 23:35 -0500 (2020-12-12T04:35 GMT)
Project Wyvern

Wind dripping with Gulf Stream humidity flutters my hood and blows toward the pure-white rocket lit up by countless LEDs. Am I moved or afraid? Before I know it, I'm hugging my own shoulders.

Seeing me shiver, my father, Ronnie Smark, puts a parka over me. "Behold, Judy. See how far humankind has come!"

Nice literary way to start off, don't you think? No? Okay. I know, I know. But seeing that rocket just moments before takeoff, I just had to write it, though I know I'm no novelist. If only I had Tiptree Jr.'s talent.

Tomorrow, the white tower looming thirty meters tall before me will shake off gravity to carry my father and me to a height of 350 kilometers.

Have you ever tried to imagine such a great dis-tance? I'm five foot eight, and when I stand on the beach looking out to sea, the distance to the far-

thest visible horizon is a mere 4.5 km. If I were
to stand at the highest point on Earth, the peak
of Mount Everest, the horizon would be 356 km away.
In other words, it is the farthest distance you can
see on the surface of the Earth. Can you picture it?
Try to see that distance going straight up. That's
where I'm going.

I'm sorry my units of measurement are all mixed up.
The Project Wyvern space people refuse to count the
distance for me in the miles and yards that I'm
familiar with. In this blog, I'm hoping to give you
a sense of what it's actually like being here.

I have one more thing to apologize for. I've taken
some dramatic liberties with the words of my father
in the introduction. Father forgot I was even there,
and raising his hands to the sky, he screamed, "Look!
See how far the power of the market has come."

Which goes to show you how each person gets excited
about something different. But I want you all to
understand the miracle that occurred in that moment.
When my father screamed, the fuel-replenishment
hose pouring in LNG made from shale gas came loose,
creating a small cloud of liquefied fuel. Then Loki
9, raising its head above the cloud, seemed to me
like a monument standing in a dream. It was a spectacular scene.

Father held his breath, as transfixed by the rocket as I was, and then immediately squeezed his hand into a fist, saying, "Orbit is just down the street, but I'm going to leave this whole neighborhood behind."

Father has reached almost the pinnacle of success as a financier, blessed with incredible luck and the vision to see just a bit further than anyone else, but he intends to go further yet—much further. How much of this is empty boasting? Might he make it to the moon? Mars? I guess both would probably be impossible during our lifetime, but the next generation might go.

I can see that the possibility of that one day coming true rests on the success of tomorrow's launch and our sojourn in space.

I must rest up.

Though I'm sure I'll be too excited to sleep.

—Judy Smark and Father

3   The Launch

Sun, 13 Dec 2020, 09:45 +0900 (2020-12-13T00:45 GMT)
Main Conference Room, Fool's Launchpad, Shibuya

"Sorry to drag you in here," Akari said to Kazumi. "I thought 'radio telescope' meant there would be visuals, but no such luck, I guess."

Uncharacteristically, the spacious conference room at Fool's Launchpad was empty except for Akari and Kazumi. It was always booked for most of the work week, but even their office mates usually drew the line at working on Sundays. Akari and Kazumi had only come in themselves because of Ronnie Smark's big launch. Loki 9 was scheduled to blast off that evening, insert the spacecraft Wyvern into orbit, and then slowly descend to the Atlantic Ocean so that its expensive, newly developed engine could be reused. Kazumi had been sitting at his regular desk intending to post the rocket's predicted positional data to Meteor News when Akari had shown up later than expected and immediately brought him here.

Smart monocular display poking out from her orange mass of hair and a keyboard strapped to her arm just like yesterday, Akari arranged three palm-sized projectors on the table before connecting each one to a miniature Raspberry computer, explaining that a single computer and projector wasn't enough to display the data. She switched on and adjusted the projectors one by one, overlaying the three images on the conference room whiteboard.

"You've already processed 150 gigs?" Kazumi exclaimed. "Wow."

"The size of the data was inflated because it was all stored as strings," said Akari. "Once I converted it into pure numeric data, three Raspberries were enough. Turns out there were three types of data in there, so I graphed each one in a different color."

Red, green, and blue graphs were now projected across the full sixteen feet of whiteboard. The red line was valley shaped, dipping deeply in the middle, while the green line had a peak at around the same place. The blue line was discontinuous, rising slowly as it moved from left to right until it reached the top of the whiteboard at about the center, at which point it reappeared at a much lower position and began rising again. Unlike the smooth red line, the green and blue lines both oscillated rapidly around the center of the board.

"Is this everything?" asked Kazumi.

"This is the data for ID number zero," said Akari. Should I overlay the other 1,023? They were basically the same."

Akari reached across with her right hand to hit the return key on the keyboard strapped to her left arm. A torrent of data poured onto the whiteboard overlay. The many red lines all followed more or less the same path, but the blue and green lines seemed to grow thicker toward the center, where countless overlapping lines spanned a vertical band of one or two inches.

Kazumi peered at the graphs. If Ozzy's blog was releasing useful observational data for SAFIR 3, there should be information about its orbit in here somewhere. Or perhaps this data was just nonsense?

"I'm getting ahead of myself," said Akari. "Let me explain how to read the graphs. The horizontal axis is time. Zero ranges from 2:15 a.m. standard time to 2:15 and 24 seconds—"

"Wait, 2:15 GMT? In that case, it's definitely observational data. That's exactly when SAFIR 3 would have been visible to Ozzy."

"Oh, good. So it probably is meaningful." Akari smiled. "Moving on, the red parameter varies from a maximum of two million to a minimum of about 290,000."

Kazumi grasped the import of this at once. "Red is the distance in meters to the observed target," he said.

"Two million meters is . . . two thousand kilometers. And the closest is just 290 kilometers. Isn't that range a bit too wide?"

"Hold on," Kazumi said. "Let me check." Rising to his feet, he half-closed his eyes and stretched his right arm out straight in front of him until his middle finger touched the wall. The sixty-four centimeters from his shoulder to the end of that finger became the 6,400-kilometer radius of the Earth, a convenient 100,000-to-1 ratio. He visualized himself as an observer at the end of his middle finger. The wall was the horizon. He could only see things beyond that plane. Now he just had to calculate the distance to SAFIR 3, sailing through space 290 kilometers—just under three centimeters—beyond his middle finger, when it emerged on this side of the wall.

He lowered his right arm slowly, stopped it once the tip of his middle finger was three centimeters from the wall, and then calculated the distance back to where it had started. Right about twenty centimeters, which came to two thousand kilometers under the 100,000-to-1 ratio.

"It fits," he said. "When SAFIR 3 touches the horizon, it's two thousand kilometers away. When it's directly overhead, the distance is just its altitude—290 km. The range fits. Red is distance."

Akari was staring at him. Kazumi felt the blood rushing to his cheeks. Now he'd done it—performed the ritual when somebody else was watching. Using your body as a visualization tool was a quick and convenient way to estimate the position of objects in orbit, but it was also crude and not very accurate.

"It's just this visualization I do," he mumbled, flustered. "I'm not good at working through equations. Probably a fair bit off . . ."

"You do that too?" said Akari.

"Huh?"

"My mentor, the one who joined JAXA, he used to do the same thing. I don't think he ever calculated in as much detail as you just did, but still. It's an amazing thing to be able to visualize!"

"You think? Wouldn't it be better to be able to calculate properly?"

"No way! Listen, if there's some visualization you use especially often, just let me know. I'll whip up a smartphone app to make it as easy as using a calculator."

Now that they were certain Ozzy's observational data had something to do with SAFIR 3, Kazumi had Akari switch off the red altitude graph. That left two parameters to account for.

Akari stood in front of the whiteboard and used both hands to point at the upper and lower bounds of the blue and green lines.

"Green's maximum and minimum are about plus and minus 1.5. All the blue lines rise to 6.283, then go right back to zero. Oh—radians!" Kazumi had a realization. "Blue is an angle!"

A full 360-degree angle—a circle, in other words—was defined as 2π radians. Twice π, in turn, was roughly equal to 6.283, which was exactly where blue went back to zero.

"It must be the azimuth. The value resets to zero when the object passes to the north. Green is an angle too. About 1.5 radians means ninety degrees—it's elevation. I see it now. These are spherical coordinates!"

So this was the data that Ozzy had put on the Seychelles Eye blog. Tracking logs for 1,024 objects that recorded their distance from the Earth and the direction they were moving. Kazumi was just starting to wonder if he could get permission to use the data on Meteor News when Akari appeared before him, hands clasped together.

"I can make a planetarium out of this! Wanna see?"

There was a video game engine called Unity, she explained, that had a library for processing spherical coordinates.

"Wouldn't that be too much trouble?" said Kazumi.

"I'm already using Unity to make these graphs. Hold on a sec. I'll rig up the VR API."

Akari sat at the table and began tapping away at the keyboard while turning her head this way and that. Kazumi had never imagined that she would know how to use a game engine that had absolutely no application in web design.

"I'll be looking at the graphs," Kazumi said. He approached the whiteboard and examined the regular oscillations of the green and blue lines, tracing them with his finger. It obviously wasn't noise from the observational equipment. Kazumi let his eyes fall half-closed again and tried to visualize the combination of the two angles, but their complexity resisted his methods. What kind of movement *was* this?

"Finished," announced Akari. Kazumi turned to see her offering him a two-lens goggle display. The LED on the frames was already lit.

Kazumi slipped the goggles on. There was the horizon, at about shoulder height. He turned his head and saw marks indicating orientation scroll across his vision. The data from the motion sensor in the goggles was being used to determine which way he was facing and to adjust the display accordingly.

"You just threw this together on the spot?" he asked.

"It's easy when there are already libraries for it," Akari replied. "Ready for the animation? I checked it up until the point that the dots come out of the west."

Kazumi looked in Akari's direction to see a small white dot rising above the horizon. It was a satellite rise like countless others he'd seen before.

"There are 1,024 objects, but their locations are all so close they just look like a single dot," Akari said. "I wonder if this is right."

"It must be," Kazumi said. "We figured out the data format. It is a very dense cluster though. Is the scale right on this thing?"

"It should be accurate," Akari said. "Why?"

As Kazumi watched, the gradually rising white dot smeared into a thick line. The line slowly picked up speed, growing longer and wider as it did, moving up the wall and onto the ceiling.

"Can you zoom in?" he asked. "I want to see the separate points." Looking straight up was starting to hurt his neck, so he lay down on the conference table to stare at the ceiling. He heard Akari typing, and then what had appeared to be a smeared line became clearly visible as a cluster of points like a hazy cloud.

"That's a 100-to-1 zoom," Akari said. "Can I start playback again?"

As Akari spoke, the white points began to slowly move again. Most of them seemed to move in pairs, each partner chasing the other. Kazumi guessed that this had to be the source of the oscillations in the graph.

"Could you zoom in a little closer? Until each point is clearly distinguishable."

"Okay. Zooming in to two thousand to one."

The zoomed-in planetarium was now displaying five pairs of points moving across the sky.

"What *is* this?" Kazumi muttered.

"That's so cool, " Akari said. "It's like they're holding hands."

Akari was right. Each pair whirled around and around in orbit as if holding hands. But there was nothing *cool* about it from Kazumi's perspective. Objects in orbit moved according to simple physical laws. To spin in circles, they would have to be constantly expelling something to drive that motion. What artificial satellite would use its limited fuel that way? It made no sense.

"Hey!" Kazumi exclaimed. "Where'd it go?" The point he was watching had vanished. Then, not far away, another appeared and began whirling in circles like the others.

"Oh, I forgot to mention that," said Akari. "The data set's full of discontinuities. One thousand and twenty-four, that's two to the power of seven. Probably the maximum number of objects that the— telescope, was it?—the maximum number the device that recorded this data can track. To judge from the gaps in the data, I'd estimate that the true number of objects was at least ten times as high. More, probably."

"Ten *thousand* objects?" Still lying on the conference table, Kazumi felt a chill run down his spine. Ten thousand objects in orbit, all crowded very closely together as they whirled. Nothing like that was recorded in the TLEs from USSTRATCOM. He'd never heard of anything like it on any of the sites run by amateurs either. "That's impossible. Unheard of."

"So are these dots debris? If they're unheard of, this is a new discovery, right?"

"I don't think they're debris. I've never seen anything like this in the catalog."

The UN's Committee on the Peaceful Uses of Outer Space published an extremely reliable catalog of debris. It was precisely this reliability that had enabled many of Meteor News's successful shooting star predictions, in fact.

The Debris Catalog was updated constantly based on data from all kinds of sources, from ground radar observations to debris-sensing satellites in stationary orbit. Everything in orbit more than two inches long was supposed to be in there. Ten thousand bits of debris that no one had ever noticed would pose a serious hazard to satellite and space station operations. Not to mention the bizarre way they were moving . . . Just what were these things that Ozzy had seen through his radar telescope?

"Can I see a bit more?"

"Sure," Akari said, unstrapping the keyboard from her left arm and handing it to him. "Arrow keys are Time and Zoom. Hit H for Help. I'm going to get some sleep."

Akari pulled her monocular display out of her Afro and placed it on the table, then pushed some chairs together to lie down on.

"Thanks," Kazumi said. "I'll wake you around noon."

A hand with orange fingernails rose from behind the table and waved in acknowledgment. Moments later, Kazumi heard snoring. Akari's all-nighter was catching up with her.

Tying up the conference room unnecessarily was frowned upon, but no one else would want to use it today. Kazumi suddenly remembered why he was at Fool's Launchpad in the first place. He was supposed to be preparing the Meteor News orbital predictions for Ronnie Smark's rocket, Loki 9. But now he had a bad feeling about the whole thing.

The intended path of Loki 9 and the orbital hotel were completely different from SAFIR 3's current orbit. Neither should have any effect on the other. But then, SAFIR 3's second stage should have come down normally. Instead, it had gained altitude, and now more than ten thousand objects not listed in the Debris Catalog were swarming around it, moving in a way that could not be considered normal at all.

What was going on up there?

And was the Project Wyvern team aware of the ten thousand objects they were sharing low Earth orbit with?

Sun, 13 Dec 2020, 06:13, +0400 (2020-12-13T02:13 GMT)
Desnoeufs Island

Light spilled through the gaps between the array of four monitors, projecting a shining cross on Ozzy's face. Sunrise. As he shifted in his long-suffering Aeron chair, Ozzy heard a squelching sound across the room. Friday must have been night fishing.

"Good morning, Mr. Cunningham."

"Wipe the floor, would you?"

Naked to the waist and carrying a beverage cooler, Friday was walking across the gigantic room toward the kitchen alcove. His sandals, still waterlogged from the ocean, squelched with every step he took. Drops of water rolled like jewels down his ebony skin.

Friday pointed at the breakfast on Ozzy's desk. "Hot dogs again," he observed. "Every day the same thing. Your health will certainly suffer."

"I don't need to hear that crap from you," Ozzy shot back. "I only took you on because you said you could cook, but you haven't made me so much as a bowl of freakin' spaghetti."

"I said that?" Friday smiled. "In any case, it is you, Mr. Cunningham, who refuses the seafood I go to such pains to obtain. Just look at today's catch."

Having reached the kitchen area, Friday turned the cooler upside down and let the bright-crimson fish it contained tumble onto the counter. Ozzy had no idea how anyone could think of eating a fish that looked like that.

"Could I interest you in some sashimi?" Friday asked. Ozzy snorted and waved him away dismissively. Cheerfully ignoring him, Friday produced a long knife and thrust it into the fish's gills without hesitation, beginning to gut it.

An accomplished man, Friday, but not one to keep his opinions to himself. Fluent enough in English to trade barbs with Ozzy, he also spoke Seychellois Creole and French, had a PhD in astronomy, and was licensed to operate a helicopter, boat, and ham radio. It would be hard to find a better assistant for someone in Ozzy's position, one resolved to live on a remote island.

When they had met for Friday's first interview in Victoria, the capital of Seychelles, Friday had simply announced that as long as he was permitted free use of the three-meter optical telescope and high-output radar tuned to track objects in low orbit, he would be delighted to be Ozzy's companion on the island. Ozzy had been half-joking when he'd first called him "Friday," but the man had cheerfully accepted his new moniker and it immediately stuck.

"Take a look at this," Ozzy said. "We struck it big this week."

He connected the monitors into one large display showing a single six-digit figure. *One hundred thousand dollars!* No matter how many times he looked at it, he couldn't believe it. To make that much from advertising in just two days!

Hundreds of thousands of visitors had followed the links in the Geeple story about the Rod from God to its source, Ozzy's blog, and when he'd uploaded the illustration request to MegaHands, a Hollywood storyboard artist had picked up the job. And that wasn't all.

With perfect timing, some cat food company had set up click-through advertising at a rate so high he could only assume it was a configuration mistake. No doubt whatever bright spark in Marketing had come up with the idea of trying to sell cat food to the stargazing nerd community would soon be out of a job, but that was no concern of Ozzy's.

I'm on a roll, he thought. *Might be time to give Friday a bonus . . .*

Spinning his creaking chair to face the kitchen, Ozzy saw Friday approaching him, wide-eyed and shaking his head.

"Telephone, Mr. Cunningham."

"Telephone? That's a word I haven't heard in a while." Ozzy reached deep into his desk, groping for the cordless that had only rung twice since he'd arrived on Desnoeufs, before realizing that he hadn't actually heard the phone ring.

"Not that one, Mr. Cunningham," Friday held up an aged blue Nokia. "They called mine instead."

"Who did?"

"I should like to ask the same question."

Friday pushed the phone, still sticky with fish scales, into Ozzy's hands. Ozzy wiped the face of the phone with one of his hot dog napkins and put it to his ear.

"Ozzy here. What are you doing calling Friday's phone?"

"Ah, good," said a male voice at the other end. "Ozzy Cunningham, tech billionaire, I presume. Read your email once in a while, would you? We've been trying to get in touch."

Whoever it was spoke in that rapid-fire way unique to Americans trying to use their high IQ to dazzle their audience. Not West Coast, this guy. He was from back East.

"You call your partner on that desert island 'Friday'?" the man continued. "Terrible, just terrible. I recommend switching to Johansson. Wouldn't want to give anyone the idea that you were violating his human rights." There was a pleasant, if practiced, laugh. So he knew Friday's real name—the one that even Ozzy sometimes forgot.

"Who the hell are you?" Ozzy asked.

"I don't care to talk on this line. How about you take a video call?"

"Why didn't you—" *Call me directly,* Ozzy started to say, before realizing that the point of the exercise was to make a visible show of power. *I know everything,* the man was saying. *You'd better do as I say.*

"Fine," Ozzy said finally. "My ID's—"

The line went dead, and a pop-up appeared in the lower right of Ozzy's display. A videoconference request from "Unknown." Whoever they were, they knew Ozzy's video ID too.

Ozzy pointed his web camera at himself and hit the Return key. The screen filled with some kind of visual he'd never seen before, then cleared to reveal an impeccably dressed black man. His close-cropped hair and goatee shone in the ruddy sunlight that lit his face from below.

Ozzy calculated the time difference based on the angle of the light. The sun had just risen over the Indian Ocean, so that put his caller somewhere in the Americas at sunset.

"Pleasure to meet you, Mr. Cunningham," the man said. "Name's Bruce. Give Johansson my thanks too, for lending his phone. Back here is Chris."

The man who had introduced himself as Bruce moved his chair, revealing himself to be in a well-appointed room with a white-haired woman seated behind him poring over something in a binder. The woman named Chris raised her head and waved to the camera with a smile. The sunset glare was dazzling on the natural-wood panel-ing and crisp white walls. The table looked to be mahogany. A huge amount of money had obviously gone into this room. Ozzy didn't care much for the low ceiling, though. *Small windows too*, he mused, before realizing where his interlocutors were calling from.

This wasn't somebody's home. The room with the sun shining into it from below was the cabin of an airplane in flight. And not just any airplane—a private jet.

People in expensive suits with unremarkable names. Superficial friendliness, high-quality furnishings. There was really only one way to sum up the scene Ozzy saw through the video call.

"What is this, a spy movie?" he asked.

Bruce laughed, revealing white teeth. Behind him, Chris narrowed her eyes.

"You win, Mr. Cunningham," said Bruce, clapping his exquisitely manicured hands together and leaning toward the camera. "We are, as you suspect, with the Central Intelligence Agency."

Ozzy nodded.

"We'd like to ask you some questions about that article of yours Geeple picked up, and the illustration of the Rod from God by one Jose Juarez. Is now a good time?"

Sat, 13 Dec 2020, 20:04 +1700 (2020-12-13T03:04 GMT)
Peterson Air Force Base

Freeman had had a bad feeling about this meeting ever since arriving at Colonel Lintz's habitually open-door office to find the door closed.

Entering the office, he saw the colonel and Major Fernandez on a sofa opposite a man and a woman in expensive suits sitting with their legs crossed. The man was black and tall enough for his legs to look uncomfortable in the limited space available. The woman was in late middle age and had her silver hair in a flawless coiffure. Both of them smiled and stood to welcome Freeman as he walked in.

"So nice to meet you, Staff Sergeant Freeman," said the woman. "I'm Christina Ferguson. You can call me Chris."

The man, standing behind her, reached out to offer Freeman his hand. "Bruce," he said.

Chris urged Freeman to be at ease. "We're here from McLean," she said. "You may not have been at this job long, but I suppose you understand what that means."

McLean, as Freeman did indeed know, was the city in Virginia where the CIA had built its new headquarters. Of more concern to him, however, was the reason he had been summoned to this meeting, and on that score he had no idea. Nor did it bode well that both Colonel Lintz and Freeman's own direct superior, Major Fernandez, were present at the meeting.

Chris and Bruce lowered themselves back onto the sofa, and Freeman took up a position at ease beside the table.

"Our apologies for the interruption at such a busy time, Sergeant," Lintz said. "It seems our two guests have some questions for you about a certain Rod from God."

Freeman cocked his head quizzically and asked, "Are you referring to SAFIR 3, sir?"

"Here we go again," Bruce said, raising his palms. Lintz sighed. Apparently this topic had already been discussed.

Chris glanced at the two of them and then turned to Freeman with a smile that didn't reach her eyes. "Staff Sergeant Freeman—may I call you Daryl? A bit less formal."

"Yes, ma'am."

"Please don't be offended. It's just that we've heard the same story five times since this morning. We dropped by Cape Canaveral and they were quite emphatic—firing an ICBM is overwhelmingly more efficient than dropping something from orbit. Correct?"

"Yes, ma'am," Freeman nodded.

Chris went over the proofs NASA had offered, counting each one on her fingers as she went. One, the cost performance for a weapon that lifted objects into orbit only to drop them again would be pitiful. Two, an orbital weapon intended to cause mass destruction would by its very existence violate various space treaties. Three, even if a Rod from God could be put into orbit, it would be exceedingly difficult to guide a dropped projectile to a precise location. A ballistic missile would be many times easier.

Freeman listened closely to Chris's review of the facts. The jargon didn't give her any trouble at all. Apparently she had done her homework. At the very least, she clearly understood better than Major Fernandez, who was nodding along in the chair diagonally opposite. His area of expertise didn't extend above the limits of the atmosphere.

"Four," Chris continued, folding her fourth finger over. "Unlike in years past when only the US and the Soviets had high-resolution radar, nowadays every object in orbit, large or small, is logged in a database so that even private citizens can track satellites. An orbital weapon operating in secret simply could not exist. Therefore, a Rod from God is impossible. Does that about sum it up?"

"Yes, ma'am. That is also my understanding."

Freeman was pleased to hear that the specialists at NASA agreed with his analysis but remained wary. Chris had gotten the facts from NASA straight and understood them well enough to repeat them in her own words. So why had she even brought the topic up with him?

Bruce produced a folded piece of paper from his pocket and spread it out on the table. It was X-Man's article. Chris tapped the illustration with one tastefully manicured finger, the nail painted a soft pink.

"What bothers us," she said, "is this illustration."

Fernandez craned his neck over the table to see. "Not a bad job," he remarked. "Lots of fine detail. Looks almost real."

"I should hope so," Chris said. "It *is* real."

Fernandez looked up at her sharply. Lintz and Freeman took another, closer look at the picture.

"This illustration," Chris continued, "is based on plans for an antisatellite weapon that were extracted from SDI and provided to an operative in North Korea in 1989."

"I *knew* it looked familiar," Lintz growled. He looked up at Chris. "So it was the CIA that leaked SDI plans to the Communists, was it? Which side were you on, anyway?"

"Colonel." Bruce uncrossed his legs and opened his palms. "If you're still hung up about the Cold War, write a book about it. I'd love to read what you come up with, and I'm sure our countrymen would too. But for the moment, we need to stay focused on this Rod from God floating around up there as we speak. That's the real threat right now."

Lintz snorted and sat back in the sofa, apparently not interested in pursuing the matter.

"If I may, sir—Bruce?" Freeman said, choosing his words carefully. "This object you call the Rod from God is the second stage of SAFIR 3, launched from Iran. It's a used-up rocket shell."

"Yes, that's the other thing everyone keeps telling me," Bruce replied, one eyebrow raised.

Freeman was surprised at how nonpatronizing the gesture looked. This man had total mastery over his expressions, and Freeman could tell he was not the sort of person who could be beaten in an argument.

"But that object is speeding up," Bruce continued, "And its altitude is increasing. True?"

"Yes," replied Freeman.

"Can a spent rocket shell speed up?"

"No. But—"

Bruce raised his hand with impeccable timing to cut Freeman off. "What I'm saying is all direct from you rocket jockeys," he said. "For the second stage of SAFIR 3 to move into that orbit would have been impossible. That leaves only one conclusion: that object zipping around up there on its thrusters isn't the second stage of SAFIR 3."

Freeman was appalled. The facts about how SAFIR 3 was moving were exactly why it was vital to find out what was making it move.

"Think about it," Bruce continued. "Just as the object is discovered, the leader of North Korea gives a speech hinting at the existence of orbital weapons. And to make sure his meaning gets across—" He paused to point at the illustration. "This picture. A drawing based on plans the North Koreans got from us, the CIA. They're trying to make a statement. They have something."

Freeman looked at Bruce's hands, which were as neatly manicured as Chris's. In the hangar earlier, spreading out the pressure suits, he had noticed the oil that had already seeped into his own fingers. He balled his hands into fists, hiding the stains.

"You think this is just politicians and the intelligence community seeing what they want to see, right?" Bruce asked. "Well, fine. But when we receive a message this loud and this clear, we have no *choice* but to respond."

He was now leaning forward over the table. Chris held up a smartphone behind him. On the screen was a picture of a hugely overweight man in a tank top.

"This is the source of the Rod from God story," she said. "Ozzy Cunningham, a.k.a. X-Man. We got in touch with him earlier. He said he didn't know anything, but we'll be poring over all of his communications for the past three years." She held her upright posture, shoulders straight. "At the beginning of next week, Bruce will pay a visit to Jose Juarez, the LA-based illustrator. Either Cunningham or Juarez is definitely getting information from North Korea. Do you understand? We are serious about chasing down this Rod from God."

Bruce got to his feet, standing beside Chris.

"We also want details about the plausibility of the Rod from God as an orbital weapon," he said. "For that, we need someone who knows space. A professional. NASA can't help us; most of their work is done by civilians. So we came to NORAD, where we won't need secrecy agreements."

Lintz, arms folded, turned his head to face Freeman. This was it—the source of the bad feeling Freeman had had since seeing the closed door. He was going to be asked to babysit a couple of spies chasing down a fantasy.

"Daryl," Lintz said. "I have a favor to ask of you."

Bingo.

"Could you analyze the data based on the assumption that SAFIR 3's second stage is actually a Rod from God and estimate its capabilities in that case? You can assume that the design shown in that illustration is accurate. We want to clarify exactly what sort of tactical maneuvers a weapon of that sort could perform."

Freeman did not relish the prospect of writing a report based on false premises, but it might be better than sorting through Cold War–era documents and trying to make nice with pilots nearing retirement. "Yes, sir," he said. "What should I do about the ASM-140 report?"

Fernandez raised his hand in acknowledgment. "Freeman," he said, "The experimental phase at NORAD is over. The ASM-140 has been adopted by and will see actual operation under USNORTHCOM. I'm sure the handover will proceed without a hitch, thanks to the documentation you prepared."

Actual operation? Were they really going to attach the engines when they'd only just finished testing them? More importantly, the ASM-140 was a weapon that violated the debris-reduction guidelines of the Committee on the Peaceful Uses of Outer Space. It might be permitted for research purposes, but it was hard to believe it would see active service.

"Oh, were you involved in the ASM-140 project too?" Chris asked. "Perfect. We wanted to learn more about how well Operation Seed Pod works, too."

Operation Seed Pod?

Fernandez rocked backwards, slapping his forehead. "How exactly does the CIA know about Seed Pod?"

"Of course the CIA knows about it," said Chris. "We were the ones who proposed using the ASM-140 to destroy satellites in the first place. Just imagine—an antisat weapon whose operation we can restrict to North American airspace. We've already started working on the Russians and the Chinese to make sure they won't complain about the breach in the guidelines."

Chris paused for a moment to glance at the box the Santa hat had come in, still beside Lintz's desk.

"To be honest," she continued, "Operation Seed Pod is the sort of proposal that really should have come from NORAD as part of your weapons-development program. I know you're busy tracking Santa right now, but perhaps you could be a little more proactive about your defensive role."

Ignoring the dark expressions that clouded Lintz's and Fernandez's faces, Chris held up her arm and checked her watch, casually conveying that her business with them was over. "Is the guest house ready?" she asked.

"Major Fernandez will show you the way," Lintz said. "Staff Sergeant Freeman, it's getting late. You can get started on that project tomorrow."

Freeman clicked his heels and saluted. "Yes, sir," he said. "I will support our two guests in whatever capacity they may require. Where should I report in the morning?"

"We'll use this room, Colonel Lintz," Chris said. "You can reach the hotline anytime you like, after all, just by reaching under your belly."

Bruce stood up and put his arm around Freeman's shoulders.

"Skip the uniform tomorrow, Daryl. We might need to take you off base. Can you whip up a short list of Denver's best restaurants?"

These two were no doubt very good at what they did. But they were laboring under a serious misconception. Poring over all of X-Man's—Ozzy's—communications? What they needed to do was study his photographs. Whatever was making SAFIR 3's second stage move that way was many times more important than this mythical Rod from God.

As Freeman was turning toward the door, Bruce's arm still around his shoulder, he noticed Lintz trying to catch his eye. Lintz's index fingers were both pointing up. Fernandez, standing beside him, was doing the same thing.

"See you tomorrow, sergeant," Lintz said. Together with Fernandez, he raised his hands and then let them fall to the left.

"Yes, sir," Freeman said. "See you tomorrow."

He recognized the gesture now. It was one of the hand signals used to communicate with aircraft on the runway.

Proceed at your own discretion.

Sat, 12 Dec 2020, 10:55 -0600 (2020-12-13T04:55 GMT)
A Hotel in Seattle

Shiraishi put his glasses back on, produced a postcoital cigarette from somewhere, and lit up. His brow, still sticky with sweat, shone briefly in the lighter's orange glow.

"That's against the rules here," Chance said.

"Whatever," Shiraishi replied. He propped himself up on one elbow and took a deep drag as he gazed down at Chance's naked body. "It's not like we ever use the same hotel twice. Shame about that, actually—the beds here are quite comfortable."

Without getting up, Chance stretched out her right hand and snuffed out the cigarette without even removing it from Shiraishi's mouth. The sharp tang of melted latex mingled with the tarry smell.

"Plastic fingers, huh?" Shiraishi raised an eyebrow. "Torture or something?"

"It hurt. The rest is covered by a nondisclosure agreement."

Chance's fingers were equipped with resin sacs instead of flesh, the latter having been grated off with a rasp after she was caught spying in Syria. It had been a blow to lose her grip strength at the height of her powers, but being able to painlessly extinguish cigarettes with her fingers had its advantages.

"What an age we live in," said Shiraishi. "Even spies respect their NDAs."

Ignoring his attempt at humor, Chance sat up to toss the cigarette butt into her editor's bag and then lay back down. She slid her right arm under the pillow, fingers curling around the grip of the SIG-9 that had been specially modified to allow her to fire it with her weakened grip.

The gun was no secret from Shiraishi, who cringed theatrically, still up on one elbow. "Relax, would you?" he said. "I'm being good."

"I wonder," Chance said. "By the way, did you hear about Kitten Master? Looks like they'll be bankrupt by the end of next week."

"Is that right?"

"They weren't the most financially stable company to begin with. Throwing a million dollars at Internet advertising in thirty-six hours could hardly cause anything but a panic. Did you have to set the click-through rate to fifty dollars?"

"You're the one who chose Kitten Master," said Shiraishi, "and their CEO is the one who didn't change his password even after losing his phone." He chuckled at the thought. "Anyway, no one's even come close to figuring out what the Cloud is yet."

"What if someone does?"

"What if they do? They couldn't do anything about it anyway. We released forty thousand of those things. No one's going to figure out how to get rid of them all."

"Not even Dr. Jamshed Jahanshah?"

Shiraishi sat up straight. "Jahanshah got his PhD? Is he still in Tehran? Tell me how I can get in touch with him."

"Well, this is a surprise. Shiraishi, showing an interest in someone other than himself?" Chance said. "All right, are you ready? Here's his phone number . . ."

Chance recited the contact information she had, counting off each item on her fingers: phone number, email address, videoconference account name. Shiraishi held one finger up before his eyes as well, gaze darting left and right as he concentrated on her voice. This was some kind of mnemonic technique he'd no doubt learned to avoid leaving any written notes behind. Once she had told him what she knew, Chance added by way of warning that the CIA and NSA had people monitoring all calls to Iran around the clock, while the Iranian government blocked all Internet connections from the US and EU.

"Thinking of sending him a thank-you note for the idea?" she asked.

"He's the one who'll be thanking me," said Shiraishi. "He knows better than anyone that ideas don't get into orbit on their own."

Shiraishi raised his index finger again and repeated Jamshed's email address. Chance listened and confirmed that he had it right.

"There aren't many people gifted enough to get as far as he did with his idea in a country where you can't even use the Internet," said Shiraishi. "But he had bad luck."

"You feel sorry for him?"

"Please. The world's practically overflowing with unlucky geniuses."

"You, for example."

"Exactly. I'm as unlucky as they come. By rights I should be at NASA leading the design team for the third-generation shuttle . . . Hey! No laughing!" he said. "Come on, just one cigarette. What do you say?"

Chance pointed at the window. "One. With the window open."

"Are you crazy? It's freezing out there."

Chance watched the muscles in Shiraishi's back move as he padded naked and grumbling toward the window. He was over forty, but his physique betrayed no hint of his frequently unhealthy life undercover.

Shiraishi opened the window and lit up. Powder snow and cold air swirled into the room, mingling with the white smoke from his cigarette. Chance let her eyes rest on the tattoo on Shiraishi's right arm. A dragon of some sort. Perhaps he'd gotten it done in China. What was that written in the middle of its serpentine body? Rising to her feet, she walked across the room to stand beside him, then wrapped her left arm around him to hold him close.

"Here to warm me up, eh? Appreciate it."

"Not quite," she said, lifting up his right arm. The writing on the tattoo wasn't a word—it was a mathematical formula.

$$\Delta v = v_e \ln\, {}^{m_0}/{}_{m_f}$$

"Ah, the Tsiolkovsky equation," she said. Shiraishi shivered. The Tsiolkovsky equation was a formula that determined how much acceleration a rocket of a given mass could attain by expelling a given amount of propellant. It applied with cold impartiality to everything that moved through space using that method.

"Correct," Shirashi finally replied. "I'm impressed that you know it." He covered the tattoo with his left hand.

"Aerospace engineers have been reciting it as their mantra for a century," Chance said. "Are you sure you don't still have regrets about not being among their ranks anymore? You wouldn't rather be flying proper rockets or spacecraft, would you? Or can I interpret this as just a youthful indiscretion?"

Shiraishi was silent. His hand gripped the tattoo tighter.

"You haven't forgotten the goal of the Cloud, I hope," Chance pressed him.

Shiraishi's body tensed for a moment. Then he slammed Chance against the window with explosive force. "Forget?" he snarled. "It was my idea in the first place. For the Great Leap."

Chance detected no trace of his usual ironic detachment.

"I'm going to destroy that hundred-year-old mantra forever," he continued. "I got this tattoo so I wouldn't forget that."

Shiraishi's arms strained, and Chance felt her back being pressed against the window. Icy rills trickled down the underside of her arms as her body heat melted the frost.

"Your phone?" she asked.

Blue-white light spilled from Shiraishi's coat by the bed. Rubbing his shoulders, Shiraishi went to extract his phone from the coat's pocket. Chance saw that ironic detachment in his expression again as the pale light from the screen lit up his face.

"Looks like we've attracted attention from someone a little sharper than usual," he said. "A blog post's turned up with the keywords we were looking for—'SAFIR 3,' 'large numbers of objects in orbit,' 'circular motion,' that sort of thing. They noticed the tethering around SAFIR 3."

Shiraishi's lips curled into a smile as he read on.

"A Japanese blog. Chance, let me look into this. It's a shooting star forecast site called Meteor News, apparently. Interesting idea for a service, wouldn't you say?"

Yekshambe, 23 Azar 1399, 09:05 (2020-12-13T05:35 GMT)
Tehran Institute of Technology

"404 File Not Found."

Jamshed cursed. "You expect me to believe that this came from a US server?" he cried, jabbing at the cathode-ray monitor with his finger.

The error message telling him in Persian that the page could not be found was one that Jamshed was all too familiar with. He saw it every time he tried to access a site run by someone from the US or the EU. This time, he had run into it while attempting to download the original observation data linked by the intriguing Meteor News blog post entitled "Thousands of unknown objects around SAFIR 3?"

No one took the 404 message at face value. It came not from the server in question but from the firewall placed on ISPs by the government. How were they supposed to conduct research like this? It wasn't surprising in the least that Alef should be agitating for azadi interanet, Internet freedom.

Seeing no other option, Jamshed returned to the Meteor News blog, to which access was permitted, and began to laboriously copy the data excerpted there into Windows Notepad.

"Yes, I see . . . Spherical coordinates, in radians. Time resolution, one thousandth of a second."

Jamshed turned to the drafting table beside his desk to plot the data, then sighed. His last piece of paper was already densely covered with hastily scribbled lines and equations.

"No Internet access, no paper . . ." he muttered, retrieving a crumpled sheet of paper from the dustbin. He smoothed the sheet out and laid it on the drafting table, placing a magnet at each corner to hold it in place. Then, wondering if there might be more paper in the lab next door, he got to work. Drawing freehand, he sketched four concentric circles, then added a cross through the center to divide them into quadrants. This done, he began to plot the coordinates he had copied into Notepad on his diagram with small Xs.

After a few minutes spent struggling with the creases in the paper and marking each azimuth and elevation, Jamshed was struck with a sense of déjà vu. The next point would be . . . here. And the next . . . yes, right there. As if the two points were holding hands and whirling in a circle. Even the slight quiver in the circle was the same as the oscillation he'd observed in his experiments back then.

"This . . . this is my space tether. What's it doing up there in orbit?!"

"Alef!" Jamshed cried. "Are you in here?"

The students gathered in the student center turned as one to stare at him. Most of them were young, dressed in jeans and dirty jackets.

Many wore scarves to conceal the lower parts of their faces, no doubt fearing identification and arrest.

Jamshed buttonholed a student carrying a yellow poster so new it still smelled of ink. "Where's Alef?" he asked. "Alef Kadiba."

After a brief pause, the student lowered his scarf. "Over there," he said, turning to point at the tarp that hung from the roof in the middle of the hall, dividing the space in two.

As Jamshed craned his neck to see, the friend he was searching for lifted up the sheet and poked his head out.

"So, have you come to join us after all?" he asked.

"Alef!" Jamshed said. "My tether's in orbit!" He thrust the student with the poster aside and started to run toward Alef, only to be intercepted and held in place by other students around him. "Let me go!" he said. "I'm not with the government."

Hands raised, Alef walked calmly toward the mass of students, which parted as he approached. "Let him go, everyone," he said. "He's a friend of mine. You," he added, turning to a nearby student. "Bring us two cups of chai."

Ushering Jamshed into the makeshift office behind the tarp, Alef handed him a small cup of chai on a porcelain saucer. "Drink, drink," he said. His pliant voice alone had a calming effect. "Now, what's gotten into you? Your tether, you say? Those balloons you were launching a few years ago—you got that thing into orbit? Congratulations, my friend!"

"No, that's not it," Jamshed said. "Someone got my papers somehow, and they're using them to fly it on their own!"

"Are you certain? Maybe they just had the same idea as you."

"No, that's impossible," Jamshed said. He explained how closely the observation data posted on Meteor News matched his own papers. His tether propulsion theory had a few "magic numbers" in it, numbers he'd painstakingly extracted from experiments that involved dropping test units from balloons and seeing how far they could move off course. The same numbers could be found in the observation data. The chance of another experimenter coming up with them independently was practically zero.

Alef nodded receptively, long eyelashes lowered. Jamshed doubted his friend understood one tenth of what he was saying but appreciated that he was making the effort to listen.

"Tether propulsion is such a fringe idea that no one else is looking into it anyway," Jamshed said finally. "No, there's no mistake. Those are my space tethers up there."

"I see," Alef said cheerfully, one hand at his chin. "And so?"

"I want to tell someone." Jamshed pointed at the yellow case slung from Alef's shoulder. "Will you lend me your tablet? Just for a day. If I don't let NASA or the European Space Agency know about this, whoever stole my papers is going to get the credit for inventing the space tether."

"I'm sorry," said Alef, placing his hand on the tablet case. "I can't do that. It's true that this SIM could get through to them, but it's being monitored. I can't afford to attract any attention right now. Not with the demonstration next week."

Jamshed hung his head. "I see," he said.

A web camera came into view before his downcast eyes.

"You can still get through to Japan, can't you?" Alef said, offering him the camera. "Why don't you get that Meteor News site to pass on your message?" He turned over his wrist to check the time—11:12. "You'd better hurry, though. Word is that the government's going to lock down the whole Internet at noon today. And once that happens, even Japan will be out of reach."

Sun, 13 Dec 2020, 16:19 +0900 (2020-12-13T07:19 GMT)
Fool's Launchpad, Shibuya, Main Conference Room

The image of a white tower brightly lit against the night sky covered the conference room's whiteboard. The tower was Launch Complex 36 at Cape Canaveral, where Ronnie Smark's rocket Loki 9 was awaiting liftoff. The swollen, metallic gray fairing at the top of the rocket held the partly exposed spacecraft Wyvern.

Launch Complex 36 had a long and respectable history, having been used for everything from the Apollo program to the Space Shuttle. Ronnie's company, Project Wyvern, had bought it outright and maintained it impeccably. Even the clock at the corner of the screen, counting down the minutes until launch—00:19:13, 00:19:12 . . . — was an original NASA model from the days of the Apollo program.

Kazumi was sitting on two chairs he'd lined up in the conference room, one to sit on and one for his feet. He had just finished his work on the site for the day, having posted some brief comments on Ozzy's data on his blog followed by a teaser for the post Akari had just suggested, predicting where Loki 9 would fall back to Earth.

Watching the circles appear on the world map that showed where the hits to his site were coming from, Kazumi added some words of appreciation for his anonymous visitors who were taking the time to check his shooting star forecast even as Project Wyvern's launch broadcast held the world's attention. Hits were coming from all over the world, but the circles from Seattle and Seoul were largest. Perhaps a dozen or so in each city. There was even one person connecting from right in the center of the Middle East. And that circle in the Indian Ocean had to be Ozzy "X-Man" Cunningham.

Kazumi murmured a word of thanks to Akari, still fast asleep, and raised his cup of coffee, long since cold and sour, to his mouth. As he took a sip, a notification popped up on his laptop screen. A chat request.

"Who could this be?" he muttered. The account name on the pop-up just read "JJ." Kazumi wondered if those were initials or a pseudonym.

With only fifteen minutes until launch, Kazumi decided to ask whoever it was to wait until afterwards.

Clicking the speech bubble next to the account name to enter the chat, Kazumi found that "JJ" had already started talking.

>EMERGENCY!
>HAVE NEWS ABOUT SAFIR 3
>VIDEO CALL PLS. NO TIME. HURRY

Kazumi smiled. Whoever it was, their English wasn't easy to understand. According to the map in the connection information, the call was coming from off the west coast of Africa. Ghana or Nigeria, maybe? Email from X-Man in Seychelles yesterday, a videoconference with someone in Africa today . . . Meteor News was becoming quite cosmopolitan.

>OK

Kazumi hit enter and clicked the camera icon. He would just tell "JJ" face-to-face to wait until the launch was over, or perhaps suggest that they watch it together. It wasn't every day that Loki 9 took Ronnie Smark into orbit, after all.

The window for the video call opened on Kazumi's display.

Heavily accented English came through his speakers before the video even came online.

"Thank you for taking my call. You are the owner of Meteor News?"

"Yes. I am Kazumi Kimura, owner of Meteor News. It's nice to meet you."

"I am relieved I am getting through. Please listen to me for just a few minutes. My name is Ja— . . . Jay. I am calling you in Japan because I can only—"

The end of the sentence was too garbled to catch. The audio was very choppy, and the video still hadn't come online. A network problem?

"Jay? I can call you Jay?"

". . . fine, fine. Jay is fine."

Kazumi glanced at the whiteboard. The broadcast being projected there was coming over the Internet too, and it was coming through fine at thirty frames per second. If network speed was the problem, it certainly wasn't on his end. Jay must have been having problems with uplink speed. Perhaps that was par for the course in Africa.

"Thank you. Kazumi, please . . ."

Again, his words dissolved into unintelligibility, but the video finally came on as they did. The image was noisy, but Kazumi could make out a man in a dark room with a patch of blue sky showing through a window in the upper right. The windowsill was clearly illuminated by the sunlight, but it was difficult to make out the man's face in the gloom.

"I can't hear you very well, Jay," Kazumi said. "I'd like to propose that we talk again in thirty minutes. I'm waiting for the launch of Ronnie Smark's rocket, Loki 9. Are you watching it too?"

"No! I cannot wait. Please, hear me out!"

The man moved violently, setting off a swirl of pixelation that danced around him. Kazumi could just make out what looked like a beard.

"I have only until noon," the man continued. "Just ten minutes. Will you listen?"

Kazumi cocked his head. The African countries displayed in the connection status were directly under London. It should be about six in the morning there, nine hours behind Japan.

"Jay, where are you calling—"

"Who is there?" Jay interrupted, either intentionally or because of lag in the connection. "Is that one of your staff behind you?"

Kazumi turned to see Akari standing behind him. Her display goggles were on, and a keyboard was already strapped to one of her arms.

"Sorry," Kazumi said to her. "Did I wake you up? I borrowed your projector."

"No problem," Akari said. "But it doesn't sound like we have time to discuss that right now." She crouched down so that her face was visible in the frame alongside Kazumi's. "Hello there. I'm Akari, engineer at Meteor News. Nice to meet you, Jay."

So Akari could speak English too. It didn't seem like Jay had anything too complicated to say, but it was a relief to have someone help him with the listening. Akari pulled up a chair and sat beside him.

At the other end of the call, Jay looked taken aback. "An honor to meet you," he said finally. "Here is what I want to tell you. It is about the objects around SAFIR 3. Listen closely, yes? They are spacecraft with a tether-propulsion system of my invention, known as the 'space tether.'"

"Space tether?" Akari whispered to Kazumi.

Kazumi shook his head. What Jay had just said was impossible. They must have misheard him. "These objects," Kazumi said, taking care to separate his words, "are electrodynamic—*space tethers*—made by you?" He pronounced "space tethers" especially slowly and clearly, so that there could be no mistake.

This wasn't the first time Kazumi had heard of this technology, referred to variously as electrodynamic tethering, inductive tethering, and tether propulsion. But it was still only supposed to be in the early experimental stage. Even Japan's space agency JAXA, despite its reputation for eagerly exploring new propulsion systems, had only run a few trials so far. It was the latest idea for spacecraft propulsion, but at this point it was more fantasy than reality.

"Electrodynamic . . . ?" Jay repeated. "Yes. Exactly."

Kazumi stared.

"But," Jay continued, "Also, no. I did not make them."

"What do you mean? You are—"

"I do not know who made what is up there now," Jay said, interrupting Kazumi for the second time. Akari reached out unobtrusively to click RECORD on the video call. "But the system is of my design. Please, tell someone! The idea came from me!"

"Why did you contact us, Jay?" asked Kazumi. "Why not tell this to NASA or the space agency in your own country? I am sure they would listen."

If Jay really had designed a space tether that was currently in orbit, a Japanese shooting star forecast service was hardly the first place he should contact.

"Please, Kazumi. There is no time. It is impossible. Ir— . . . —lease." His voice began to break up. ". . . send . . . papers . . ."

"Sorry, Jay," Kazumi said. "I could not hear you. Can you repeat—"

As if by way of reply, a file transfer request appeared in the chat window. Kazumi clicked the Accept button, but the file didn't begin downloading. Akari began to tap furiously at the keyboard on her left arm, eyes never leaving the screen.

"What is this, Jay?" asked Kazumi. The sound came back clearly for just a moment.

"Proof. My papers on the space tether, from five years ago. They are not reaching you?"

"No, they aren't," Kazumi said. The file transfer dialogue was open, but the download still hadn't begun.

"Thirteen, fourteen." Akari said. "Too slow." She leaned in close to the camera.

"Jay, this file you are sending is being censored. Censored!"

"*Mahhodotsiman!*"

As Jay buried his face in his hands, the download finally began. It was a PDF, about 130 kilobytes. The progress bar moved agonizingly slowly.

"I don't know any African languages," Kazumi said quietly to Akari.

She shook her head. "What are you talking about? That's Persian. Jay's in Iran."

No, he isn't, Kazumi protested, pointing at the connection information showing a connection in Africa, but Akari grabbed his arm and pulled it back. Kazumi saw pages of text scrolling across her eye display.

"Later," she said. "Move."

"What?"

"Move, please! Now! There's no time!"

Akari pushed Kazumi out of the way and seized the laptop.

"What are you doing?" Kazumi demanded, trying to snatch it back. Akari held up one palm to silence him, typing something into the chat window with her other hand as she shouted into the camera.

"Jay, click on the URL I'm about to send you!"

"Got i—"

Jay's image froze as the sound cut out midword. The file download stopped. The connection had been terminated.

"Now look what you've done!" Kazumi said.

"It wasn't me," Akari said, pointing at the whiteboard. "Your call with Jay was cut off by the Iranian government."

A new window had been added on the conference room's screen, beside the launch livecast. A woman was looking at the camera with a pained expression. At the bottom of the screen was the station's logo: Al Jazeera.

". . . confirm that as of noon today," the woman on the screen said, "the Iranian government has severed the country's Internet from the rest of the world."

The camera panned to one side, revealing a city street. In the background, a man with a potbelly was pulling the shutters down over a window full of computers.

"Internet cafés have also been closed down," continued the black-clad anchorwoman. The potbellied man yelled something at the camera and then pasted a green poster over his shutters.

"The government has made no public announcement about the disconnection," said the woman. "Student groups have declared that they will stage protests to demand free access, but if the Internet remains unavailable for too long, the possibility of the demonstrations turning violent cannot be discounted."

A caption appeared: INNER TEHRAN. The streets were full of

colorful strips of paper, as if countless posters had been torn to pieces. A woman with her face covered by a scarf hurried past. *Iran*, Kazumi mused. So an engineer from this Islamic nation had developed the working theory behind the space tether? While unable even to connect to the Internet? Kazumi had never even imagined such a thing.

"Al Jazeera reporting via satellite link," the anchorwoman continued. "This is Tehran, signing off."

"Sorry about that, Akari," Kazumi said. He should have paid more attention to Jay. But it was too late now. Jay couldn't get in touch with anyone outside Iran. Would that half-downloaded file they'd received from him even be readable?

"No problem," Akari said. "But forget about that. Let's see if we can find Jay. He hit that URL just before his connection dropped out, so he should be in the access log. I'll reconstruct the PDF we got half of too. You want to read it, right?"

"Yes, please," Kazumi said.

"I guess the launch is over by now."

Akari was right. On the conference room screen, Loki 9 was soaring into the clear night sky, long white trail behind it. The launchpad was still roiling with a mass of steam. It looked like all had gone well.

"That's okay," Kazumi said. "I'll watch the recording."

He turned his thoughts back to the space tether. If Jay was right about those objects floating around SAFIR 3, they made up a cloud of miniature spacecraft, each one capable of moving freely in orbit. He had to tell someone what was up there waiting for Ronnie. With Jay's name attached, of course.

But who?

He thought back to the hackathon where he'd developed the first prototype of Meteor News. Who was that JAXA employee he'd met

there? That was it: Kurosaki. And Kazumi was pretty sure he still had
his private contact details, too.

Sun, 13 Dec 2020, 08:45 +0000 (2020-12-13T08:45 GMT)
Project Wyvern

Pure excitement!

I have no words. Does that make me a failure as a
journalist? No way! Sometimes there *are* no words.
And a rocket launch is one of those times.

Have you ever seen one in person? This wasn't my
first. Back in 2000, when I was eight (no calculations, please), Ronnie took me to see the Space
Shuttle go up, headed for the ISS.

We were on the observation deck, three or four miles
away from the rocket. Ronnie was standing, and I was
on his shoulders.

There was a cloud of steam and light big enough to
hide the shuttle. I thought I heard a whoosh, and
then suddenly the loudest noise I had *ever* heard
rumbled right through me. Ronnie lost his balance
and dropped me onto the floor of the observation
deck.

I sat there on my butt watching as an arrow of light
stretched up into the clear blue sky, until the

white clouds had disintegrated and the last glittering point winked out.

That was my first rocket launch. I made a presentation at school about how exciting it was, but I could
tell that my classmates didn't really get it. I swore
that I would find a way to explain it to them—that I
would make them understand how life changing it was.

Today, I looked back from the opposite perspective.
I was up in the tower at Launch Complex 36, and
there was the observation deck. It was lit up, but
it was so far away that it just looked like a thin
line. Amazing to think that the shock of the launch
had been powerful enough to knock a full-grown man
off-balance that far away! Well, if I'm honest, I
don't mean "amazing." I mean "terrifying." Because
this time, that same energy would kick me right in
the back.

I waved for the cameras, but my legs were shaking
the whole time. I entered the Wyvern through the
hatch, took my seat, and began running through the
launch protocol. I didn't stop shaking once.

I felt ten times the energy of the loudest noise
I had ever heard in my life vibrating beneath me.
Then the countdown from Mission Control began in
my helmet.

Three. Two. One. Liftoff!

The vibration stopped for just a moment, then there was an even *louder* noise in my helmet and my whole body was slammed back into the seat. I tried to cry out. No—I couldn't not cry out. I couldn't tell you if it was closer to a yell or a scream. But it was the loudest noise I could make. I hope it didn't worry Ronnie or Mission Control. The camera should have told them that I wasn't scared, but shaking with joy. Still . . .

*

When the noise cut out again, we were in space.

It first hit me when I saw blue light through the Wyvern's cupola.

We were in space.

That light was from Earth!

My instructors back at journalism school always dinged me for overusing repetition. They agreed with my textbooks—useful tool, must be used in moderation. But I'm going to ignore what they taught me now.

I'm in space! Space! In SPACE!

Next time, I hope to report on the experience of
zero G. Should be a stimulating one! Ronnie is
as excited as a little boy—nothing like his usual
impatient, irritable self.

Wow! There goes a shape I'd only ever seen on maps
before. The Americas!

Note for editors: Now that I'm in space, please use
GMT format for my dateline.

— Judy "Columbus" Smark

4 Standby

Sun, 13 Dec 2020, 02:03 -0700 (2020-12-13T09:03 GMT)
The Buffalo Café, Colorado Springs

". . . Two! One! Liftoff!"

The shining white rocket on the television screen burst through pale cloud cover into the night sky. The patrons in the Buffalo Café raised their glasses as one and cheered. Though it was the middle of the night, this steak house five minutes from Peterson Air Force Base was alive with celebration. Beer foam flew as the clink of glass on glass rang out across the room.

Freeman could only shrug at the racket. Bruce had his fingers in his ears. Beside him, Chris sipped her martini with unbelievable composure.

The television cut to a close-up of Judy Smark screaming with joy as tears ruined her makeup. A merciless chorus of whistles and boos rose from the audience in the steak house as they rewatched the special news feature on Loki 9's launch that had played half an hour earlier. Then the television cut again, to an ex-chief of NASA rhapsodizing on the dawn of private space tourism, and the crowd began to settle down.

Bruce, wearing a leather jacket instead of his usual suit, raised his glass perfunctorily to another patron coming from the counter. "Should have expected this from a NORAD town," he said.

"No kidding," said Chris, looking up from her martini glass. "And it's been how many years since Cheyenne Mountain closed down? Amazing." Her white hair was down, and she'd changed into a floral-print dress that made her look like a retiree come to drag her irascible husband home from his local watering hole. No one would have imagined that she was with the CIA.

She turned to Freeman, setting her glass down with a smile. "Sorry about calling you here in the middle of the night," she said.

"There's no need to apologize, ma'am," Freeman replied. "How can I be of assistance?"

"First of all, by explaining this," Bruce said. Without putting down his glass, he pointed both index fingers at the ceiling, then at Freeman, then off to the left. "Lintz and Fernandez did this routine for you. Tell me what it means."

Freeman scratched his head. Of course they'd noticed. He saw no point in lying. "It's a runway hand signal," he said. "You actually do it like this."

He set his glass on the table and showed them the signal with both arms fully outstretched. This caught the attention of a bearded man leaving the counter.

"Hey, you with the air force, pal?" he asked. "'Proceed at your own discretion.' My favorite signal too!"

"Cheers, Pops," Bruce said, inclining his glass and flashing a dazzling smile at the man. Then he turned back to Freeman. "Got it," he said. "'We leave it up to you,' basically?"

Freeman nodded cautiously.

"Don't worry," Bruce said. "We've been around the block a few times ourselves."

Chris pulled out her phone, apparently no more concerned about the subterfuge than Bruce was. "We don't care what you do on the side as long as you get that Rod from God research done," she said. "We didn't come here to make friends."

"Rod from God?" Freeman repeated. "You mean that idea about bombarding Earth with tungsten spears? Like I said earlier today, the very idea is absurd."

Bruce tossed back the last of his martini. "Hold up there," he said. "We don't just want to know if it'd really make a good weapon or not. We want to know everything. What kind of strategic range its movement implies. How long it can keep maneuvering. Whatever you can tell us."

"You want an assessment of the object as a spacecraft," Freeman said.

"Starting to sound more interesting?"

"A little," Freeman said, with a calculated laugh. He brought his ginger ale to his lips, but Bruce raised a finger.

"One more thing," Bruce said. "The ASM-140. You wrote the report, so let me pick your brain directly. Why was such a brilliant idea mothballed in the first place? We could have been shooting down enemy satellites with fighter planes right now. How awesome would that have been?"

"Debris," Freeman said. He leaned in toward Bruce so that he could speak more quietly. Chris casually huddled in closer as well. "You might say that the whole problem of space debris started with 'the flying tomato can'—the predecessor to the ASM-140."

"Solwind," Chris said.

"You're already familiar with it?" Freeman asked.

"Just tell us about it," said Bruce. "We want to hear it from a real, live human."

Freeman gave them the basics. In 1985, the ASM-135, a.k.a. "the flying tomato can," had been tested on P78-1, a decommissioned solar-observation satellite also known as Solwind. The test of the flying tomato can as an antisatellite weapon was successful—the satellite had been destroyed. The resulting dispersal of fragments and debris, on the other hand, had posed a threat to the burgeoning private space industry. Not to mention the fact that even the army had been horrified to see how easy, cheap, and effective the ASM-135 was—an ASAT weapon that didn't even need a launching facility.

The ASAT plan had been canceled, with the army citing that old cliché, "budget overruns." The truth had to be kept from the Soviets at all costs, though hiding things that were already in orbit wasn't easy.

"Okay," Bruce said. "So what's the takeaway? Can we throw this new ASM-140 at the Rod from God?" His smile didn't reach his eyes.

Freeman felt something at his back: the sofa. He must have gone weak with surprise. "You mean," he said, "you put together that plan—'Seed Pod,' was it?—without even looking into that?"

"Well, it wasn't *my* plan," Bruce said. He took a gulp of the bourbon that had just arrived for him. "It came from somewhere higher up. We're just the worker bees. When we went to ask NASA about SAFIR 3, we got the debris lecture. It's a bit unnerving to have the Smarks up there too. We could hardly ask Colonel Lintz about that." He gave Freeman a disarming smile. "Come on, give us the lowdown. How does the ASM-140 tick?"

"Can I leave out everything up to the launch?" Freeman asked. "That part's exactly the same—take it above twenty thousand klicks and point it at the target. The first stage can accelerate to Mach 7. The second stage is an Altair 3 rocket that can reach Mach 14. That's 40 percent faster than the ASM-135."

Bruce wasn't writing anything down, but Freeman could see the gleam of understanding in his eyes. He couldn't help but think back on the time he'd given the same explanation to Major Fernandez with less satisfying results.

"Let's say this is the target satellite," Freeman said, holding up his index finger and moving it in a slow horizontal line. He then let his left hand approach it at an angle from below. "The ASM-140 closes with its target from below and hits it from the front. If the target is the Rod from God, the final relative velocity would be ten klicks per second. But . . ." He opened the fingers of his left hand as if to grasp his right index finger. ". . . five klicks from the target, the ASM-140 launches an electronic attack. Two klicks from the target, it fires a volley of slugs, like a shotgun. The aim isn't to destroy the satellite, just to render it inoperative, either with ECM or by riddling it with holes."

"So that's why the plan's called 'Seed Pod,'" said Chris, nodding.

"It's not a bad name," Freeman said. "The slugs are just three millimeters in size. The attack really is like a barrage of seeds from one of those plants with an explosive pod."

"Three millimeters, though?" Bruce held his thumb and finger close together. "If slugs that tiny hit at that velocity, wouldn't the energy just vaporize them? They couldn't get through composite armor."

Freeman was startled that Bruce knew as much as he did. Not to mention the fact that he was right. Armor was standard in orbit. The International Space Station had three layers protecting its front end: an innermost airtight wall, a Kevlar fiber layer, and a thin shield of gold known as a Whipple bumper on the outside. Any tiny pieces of debris that hit the station were vaporized by the heat of the collision.

They might punch a hole in the bumper and the Kevlar layer, but the airtight wall would never suffer more than a dent. And a Whipple bumper was standard equipment even on an unmanned satellite. It worked on the same principle as composite armor.

"Bruce used to drive a tank," Chris said. "The CIA took pity on him and took him in because he looked so cramped in there."

She was joking, but it was true that the ASM-140's armor-piercing slugs worked on a similar principle to antitank missile warheads designed to penetrate the composite armor of their targets.

"Let me guess," Bruce said. "There's '*heavy* metal,'" Bruce said, making quotation marks with his fingers, "at the core of each slug. Am I wrong?"

"No," Freeman said. "The cores are heavy, all right."

Bruce scratched his head. "But that doesn't make any sense. Depleted uranium in new technology?"

This was the dark side of the ASM-140. There was no way around it: depleted uranium was notoriously harmful to human health. The plans had originally called for tungsten instead, but Lockheed, who owned the patent on depleted uranium, had craftily pointed out that tungsten was produced in a competing nation: China.

"One small consolation," Freeman said, "is that the slugs have basically no orbital velocity. They fall into the atmosphere and burn up right away."

"And become shooting stars," Bruce said. "Okay, next: What happens at the moment we kill the satellite? Can other countries see what's happening?"

"Surely the CIA must know better than me?" Freeman said. "Military satellites from all over the world are constantly watching the North American continent. The launch of ASM-140 will be out in the open for everyone to see."

"Daryl," Chris broke in. "To keep North America under constant observation, you need geosynchronous satellites in the right place. Only a handful of countries operate satellites like that: Russia, China, the UK, and France. We just need to make sure everyone gets the right message behind the scenes."

This was news to Freeman.

"Besides, if we can get a UN resolution to eliminate the Rod from God, it doesn't matter whether we're spotted doing it or not," Chris continued. "That's why we need you to prove that this object SAFIR 3 is an orbital weapon. It's a big responsibility."

Freeman looked up at the soot-smudged ceiling. *I should have known.*

How could he get them to understand how ridiculous it would look to send up a cutting-edge weapon to take care of a single empty rocket body?

Sun, 13 Dec 2020, 02:14 -0800 (2020-12-13T10:14 GMT)
A Seattle Hotel

The commercial for some local business ended, and the screen filled with yet another shot of Loki 9 blasting off while the announcer groped for yet another way to say "amazing." The third or maybe fourth "cool" was the last straw for Shiraishi.

"We're in a hotel," he said. "Can't we at least watch cable?"

"No," Chance replied. "And even if we did, you'd just complain about their coverage instead." One of her first acts as Shiraishi's handler had been to cancel his cable subscription. Not only did the contract contain a record of his address, the cable company also had a deal with the CIA to supply data on everything their customers viewed. Even in hotels, Chance herself only watched broadcast television.

If you couldn't receive it with a regular television set, she wasn't interested.

As Chance reached out for the remote to switch the television
off, she noticed light spilling from her editor's bag. She pulled out her
tablet and checked the notifications.

"It's here," she said. "The results of our investigation into Meteor
News."

"They work fast at the Cyber Front, I'll give them that. It hasn't
even been four hours. So what did they learn?"

"All they've found out is that it's run by a single person, one
Kazumi Kimura. Domain registrations and all other public information use the details of a shared office space attached to Shibuya
Station in Tokyo. The phone number and address are both just for-
warding services, untraceable to any particular address. He's well
hidden."

Taking the tablet from her, Shiraishi rubbed his chin. "So either
he's a security freak, or he's hired an engineer who knows what he's
doing in that area . . . Probably wouldn't fall for a spear phishing
attack either. Hey, what about this number?"

He showed Chance a web page he'd found after a few searches:
Mary@Fool's Launchpad. With a smile, he reached out and tapped at
a phone number on the page.

" 'English customer support,' it says here. Give her a call, Chance.
I think this just might be the chink in Kazumi's armor we're looking for."

Chance pulled out her phone, set it to speakerphone, and tapped
in the number. They heard it ring three times before the other end
picked up.

"English reception, Fool's Launchpad, this is Mary Nomura,"
came a voice in smooth English.

"Hello, Mary."

"Our business hours for today are over," the voice continued. "If you would like to leave a message for an individual service, please press . . ."

Chance listened for a few more seconds, then muted the mic.

"Meteor News is number five. Can I hang up?"

Shiraishi nodded, closed his eyes lightly, and turned his head gently from side to side.

"Let's see . . . Right now in Tokyo it's Sunday night. After dinner tomorrow, let's try to get all the information about Kazumi we can out of our new friend Mary. I've dealt with these outfacing English-speaker types before. They don't care who their client is—they'll take the side of whoever speaks better English. They'll blab anything if they think it'll impress. Notification for you, by the way."

A new message alert had appeared on the tablet: SURVEILLANCE TARGET DOCTOR JAMSHED JAHANSHAH HAS MADE CONTACT WITH AN INDIVIDUAL OUTSIDE IRAN.

Chance took the tablet back from Shiraishi and checked the details. It seemed that Dr. Jahanshah had sent the space tether paper to a recipient outside Iran. The Iranian authorities had detected the transmission and shared the information with North Korean intelligence.

Her hand tightened around the table. The IP address the papers had been sent to was linked to a shared office space in Shibuya called Fool's Launchpad.

"Not bad, Kazumi," Shiraishi said, chuckling and shaking his head. Chance shot him a look before deciding on a particular operative they had stationed in Tokyo.

"I'll have someone pay them a visit when we call Mary," she said. "I think this is something we need to discuss in person."

Mon, 14 Dec 2020, 09:25 +0900 (2020-12-14T00:25 GMT)
Fool's Launchpad, Shibuya

Kazumi sat in the window seat he'd managed to snag and spread out the supplies he'd bought at the Tokyu Hands department store the previous night just before it closed. A magnetic sheet, two foot-long copper rods, a battery box complete with a switch, an acrylic plate, double-sided tape, and a sewing needle.

He got to work. First, he used the double-sided tape to stick the two well-polished copper rods to the acrylic plate. He arranged them in parallel, like two rails. Next, he laid down a narrow strip of magnetic sheet in the gap between the rods. Finally, he connected the copper wires extending from the battery box to the ends of the rails.

Done. All that remained was to place the needle across the rails and turn the device on.

What he had created was a miniature version of the design at the top of the PDF he'd received from the man calling himself Jay the previous night: "An Overview of the Continuous Space Tether, with Experimental Results." The paper was credited to Fahim Hamed and Jamshed Jahanshah as coauthors, and Kazumi suspected that it had been the latter who had contacted him. Only about a quarter of the PDF had been recoverable, but he could tell even from the abstract that the ideas in it were quite advanced. Having no background in electrical engineering, Kazumi had not really been able to understand the circuit diagrams and equations that filled the second half of the paper, but he was still buzzing with the thrill he'd felt when he had worked out what Jamshed's awkward English was getting at.

Kazumi carefully placed the sewing needle on the rails, then flipped the switch on the battery box to ON.

The needle quivered, then began to roll along the rails. A body had been set in motion through electric current alone. Success! He understood the theory, but seeing the needle move in front of his eyes made it real. It was barely as strong as a breath, but this was the Lorentz force—the force that drove Jamshed's space tether propulsion system.

"What's that, a rail gun?" Watanabe was peering over his shoulder.

"Sorry, I've made a bit of a mess. I'll clear it up before I go home."

"It's no problem. You're here every day anyway. Just leave a reservation card on the desk. You sure were concentrating hard, though. Actually, I have a favor to ask . . ."

Watanabe showed him a tablet displaying a wireframe website layout. He always had multiple website contracts going on at once and made a point of sharing them with other members of Fool's Launchpad. Kazumi had accepted his share of the subcontracting as well.

"I'm sorry," Kazumi said. "I appreciate the offer, but for the next month or so I'm going to focus on this. I've already got enough to cover my expenses."

"That's too bad," Watanabe said. "You do great work on these sites—the little details, you know?" He peered at the experimental apparatus again with obvious interest. "This is a model rail gun, right? Is Meteor News expanding into weaponry now?"

"Good morning, Watanabe-san!" A miniature landslide of electronic devices clattered onto the table opposite Kazumi. Akari had arrived.

"Good morning, Akari," said Watanabe. "Thank you so much for last week—that settlement business. The client understood when I put it to them the way you told me to. Please don't hesitate to set me straight again in the future."

Kazumi was impressed with how quickly Watanabe could admit that he had been wrong, especially after how thoroughly Akari had embarrassed him at the AMX last week. Here was a real adult.

"No, no, I should have been more tactful about it," said Akari. Then she turned her eyes to the experimental apparatus, two copper rods hooked up to batteries. "What's that?" she asked Kazumi.

"An experiment," Kazumi said. "I'm trying to get my head around this space tether thing."

"What's a space tether?" Watanabe asked, looking to Kazumi for answers. The man could hardly be expected to just walk away at this point, so Kazumi decided to use this as an opportunity to learn how well he had come to understand the space tether. Trying to explain something to other people, he knew, was the truest test of your own understanding.

"The space tether is a kind of conductive tether system," he began. "An engine for use in space, especially in orbit around planets with magnetic fields. Have you heard of the Lorentz force?"

Akari shook her head, but Watanabe nodded. "This thing, right?" he said, holding up his left hand with a hint of smugness. His thumb was pointed at the ceiling, his index finger straight forward, and his middle finger off to the right: each digit was orthogonal to both of the others. "Fleming's left-hand rule. Middle finger is the direction of the current, index finger is the direction of the magnetic field, thumb is the force on the object. What? Engineering was my major."

"Sorry," said Kazumi. "I didn't realize that."

"It's fine, it's fine. So, what about the Lorentz force? If that's your engine, then I guess the lines go like . . ." Watanabe twisted his wrist to get his thumb parallel to the rails. His index finger—the magnetic field—pointed straight down, while his middle finger—the electric current—pointed in the same direction as the needle.

"Thanks. That's right," Kazumi said. He put the needle on the rails again and hit the switch. The needle trembled and rolled along the rails. "So what this experiment shows is the needle moving through the magnetic field created by the magnetic sheet as current flows through it. The space tether does this too, but in space."

Kazumi picked up the needle between his right thumb and index finger. After a moment's thought, he held it vertically.

"Let's say that this is a metal cord—a tether—floating vertically in orbit around Earth."

Watanabe and Akari nodded.

Kazumi moved the fingers of his left hand in a plane that passed through the needle. "This is the magnetic field," he said. "It's guaranteed to be there if you're close enough to Earth. So, you pass a current through the tether, and the Lorentz force comes into play."

Kazumi moved the needle to the left.

"I get it," Watanabe said. "But wait. It's a current, right? If there's no circuit, how can electricity flow?"

Akari tilted her head in confusion, but Kazumi appreciated the question.

"You put an electron gun at one end of the tether," Kazumi said. "The tether spits out electrons from that end and attracts free electrons from its surroundings at the other. The result is a direct current."

The propulsive force was small, but because no fuel was required at all, you could use the tether to keep satellites in low orbit from losing velocity to the atmosphere and falling to Earth. JAXA was also investigating techniques for attaching the tether to debris objects and intentionally propelling them down into the atmosphere to burn them up.

"What I'm investigating is a slightly unusual system thought up by an Iranian scientist. In orbit, tidal forces mean that a long object like a tether stands upright. But that means that the direction of the Lorentz force is decided by the magnetic field."

Kazumi turned the needle over onto its side and pointed it in one direction, then another.

"So Dr. Jahanshah thought up a self-rotating tether-propulsion system. And he called it the space tether."

If the tether could be turned horizontal, the Lorentz force could be made to act in any direction. The concept of a self-rotating inductive tether wasn't original to Jahanshah, but what made his unique was that the weight that moved on top of the tether was constantly unstable. The system was constantly trying to right itself under the tidal forces; if you kept it unstable and in motion, slight Lorentz forces were continuously being generated, and these could be fed back to drive rotation.

Akari's eyes sparkled. "If it can rotate itself, then it can move anywhere in orbit, and it'll always be pulled tight. Using a moving weight to make it unstable is a bit brute-forcey, but I bet it works fine. Wait—so that's what . . . ?"

"Right," said Kazumi. "That's what the objects flying around SAFIR 3 are."

Noticing Watanabe's quizzical expression, Kazumi explained about the ten thousand–plus objects in orbit, mentioning that they weren't in the catalog that contained everything ten centimeters or longer.

"Well, they must be smaller, then," Watanabe said. He reached into his pocket and pulled out his smartphone. "All a tether needs at its end is an electron gun, a GPS, and a gyro sensor, right? That would all fit on a smartphone board. Use a Qualcomm chipset and it'd be the size of a five hundred–yen coin."

Akari nodded.

All at once, the space tether appeared before Kazumi in his mind's eye. He could see it: a line two kilometers long with a tiny object at each end, maybe a two-inch cube. A resin case. That wouldn't show up on debris-tracking radar, which explained why it wasn't in the catalog. It was unnerving to not know who was flying those things, and why, but there wasn't much he could do to remedy his ignorance in that area.

"Well, you've got an interesting problem there, Kazumi," Watanabe said cheerfully. "Congratulations. The month will fly by. If there's anything I can help with, let me know. And—"

There was a flash of light and a noise somewhere between a pop and a click. As they turned their heads to the source of both, they heard Mary scream. There she was, hugging the counter she'd redecorated to look like a café.

"Shit," Watanabe said. "Not again. Excuse me."

He ran off toward the counter, calling out to see if Mary was okay. The fire alarm shrieked. Watanabe quickly told one of the other Fool's Launchpad residents what to do, then went to hold back the security staff running toward the commotion. "It's just the microwave!" he said. "False alarm!" Watanabe wasn't paid to deal with situations like this, but his sense of responsibility wouldn't let him ignore them.

"Mary was probably trying to dry out some papers in the microwave but forgot to take the paper clip off," Kazumi said with a grimace. "You probably didn't know this, but this'd be the third time she's done that. When she isn't too busy spilling her coffee."

"It's no joke," Akari said. "What if she really does start a fire? Just how dumb is she?"

Kazumi decided to let that one go.

"Why do sparks fly when you microwave something metal, though?" Akari wondered.

"When you switch the microwave on, current runs through the metal. The sparks are the discharge. Which reminds me." Kazumi put the needle back on the rails and rolled it with his finger. "A conductor passing through a magnetic field generates an electric current too, right? So if a space tether is in orbit, that orbit alone would generate current. In this paper by Jahanshah, he recommends using that to charge it for later use."

Akari's eyes went wide. "You mean it could stay up there forever?"

"In theory, yeah," Kazumi said. "Battery degradation would bring it down eventually." That would take decades, though.

"So it can move around freely and stay in orbit indefinitely. That's amazing. Scary, too."

"I'm going to try to get in touch with JAXA. If I can set up a meeting, can I borrow the planetarium from yesterday?"

"Sure, but can I ask a favor in return?"

Akari pulled a tablet out of her mountain of gadgets and woke it up. The screen showed the Meteor News web page. Akari pointed at the Kitten Master banner in the advertising box.

"This ad pays really well, but can I set the page to not display it for a while?"

"Huh?"

"There's something funny about it. It looks like the image has script fragments embedded in it."

"Could it be a virus or something?"

Only strictly vetted items were transmitted for web advertising. Was it possible that some executable fragments had made it through that screening and onto his page?

Akari put the tablet to one side and swept her gadgets out of the way to make room to work. "Maybe. I'll look into it."

Mon, 14 Dec 2020, 10:03 +0900 (2020-12-14T01:03 GMT)
JAXA Tokyo Office, Ochanomizu Sola City

"Wish there was more to do around this place," sighed Sekiguchi, tapping aimlessly at his tablet in the seat opposite Kurosaki.

Kurosaki looked up. Sekiguchi had only been in the office an hour. "Don't you have work to do? Did you reply to the observatory?"

"I got the techs to reply on Friday. You were in CC."

Kurosaki shrugged. Sekiguchi was a fast worker and a solid thinker. The Japanese translation of North Korea's declaration he'd prepared for the space policy minister's talking points had saved the minister serious embarrassment. Kurosaki wondered if everyone on the bureaucratic career track was this sharp. Sekiguchi wasn't exactly polite, but he was tactful enough not to hound his superiors about whether they'd read the mail he sent or not.

"I didn't spend much time on the reply from our side," Sekiguchi continued. "Do you want to take a look?"

There was a mischievous look in his eyes. He was trying to draw Kurosaki in. The mail had probably been overfamiliar—Sekiguchi thinking he could skip the politeness because of a shared interest in space.

"I'll pass," Kurosaki said. "What about Wyvern, then?"

"Already on top of it," Sekiguchi replied. "Good for them, getting into orbit, right? I guess they'll open the hotel soon. Here's hoping all goes as planned."

No doubt he was collecting information on Ronnie Smark in English. Not that he would brag about that. For Sekiguchi, English was a bare-minimum skill. He'd mentioned once that he'd traveled around the world as a student, and Kurosaki could see him cheerfully getting his way wherever he went, just like he did now.

Sekiguchi sighed. "What a life, right? Private spaceflight. Wish we could publicize some of the Japanese tech on the Wyvern. The orbital hotel Miura folds for storage, doesn't it? Was it the IKAROS that used Miura folds too? . . . What, did I say something wrong?"

"No," Kurosaki said. "Just surprised you know about that."

"I'm only going to be in JAXA for four more years. I have to bone up while I can. I learn a lot from Judy's blog, too."

"Better make sure no one else hears you say that."

There was grumbling throughout the office, right down to the smoker's area, that there wasn't a more substantial source chronicling the historic human achievement taking place in orbit right now. Fair or not, it didn't help that the Japanese translation was being published on a news site marketed to women.

"Really?" Sekiguchi asked. "But why? A lot of information about Wyvern is released for the first time on that blog. Like how its fuel comes from shale gas. I was actually surprised that Wyvern can connect to the Internet at all."

Kurosaki was taken aback. You could find stuff like that on *that* blog? Not even the engineers had mentioned that to him.

"Judy's blog is written in perfect PR style," Sekiguchi continued. "I've read some of her work for political journals, and it was the real thing. Can't wait to see what she puts up about the orbital hotel. A soft-shell spacecraft? There must be all kinds of trade secrets in there."

Sekiguchi was already looking back down at his tablet. Reading the blog in question, maybe?

"She's no lightweight, that's for sure," said Sekiguchi. "This is a mission planned by *the* Ronnie Smark. He's not the type to bring his daughter along just because she asked nicely. I mean, he divorced her mother fifteen years ago, so this isn't your standard parent-child relationship."

Kurosaki opened the Project Wyvern website and clicked on Judy's profile. Her picture smiled back at him from the page.

"She might be related to him by blood, but she's only up there because she showed real ability," Sekiguchi added.

Kurosaki knew he was right. Judy Smark had been competing with every other journalist in the world for the gig as embedded writer on the first-ever commercial space journey. She clearly knew what she was doing.

"This 'iron hammer' and 'Rod from God' thing couldn't have come at a better time, that's for sure," Sekiguchi said.

Kurosaki nodded. Over the weekend, the comments section on the Geeple article had exploded. The most popular topic had been whether the Rod from God was aimed at the ISS or Ronnie's orbital hotel.

"It'd be scary to think that someone might have it in for you like that," Sekiguchi said. "The orbital hotel is supposed to connect to the Internet today, so they're about to learn all about it. Let's hope Astro-girl is up to the challenge."

"Yeah," Kurosaki said. "Maybe I'll start reading, too. Whoa— excuse me."

His jacket pocket had vibrated. His private phone, not the one from JAXA. He stood up. Sekiguchi made fun of him for it, but he hated dealing with private business in front of coworkers. He turned his face toward the document cabinets and pulled out his phone. The mail subject line hit him at once:

Information on multiple orbital objects around SAFIR 3 / Invented by Iranian scientist

From . . . Kazumi Kimura. He knew Kimura. A younger man. Came to JAXA's data hackathon every year.

"What a coincidence," Kurosaki said. "It's from Japan's own Astroboy."

"You move in exalted circles, Boss," Sekiguchi said.

"What can I say? According to this, our friend's got information about SAFIR 3."

He raised his hand so that Sekiguchi could see the screen from behind him and unlocked the phone. The mail appeared on the screen. It was in Kimura's usual polite style, but it started off with a string of terminology Kurosaki was unfamiliar with.

"Inductive-tether system? Space tether?" Kurosaki said.

"Oh—that's that thing they were working on at Sagamihara," Sekiguchi said.

Kurosaki turned to face Sekiguchi.

"That research about deorbiting debris, wasn't it?" Sekiguchi said. "They had a prototype but no budget. Did an experiment using the HTV a few years ago but never followed it up."

"I remember now," Kurosaki said. The memories that came to him were not pleasant ones. An old friend who would later abandon Japan had argued passionately for the spacecraft, but even within JAXA it had essentially been buried. The three remaining researchers on the project had to keep up their maintenance on a satellite that would never fly, just to hold on to what amounted to a pity budget. Five, no, ten years wasted, for everyone involved.

"So the tether—what about it?" asked Sekiguchi.

"It's in orbit," Kurosaki said. "Times ten thousand."

Sekiguchi leaned forward. "Who's the mail from? Where'd they get that idea?"

"Kazumi Kimura. Runs a website called Meteor News."

Kurosaki was about to read off the URL, but Sekiguchi beat him to it with "Found it!" A fast typist, too.

"Wow, this is hard-core," Sekiguchi said. "Is this guy Japanese? We need someone like him on our site's design team. Looks like the most recent blog entry is the one we want. Says he found something unusual in the data from the X-Man—the guy who discovered the Rod from God. Nothing about any space tether, though."

"When was it posted?"

"Two days ago. Saturday."

"Maybe that's what this Iranian scientist saw. Apparently Kimura got a video call from Iran yesterday—a scientist who told him that the mysterious objects up there were running on space tether technology. Sent Kimura some papers, too, but the connection was cut halfway through. Sounds fishy to me."

"Do you know what time yesterday?"

"Evening, I guess?"

"Case closed," Sekiguchi said. He turned his tablet to show Kurosaki his screen: video footage of a man pulling blue shutters down over an Internet café. "Yesterday, at 5:30 p.m. Japan time, Iran cut off all access to the Internet. Kimura's story checks out. We may as well see what he has to say. What have we got to lose? I'll set up a meeting."

"Not too boring for you?"

"Even if it is a red herring, it's an interesting one. I like this Meteor News site, too. Maybe we can hook him up with some JAXA data, use our kind donation for PR somehow. You're free first thing this afternoon, right?"

"Uh . . ." Kurosaki opened his groupware schedule with a sigh. His eyes opened wide when he saw that a trip to Shibuya was already scheduled for 1:00 p.m. "Hey!"

"I took the liberty," Sekiguchi said. "Looks like Kimura's office is in a building connected directly to Shibuya station. Let's get lunch on the way."

2020-12-14T01:30 GMT

Project Wyvern

Good morning! Good evening!

I just woke up. I'm looking at America for the fifth time today through the Wyvern's sole port-hole. Seeing the outlines of Earth is such a shock to the system. The atmosphere's a crisp blue line no thicker than a fingernail. At sunrise and sun-set, the hills and valleys of the clouds and the ground below are all thrown into relief by bright scarlet light.

And we're in zero gravity! . . . is what I want to write, but my science grip Rob would get mad at me, so I'd better explain it properly. It's true that if I let go of the mission check sheet I'm holding, it floats. I feel weightless myself. My ponytail's waving back and forth. But even here in the Wyvern, orbiting the Earth at seven kilometers per second 350 kilometers up, gravity isn't entirely absent.

Technically, we're in free fall. The Wyvern is falling toward Earth, pulled down by about 80 per-cent of the gravitational pull at the surface. But it never gets any lower, because we received enough

velocity from Loki 9 and the rotation of the Earth
at blastoff to keep moving sideways instead of just
down. Imagine throwing a ball as hard as you can—it
lands pretty far away, right?

We're basically an orbital-scale home run.

I wish I could write more, but Ronnie is giving me
one of his looks, so I'll wrap it up. It's going
to be a busy day. We're going to unfold the orbital
hotel in the docking bay and get it connected to the
Internet. I was involved in the decision-making,
but our access might be even faster than what you
get on an airliner. A high-speed connection through
a combination of Elysium and Global Satcom lines!

And why will *I* be busy, you ask? Because a certain
IT billionaire glaring at me right now doesn't know
how to set up his own wireless router. Oops—did I
just violate my NDA?

See you all in six hours!

I hadn't planned to write more, but I guess I can't
stay silent on this one. Yes, I saw the launch
video. According to this one email from the project
staff, my screaming has been viewed more than two
million times. I do wish I hadn't looked *that* much
like a zombie with the drool and the tears . . .
No, I'll be honest: it's *incredibly* embarrassing.

I'd be happy never to see that video again. But I
guess it's destined for the textbooks of the future.

Which gives me a new goal for the mission: do something impressive and meaningful enough to make *that*
the image people have of me. Wish me luck!

Yours from 350 km up,
Judy Smark

5   Evasion

Mon, 14 Dec 2020, 13:02 +0900 (2020-12-14T04:02 GMT)
Fool's Launchpad Conference Room, Shibuya

Dressed in jeans and a button-down shirt, Kazumi Kimura stood in front of the whiteboard and nodded politely to Kurosaki, then Sekiguchi. The woman with an Afro sitting in the chair beside him—Akari Numata—nodded as well. Kurosaki and Kazumi crossed paths once a year at an event they both attended, but this was the first time Kurosaki had seen Kazumi give a formal presentation like this.

"Thanks for coming, Kurosaki-san, Sekiguchi-san," Kazumi said. "And sorry about the handwritten agenda."

"Doesn't bother us," said Kurosaki. He jerked his thumb at Sekiguchi. "It's this guy's fault for rushing you, anyway."

Kazumi responded to Kurosaki's informal manner with an easy smile. "No, I appreciate the quick reply," he said, and then turned to the whiteboard.

Akari, acting as notetaker, sat up ramrod straight and tapped at her keyboard. Kurosaki felt himself in a very strange situation. Despite their casual dress, both Kazumi and Watanabe, who'd met them at reception, displayed perfect business manners. Even Akari, with her shock of orange hair, behaved exactly like a regular office worker. Especially surprising was how clear and easy to understand the materials Kazumi had sent in advance had been. What was a guy like this doing in freelance web design?

Kazumi turned back to his audience and replaced the cap on his marker.

"These are the three things I want to share," he said.

- Jamshed Jahanshah's space tether
- SAFIR 3 R/B—irregular orbit
- Objects near SAFIR 3

"Excuse me," Sekiguchi said, rising to his feet. "I realize that this is outside your field, but I'd like to get opinions from you two on one other issue." He borrowed the marker from Kazumi and added a fourth bullet point.

- Q: Translation of *cheolgwon*?

"There's no need to ask these two—" Kurosaki began to object, only to be interrupted by Akari raising her hand from the seat directly in front of him.

"In that case," she said, "I have one too."

Kurosaki noticed that she had a metal keyboard strapped to her left arm, the sort of device he'd seen only in high-tech war movies. She tapped on the keys, and one of the miniature projectors on the table came to life. The sentence she had typed moved into place beneath the one Sekiguchi had added.

- Report: Shadow-ware

Shadow-ware? Kurosaki was mystified. Some kind of computer software, maybe?

"One surprise addition from each side," Sekiguchi said, handing the marker back to Kazumi. "Seems fair." He returned to his seat.

Kazumi looked at the two newly added points and tilted his head for a moment as though in thought. "Well, here's hoping I can be of some use on these too," he said. "Let's start with the space tether. This is all based on papers I received directly from Jamshed Jahanshah in Iran—there was no title for him on the paper I read, but he might have gotten his PhD and be Dr. Jahanshah by now."

Kazumi began his explanation, using the Lorentz force experimental apparatus on the table to demonstrate the effect. Kurosaki shook his head in amazement. The guy made it so easy. It was like they were up in orbit looking at the space tether itself. Everything was new to him, but he understood it perfectly already.

Kazumi must have developed a knack for explaining the unfamiliar in simple terms while writing English posts for Meteor News, Kurosaki mused. The service catered to amateur astronomers around the world.

Kazumi's presentation moved on briskly to the observational data from Ozzy "X-Man" Cunningham. When the projectors on the table turned the conference room into a planetarium, projecting images onto the walls and even the ceiling, Kurosaki couldn't help grunting in admiration. Even Sekiguchi was stunned to hear that

Akari had thrown the planetarium together just the day before. Having Kazumi around to clarify the astronomical side of things must have helped, but to get something like this running in a single day was impressive.

Kazumi pointed to a spot on the ceiling. Akari spread her arms, and countless white dots came into view clustered around a red dot.

"This is the sky that X-Man saw in the Seychelles," Kazumi said. "The red dot is SAFIR 3, and the white dots around it are probably space tethers. That's the conclusion that follows from the orbital data, at least. Something interesting happens right around the time of the acceleration that X-Man reported. Numata-san, can you advance the frame to two minutes, thirty-four seconds? Put the velocity and acceleration graphs up on the whiteboard, too."

With a nod, Akari followed Kazumi's instructions, controlling the graphs and planetarium through keyboard and gesture control. It was like watching someone play a musical instrument.

"Now that's cool," Sekiguchi murmured, forgetting for a moment to play it cool himself.

On the whiteboard Kurosaki saw two lines, green and blue. Around the center of the board, the green one took a sudden step upwards, while the blue one came to a sharp point.

"Here," Kazumi said, indicating that central area, "is where the velocity increases by about three meters per second."

"So it still had some gas in it," Kurosaki said.

It was certainly unusual for an empty rocket body to accelerate, but it wasn't unheard of for leftover fuel to be expelled for some reason and to propel the rocket in the opposite direction. To an amateur, this might appear to be an orbital correction.

"Normally, that would be the assumption," Kazumi said. "But . . ." He pointed at the place on the graph where the green line went up so sharply it looked vertical. "The time span is too short for that. Less than five milliseconds."

Kurosaki leaned forward in his seat.

All spacecraft moved as a side effect of expelling fuel called propellant. A trickle of fuel leaking from a cracked tank could not cause acceleration that fast. But what could give such a kick to a booster that weighed tons in just five milliseconds?

"It's like—pow!" Sekiguchi said, punching his open palm. "Isn't it? Almost like a collision." He was right: that much acceleration that quickly was consistent with an impact. "Orbital debris, maybe? Scary idea."

"There isn't that much debris up there," Kurosaki said.

The figures for 2020 estimated only five hazardous collisions per year throughout the entire low-altitude orbit zone.

Kazumi agreed. "Given the current density of orbital debris, a series of impacts at this rate would be impossible," he said. "In only five minutes of data, we see five velocity changes like this. And the acceleration is always along the direction of its orbit."

Kazumi paused for a moment, apparently unsure how to continue. Finally he turned to face Kurosaki and spoke again.

"I think that what's colliding with SAFIR 3 here is Jahanshah's space tethers," he said.

"Hold on," Kurosaki said. "We're talking about things that aren't even big enough to show up on radar. Could they really move SAFIR 3 like that just by colliding with it?"

"The apparatus at either end of the tether—I call it the terminal apparatus—moves faster than three kilometers per second. That's several times faster than a bullet fired from a rifle and probably five to ten times heavier. It wouldn't be so strange for an impact from something like that to cause some amount of motion."

A chill ran down Kurosaki's spine.

This was no ordinary debris. The space tethers were rotating, and fast. They didn't need a high relative velocity when they crossed paths with something to damage it. All they had to do was match the orbit of a satellite or space station and approach it at their leisure—the energy in their rotation would be enough to smash the target apart.

"Fortunately, we were able to pick out the terminal apparatus that we think collided with SAFIR 3 at this point from the data," Kazumi said. "Numata-san, please show us the orbits for objects 156 and 643. Enlarge number 156."

"All right," Akari said a moment later. "Starting the animation."

She pointed at the ceiling, where a red dot began moving from the front of the room toward the center of the ceiling.

"First," Kazumi said, "please note the motion of SAFIR 3."

He pointed at the center of the ceiling, where a white dot had appeared. As they watched, the white dot approached SAFIR 3's orbital path directly—but then dropped back, describing a circle. Even after Kazumi's explanation of the space tether, Kurosaki couldn't believe his eyes. Could it really be possible for something to move like this in orbit?

As Kurosaki stared wordlessly, Kazumi continued. "The object that collides with SAFIR 3 is about to appear," he said. "There it is."

A slightly larger white dot appeared at the edge of the wall where Kazumi was pointing and began to rise toward the ceiling as if holding hands with the white dot that had appeared first. It seemed to be in pursuit of SAFIR 3.

Kazumi pointed slightly ahead of SAFIR 3.

"Here it comes," he said. Then: "There. That was the collision."

The larger dot had caught up with SAFIR 3 and disappeared. SAFIR 3 seemed to tremble slightly, but that might have just been

Kurosaki's imagination, since he was expecting a collision. The original white dot, having lost its partner, drifted away.

"As you can see," Kazumi said, "Jahanshah's space tether caused SAFIR 3 to accelerate. At least, that's how I see it."

His nervousness was obvious. He couldn't be entirely sure that he was correct. Anyone would be reluctant to report something as outlandish as a collision from an unknown spacecraft to an organization like JAXA, even to nontechnical staff like Kurosaki and Sekiguchi.

"This hypothesis relies on a lot of assumptions, and I'm unable to check them all," Kazumi continued. He started to list the assumptions on his fingers: one, that the observational data from Ozzy Cunningham was accurate; two, that Jahanshah's space tether theory was viable; and three, that space tether technology had indeed been launched into orbit.

"That about covers it," Kurosaki said. He saw Kazumi and Akari for what they were now: an exemplary pair of young IT professionals.

The two of them couldn't possibly be making a living off Meteor News. Realistically, they had to be doing it in between web design work. In other words, they'd made what might be the discovery of the century in what amounted to their spare time, and they still coolly recognized their own limitations as amateurs. If Kazumi were able to tackle this problem full-time, with Akari's support, who could guess what they might achieve?

Sekiguchi rose to his feet. "Thank you very much," he said. "I think it's my turn now . . ."

He trailed off, looking at the conference room's glass wall. A partition made of clouded glass for privacy. The people outside were visible as vague murky forms, moving busily in the Fool's Launchpad lounge.

"My apologies," Sekiguchi said. "I'm a bit stiff from all that looking at the ceiling."

With his briefcase in one hand, he walked around opposite the whiteboard and stretched as he passed the partition.

"You're only twenty-eight," Kurosaki said.

"Age is nothing but a number," Sekiguchi replied. "Let's get started."

The North Korean leader's speech appeared on the whiteboard, played through a projector that Sekiguchi had borrowed from Akari.

"Look at the machine-translated English subtitles," Sekiguchi said. "There's a lot about them that strikes me as odd." He stood in front of the whiteboard and drew a circle beside the subtitles, then turned to Kurosaki. "This is handy, eh?" he said. "We should get one of these high-reflectivity whiteboards for our conference room, too."

"Just get on with it," Kurosaki said, waving his hand. Sekiguchi's outgoing manner had helped warm the room up, but Kazumi and Akari probably didn't have all day.

"Sorry, sorry," Sekiguchi said. "Okay, this is the part that bothers me. The word in Korean is *cheolgwon*, which literally means 'iron fist,' although this is really just a metaphor for a strongly clenched fist. But the English subtitles read 'iron hammer.'"

He replayed that part of the video, filling in the circle he'd drawn earlier. Kazumi watched with obvious interest. Akari leaned forward in her chair.

"The translation has a lot of other strange word choices in it, but the real issue is that it's much more fluent than any machine translation has a right to be."

Akari pointed one orange-nailed finger upwards and said, "Maybe the translation engine's corpus is contaminated!"

Kazumi noticed Kurosaki frown and tilt his head at the word *corpus*. "The database of translation pairs that the translation engine uses," he explained. "As for what the 'contaminated' part might mean, no idea."

"Try this," Akari said. She turned her laptop to face Sekiguchi. He peered at the screen and saw that she had opened a well-known translation tool and set it to translate from Korean to English. "Enter the Korean for 'iron fist' in the left," she said. "It's set to hangul entry. Go ahead."

Sekiguchi thought for a moment, then muttered "*Cheolgwon, cheol-gwon . . .*" to himself as he typed 철권. On the right side of the screen, a single word appeared: TEKKEN.

"Huh? But that's just Japanese in Roman characters," Sekiguchi said.

"And it's all in uppercase," Akari observed.

The two of them stared at the screen, puzzled.

Kazumi clapped his hands. "I get it," he said. "It's that fighting game series. They use the title *Tekken* in English too. Is this what you meant by contaminated, Akari?"

"Yes," Akari said. "That's exactly it."

According to Akari, most cloud-based translation engines relied on translated content on the Internet to compensate for the fact that the meaning of words changed depending on the context. In theory, a single word might have many possible translations, and a machine could not know which was appropriate. To solve this problem, translation engines used online material available in two or more languages to see which words were more likely to correspond in certain contexts.

"It makes sense, I guess, that the online engines would chose *cheolgwon* over the alternatives," Kazumi said. "As a single word, it's probably used to refer to those games more than anything else. Ugh."

"Sekiguchi-san," Akari said. "Try entering more of the speech. Leave *cheolgwon* just as it is."

Sekiguchi moved the cursor to after *cheolgwon* and mumbled to himself in Korean as he typed the rest of the sentence in hangul.

"Hey! There it is!"

The text on the right had been updated to STRIKE WITH IRON HAMMER—the same phrase that appeared in the English subtitles still visible on the whiteboard. The source word CHEOLGWON itself had been left exactly as it was, but presumably its interpretation had changed from "Tekken" to "iron hammer."

"I knew it. It's corrupt," Akari said. "Let me track down the original translation data."

She spun the laptop back toward her. After a short burst of typing, she projected the contents of her monitor up on the whiteboard. She had done a web search for STRIKE WITH IRON HAMMER. Most of the results were on sites in the .kr domain. A lot of Korean results, in other words, for an English search term.

Akari clicked on one and arrived at a product release announcement on a cell phone manufacturer's website. They all stared at the top of the page.

"Why is the English version of a North Korean speech at the top of this page?" asked Kurosaki.

There it was, like a heading at the top of the press release. It didn't seem to have anything to do with the product.

"Can you show us the Korean version of this page?" asked Sekiguchi.

Akari tapped a few keys, and a hangul version of the page appeared on the whiteboard alongside the English one.

Sekiguchi pointed at the top line. "This is what the North Korean leader said in his speech," he said. "Word for word. Can we see the other results?"

Akari opened a few of the other hits from the web search, but all contained a line from the speech. An official site for a television program, an interview with a musician, a fashion blog . . . The only thing they had in common was language: they were all pages on a Korean site with a corresponding English version available.

Sekiguchi nodded eagerly. "I see what's happened," he said. "Someone's been fiddling with these websites. They've chopped up the leader's speech and injected individual lines into bilingual websites for the translation engines to pick up."

"So 'iron hammer' is actually a human translation," Kurosaki said. "But then why is it wrong?"

"Whoever did this wanted the phrase 'iron hammer' to spread," Sekiguchi said.

Kurosaki's coffee turned sour in his mouth. "Why?" he asked. "And who?"

Akari was still paging through the search results. "I know how they did it," she murmured. "Site vulnerabilities. All of these web pages are using an old version of PHP. They just had to reach through known security holes and rewrite the content directly."

Was she talking to herself? All signs of her business-grade politeness had vanished. Looking at the projection of her screen on the wall, Kurosaki could see her opening one browser window after another. Hangul page, English page, web search . . .

"The total number of sites affected is . . . about three hundred thousand," Akari said. "The same source-translation pair on that many unrelated sites might well be enough to contaminate the corpus. The time stamps on the pages all show that they were updated after noon on Friday. Ugh . . . How can anyone run a website without patching such a terrible cross-site scripting vulnerability?"

"Wait," Sekiguchi asked suddenly. "What did you just say?"

"Three hundred thousand sites, all wide open," Akari said. "I can't believe it. This problem was discovered three years ago."

"No, before that. The time stamps. Friday, did you say?"

Akari nodded absently, clearly already slipping into work mode.

"That's *before* the speech," Sekiguchi said. "*Dianwang zhan-xian . . .* ?"

"Dianwang—what did you say?" Kurosaki asked.

Sekiguchi smiled. "The Cyber Front," he replied. "North Korean cyber command. If the corpus corruption was done before the speech was delivered, it could only be the work of a group that knew what would be in the speech beforehand—a North Korean group. They want us to believe that their leader said 'iron hammer.'"

According to Sekiguchi, the speech wasn't especially menacing in Korean. Countries friendly with North Korea, like Iran and Pakistan, would receive translations made directly from the source language and see nothing remarkable about it. But the English-speaking world would get the alarming "iron hammer" translation. Even if the Pyongyang watchers in those countries assured their leaders that the speech wasn't as bad as it sounded, there would still be speculation on what the North Koreans really meant just in case the experts were wrong.

Collecting a list of websites with security holes, then hacking them all at once when the time was right: this, Sekiguchi explained, was exactly the sort of thing the North would do.

It sounded like something from a spy movie, but his voice was completely serious. And Kurosaki had to admit that if Sekiguchi hadn't noticed something funny about the English translation, and if they hadn't discovered the corruption in the translation engine, the question of what the "iron hammer" was would have made him very uneasy.

"Could the Rod from God article have been faked too?" Kazumi asked. "Cunningham doesn't strike me as the sort to do that. He's not, you know, together enough."

Sekiguchi shook his head. "Cunningham's discovery might have been a coincidence. But drawing the connection between the Rod from God and the iron hammer in the public mind—that has to have been the work of the Cyber Front. I *knew* the timing of those comments on the Geeple article was too perfect."

Kurosaki thought back to the alleged NASA engineer's profile Sekiguchi had shown him last week. That had been the source of the original comment linking the Rod from God to the iron hammer, made right after the speech had been broadcast. Sekiguchi had been right to be suspicious.

Sekiguchi stood up and turned to Kurosaki. "Do you have any contacts in the National Security Council?" he asked.

"Afraid not."

"All right. Then I'll get in touch with a guy I know from my intake group." Sekiguchi pulled his cell phone from his pocket and turned to face the door.

There was a knock. The door slowly swung open. Sekiguchi froze.

A woman in a suit poked her head in. "Kazumi, phone call in English for you," she said, looking around the conference room. She waggled a cell phone decorated with beads at Kazumi. "Sorry to interrupt your meeting," she added. "They say they want to send you a check and need your current address. A fan of Meteor News, apparently. They're also after a recent head shot and your cell phone number. Should I oblige?"

She pushed the door farther open and entered the conference room. Kazumi sighed and started to get up, but Sekiguchi quickly pushed him back into his seat and walked toward the door, spreading his arms wide to block the view of the room from the doorway.

"Sorry," he said. "This is important business."

Kurosaki craned his neck and saw a man in a moss-green coat standing outside the door. He had a camera in one hand, and he was clearly trying to angle it for a shot into the room past Sekiguchi and the woman.

The woman stopped in her tracks, unsure of what to do. Sekiguchi put his hands on her shoulders and gently moved her into position to block the camera.

The man's camera shook. Sekiguchi spun the woman around and pushed her out the door, then closed it immediately and leaned his back against it to hold it shut. In his hand was the woman's smartphone. He'd taken it from her.

"Sekiguchi?" Kurosaki said. He started to get up, but froze at the sharp look Sekiguchi threw at him. Sekiguchi put the bead-adorned smartphone to his ear and spoke in Korean.

For a moment, Sekiguchi peered at the phone with a look more serious than Kurosaki had ever seen on him before. Then he furrowed his eyebrows.

"They hung up," Sekiguchi said. "But before they did, they answered me in Korean. Whoever it was, they were a native speaker of the language, or have at least been trained to conversational fluency." He wiped the smartphone's screen with his sleeve. "We have to get out of here, Kimura-san," he said.

"Huh?!"

"What are you talking about?" Kurosaki said, standing up for real this time.

"Give me back my phone!" called the woman outside, knocking on the door.

"In a minute!" Sekiguchi called back through the door. "Very sorry about all this!" He silently beckoned the others toward him. Akari, apparently already having grasped his plan, was sweeping the projectors off the table into the pockets of her cargo pants. "Someone's been out there for a while trying to see into this room," Sekiguchi said. "I tried to keep my guard up, but they got a photo through the door just now. A spy, I assume. We have to leave now. Does this office have an emergency exit?"

Sun, 13 Dec 2020, 21:01 -0800 (2020-12-14T05:01 GMT)
Pier 37 Warehouse, Seattle

Shiraishi pointed at the blurry photograph on the television screen.

"That one in the middle must be Kazumi," he said.

The agent they'd sent to Fool's Launchpad had managed to take one usable photo. It was too blurry and out of focus to make out much about the space itself, but you could still see how many people were there, their height and weight, and so on.

"He's a serious player, this kid," Shiraishi went on. "Ozzy's paranoid rantings were enough for him to identify the Cloud, and then he got those papers from Dr. Jahanshah. He's already put most of the pieces together. Compared to him, these two officials might as well have been twiddling their thumbs."

"Quiet," Chance said through gritted teeth.

She'd slipped up.

She hadn't expected anyone in the room to have such fluent Korean. So fluent that when he'd said "Are you ready?" she'd replied

"Yes" automatically. And in that moment she'd allowed the shadow of
North Korea to fall over the whole thing.

Chance looked down at her hands, balled into fists on her knees.

"Don't look so grim," Shiraishi said. "It's a waste of a pretty face."
He put his index finger under her chin and tilted her head until she
met his eyes. "You made a mistake, but I'll make up for it. We can
track them in real time now. I'll use the Sleeping Gun I left in JAXA's
systems."

"JAXA? What do they have—"

Shiraishi silenced her with an upraised finger, then directed her
attention back to the screen. He pointed at the middle-aged man in
a suit.

"This photo might be blurry," he said, "but I recognize this man.
I used to work with him. Name's Kurosaki."

2020-12-14T05:22 GMT
Project Wyvern

It's almost time for me to check in to the first hotel
of its kind the world has ever seen. No bellboys, but
who needs them when your luggage floats to your room?

The orbital hotel we had folded up in the Wyvern's
docking bay is now fully unfurled. I can see how big
it is even looking through the tiny windows here.
The outer shell was folded using Miura folding,
which was invented by a Japanese researcher. Now
it's all spread out without a single wrinkle. The
space beneath this soft outer shell was pumped full
of water. It took three whole hours.

The outer shell is covered in thin gold foil. Inside there's a two-layer outer wall woven of Kevlar fiber that protects against small debris. Even if both of these layers are torn, the water pumped between them and the inner wall should be enough to keep the hotel airtight—it can stop incoming objects moving at up to ten kilometers per second.

The water will also protect us against another kind of unwelcome invader: cosmic radiation. The radiation levels 350 kilometers high are several times higher than they are at ground level, because down there we're protected by the Earth's magnetic field. The best protection against all those rays is, hands down, the same water that protects us from debris. Two birds with one stone? Three, actually! When we arrive at the ISS, they'll add this water to their drinking-water tanks.

See? It all fits together logically!

Let me give you a quick rundown on my physical condition. When you're weightless—well, in a state of free fall—the blood goes to your head. It's a refreshing new feeling, but it also makes your face look a bit chubby. Makeup is restricted, too. I should have lost more weight before I came.

There's definitely a need for some makeup than can alleviate "space face." We don't want any couples

choosing the Wyvern Orbital Hotel for their honey-
moon and being disappointed with the view, so to
speak. Anyone want to talk to me about a licensing
deal?

*

And now, the long-awaited check-in! As soon as we
took off our space suits (at last!), Ronnie jumped
in, shouting "My hotel!" He's as happy as a child
at Christmas. I undid my harness and followed him.

Does it sound like all we do is play around? Don't
worry, rocketeers, this "first frolic" was included
in the project sequence, with properly allotted
time and everything.

It counts as R&D time, in fact. The hotel's soft
structure is the first of its kind. As we bounce
around, changes in the shape of the rooms and their
center of gravity are monitored and sent back to
staff on Earth. They, in turn, check that the parameters of the orbital hotel's tensioners are correct
to maintain its orbital shape, research whether the
docking bay could be made lighter, and so on. Oh,
which reminds me—we'll also be testing the engine
that will drive us into a rendezvous orbit with
the ISS.

Here's some trivia for the non-space buffs out
there. The difference between an engine and a motor

is simple: fuel. A motor uses solid fuel, and an engine uses liquid fuel. Solid fuel is like fireworks: once you get it started, it's hard to stop, but it's simpler to use and can give you quick access to large amounts of energy. For this reason, motors are often used for liftoff from Earth. But from now on, the orbital hotel will be making delicate maneuvers to dock with the ISS, which calls for an engine. The more you know, right?

Anyway, I'm off for some mission-critical experimental play—or so it reads on the project sequence. I suspect Ronnie just had them put this in the schedule because he wanted some time to have fun.

Next time: Breaking free from the Wyvern, and what the hotel's like inside!

Judy Smark
A suite in low Earth orbit

Mon, 14 Dec 2020, 15:23 +0900 (2020-12-14T06:23 GMT)
The Nippon Grand Hotel, Iidabashi, Tokyo

As Kazumi sank into the soft leather of an immaculate sofa, Kurosaki tipped the sofa facing it back at an angle and ran his hand along the bottom.

Sekiguchi smiled as he watched from the built-in bar counter. "I told you already," he said. "There's no need to get all paranoid. This hotel is used by Chinese officials too. So please forget the couches and tell me what you want to drink."

Sekiguchi ducked beneath the counter, made of a single slab of natural green stone. The wall behind him was lined with crystal glass brandy bottles. The wood of the shelf showed a complex grain.

Akari sank hip deep into the same sofa as Kazumi and swept her gaze around the room curiously. Of the four of them, only Sekiguchi seemed accustomed to the sophisticated decor.

"Will cola do?" he asked them, placing a plastic bottle moist with condensation on the counter.

They were at a luxury accommodation called the Nippon Grand

Hotel, right near Tokyo's Iidabashi Station. After hailing a cab from Fool's Launchpad and riding it in circles all over the downtown core to lose their tail, they had had the driver bring the car up beside the entrance to a secret elevator in the semi-underground employee parking lot before being escorted up to this windowless suite.

For the first time, Kazumi understood the true meaning of the expression "nothing but the clothes on their backs." He'd managed to bring the laptop he'd been using in the meeting room but had left behind the bag he kept his writing implements in, and Akari had had to rush off without the cart loaded with her larger luggage.

"Who's paranoid? I bet spies stay here all the time," said Kurosaki, righting the sofa irritably but softly so as not to scratch it and sitting down on the carpet.

"I'm telling you it's fine. There are probably bugs in here, but there's no way amateurs like us will find them," said Sekiguchi with a smile as he poured the cola evenly into four mugs. "Our top priority right now is to protect these two from North Korean agents, right? And since this place is basically a safe haven used by Chinese government agencies, there's simply no chance Northern agents are going to sneak in here undetected."

Sekiguchi's point sounded plausible enough, Kazumi thought, but surely Japan had its own intelligence agencies. Kurosaki seemed to be one step ahead of him, saying, "Sure, but why on earth do we have to seek refuge with China? Didn't you say earlier that you were going to call someone you knew at the National Security Council?"

Inside the taxi, Sekiguchi had explained to Kazumi and Akari that he was a career bureaucrat on temporary assignment to JAXA as of the beginning of the year.

"I did. This is where he said to go."

"What?! A Japanese spy told you to use a Chinese safe house?"

Kurosaki let his shoulders sag as his gaze paused on something atop the coffee table between the matching couches: an ashtray. Seeing the troubled look in his eyes, Kazumi and Akari both told him to go ahead. Kurosaki got up from the floor and started to reach for his breast pocket but then sighed, seeming to change his mind, and sat on one of the couches. "Thanks, but I'll light up in my bedroom later," he said. "Just knowing I can have a smoke if I want one is good enough for now."

Sekiguchi placed the mugs of cola on a silver-colored tray and brought it to the table. "Let's just have a breather here for a moment," he said. "Once we've calmed down a bit, we can contact each of the agencies. I'm going to get in touch with our superiors at JAXA. Oh— Kimura-san, Numata-san, please don't use the hotel Wi-Fi."

There was no need to give any information away to China for free, he explained, recommending that they use their cell networks instead. There might be no way to know how far North Korean intelligence operations had penetrated, but Japan's information infrastructure was likely safe. Akari nodded, apparently convinced, which told Kazumi he could probably trust the logic behind Sekiguchi's risk assessment.

"Kurosaki-san," Sekiguchi continued, "as I requested earlier, I'd appreciate if you could inform some foreign space agencies about Kimura-san's report and current situation if that's possible. Please try to find somewhere that will provide protection for these two."

"How about NASA? I can contact high-level officials there."

"America would be great. But it might take a bit too much time . . ." NASA, it seemed, was not an organization particularly well suited to dealing with messes like the one they were in.

Sekiguchi scratched his chin. Kurosaki took out his smartphone and squinted at his list of contacts.

Kazumi thought back on the small number of communications

he'd had with government officials. The UN manager he'd exchanged emails with when posting the Debris Catalog data worked at the lowest rung of his organization. Not useful at all in the present case. Then there was the man he'd contacted at USSTRATCOM when asking them to disclose the TLEs . . . The email address had belonged to a high-ranking officer, but the body had just been a template response. Kazumi doubted the guy even remembered who he was.

Then he remembered another organization. Also American military. Kazumi had never contacted them personally, but he expected JAXA would have some connections. "How about NORAD?"

"Ah. I know someone there," said Kurosaki. "I can contact Colonel Lintz in Orbital Surveillance. We've already exchanged PGP keys, so I can send him encrypted emails. How's that sound?" He looked toward Sekiguchi.

"Sounds good," said Sekiguchi. "No less than I'd expect from the head of international cooperation."

Kurosaki smiled wryly. He seemed to be wondering which one of them was in charge. For his part, Kazumi appreciated the way Sekiguchi had taken the reins to keep them on track. Fleeing Fool's Launchpad, Sekiguchi had seemed like a different person. Now he was back to his cheerful self again, but he continued to lead them as though savoring the unusual situation they found themselves in. By calling the shots decisively, Sekiguchi prevented the other members from succumbing to anxiety. Though he and Kazumi were around the same age, Kazumi saw this confident side of Sekiguchi and found himself beginning to look up to him.

Sekiguchi inserted his index finger into the knot of his necktie and pulled it off in one tug. "All right, let's take a break and maybe have a little chat for a while. I know we'll probably start to worry about everything if we don't keep ourselves busy, but it's not over yet, and we won't hold up if we don't rest."

Kazumi picked up his glass of fizzing cola and took a sip. He tasted nothing. As though in reaction to the cold liquid, a chill ran from his thighs up his spine. Kazumi began to wonder what he was doing in this luxury hotel. According to Sekiguchi, the agent at Fool's Launchpad had likely located Kazumi by calling Mary and had been trying to take a picture of him. He had also asked for his address and cell phone number. If Kurosaki and the others hadn't been visiting, he would've been photographed and then—kidnapped?

Kazumi trembled. It wasn't even 4:00 p.m. yet. Kurosaki and Sekiguchi had stopped by just after noon, but already they were in a suite used by Chinese spies. It was just as Sekiguchi had said. They were still in the thick of it.

Kazumi found himself staring at the floor. Looking up, he noticed a relief of two female gods adorning the wall below where a clock hung. Their legs were slender like snakes and intertwined with each other like the strands of a rope. One of them held up a square ruler, while the other had a scale dangling from her hand. The relief had been carved out of some sort of pottery that looked like hardened sand, but the ruler and scale were made out of metal.

"What's that?" Kazumi asked.

Sekiguchi, who was loosening the buttons on his shirt, glanced at it and said, "Looks like Fuxi. One of China's first emperors . . . More like a god, really. That scale is strange. Usually they should have a *compass* and a ruler."

Kazumi approached the wall and touched one of the pans of the scale, making the chain held in the god-emperor's hand shake and the other pan sway. Looking at the seesawing beam of the scale, Kazumi remembered the space tether. Constructed of two devices tethered together, this spacecraft revolved in orbit like a pair of dancers holding hands and could move around freely without using any propellant. Most likely North Korea was behind it, but what was the purpose of having so many of them floating around near SAFIR 3? The tethers that collided with it were scattered in all directions and lost forever. Was this just a demonstration of what North Korea was capable of or a rehearsal for terrorism? An uneasy feeling rose in Kazumi's chest.

What a waste, he thought. Jamshed's space tether could be put to much more practical use. His design had been painstakingly tested through the crude method of sending up balloons in Tehran, where both funding and research facilities had to be sorely lacking. It didn't seem right that it would be used as a tool for anything to do with terrorism. To Kazumi, its potential seemed so much greater than that.

Sticking out his index finger, Kazumi raised it in front of his face and stopped it in the spot where it overlapped in his visual field with the center of the scale's beam held up by the emperor. He imagined the two pans as the devices on each side of the tether and rotated them parallel to the ground in his mind's eye.

If Ozzy's observational data was correct, the space tethers would spin at a velocity of one rotation every two seconds. If the radius was 1 km, the velocity of the terminal apparatuses would be 3 km/s. If the tether was long enough or rotating even faster, it might be possible to hurl an object into an even higher orbit. If you adjusted the tether's velocity of rotation and tied it to a habitation such as Project Wyvern's space hotel, you could generate an analog of gravity inside the room. Kazumi wondered if there was some way to discuss this possibility with Jamshed, who had surely spent years thinking about the space tether and—

"What's he doing? Calculating the time difference or something?"

Kurosaki's voice suddenly broke into Kazumi's thoughts. Apparently he had been concentrating so hard that the conversation around him had not reached his ears. Looking toward the sofas, he saw Kurosaki pointing at him smiling.

"Time difference? Sorry about that. I know I was supposed to be taking a break, but I was thinking about the tethers."

"Oh. So you can hear what we're saying down here again, eh? Welcome back to Earth," said Kurosaki with a laugh. He motioned Kazumi toward one of the empty spots on the couch. "Seeing you concentrating like that reminded me of an old colleague. He wore an expression just like yours when he was calculating time differences. He also helped send up satellites and such."

Akari gave him a quizzical look and said, "You don't by any chance mean Uncle Ageha?"

"You know Shiraishi?" said Kurosaki, staring at Akari.

"He's my uncle. I knew already that he used to work for JAXA."

"What a coincidence. Who could have guessed I'd run into his niece in a situation like this? Did you by any chance pick up your computer trade from him?"

"Yes. He was my mentor," said Akari, suddenly looking happy, and Kurosaki nodded as though something that had been puzzling him now made sense.

"I see. Well, that explains your planetarium. That's just the kind of design I'd expect from a protégé of Shiraishi's."

"If it compiles, it's correct!" said Akari and Kurosaki at once and then laughed together.

"What kind of person was he?" Kazumi asked, and Kurosaki narrowed his eyes wistfully.

"He was an engineer who entered JAXA the same year as me. An astoundingly intelligent character. Numata-san seems to have inherited the same hacker's mind. But he also loved grappling with urgent problems, and that side of him kind of reminds me of Sekiguchi . . ."

"What are you saying? I hate problems!" said Sekiguchi, kicking his legs out onto the footrest in exaggerated denial of the claim.

"Then get back to Ochanomizu and do some paperwork. Nothing doing, right?"

"Not going to happen."

"See? That's just what I mean."

The suite filled with laughter. When it died down, Kurosaki began to tell them what had happened to Akari's Uncle Ageha. Shiraishi's first assignment at JAXA, Kurosaki explained, was an information-satellite project managed by the cabinet. The enormous amount of observational data transmitted from their four groups of reconnaissance satellites was too great for the mere two hundred or so regular workers who staffed the Satellite Intelligence Center to analyze. Meanwhile, the team of bureaucrats in charge handed over responsibility for everything about the satellites, from their design to their operation, to domestic corporations and lacked even rudimentary knowledge about orbital objects. Soon it became clear that they needed someone with expertise in both IT and analysis of the steadily accumulating satellite data to work as a go-between for the engineers and bureaucrats. It was for this job that Shiraishi was specially selected.

Torn between the demands of the manufacturers who insisted on sticking with the technical specifications in their original work orders, the unrealistic expectations of the analysis team, and the ignorance of the bureaucrats, Shiraishi was constantly instigating squabbles. It was in this context that the minister of space policy, who'd been shown pictures of a spy satellite taken by an amateur astronomer, ordered JAXA to make orbit confidential.

"He was panicked that North Korea might find our spy sats."

"Was he an idiot?" asked Sekiguchi.

"That's exactly what Shiraishi called him, right to his face."

Military satellite or not, it wasn't possible to keep objects above a certain size secret in orbit. Kazumi was shocked to hear that such ignorant politicians and bureaucrats were pouring hundreds of billions of yen annually into operating the spy satellites.

"It's okay to laugh, Kimura-kun. I happened to be present at one of their meetings, and all the government engineers in attendance were trying not to laugh too."

Once Shiraishi was removed from his post, he was banished to a window-gazing position in the "Reserves" and became involved with maintaining JAXA's IT infrastructure. Apparently, he did a lot of exceptional work there given the circumstances, including facilitating the adoption of smartphones.

"So that's why he was suddenly so absorbed in security work," sighed Akari. "I had no idea."

"Today, JAXA spends a third of its budget on those spy satellites. I wonder if those costs will go up yet . . . Anyways, Japan's space development isn't exactly all rosy. Projects in this field take a long time to get off the ground. With most of them, it's ten years before they even reach the experimental stage, but the Ministry of Science and Education rotates civil servants through different departments every five years, so none of them have the chance to really understand what they're doing."

"I'm sad to say that I'm one of them," said Sekiguchi. "However much I learn about astronautics, I'm set to be transferred in four years. Then I'll just move from ministry to ministry for the next twenty years or so, though I might be able to come back someday if no young workers come in to replace our aging workforce."

"You're doing a great job here," said Kurosaki. "Anyways, to get back to my story, one day, without saying anything to anyone, Shiraishi quit and went to China. I guess the fact that the inductive-tether project he supported hit a snag may have had something to do with it . . ."

Kurosaki tried to insert his fingers into his already loosened necktie and then gazed at his fingers gripping empty space. "I'm exhausted. Must be getting old . . ." He gave a wry smile. "The truth is, it wasn't just Shiraishi. China got a number of other engineers as well. Thanks to the Tiangong-2 space station, the space industry is booming over there. Japanese engineers are probably highly attractive to China because most of them have become jacks-of-all-trades from working on small teams."

"Don't any of them go off to America?" Kazumi asked.

"I hate to admit this, but us government engineers aren't seen as valuable over there . . . or maybe that's just our perception. We probably see it that way because private enterprises like Project Wyvern are just full of specialists from NASA and Lockheed. What they're ultimately looking for is people with the design skill to come up with outrageous plans like orbital hotels. If you can pull off a Dr. Jahanshah and develop a known technology like an inductive tether into something like those space tethers, I bet that would get you in the door too . . ."

Kazumi looked at the scale hanging from the relief on the wall. Kurosaki was probably right, he thought, that something like the space tether would pass muster in America.

"I don't know who's scouting them out, but since the beginning of the year, twenty of us have already gone over to China. And they've all left knowing they'll be highly disposable. That's how little of a future they see in Japan . . ."

"Well, it's not all that bad." Sekiguchi swirled the cola around in his glass, tinkling the ice cubes together. "The staff who've gone over are probably enjoying it."

". . . Let's hope so, for their sake. And I hope that's true for Shiraishi too, wherever he is and whatever he's doing. You know I check

Chinese academic journals now and then to— But excuse me. I'm going to have a smoke."

Kurosaki stood up, raising two fingers as though holding an invisible cigarette.

Mon, 14 Dec 2020, 01:12 -0800 (2020-12-14T09:12 GMT)
Pier 37 Warehouse, Seattle

"So the young guy who threw you for a loop is a rookie named Sekiguchi. Come on, Chance! A pencil-pushing bureaucrat?" Shiraishi pointed to the TV screen.

"Makoto Sekiguchi, hmm? Entered this year? I'll have our team look into it."

"Forget about him. He doesn't matter. What's important is that we know where Kurosaki is! So send in Mr. Park!"

Shiraishi hit the keys a few times, and a large intersection with half a dozen intersecting roads appeared on the screen. Several arrows pointed to a hotel in the vicinity of Iidabashi Station. Once Chance saw the building, she shook her head.

"Isn't that the Nippon Grand Hotel? If so, our hands are tied. That's a Chinese safe house."

As Chance explained to Shiraishi, half the staff were either soldiers or spooks. Sending agents in there would be sure to stir up serious trouble. The Clouds and the Great Leap that would follow had been kept secret from China. There was no way they could compromise that secrecy for such a minor operation.

"The best we can do is have people watch the perimeter," said Chance. "Also, China isn't our only worry. With America beginning negotiations to partially relax space treaties and guidelines concerning debris—"

Suddenly Shiraishi grabbed Chance's shoulders and spun her around. "You didn't think to tell me? Since when? Who's your source? Give me the details!" Shiraishi's grip on Chance's shoulders tightened as he glared at her with an unwavering gaze.

"It was a cable sent to WikiLeaks. An anonymous tip. It all began immediately after the Supreme Leader's speech. America wants to initiate discussions to relax a section of the regulations, that's all."

Shiraishi stared up at the ceiling, apparently thinking. "The part of COPUOS they'd be relaxing is guideline 4: 'Avoid intentional destruction and other harmful activities.'"

Looking at Chance, Shiraishi curled his lips in a smirk.

"This is fantastic!" he said. "It looks like the CIA has fallen for the Rod from God. Just to be sure, send someone into the Smithsonian National Air and Space Museum. The ASAT weapon ASM-135 and fire control system should be on display. If not, have them ask when they took them off display and if the display item is a model or the original. If the agent poses as some kind of space geek, the staff will be glad to answer all their questions."

As Shiraishi briefly explained to Chance, the ASM-135 had been developed and tested in the eighties. It was one of the best weapons available for disposing of orbital weapons like the Rod from God. But destruction of orbital objects violated space-debris reduction guidelines. Shiraishi's guess was that America was trying to get around the rules by changing them in advance.

"If we give them one more push, they're bound to panic and fire off something, whether it's the ASM-135 or one of its predecessors. Oh, the embarrassment!"

"What kind of 'push' do you mean, exactly?" Chance looked at him quizzically.

"I mean we'll bring the Rod from God within range of the Wyvern Orbital Hotel."

". . . I don't think I understand. The Rod from God is just X-Man's wild fantasy, right?"

"Nope. The plans used as the basis for the illustration may never have actually been realized, but it was conceived as a serious possibility. Its range as a weapon could be calculated."

Chance shrugged. "Your plan is hopeless. Do you seriously think the American military and the CIA believe in the Rod from God? Even amateurs like Kazumi see right through it."

"They may have their doubts, but I bet they haven't totally ruled it out. That's why I'm saying we give them one more push. The Rod from God illustration is modeled after an American military orbital weapon that hurls a tungsten projectile at Mach 22 into the Earth's surface. Let's redirect their sights on to this wild goose. Then they'll be desperately thinking up a way to stop it."

"You really expect everything to go so smoothly? First, we have to silence Kazumi. And I'm sure NASA experts will talk sense into the CIA."

"No one's going to listen to a bunch of rocket geeks."

"How are you so sure?"

"If politicians paid any attention to engineers, I'd still be building rockets in Japan. Science, technology, reason—people simply aren't wise enough to entrust their lives to such cold ideals. Tell the general and the Supreme Leader: pretend to be scared. Those fools are going to take my ruse—hook, line, and sinker!"

Chance shrugged and let out a sigh. "Understood," she said. "But how about you sleep for a bit?"

Shiraishi turned toward the television displaying the map of

Iidabashi. "No sleeping just yet. The night is getting on in Japan. Right! So how about we wait until our targets stop moving? Then we can get it on too, Chancey babe."

"Sounds good! It's six hours until the date changes in Tokyo . . . I'll go pick up some coffee."

Mon, 14 Dec 2020, 19:20 +0900 (2020-12-14T10:20 GMT)
The Nippon Grand Hotel, Iidabashi, Tokyo

Kazumi stared at the large slips of paper stuck all over the whiteboard he'd had brought into the suite. They charted the structure of the email they were planning to send to Colonel Claude Lintz, head of Orbital Surveillance at NORAD. Written on each slip were sections they intended to include, such as "Greeting," "Request for Protection," "North Korea," and "Space Tethers," and they had been arranged into a particular order by Sekiguchi.

"I'm going to write up the request to have Kazumi-san protected personally," he said. "Kazumi-san. Can you draft an analysis of the objects around SAFIR 3 in a register suitable for engineers and also draft a summary of the space tether?"

"Yes," said Kazumi with a nod. "I can handle that." All he had to do was reorganize the presentation he'd given today. And he wasn't expecting it to take very long, either, because most of the documents he was relying on were in English.

Sekiguchi nodded to acknowledge Kazumi's reply, peeled off two notes from the whiteboard, and turned to Akari. "About the contamination of the translation engine . . . Can you take care of that?"

"I'll write it up if you don't mind correcting it for me later," she replied.

"Please," said Sekiguchi, putting his hand to his chin and staring at the list of items lined up on the board. During their break, Sekiguchi seemed to have decided to call Kazumi and Akari by their given names. The first time he addressed them in this more familiar way, Kurosaki gave him a sour look, but Sekiguchi brushed off his disapproval with a vague excuse, saying, "From here on out, we're all going to be writing emails in English, so we'd better get used to it."

Akari raised her hand. "In the information we send them," she said, "should we mention the advertisement and the shadow-ware?"

"Can you remind me about that again?" asked Sekiguchi with a puzzled look.

"I was planning to explain it to you at Fool's Launchpad." When Akari tapped at the keyboard on her left arm and pulled the Geeple Rod from God article up on the whiteboard, the cat in a banner advertisement leaped out. "This cat food ad can be found on numerous websites related to the Rod from God, and I've figured out what conditions make it appear."

Akari pulled up another display on the whiteboard. On a page with a white background was English text—regular words that didn't serve as advertisement keywords. Written in the page's title and caption was the name "Jamshed Jahanshah." And in the upper-right advertisement area the familiar cat banner was displayed.

"'Rod from God,' 'space tethers,' 'SAFIR 3,' and then 'Jamshed Jahanshah.' On every page with any one of these strings of text, the advertisement appears."

Kazumi and Sekiguchi stopped what they were doing and stared intently at Akari.

"So, Akari-san," said Sekiguchi, "you're saying this advertiser is . . ."

"Exactly. Whoever's placing ads for Kitten Master knows about Jamshed Jahanshah and the space tethers."

Kurosaki finally seemed to clue in and opened his eyes wide. "You mean they know Jahanshah's name? So who on earth . . . Well, I guess we're pretty sure it's North Korea, but why?"

"To lure whoever reacts to these keywords out into the open." Akari dragged the cursor over to the advertisement and opened a menu item called Display Element Details. "I discovered a program built into the advertisement. Do you understand what this means? A fragment of an executable file is included in the image data."

Web Inspector, which Kazumi often used himself, popped up. When Akari dumped out the raw image data and scrolled down to an area near the bottom, there, mixed in with the image's color information, the code for a script could be deciphered.

"Of course, this wouldn't pass the screening if the program were operational. But only half the code is included in this image. The rest has been built into a separate banner ad." Akari pointed to a less flashy advertisement. "When these two advertisements are displayed together on a single site, a shadow awakens."

"A . . . shadow?" said Sekiguchi. "What does the program do?"

"What I've been able to determine so far is that it transmits the IP address, browser type, display size, and so on of any computer that views it to a server in America."

"Hmm," Sekiguchi said with concern. "This sounds like some sophisticated stuff. But I've never heard of shadow-ware. What does it mean?"

"Tracking," Akari replied, and Sekiguchi looked at her perplexed. Kazumi felt the same way. From what he knew, a better word for something that functioned in this way was "tracer."

"Oh, so you don't know," said Kurosaki, looking toward Kazumi, and then turned to Akari. "Did Shiraishi teach you that, about this shadow-ware?"

"Huh?" Akari's face tensed up.

"It's an old expression. You hear it sometimes in Cold War spy films and such. Shiraishi and I used to talk about movies like that all the time. I hit the mark, didn't I?"

Akari began to shake her head, but then, seeming to reconsider, she nodded. ". . . Yes, Uncle Ageha came up with the idea."

With apparent resignation, Akari began to explain. During a period when Shiraishi was absorbed in the task of finding security holes, he came up with a method for activating a program by linking two advertisements together. Shiraishi and Akari created a program to verify that it would work and then reported the system weakness to a company that propagated advertisements, but they were dismissed because the company deemed the cost of fixing it unrealistic. The truth was, there was no small number of security holes left unfilled due to the apparent lack of economic and political feasibility to do so. Even from what Kazumi had heard, there had been a case in which a smartphone and PC manufacturer bought out by a Chinese corporation had unknowingly installed Trojan horse viruses in their devices.

"But until I saw this advertisement," Akari continued, "I didn't think there was anyone actually using the method."

"Well, yeah, having two advertisements appear side by side costs a huge amount of money, doesn't it?" said Sekiguchi.

Most websites had fixed widgets for displaying several advertisements, and apparently someone was using this convention to merge fragments into a program and steal personal information.

"So where's the information going?" asked Sekiguchi.

"The IP address is assigned by AT&T in Washington." The MAC address containing the manufacturer name, device name, and serial number for the receiving server, Akari explained, indicated that it was a Chinese brand of mobile router. The information was probably being received with a laptop or tablet rather than a virtual server in a data center.

"We definitely need to report this," said Sekiguchi, and wrote "Shadow-Ware: Transmission Destination Washington State" on one of the slips of paper on the whiteboard. "Let's have NORAD contact the CIA or FBI about it."

Sekiguchi went on to explain that the CIA and NSA held on to the web connection records of AT&T. If they had NORAD inquire with these two organizations about it, they would know immediately which antenna had been used to go online at that time.

"There's also the phone number and voice record," said Akari, projecting a fourteen-digit number starting with 01125 onto the whiteboard. After a pop from the projector speakers, Kazumi heard the cheering of a familiar voice. Next was the voice of someone who sounded like an announcer. Overlaid on this was faint breathing and a woman saying in English, "Hello, Mary. Mary? Can you hear me?"

Sekiguchi stared at Akari in wide-eyed astonishment. "What? How? Numbers with 125 after the country code 01 are for Chinese cell phones. They must have been using a roaming SIM card!"

"I'm the one who set up the call tracking system that Mary uses for customer support. This recording is an answering machine message left last night. Sekiguchi-san, do you recognize the voice?"

"Yes, it's the woman from earlier. She called once to scope out the situation. Please play it again. When I heard it before, there was no background noise."

The cheer played again, and Kazumi realized who it was. The voice was Judy Smark's. And the announcer was praising the success of the Loki 9 launch. Whoever the woman was, she had called Mary from a room with a television.

"The television is playing KFFV Television, right, Akari?" said Sekiguchi.

"Yes, Seattle," Akari replied immediately. "Apparently KFFV is a local, independent terrestrial station. They seem to have a weak signal because there are some reviews online complaining that it's difficult to tune in from other cities."

"You're incredible," said Sekiguchi, "figuring all this out." On the whiteboard he wrote "Agent Hideout: Seattle."

Akari stood up, pulled a display out of her 'fro, and put it on the table, as text continued to flow across the screen. "I'm going to Seattle, too," she said. "We're going to catch whomever the shadow-ware is transmitting to."

Kurosaki leaned forward in his seat and said, "Hold on! What are you thinking here? You think I'm going to let you play spy like that? And—right! Passports. Do both of you have passports?"

"I have one," said Kazumi, pulling his passport out of his pocket. Akari also held out the red-covered booklet of a Japanese passport, and then Sekiguchi produced his as well with a smile.

"Kurosaki-san," he said. "People these days use it instead of a driver's license. It's one of the few photo IDs available. And it's not such a bad idea for Akari to go to Seattle."

"Hold on! Sekiguchi—"

"Either way," Sekiguchi interrupted, "we were planning to have Kazumi flee overseas, right? In that case, I think it makes sense for Akari, who can provide engineering support, to accompany him. But more importantly than that, she says she wants to go."

Akari pointed to the word *Seattle* on the whiteboard. "If I go,

I can help out in all kinds of ways. The only way I can figure out the rules AT&T uses to supply IPs, for example, is by being on the ground in America."

"So you think Shiraishi has something to do with this, do you?" said Kurosaki, staring at Akari.

Kurosaki's low voice made Akari tremble. ". . . That's not it. It's the shadow-ware destination, I—"

"Just hypothetically speaking," said Kurosaki, "if you did find Shiraishi, what would you do?"

Akari bit her lip and cast her gaze down. It wasn't just about the advertisement. It was also about the successor for the tether-propulsion system, the space tether, that Shiraishi was said to have been involved in.

Sekiguchi broke the tension in the air with a clap. "Let's definitely have these two head off to Seattle," he said. "It's a nice town. Maybe a bit cold, but the coffee and clam chowder are delicious. As long as it's okay with Kazumi, that is."

"If Akari doesn't mind," said Kazumi. "I'd be happy to have her along." He was going to need her help with analysis of the space tethers. And if she was going to search for the man called Shiraishi, he wanted to help with that, too. Then Kazumi might be able to discuss the space tethers with him.

"Sekiguchi," said Kurosaki. "Do you have any idea what you're saying?"

"Kurosaki-san, let's not waste time like this," said Sekiguchi. "We still have no idea what North Korea is after. The English translation of the speech was saying they might target the ISS, but it's hard to imagine they'd do that with Russia's involvement in it. We'd be best off teaming up with America, since its relationship with North

Korea is frigid to begin with. We can't overlook the possibility that the Wyvern Orbital Hotel could be their target. If they're planning something, they're bound to strike this week while the two Smarks are aboard."

Sekuguchi went on to outline the rest of his plan. The two JAXA employees, Sekiguchi and Kurosaki, would be in charge of contacting the Ministry of Defense, the cabinet, and other relevant foreign organizations. That way, they could seek the cooperation of specialists in analyzing and observing the space tethers. However, while they spent their time bringing these specialists up to speed with the knowledge already held by Kazumi, the space tethers would continue to fly around freely in orbit.

Crossing his arms and closing his eyes, Sekiguchi said, "Let's narrow down our potential collaborators to the ones who can actually get things done. NORAD is ideal. Also, if we take refuge overseas, we can force North Korea to start their hunt over again from square one. And if Akari accompanies Kazumi, she can take care of his Internet security. Really, if we start fresh in a new location, anywhere will do. So how about Seattle, then? I doubt the agents we're looking for would expect us to come right to their doorstep."

With inquiring eyes, Kurosaki looked at Kazumi, then Akari, then Sekiguchi in turn. "Fine. The responsibility for all this . . . As if there was a way for anyone to take it in our situation . . . Count me in! Seattle it is!"

"Excellent," said Sekiguchi. "Now that that's settled, I'll book the flights and arrange for all the things we might need. Everyone else, please get your documents together."

Sekiguchi put on the jacket he had draped over the sofa and dashed out of the room.

Mon, 14 Dec 2020, 06:58 -0700 (2020-12-14T13:58 GMT)
Peterson Air Force Base

"Kurosaki, eh? How unexpected."

Colonel Claude Lintz was looking over the list of emails Jasmine had sorted for him when an unexpected name caught his eye. Kurosaki was his counterpart at JAXA. Since NORAD's international operations had been cut back several years ago as part of restructuring, they hadn't been in touch, but Lintz still remembered his dedicated work ethic.

The email's subject was "Urgent: Unusual SAFIR 3 Orbit Caused by North Korea," and its body was encrypted with PGP. Lintz and Kurosaki had exchanged a PGP key in accordance with military protocol, but he couldn't recall their ever having used it for normal communications. That he was using it now told him it must be a highly urgent matter.

Lintz reopened the email in a separate window. It had two attachments. Rare for an email written by a Japanese person, Kurosaki's greeting was short, but as Lintz read through the rest of it, that wasn't his only surprise. *Space tethers? Iranian scientist? North Korean agents?*

"What on earth . . . ?"

A Japanese engineer had analyzed SAFIR 3's abnormal behavior using his own personal resources and, with the help of an Iranian scientist, had uncovered the existence of a spacecraft composed of over ten thousand separate units that were all floating in orbit. At the same time, their efforts to interfere with North Korea were progressing.

The attached report was remarkable, and the engineer who wrote it was obviously highly capable. He had skillfully summarized all the central points and, most importantly, grasped the space tether, an unknown craft, with such completeness it was as if he'd built it himself.

Reading the final sentence, Lintz sighed. Why did Japanese people always put the most important part of their emails at the end?

"I'm sending two key members of our team who are being hunted by North Korea to Seattle. Would it be possible to place them under your protection?"

Linz glanced at the Speedmaster on his wrist. It was currently 11:00 p.m. in Tokyo. *If I send a response now*, he wondered, *will Kurosaki have a chance to read it?* But forget about that. First he had to arrange for a security escort.

Lintz raised his voice and called through the open door, "Jasmine! Send over Sergeant Freeman, would you?"

"What's this?" she replied. "Don't tell me you haven't noticed? He's already here!"

"Is there something I can assist you with, sir?" asked Sergeant Daryl Freeman, poking his head in from one side of the doorway with an orange backpack slung over his shoulder.

Suddenly Lintz remembered. Freeman had been dispatched to Lintz's room to babysit the CIA. There was no need for him to be there so early, but he'd probably felt pressured when the two early bird operatives made snide remarks about NORAD's work ethic.

"Sergeant, I'm going to have Second Lieutenant Fisher take over for you in looking after our CIA friends."

"I beg your pardon, sir?"

"Some Japanese who've solved the riddle of SAFIR 3 are coming to Seattle, and you're going to make sure nothing happens to them."

It took several seconds for Freeman's look of suspicion to shift into a broad smile.

Papers piled up before Daryl's eyes: request to travel on duty, plane ticket, hotel reservation chart, application to use a credit card . . . Lintz's assistant Jasmine laid on the documents one after the other.

Lintz placed a credit card on the desk. Stuck to it was a Post-it with a four-digit number on it. This Chase MasterCard, with a white star and yellow wings on a deep-blue gradient, was for use by air force staff only.

"I'm not expecting too many expenses, sir . . ."

"Our guests will arrive here with nothing but the clothes on their backs. They had to leave everything behind, from their computers to their toothbrushes. Seattle is freezing. We'll probably even need to buy them jackets."

Jasmine put another paper folder on the desk in front of Daryl. It contained a receipt from a travel agency he recognized.

"I borrowed the car from Air Force Travel Zone," said Jasmine. "It's a Chevy wagon. You can drop it off at any federal facility. I've booked a block of three rooms in the Western Days behind the Needle. One is for our Japanese guests, one is for you, and one will serve as your operations center."

"'Guests' plural?" asked Daryl.

"According to the email from Kurosaki," said Lintz, "Mr. Kazumi Kimura, who is investigating SAFIR 3, will be accompanied by a female engineer named Akari Numata. I'll explain the situation to Chris and Bruce."

"Understood."

"Proceed with the utmost caution, Sergeant. I doubt those North Korean agents will make any big moves out in the open here in America, but the moment you sense danger, take the two of them and run!"

Daryl continued to sign the growing stack of papers, mentally shouting for joy. *Fantastic!* He'd never guessed that SAFIR 3 might have been driven by impacts. But that was the least of his excitement. *Space tethers?!* He'd heard of tether-propulsion systems before, but what could be more thrilling than the chance to analyze real ones in action?

Mon, 14 Dec 2020, 07:22 -0700 (2020-12-14T14:22 GMT)
Guest House, Peterson Air Force Base

Sitting across from Chris as she worked on her salad, Bruce wiped some latte foam from his trim mustache, flicked his eyes to his smartphone, and said, "Hey, Chris. Is it just me, or does everyone in a uniform have muscle for brains?"

Staring up at him from the reservation chart for Air Force Travel Zone, a business under surveillance by the CIA, was the name of a hotel and a Chevy wagon rented in the name of NORAD. Beginning yesterday, all communications related to Freeman had been flagged for monitoring.

Interestingly, the email sent to Lintz from Japan had been encrypted with PGP. It had been decoded with Lintz's private key and provided to the CIA by the air force, and the plaintext version had been relayed over. The care taken by the JAXA official, Kurosaki, to use strong encryption had been pointless in the end, but as a result Lintz's sloppy operations had been exposed. In other words, the surveillance had paid off: Bruce and Chris would be able to protect two private citizens coming from Japan, Kazumi Kimura and Akari Numata.

"I can't imagine what's come over them that they would rent a car that might as well have 'Soldiers On Board' spray-painted on the doors when they're picking up two private citizens chased by spies!"

said Bruce. "And separate hotel rooms to boot! What are they going to do if someone comes for them? Unbelievable!"

Even assuming that Lintz was right to change Daryl's assignment under his own authority and have him escort these guests carrying secret information, sending his subordinate off to rent a car at a military travel agency like Air Force Travel Zone revealed a serious deficit of imagination. Bruce himself had used the service back when he was in the army, but when they brought out a drab olive Land Cruiser with a huge white star plastered on the side, he'd been simply appalled.

"They just aren't grasping how serious it is that they're being targeted by enemy agents," said Chris. "It can't be helped." She picked up a cracker, crushed it in her hand, and sprinkled the crumbs on her bland salad. "This Japanese guy comes out of the woodwork, and all of a sudden he's this incredible information hub. He's got JAXA and even the Iranian professor involved. Do you remember what Daryl said yesterday?"

"About what?"

"About instantaneous acceleration. An identical phenomenon was recorded in the data Kimura extracted from Cunningham's observational data. We were so focused on Cunningham's involvement with North Korea that we completely overlooked the activities he himself was engaged in."

"Well, there's no point in worrying about that now." Bruce shrugged. In the investigation being conducted at the McLean CIA headquarters, they were treating Ozzy Cunningham as either a spy or a puppet and trying to uncover traces of North Korea in his communications. No one had even considered the possibility that clues might be found in his observational data already available to the public online. So while it was true that the CIA could monitor everything, they could still go way offtrack without the right search method.

"What do you think of Kimura's space tether hypothesis?" asked Chris. "That's the line of inquiry I'd personally like to follow."

"Sounds good to me. If the Rod from God is really the diversion it seems to be, that would iron out a lot of inconsistencies. But, wow, did they ever fool us!" Bruce thought back on his exchange with the NASA officials. When asked about the Rod from God, astronautics specialists could only state that the whole idea of an orbital weapon targeted at Earth was ludicrous. But Bruce and his team had been so distracted by the illustration created with information held only by North Korea that they had bent this explanation to match their own perception of the situation. "The North Korean strategist behind this is a capable fellow indeed. Even just looking at the IT tricks that woman Numata uncovered, you can tell he's like no one we've ever dealt with before."

Bruce brought his mug of latte up to his nose and let the steam rise into his mustache. The translation corpus contamination that the engineer Numata had discovered had definitely jumbled the decision-making of everyone concerned. The phrase "iron hammer" that had appeared in the English subtitles of the North Korean leader's speech suggested a specific weapon of some kind. Even after learning that no such nuance could be found in the original text, the expectation that those words had instilled in them only bolstered their belief in Cunningham's Rod from God report.

"This shadow-ware that piggybacks on advertisements is an incredible piece of workmanship, too. It might be the first time that the Cyber Front has employed such a sophisticated method in their operations."

The services provided by private corporations such as Google and Amazon now covered the entire world and had changed the way that information flowed. Even an organization like the CIA, said to command twenty thousand regular employees and 1,600,000 contractors, used Google to check maps. Bruce had never suspected that North Korea's intelligence capabilities had grown so strong that they could pull off an information attack capable of causing such widespread misunderstanding through contamination of these services.

"So should I call a halt to Seed Pod, then?" asked Chris.

"Can't be done. The military unit will be assembling today."

The American military was superbly organized. It should have been cause for celebration that after only two days NORAD's test-run team was already on standby waiting for an order to engage, even though on paper all that had happened was that they had been transferred. No matter how rapid the preparations, however, it was all irrelevant if their objective wasn't right.

"I'll leave them as they are," said Chris. "I have no idea how much North Korea knows about the ASM-140, but we might as well act as though America still believes in the Rod from God."

"And the second stage of the SAFIR 3 is still a pain in the ass either way."

"Good point," said Chris with a laugh. "Okay, then, I'm going to Seattle."

"I'm relying on you to stick with Daryl." They couldn't leave the protection of their Japanese guests to amateurs.

Chris brushed cracker crumbs off the tablecloth and picked up her glasses. "Can I count on you to track down the illustrator from Los Angeles?" she asked. "Even if the Rod from God is just a diversion, he did receive the plans, so he must be involved somehow."

"Jose Juarez. Leave it to me. I'll get a commercial flight. You take the Gulfstream we came here on."

The comfort of a private jet was tempting, but even on a regular commercial flight, he could arrive by ten o'clock local if he left now. Then he could round up some operators in the area, raid the man's residence, and question him about where he had gotten the confidential documents that were the basis for the Rod from God.

Mon, 14 Dec 2020, 23:45 +0900 (2020-12-14T14:45 GMT)
The Nippon Grand Hotel, Iidabashi, Tokyo

With two small brand-new suitcases and the bags Kazumi and Akari had left at Fool's Launchpad piled on a cart, Sekiguchi pushed open the door with his back and entered the room.

"Sorry to keep you waiting," he said. "I had to get Watanabe-san's help bringing your stuff here."

Kazumi got up to help him with the luggage, but when Kurosaki told him to relax and stood up to do it himself, he took advantage of the offer and sat back down.

Now that everyone was there, Kazumi decided it was time to tell them his one lingering worry. "In the email I sent to Colonel Lintz, I forgot to mention how Dr. Jahanshah got in touch with us."

"Ah," said Sekiguchi. He gazed up at the ceiling with chin in hand. Apparently he had let it slip his mind too.

"We only received a portion of Dr. Jahanshah's paper, and the expanded orbital hotel will detach from the Wyvern soon. To speed up our analysis, I'd like to ask for his assistance. Would it be possible for you to contact someone at NORAD for me?"

"I don't think so," Kurosaki responded immediately. Iran and the US had tried to restore diplomatic relations six years ago, but the new president had halted it. There wasn't even an embassy, so their hands would be tied if they proceeded through official channels. "We might be able to work out something if we could get an intelligence agency like the CIA to understand why connecting with Jahanshah is so important, but that's not going to happen. We've got no time."

"I can get you in touch with Jahanshah," said Sekiguchi.

Kurosaki frowned. "I wouldn't go making promises you don't know you can keep."

"I've got a few connections," said Sekiguchi. "But I need your help, Kurosaki-san, so I'd appreciate your cooperation when the time comes."

It seemed unlikely to Kazumi that JAXA could put them in touch with someone in a place like Iran where the Internet was blocked off. Instead, he guessed that Sekiguchi would probably ask his colleague at the NSC to pull some strings.

"Are you sure you can manage this?" asked Kurosaki.

"Just leave it to me," said Sekiguchi. "Oh yeah. Where did I put that again?" From a suitcase, he withdrew a thin oblong box neatly wrapped in wrapping paper. He then stood up and proffered it to Akari, the orange ribbon attached to it quivering. "I wish this present could have been something more to your liking, but . . ."

Wearing a look of suspicion, Akari took the box, unwrapped it, and looked up at Sekiguchi. He pursed his lips and bowed to her in apology. It was then that Kazumi finally saw what the so-called present was: an electric shaver. Sekiguchi had a point; Akari's Afro would definitely draw too much attention.

"I'm very sorry," said Sekiguchi. "I couldn't think of any other way."

"No . . . I appreciate it," said Akari. "This should allow me to go around with Kazumi-san without having to worry all the time."

Akari looked toward the whiteboard. Written on it was "1:38 AM," the departure time for JL 293. They had two hours to go.

"You think we'll be on time if I do this now?" she asked.

"Should be okay. Please use the bathroom."

Akari stuck her empty hand inside her Afro and stirred it around. "I'm going to miss this . . ."

"In your suitcase, you'll find a hat . . . and a wig. If you don't like them, please buy replacements at your arrival airport."

Kurosaki turned away as if he couldn't bear to watch, muttered something, and pulled out his smartphone. "I'm going to hire a driver," he said. "Even with business class tickets, you have to go through the gate twenty minutes early or you won't be on time for—What?"

Sekiguchi was wagging his finger. It seemed they wouldn't be needing the driver.

"To apologize for what I've done to Akari, I'd like to show her the ultimate nighttime view of the city."

On her way to the bathroom, Akari stopped in front of the door and turned around.

Sekiguchi pointed straight to the side and said, "I called a helicopter over to the Korakuen Building next door. With this, we can be at Haneda Airport in fifteen minutes. Please forgive me."

Akari smiled at him and said, "I'm going to come out of here looking cooler then when I went in. Just you wait and see."

Now wearing a bathrobe, Akari looked at her reflection in the full-length mirror. In her right hand, she gripped the shaver that Sekiguchi had just given her. The words of Kurosaki kept echoing inside her head. *So you think Shiraishi has something to do with this?* At the time, she'd said no, but everything they'd discovered so far pointed to her uncle's involvement. In addition to the shadow-ware installed in the advertisements, she'd also heard him talk about how a translation engine could be contaminated and how to remain anonymous inside a surveillance state by changing roaming SIM cards.

"Uncle Ageha . . ." she whispered.

Though Shiraishi was more than two decades older than her, he had treated her as a friend and taught her programming. To Akari, he was the model engineer. Listening to him describe his seemingly endless supply of ideas, she had adopted his way of thinking and dedicated herself to learning his techniques of choice. Whenever one of them had uncovered a seam in the global system that now depended on the Internet and cloud services, they would dutifully send reports to the manufacturers and providers. Fixing many of the security holes that Shiraishi had found would have required enormous funding, nationwide initiatives, or some other costly investment, and his suggestions were often rejected. Even so, the two of them had often laughed together at the special efforts they had made to make the world a better place.

Shiraishi never once tried to use the skills he had acquired for selfish purposes. It just didn't seem possible that a man of his character, who had demanded a high degree of restraint from Akari and who had personally taught her engineering ethics, would exploit a security hole like the one they had witnessed. Petty little subterfuges like those with the advertisement, the translation engine, and the SIM cards would surely have occurred to someone else at some point. There was no good reason to assume it was her uncle. She was just going to Seattle to—

"To uncover those North Korean agents," Akari muttered, putting the buzzing foil of the razor to her temple and watching her frizzy curls begin to scatter before her eyes.

2020-12-14T15:00 GMT
Project Wyvern

14:39 GMT. The orbital hotel has successfully
detached from the Wyvern and became a single independent spacecraft. I wanted to blog about that
moment, but it was totally quiet, and before I knew
it an announcement came from one of the staff on
Earth saying that the separation was complete. Not
much to work with there. They could have at least
given me a *thunk* or something. Seriously.

According to our itinerary, our plan from here on
is to enjoy five days in orbit before transferring
over to the ISS and then returning to Earth on the
Soyuz.

The Wyvern spacecraft that carried us all this way
is going to remain in an orbit that will make it
easy to rendezvous with our orbital hotel in case
of a problem. Then, when we depart from the ISS on
the Soyuz, it'll dock with the ISS and become a new
return vehicle. I can't tell you how jealous I am
of the astronauts who get to go back to Earth in the
unrivaled comfort of this wonderful ship.

Through the big round windows of the orbital hotel,
I can see the body of the soon-to-be return spacecraft, the Wyvern.

No picture could ever convey to you how exciting this window is. You probably think a five-foot circle is tiny. Well, think again. From what I heard, when Ronnie came up with the idea of having a window this size, all—and I mean *all*—the architects were against it. If I'd been at the meeting, I'm sure I would have been against it too. Here in low Earth orbit—they call it LEO—thousands of bits of space garbage are zipping around at speeds between six and eight kilometers a second. Then consider that this orbital hotel moves at seven kilometers a second. This means that if there was a direct collision, one of those little bits might smack into one of the screws or solar panels at the unbelievable velocity of 13 km/s. Just like that, thirteen times the speed of a rifle bullet. The hotel has to be able to take lumps of metal flying at those speeds.

A shell made of multiple layers of metal can hold off small pieces of debris, but it's difficult to make something that strong with transparent materials such as glass and acrylic. But Ronnie wouldn't give in. And the designers actually fulfilled his request. Jammed into this window is an appalling amount of technology: a heavy water bulkhead, a shutter operated by gunpowder, and, carefully folded in so as to be invisible to the human eye, carbon nanotubes.

The view of the Earth through this window is simply magnificent!

As I write, I'm standing with the soles of my sandals on the window frame . . . This really makes me
miss the Earth. Is that the Atlantic Ocean under
nightfall straight beneath my feet? Inside the
clouds floating over the Gulf of Mexico, I can see
lights bigger and sharper than any illumination
that humans can create: flashes of lightning.

I have one surprise announcement to make. Project
Wyvern will be providing a complimentary sojourn on
the orbital hotel to heads of state. It's hard to
say how many years you'll have to wait in line, but
we look forward to your applications. We would be
delighted for all you leaders to see the countries
you've been entrusted with from 350 km up.

With-a-touch-of-that-on-top-of-the-world-feelingly
yours,
Judy Smark

PART TWO
The Tethercraft

7   **War**

Once Kurosaki had watched Kazumi and Akari disappear into the full-body scanner, he stopped waving and dragged his hand down his face. In twelve hours, the two of them would arrive in Seattle, where Sergeant Daryl Freeman, a subordinate of Colonel Claude Lintz, would pick them up at the airport. The body odor that came with old age wafting from Kurosaki's wrist reminded him of how stressful the day had been. Only twelve hours had passed since their visit to Fool's Launchpad, and already so much had happened.

Sekiguchi, who'd been looking out behind them, leaned his back on a barrier and slid down into a crouch.

"Are they gone?" he asked.

"Yeah. Anyone look like they're tailing us?"

"No one was paying special attention to those two. I think we're okay."

"Good work. You did a great job today. I'm scared to think of tomorrow though . . ." Kurosaki said, feeling overwhelmed as he went over all the things they had to do the next day in his head. He would have to report to his superiors about the North Korean plot as well as the space tether that he was still trying to wrap his mind around, and explain the expenses that Sekiguchi had been putting up for them. He could justify the change of clothes and the suitcases they'd given to Akari and Kazumi, but the cost of the chartered helicopter to Haneda and the suite in the Nippon Grand Hotel went way beyond their allowance for entertaining important guests.

"You did a great job yourself, Kurosaki-san. This is far from over, so I'm sure we'll be relying on each other more from here on out. All right. So let's go back. The train to Iidabashi should still be running."

Kurosaki nodded. Thanks to the Olympics, the trains now ran late into the night. Nonetheless, to get back to his home, he was going to have to take a taxi from Nakano Station. Kurosaki was just pulling out his smartphone to call his family when Sekiguchi waved at him to stop.

"Please don't turn on any smartphone provided by JAXA," said Sekiguchi.

Kurosaki remembered how Sekiguchi had had everyone turn off their smartphones before boarding the helicopter from the Korakuen Building. He'd thought that this was to prevent any interference with the vehicle's instruments, but perhaps not.

"We can turn our phones on when we get back to the hotel," Sekiguchi continued.

"What are you talking about? I'm going home."

"After we have a nap at the hotel, we've got to get moving right away. Our flight to Turkey tomorrow leaves at noon. Since we're taking economy, we've got to be at Narita by 9:00 a.m."

"Hold on, there. Turkey?"

"Yes. There's no direct flight from Japan to Tehran, so we're getting a connecting flight from Istanbul. At 5:00 p.m. . . . This itinerary is going to be rough." Sekiguchi put his hand on the barrier to push himself to his feet and bowed his head to Kurosaki. "I'm very sorry. There was no time to explain. We're going to Tehran."

"Tehran . . ." muttered Kurosaki and stared at Sekiguchi.

"Yes. We have to find Jahanshah. I promised Kazumi."

Sekiguchi explained that they would bring satellite phones and other devices to create a network-connection environment that would allow them to communicate with Seattle. "This is going to be my first official trip abroad since I started working for JAXA," said Sekiguchi, doing a big stretch.

"You . . . you think they're actually going to approve this trip?"

"What better time than this for me to throw my weight around?"

Within a few years, a career bureaucrat like Sekiguchi would rise up the ranks in the Ministry of Science and Education and might even enter the department that controlled JAXA.

"I used your stamp to approve the application for our trip and included your portion on— What? You said I could use your stamp 'when necessary.' I also took the liberty of bringing your passport from inside your desk."

"You fu— That's not what I meant! What—"

"Kurosaki-san, I apologize for arranging all this without consulting you. But it's of the utmost importance that we go. If Kazumi-san has a chance to speak with Dr. Jahanshah, the man who came up with the concept, our insight into the situation will only deepen further. And most importantly, this is what Kazumi-san wants."

". . . Well, that may be so. But there's absolutely no need for *us* to go."

"No, there is. We need to go into hiding."

"What's this?"

Sekiguchi lowered his voice and leaned in close to Kurosaki. "North Korea has us in their sights too."

Sekiguchi took out his powered-off smartphone.

"I had to go to Ochanomizu to pick up your stamp so we could approve the trip, but when I got there, our IT team was in a frenzy. Apparently they've detected the unauthorized use of MDM."

"MD what?"

"Mobile device management." The moment Sekiguchi said this, Kurosaki recalled that JAXA had adopted a system to centrally administer the smartphones and tablets used in their operations. In case any of them were lost or stolen, the IT department was set up to wipe out all its information. They could also check how many times certain apps were activated, where phone calls were made, and each device's current location. Employees of the device manufacturer on temporary transfer from its systems integrator were in charge of running this system, and Kurosaki supposed that Sekiguchi had heard about the misuse of MDM from them.

"There was a record of someone checking the location of our smartphones right when we were in the Nippon Grand Hotel." Pausing for a moment, Sekiguchi looked around and dropped his voice even further. "The account used to manipulate the MDM was Shiraishi's. A disgruntled ex-employee's account, still active. The password hadn't even been changed. Once this is all over, we've got to let human resources and IT know how badly they screwed up."

"Shiraishi's account?" Kurosaki was surprised that it hadn't been deleted.

"We still haven't determined 100 percent that it was Shiraishi who did it," said Sekiguchi, apparently noticing the look of dismay on Kurosaki's face. Kurosaki was having serious trouble telling anymore which one of them was older and had seniority.

"I put off dealing with the problem because I didn't want whoever it was to know we're onto them," continued Sekiguchi, "but we can't use JAXA's infrastructure until this all settles down. That's why I submitted our application to travel on paper. It'll be input into the system eventually, but this will at least buy us some time."

Kurosaki was grateful for Sekiguchi's quick thinking. "Ah . . . So that's why you had us turn off our smartphones before boarding the helicopter."

"Exactly. If they knew we were at Haneda now, there would be no doubt that our two engineers escaped abroad."

"Sorry for being so slow on the uptake."

"Don't worry about it. Let's just stay focused on what we're going to do next," said Sekiguchi, scanning the lobby. "If we rush off to one of our domestic institutions like the NPSC or NSC, they might offer us protection from the North Korean operatives. But is that what we really want? A chain of interviews, reports, questioning? We'll lose days to all that. That will mean leaving Kazumi and Akari unassisted in Seattle."

Sekiguchi lifted his hand as if to grab something and then placed it on Kurosaki's shoulder. "Kurosaki-san, listen. If we lay low at the Nippon Grand Hotel until tomorrow morning and then fly off to Turkey, we can enter a country in which not even NORAD or the CIA can move freely. And we can bring the man who came up with the space tether on to our team."

Kurosaki felt Sekiguchi's fingers bite into his shoulder. Clearly the man wasn't playing around. "Sekiguchi, that hurts."

"Oh . . . I'm very sorry," said Sekiguchi, removing his hand and retreating a step. "Whether you join me or not, I'm going. If you're going to stay, please get in a taxi now and go to the NSC in Kasumigaseki to ask for protection. I'll arrange everything for you."

With shaking hands, Sekiguchi lined up his lapels and stared at Kurosaki.

Kurosaki thought of Kazumi and Akari. They were heading to a foreign land to work with strangers on verifying their hypothesis while hidden operatives hunted them. Sekiguchi would be leaving, too, for Tehran. With faith in their as-yet-uncertain guess about the tethercraft, the three of them were plunging into deep water.

The pain lingering in Kurosaki's shoulder gradually turned to numbness. But Kurosaki could sense that the heat transferred from Sekiguchi's trembling hands had sparked some new feeling in his chest.

"All right, then," he said. "Let's go back to the hotel. It would be great if we could head off to Narita by helicopter too."

A flash of white peeked from between Sekiguchi's thin lips as he smiled. "Don't tease me with your jokes. We've got to cut costs, so we're going by bus."

Mon, 14 Dec 2020, 10:22 -0700 (2020-12-14T17:22 GMT)
Peterson Air Force Base, Colorado Springs

Major Sylvester Fernendez stretched out his long arm and pointed at some ugly orange clothes hanging in a locker. "Hey, Ricky! You really won't wear this for me?"

Straddling a bench, Captain Ricky McGillis shrugged slightly in response, keeping the gesture small enough so as not to appear rude. When he had first heard the story from Fernendez's subordinate, Sergeant Daryl Freeman, last weekend, he'd thought it was a joke. But this was the third time he had been asked.

"Just take it already! Don't you think it'll be cool to become a legendary test pilot?" Watching this exchange from where she stood in front of the lockers, Second Lieutenant Madu Abbot laughed. This Indian American woman might have been highly capable flying an F-22 Raptor, thought Ricky, but she simply didn't understand the tact required of a pilot.

"Lieutenant Abbot. Can you please be quiet?" said Sylvester, and Madu shrugged, shifting her weight from one foot to the other. She had been acting cheeky like this since the moment she had learned that Sylvester's visit was not on official orders. She was an excellent pilot but didn't understand how important personal bonds within the organization were when it came to an experiment in which life was on the line. In other words, she wasn't exactly someone who inspired solidarity.

"Come on, Ricky!" Sylvester casually puffed out the right side of his chest. The silver wings of the emblem that indicated he was an air force pilot gleamed dully under the fluorescent lights. "I'm a pilot too. I understand better than anyone that a pressure suit gets in the way when you're driving the Eagle, feeling its incredible power, but—"

"That's not it at all, Major," interrupted Ricky, looking flustered. "That suit was worn by the crew of a bomber, right? That's no pilot suit!"

Sylvester's eyes went wide and he said with a laugh, "Oh boy. You've got it all wrong. This uniform was used on the Streak Eagle."

". . . The one with the world record?" asked Ricky, and Sylvester glanced at him with a snort, as if to say, "This isn't something a little whippersnapper like you would understand." And Madu agreed completely. Any pilot who truly loved the Eagle would pump a fist with excitement the moment they heard the words *Streak Eagle*.

In February of 1975, a Streak Eagle, stripped bare of paint and gutted of weaponry, radars, fire control systems, and most other avionics, had reached an altitude of one hundred thousand feet in just

207 seconds, setting the world record at the time. The old-fashioned orange jumpsuit in the locker had in fact facilitated a historic achievement and deserved to be commemorated as prize memorabilia.

Sylvester stood up before the pressure suit, looked back, and said, "It's been forty years since Captain Smith set his record, so most of the parts have been refitted." Sylvester ran his bony finger over the components as he explained its history. The high-altitude pressure suit had been designed for the Streak Eagle. It had then been stored in the back of the warehouse, going ragged over the decades, but they had fixed it up. Though there was no time to redesign it, the rubber inner lining had been replaced with Gore-Tex, and the duralumin helmet had been data modeled with a 3-D scanner so that a mold could be 3-D printed and it could be remade in polycarbonate. As a result, the suit was lighter and more comfortable than the original.

"A transparent material was used for the helmet, so the view should be much better than with the original. Sounds like the ultimate Eagle experience to me, wouldn't you say?"

As Ricky listened to this, an idea reared its head. ". . . The ASM-140 was launched over fifty thousand feet, right?" he said.

"That's exactly right. You've really done your homework," said Sylvester with a satisfied smile, as though self-assured that his invitation had been a success.

"Seventy thousand feet," said Ricky. "We could try to send the launch to about that altitude, couldn't we?"

Sylvester frowned.

I'm going to pull it off, thought Ricky. *I'm going to show you all.*

"Request permission to top the Eagle's strategic altitude record," said Ricky. "That should set a record for the F-15C with regular equipment. Does that sound acceptable, sir?"

Sylvester gave a conspiratorial grin. "That sounds fun."

"I'm out of my depths here," said Madu, who'd been listening quietly. She let down her hair and shook her head.

"Hey," said Ricky. "Wanna do it together? You can set a record for the F-22 too."

"Not my sort of thing," said Abbot. "You go for it. I'll be down here taking pictures of the ASM's takeoff."

" 'Takeoff'? This is a 'blastoff,' baby!"

Sylvester brushed Ricky's shoulder as he passed between him and Madu. "Technically, we're planning to call it a 'launch,' " he said. "In my letter to NORAD, I'll be sure to strongly emphasize your seventy thousand–feet request."

"Thank you, sir."

At the entrance to the locker room, Sylvester turned around as though he'd just remembered something.

"There was a message from Colonel Lintz," he said. "Even fifty thousand feet is well into the stratosphere. That means you might be able to see the stars even during the day. Have a ball up there, Captain."

"Understood."

Ricky brought his fist and palm together and smiled at Madu. *Ho yeah!*

Mon, 14 Dec 19:42 2020, -0700 (2020-12-15T03:42 GMT)
Interstate 5, Seattle

When the car went over a hill coated pure white with snow, the bright red lines of tail lamps leaped into Kazumi's view. Before he could mention the traffic jam, Freeman smoothly slowed the car. The lane to the left painted with white diamonds was open, but few cars were taking advantage, and Kazumi supposed it was reserved for something.

Earlier that evening, Freeman had come to the Seattle-Tacoma International Airport to pick up Kazumi and Akari. He was a short man with somewhat dark skin whose youthful face made Kazumi think he might be younger than him. But he held his back straight and carried out tasks efficiently, making Kazumi think of an organization with which he had little familiarity: the military.

Kazumi searched for the right words and at last squeezed out an English sentence. "It is a traffic jam," he said.

"Yeah, this is terrible," said Daryl, tapping the steering wheel with his fingers. "At this rate we won't be there for about forty minutes."

As Kazumi stared at the rows of cars ahead, a silver passenger plane in position for takeoff flashed into view, and turning his head, he could see a runway stretching to the left.

"Sea-Tac is really spread out," said Kazumi.

"Um, actually," said Akari from the backseat, patting Kazumi's headrest, "that's Boeing Field. On Google it's labeled King County International Airport."

Akari's English was far from fluent, but she spoke up without any hesitation, and Kazumi resolved to follow her example.

"That was King County? I see. It has an official airport name. Thank you, Akari."

Kazumi looked into the backseat. Akari's face was hidden by the brim of the Seattle Mariners cap that Sekiguchi had given her. She was just in the middle of inserting the SIM card she had bought at the airport into the Raspberry Pi resting on her lap. This reminded Kazumi of the SIMs he had in his wallet. Akari had bought them for him when they had arrived at the airport. Raising the eyebrows of the mobile counter staff by buying ten of them, she had given three to Kazumi and told him to change them every day. It seemed unlikely that the North Korean agents would be able to monitor their communications in America, but she wanted to reduce the risk, and Kazumi had no qualms with that.

Kazumi heard the sound of another jet firing up. The silver passenger plane was just lifting off.

"Is that a domestic flight?" asked Kazumi. "I can't see any airline logos."

Daryl glanced to the side and tapped the steering wheel as though satisfied with what he'd seen. "They just haven't finished painting it," he said. "The Boeing factory is doing the flight check and paint job before delivering it somewhere. That's why it's called Boeing Field. Is this the first time in America for you guys?"

"Yes, first time," said Kazumi, and Akari said, "Me too."

Kazumi smiled, feeling disappointed with himself. He couldn't speak English fluently, so he found himself repeating whatever Daryl said. He felt like a parrot.

"While we're investigating, I'll show you around Seattle. I've heard the collections at the Museum of Flight in the back of the airport are just incredible. They even have a Concorde on display. I bet you'd really enjoy the orbiter simulator, Kazumi."

"An orbiter . . . That is a space shuttle, right? Thanks."

"You're welcome," said Daryl and tapped the wheel again. The Boeing Field runways kept sending silver passenger planes into the air in a flurry of motion. Kazumi took another look at Daryl's face and felt amazed that this man with whom he was chatting casually was a serviceman for NORAD, a military organization with a tradition of monitoring orbital objects for as long as forty years.

Here he was in America, the mecca of space development. As Kazumi took a deep breath to absorb the air of this exciting place he found himself in, he began to choke on the fragrance of a strong perfume.

"You okay?" asked Daryl. "Before we go to the hotel, I'd like to stop by a shopping center. We've still got to build an operations center for you two to perform your analysis, and I brought almost nothing with me from Seattle—oops!" Daryl smacked his forehead. "There's three of us in the car. I forgot. That means we can use the car pool lane." Pointing to the lane with the diamonds, Daryl checked behind them and turned into it with brisk motions. The powder snow that had been accumulating on the windshield puffed up.

"I'm always alone, so I forgot," said Daryl. "It's nice to be on a team for a change."

"Nice to be working on a team," said Kazumi, parroting what he had heard again. He tried to think of other words he might have used: colleague? friend? budd— He felt a smack on his headrest. Looking back, he saw Akari smiling at him with the brim of her cap pushed back by her Raspberry.

"A team! Nice!"

Pushing a shopping cart, Kazumi followed Daryl as he cut through the high-ceilinged lanes of the store. From a rack, Daryl took out six feet of aluminum, bent it to test its strength, and turned around. "It seems fine. Let's use this for the girders. I want to get a dozen—can you help me?"

Apparently Daryl was planning to use the aluminum as the base for a grid of LCD monitors in front of their desks. The cart, which looked big enough for someone to stretch out and sleep in, was chock-full of things Daryl had picked out: power tools, bolts, VESA-compliant LCDs. Kazumi was getting tired of Daryl's shopping style—he merely glanced at the packages before tossing them in, as though anything would do so long as it was compatible.

"Will that fit in the car, all that?" asked Kazumi. The English that slipped from his mouth wasn't yet natural, but as he walked around the massive Costco behind Daryl, he found the words beginning to come to his lips.

"Just barely, maybe," said Daryl. "It should be all right."

Kazumi retrieved the aluminum and glanced casually at the ceiling. Hanging there was an antenna that looked to be ten meters long. He guessed it must be used for ham radio.

"Americans really like to make everything themselves."

The store that Daryl had brought them to was an enormous warehouse of a giant mall, completely unlike the Japanese electronics mass retailer he had vaguely imagined it would be. The variety of computer accessories was somewhat limited, but they were well stocked with items seen less in Japan of late, such as hard disks and wired mouses. In the automotive zone, they had everything from car bodies to engines to maintenance cranes. Then there were the DIY items: chainsaws, wooden logs, unit baths, household power generators . . . Amazingly, they even sold helicopter blades and nuclear shelters for domestic use.

"It's surprising isn't it? I felt the same way the first time I saw one of these stores too. There are lots of people in this country who live isolated from urban infrastructure like sewers and base stations for television or cell phones, and it seems like doing things for yourself is considered a virtue."

"You were not born in America?"

Daryl let out a white-toothed laugh and said, "I'm from Indonesia. I came over here for school and then went straight into the air force. I wanted to get a green card and build up a career in the space industry."

"Sorry. I wasn't thinking."

Kazumi was reminded of what Kurosaki had said at the Nippon Grand Hotel about the engineers whose abilities weren't recognized in America and so went over to China instead. But without any career, skills, or connections to rely on, Daryl had made the leap into America from Indonesia.

"I'd like to say that it doesn't matter where you're born . . ." said Daryl. "But I feel like the people who were raised here are just different somehow. It's not like I've met all that many people, but I can tell we're not the same."

"Is it difficult to do space work? Back in your hometown."

Daryl scrunched up his face, bringing his thick eyebrows together. The expression could have been one of regret or mirth.

"There is *some* work there," he said. "When I was a child, I used to watch in awe every time we launched a rocket. When I saw one of them shooting straight up into the sky dragging a tail of light, that was when I made my decision. I was going to space!"

Kazumi tried to remember what he knew about Indonesia. He seemed to recall there had been the Pameungpeuk spaceport on the island of Java, but after a few tests they had stopped carrying out any launches to speak of.

"You might even remember it, Kazumi," said Daryl, and went on to explain that the rocket that inspired him was a sounding rocket. Used for meteorological observation, it hadn't even reached fifty kilometers in altitude. "I can't tell you how depressing it was when I learned that. Fifty kilometers is almost within arm's reach. I mean, even a balloon can rise that high. How about you, Kazumi? Have you seen a rocket before?"

Kazumi shook his head. "The launch sites in Japan are on the southern edge," he said, and then realized that he hadn't really answered the question.

"That's true of all countries in the Northern Hemisphere," said Daryl. "You're talking about the sites in Tanegashima and Uchino-ura, right? Didn't they send up an H-II Transfer Vehicle last month? A spaceship with 1 atm pressure that can also double as a manned vehicle. I think that's pretty impressive. If we had anything like the space industry that you have in Japan on Java, I wouldn't have had to become a soldier twice."

Daryl raised two fingers as though giving the peace sign and laughed. He explained that his first time in the service was when he had been drafted for two years in Indonesia, one of several countries in Southeast Asia to revive conscription after rumors began to spread that China would make incursions into the Pacific.

"After my mandatory period was over, I came to America. But I didn't have any connections here, so I decided to enter the military again."

Daryl continued to toss bolts, screws, and various other items into the shopping cart as he spoke.

"Have you ever been in the military, Kazumi? I see your hair is long and you've got a slight slouch. If you'd served, you would've turned out like me. Worrying about your hair just becomes too much of a nuisance."

Kazumi was shocked. He had no idea he had a slouch. He decided to puff out his chest.

"My shoulders . . ." he said, but couldn't think of the right word in English. "They harden."

"Sorry, did I make you self-conscious? I only meant if I pay really close attention—" Daryl cut off what he was saying and cast his gaze to the end of the lane. "That's Akari, isn't it?"

Kazumi followed Daryl's gaze. In front of the register, clinging to a massive cart, was a small figure in khaki cargoes, her shaved head conspicuous as her hat seemed to have fallen off somewhere. The cart was piled full of equipment.

Seeing her pull a credit card from her wallet, Daryl shouted, "Akari! Stop!" and began to jog toward her. Kazumi followed behind him pushing the cart.

"Obviously that stuff isn't for your daily personal use. I've got it."

"Really? That would be great. I was really worried because it looked like this was going to go over my limit."

Daryl began to push Akari's cart for her and waved over Kazumi, saying, "I'll pay for it all together."

"Wow, this is a lot," he continued. "Amazing that they had this many Raspberries in stock. And LAN cables too. But what's with this tarp and Nichrome wire?"

Daryl lined up the items in the carts on the checkout counter. The amount of merchandise Akari had piled in hers was stunning. There were three cables wrapped around drums with LAN and USB connectors. A heap of antistatic bags and cardboard boxes containing various electronic devices in the dozens. Overwhelmed by the quantity, the cashier called over help, and three staff began to beep them through. One of them, a black man close to Daryl, said "Oh Jesus" in a fed-up tone as he scanned the bar codes. "What are you getting yourselves into with all this stuff? Hey! Isn't that a display item?"

The hands of the cashiers stopped and Daryl, who had put down the object in question on the counter, shrugged. On the yellow frame above bristly tires was the brand name "Cannondale." A mountain bike.

Passing through the checkout gate. Akari, who suddenly had her Mariners cap on again, turned around. She had the tips of her fingers up on the brim and was smiling. From her upraised, unlipsticked lips came some badass words.

"We're getting ourselves into war."

2020-12-15T04:00 GMT
Project Wyvern

Have you ever seen a light when your eyes were closed? Here, 350 km above the surface of the Earth, in the vacuum of orbit, I had just such a strange experience.

Burrowing into bed after turning off the lights and tightening the Velcro straps around my blanket, I suddenly felt the sandman dragging me down to sleep. I could be indulging in a bit of hyperbole here.

Then, just when I closed my eyes, it happened. Behind my eyelids, a pure "light" flashed.

I should have been more careful how I worded this. The networks will probably just quote my introduction and broadcast it all over the news. But to all my spiritual ladies out there, this is not the guiding force of the élan vital or even an angel. Nor did an alien enter into my consciousness on its way back to retrieve its corpse from Area 51.

The true nature of this light is cosmic radiation. One cosmic ray out of the many emitted unceasingly by the sun, black holes, and the stars of the galaxy passed through the bulkhead of the Wyvern Orbital Hotel and my eyelid to strike my retina.

I experienced this as light.

In other words, I was irradiated. Most likely this radiation came in the form of gamma rays.

It has been almost two full days since we blasted off, and during that period I have absorbed two microsieverts of cosmic radiation. That's an exposure 150 times greater than on the surface of the Earth. Just like an X-ray technician, I have a dosimeter badge strapped on.

I'm going to be honest here. Oh, I really don't want to tell you how old I actually am . . . but this is for science. If a twenty-eight-year-old like me stays on the Wyvern for a week, the chances that they will die of cancer increase by approximately 0.02 percent.

Of course, all measures have been taken to protect this hotel from cosmic radiation. I've blogged about this several times already—to block it out, the space between the exterior and interior wall is full of water, and a faint electrical current is passed through a fine metallic mesh. It's even safer here than on the ISS. If someone were to step outside of the hotel, they would be exposed to hundreds of times more radiation.

The reason this radiation isn't a problem on the surface of the Earth is that the atmosphere and

magnetism protect us from it. Magnetic fields are
invisible to the eye, but you can see the atmosphere
clearly from this hotel.

The Earth is too big to view all at once from the
window, but around its outline lit up by the sun I
can see a shell the thickness of a fingernail. This
thin, gleaming blue thing is what protects terrestrial life.

And I'm able to be up here because the efforts of
science and technology have managed to re-create
a fraction of that mystical protective power. We
could go so much further.

But it looks like my writing won't be going any
further this time because Ronny has just ordered me
to go to sleep. Until next time.

Coddled-in-a-giant-cocoon-feeling-protectedly
yours,
Judy Smark

8 The Team

When the Chevy loaded with their bags and luggage passed beneath an elevated city railway, Kazumi saw a strangely familiar tower brightly lit up ahead of them.

"Windows 8!" cried Akari in excitement from the backseat, and Kazumi suddenly remembered where he'd seen the tower before. It had appeared on the wallpaper of the PC he'd used in college. In the image, it seemed to be standing by the shore for some reason, though they were now quite a distance from the ocean.

"You got it," said Daryl. "It's called the Space Needle. Our hotel is at the base. I hope you'll forgive me for booking at a cheap one."

Against a pitch-black sky dancing with powder snow, the illuminated Space Needle drew closer. This served as a vivid reminder for Kazumi that he had indeed come all the way to America. As planned, Daryl took a right when they reached the base of the Space Needle, passed through a gate labeled Western Days, and drove into the rotary. When the Chevy proceeded farther, shaking green leaves dusted with snow as it passed, two staff dashed out from the lobby to meet them: a bellboy in a blue jacket with a white belt strapped diagonally across, and a large black man in a white jacket.

"Well, this is odd," said Daryl, looking perplexed. "We seem to be getting the royal treatment."

The uniformed bellboy came around to the driver's seat and stood up straight, facing in the direction of the car's rear. The jacketed black man came around to the shotgun seat where Kazumi was sitting, smoothed out the handkerchief in his pocket that had gotten ruffled when he ran over, bowed deeply, and said in a loud voice, "Welcome to Western Days, Mr. David, Mr. and Mrs. Chan. We have come to greet you as representatives of this hotel."

"That is not us," said Kazumi, the English that came hurriedly to his lips seeming unnatural even to him. He was worried that even if the man had heard him, he wouldn't understand what he'd said, and Kazumi shook his head and hands to indicate that there had been a mistake. But keeping his head down, the man made big obvious motions with his thick lips and said, in a voice that was barely audible inside the car, "We know."

The man then glanced inside the car. "Woo-wee. That sure is a lot of luggage. Even a bicycle. Well, we'll carry it all for you, so please feel free to make your way directly into the hotel."

When the man whistled and raised his arm, several other staff members dashed out of the hotel and made a line that ran to the revolving doors at the entrance. Wearing tense expressions, they all stared intently in the direction of the outside of the rotary and the road that ran alongside the hotel.

With a sigh, Daryl unlocked the car doors and said, "So the jig is up . . . We don't hold a candle to them."

"What is wrong?" asked Kazumi.

"Let's go right on in," said Daryl. "I don't want to be a nuisance to the hotel staff."

Once the man saw that the car was unlocked, he opened the door and stood in a position that would block Kazumi from view of the road. He then led him behind the line of staff and went back to let out Daryl and Akari, shunting all three to the entrance.

"Welcome to Western Days," he whispered to Daryl and Kazumi. "The woman who arrived before you instructed us to provide our best hospitality and protection. Please enjoy a relaxing stay at our hotel."

Gently but firmly with his strong arms, the man pushed them one by one through the slowly revolving doors, first Akari, then Kazumi, and finally Daryl. On the other side, Kazumi was disgorged into a toasty-warm lobby filled with the faint scent of roses. Akari, with her hand on her freshly shaved, hatless head, swept her gaze around the room in apparent wonderment.

The space inside wasn't so different from the hotel lobbies Kazumi was used to seeing in Japan. Though it lacked the elegance of the Nippon Grand Hotel, there were rows of low sofas big enough to sleep on under the glow of evenly placed ambient lights, and he could see the flame of a fireplace enclosed by a brass screen in one wall. From the huge speakers that resembled spaceships installed in each of the four corners of the lobby came the sound of stringed instruments.

When Daryl came in through the revolving door, a suited lady stood up from the sofa where she'd been sitting in the back. Her perfectly set blond hair reflected the light of the fire and took on beautiful orange highlights.

"Just as I thought," Daryl muttered.

"You're late, Daryl," said the lady. "But good work picking these two up." She walked over and extended her right hand. "Mr. Kimura and Ms. Numata, I presume. You must be tired after your twelve-hour flight. My name is Chris Ferguson. Please call me Chris."

The lady squeezed Kazumi's hand with more strength than he would've imagined she possessed. "Welcome to the United States."

Kazumi got off an elevator that went directly to the seventh floor and realized that there was only one room there. Daryl pushed open the door to the room, glanced inside, and gave a whistle. "Ladies first," he said, inviting Akari in, but she dithered for a moment and Chris stepped inside. Peeking into the room after her, Akari muttered in awkward English, "Another suite."

If she was going to talk to herself, Kazumi thought, she might as well be using Japanese, but she seemed determined to get by with English as much as she could.

"There are not enough seats," said Akari. "If I had been told it was this spacious, I would have bought more things."

"What you going to use that silver stuff for?" asked Chris.

"For a darkroom. I will explain later."

"All right."

Kazumi was taken aback by the interior, which was decorated in the same way as the lobby but was much more spacious. A chandelier hung from a round cove in the ceiling. There was a real fire going in the fireplace between two large balcony windows. The carpet was so plush it seemed to be absorbing the legs of the table and sofa. While this room might have been a suite like the one at the Nippon Grand Hotel, it struck a far better balance between refinement and calmness.

Ahead of the others, Chris stood in front of a brand-new table with legs still in plastic wrap. It was oval shaped and big enough for about ten people to hold conference. Around it were placed six high-quality business chairs the likes of which Kazumi had only ever seen in catalogs. Beyond the table was a giant whiteboard that was also so brand-new you could tell at a glance and a glass partition with adhesive tape stuck to it like the squares of a go board. On the upper part of the partition, five digital clocks displayed the time in different cities around the world in red shining digits, and below them hung the Geeple Rod from God article.

"This is our operations center," said Chris. "We haven't brought in the computers yet, but you've picked up a few things too, haven't you, Daryl?"

"Yes, I've purchased some of the materials we'll need."

"That's my seat over there," said Chris. "Can I have you connect me with wired Internet?" She pointed to a big, hefty desk placed in a spot near the entrance from which you could view the entire room. It was the sort of desk that might appear in a drawing of "the boss's seat." Her open laptop was on top. "Kazumi and Akari, you'll be sleeping in the two bedrooms to the left. Please rest assured that both of them have been disinfected."

In the direction that Chris pointed were two doors. When a CIA agent like Chris said "disinfected," Kazumi supposed that it meant they had checked for bugs.

"You're lucky I came, Akari," said Chris. "Daryl's superior thought that you and Kazumi would sleep together in the same room."

"What? He was wrong about that?" said Daryl in surprise.

"We're just business partners," Akari replied.

"Yes. No. It's not like that," said Kazumi.

Chris laughed warmly at Kazumi's confusion about how to use "yes" and "no." "There's no need to worry about English mistakes, Kazumi," she said. "If you start talking the way Akari does, you'll get used to it right away. Japanese reserve is a vice in America."

Chris stood up tall and walked toward the whiteboard. "It's

going to take some time for hotel security to check our luggage. In the meantime, I'd like to talk to you all about something."

Kazumi noticed that Chris was suddenly gripping a whiteboard marker in her hand. Daryl's brisk movements had been surprising enough, but Chris's deft efficiency was of a different sort altogether. If Kazumi had to compare her to someone, it would be Sekiguchi at the Nippon Grand Hotel. He looked into her gray pupils sparkling beneath her perfectly set blond hair and thought, *So this is what a real CIA operative is like.*

Chris did one lap, pacing back and forth in front of the whiteboard. Then, turning her focus on Daryl, Kazumi, and Akari, who were all staring at her, she slowly took the cap off her pen. Then she wrote "MISSION" in big, spaced-out letters so that the two Japanese could read it clearly, swiftly underlined it, and turned to face the three of them.

Rule number one: if you want to command your audience's attention, never speak with your back to them. Chris knew how to write on a whiteboard behind her while facing straight ahead, but she was aware that this was not the time or place to use such parlor tricks. Surprise can only get an audience interested once. The three of them were bewildered by the shifting situation. Now was the time to hold sway over them with a strong will.

"We need to clarify our mission," she said.

"Yes, ma'am," said Daryl, standing with his feet at shoulder width and his hands together behind his back. He seemed to have decided that he was now acting under Chris's authority. But she wanted him to lose the military decorum. It was too stiff and constricting for their two private citizens, Kazumi and Akari, not to mention Chris herself.

"Please sit and be at ease," she said. Chris recognized that she had to be careful how she dealt with the two Japanese. They were new to

America, and if she was too pushy with them in seeking their obedience, they might withdraw into their shells like turtles.

Judging by the email sent by the JAXA official, Kurosaki, she could tell that the information these two had gathered was of exceedingly high quality. Particularly impressive was how Akari had exposed the translation-engine contamination that allowed them to determine North Korea's involvement, as well as the shadow-ware ad hack technique. If the CIA extended the hand of friendship to her, then they could investigate in a different way than the by-the-book headquarters team.

The unknown quantity was Kazumi. He had been the first to draw out the existence of the tethercraft using the observational data uploaded on Ozzy's blog and had even received the academic paper of Jamshed Jahanshah in Tehran. Everything he had achieved up to that point, including writing the report attached to Kurosaki's email, was remarkable, but what role Kazumi might play now was a different story. They had no need for an amateur who had enjoyed one lucky break, and she wondered how useful he would be in unraveling the true nature of the mysterious tether-driven spacecraft.

"Kazumi," said Chris, "I'm throwing in my chips with your tethercraft hypothesis."

Daryl held his breath, and Kazumi nodded slowly.

"Thank you," said Kazumi.

Chris chose her words carefully, so as not to put pressure on Kazumi, who had just entered the country a few hours ago and who, moreover, had no experience traveling abroad.

"There's no need to thank me. What's important here is that I'm starting up a team to follow the tethercraft. I'll be reporting this to CIA headquarters. I need to get the government of the United States to trust in what you amateurs have to say."

Chris noticed that this drew Kazumi's frown.

"Is it necessary for us to write up a report?" he asked.

"I'll take care of that," said Chris with a shake of her head. "What you should concern yourself with instead is convincing me of your hypothesis. I said my chips are on you, but that's only because we don't have any better ideas to work with."

Daryl went to stand up, but Chris raised her hand for him to sit back down and stared into Kazumi's dark-brown eyes.

"I'd like to hear about it directly from you, Kazumi."

Kazumi looked to Akari and Daryl, then took a deep breath and stood up.

"Akari, can you get out the projector?" he said, walking up to the whiteboard and receiving the pen from Chris.

After giving over the stage to Kazumi, Chris took her seat. As Kazumi followed her with his eyes, he was showered with light from atop the table. It was from a small projector that Akari had set up. Akari, who was now wearing display glasses and a special ops keyboard on her left arm, was beaming the presentation onto the whiteboard.

"The materials available to me are limited," Kazumi began. "The only facts we have so far are Mr. Cunningham's observational data. Everything else I'm about to tell you still needs to be verified. That task is what I'd like to ask for everyone's help with." A schematic diagram of the tethercraft was overlaid on Kazumi's body. "The tethercraft is a never-before-seen spacecraft conceptualized by an astronautical engineer in Tehran, Dr. Jamshed Jahanshah."

Kazumi began with simple English but a commanding presence. Chris admired how he could describe an unprecedented technology as though he had held it in his very hand. She was now convinced that they had found a mind that would be as useful for their analysis as Daryl's, if not more so.

Mon, 14 Dec 2020, 21:50 -0800 (2020-12-15T05:50 GMT)
Pier 37 Warehouse, Seattle

Shiraishi's pure-white breath rose into the air as he flung himself into bed. Then, taking off his glasses, he massaged the space between his eyebrows.

"It's over," he said.

"It's great that our proposal was accepted," said Chance.

"You never know what you can get by asking, huh? You have to give dictatorships credit. They sure make decisions fast."

They were in the Pier 37 warehouse control room. On the television screen, lines of digits were displayed. Chance couldn't parse what they signified, but she knew that all their arrangements for the "implementation" they had approached the North Korean military officer about and the mission to bring the second stage of SAFIR 3 close to the orbital hotel were now complete.

Shiraishi removed his fingers from his brow and looked at the television.

"So it took ten hours," he said. "Can you draw up the anticipated questions and answers?"

"Yes, no problem. They'll no doubt respond like a broken tape recorder anyways."

"It would be good to coach UN ambassador Young Nam on his part. Tell him to say it with his usual sulky face."

Shiraishi reached for Chance's breasts. Now that one task was complete, he was in a jovial mood.

Chance brushed away his hands. "What about Japan?" she said. "I mean Kazumi and the rest."

Shiraishi pointed to a small map that floated on the edge of the television and said, "Don't worry. I've been watching them the whole time. The smartphones of those bureaucrats, Kurosaki and Sekiguchi, are still in the Nippon Grand Hotel. They haven't sent any messages or made any calls. I bet they're in there cowering in fear." Shiraishi sat up and put on his glasses. "I expected Kurosaki and co. to have more backbone than that though."

Shiraishi regularly accessed the JAXA MDM system with his old account, still active long after he had quit—you couldn't get any more careless than that—but there were no indications that anyone was onto him yet.

"I checked the advertisements, and none of the other space experts have figured out about the tethercraft," said Shiraishi. "What about Afro?"

Chance shrugged. She still hadn't pinned down the identity of the person with the Afro who had been with Kazumi. They had posted three agents near Fool's Launchpad and had them check the vicinity, but none of them had spotted anyone who fit that description. Most likely she was with Kazumi in the Nippon Grand Hotel.

"I see." Shiraishi reached into the pocket where he kept his cigarettes.

"That's not allowed."

"But we just wrapped up a big job."

"This place is nonsmoking to begin with. Also, no fire as of today. Our move is on Thursday."

Shiraishi let out a big sigh and pointed to some piping squirming against the wall of the room. "Is there gasoline in there already?"

"Of course not. I only put it in the tank of the fire cistern. I'll get a smoke detector tomorrow."

"Sterilization" of the hideout they had prepared downtown was finally finished. On Thursday, they would be able to move out of the warehouse room that Shiraishi had been living in for five long years.

The plan was to leave with only their basic personal belongings and then burn down the entire warehouse.

"I stacked our inventory of the D-Fis that Sound Technica returned on the first floor of the warehouse," said Chance. "I'll burn them all together."

"I think I'd like to watch. Those cables give off the fragrance of roses when you heat them up."

"Quit joking around. It makes me want to leave Seattle altogether."

Shiraishi reached for his thermos. "I never want to leave a city where you can drink coffee this good," he said. "Why don't you have a cup yourself? Then we can watch the video of Earth taken by the tethers together."

Video, by tethers? Chance was confused. "What are you talking about?"

"I took a recording with the cameras on the space tethers."

". . . You never told me about that."

"Don't get mad. I was just rolling with what was already there." Shiraishi winked at Chance as white steam rose from the coffee he was pouring. "I reappropriated the substrate of a smartphone to use as the sensor for the tethers—actually, they *are* smartphones. They have a radio, compass, gyro sensor, GPS, and a powerful CPU that operates on minimal energy with a high-performance battery. These days, they even contain atomic clocks. Jahanshah used smartphones for his paper, so I decided to borrow his idea."

"Of course, Professor Analog may have thought it up, but he never actually realized it," Shiraishi added with a smirk. "Obviously smartphones are equipped with cameras too, so there was no way I could resist." Shiraishi's sinuous finger stroked his tablet. "I just finished making a program that stitches together all the recordings. I'm talking about an orbital video taken by the world's biggest camera. Behold!"

Chance caught her breath. An image of Earth against the blackness of space appeared on the screen. The POV appeared to be straight above the continent of Africa. Sunlight beaming down diagonally into a great valley cast sharp shadows. Far back along the shoreline visible on the far right were rows of thunderheads swelling up from the Indian Ocean. Looking closely, Chance could see the clouds moving. But that meant—

"It's real-time," said Shiraishi. "So beautiful."

"But this . . . video is—"

"Incredible isn't it? This goes far beyond even what I myself was imagining."

Shiraishi spoke with feverish intensity as he stared fixedly at the screen. Apparently, the video taken by the cameras installed in the terminal apparatus pair of each space tether was being transmitted continuously to the Earth's surface along with coordinates, attitude, and other telemetric variables. The feed from each camera was low quality, but by synthesizing the data sent down by a cloud of forty thousand tethers spread over an area three hundred kilometers long and twenty kilometers wide and coloring in space, a high-resolution 3-D model was created. Shiraishi had divided the structural units of the video-stitching program and contracted them out to freelancers around the world.

"It cost less than $1,000 in total. I was able to make this with my own pocket money." Shiraishi stroked his tablet and rotated the Earth on the screen for Chance. "Do you see the spot in the middle? It's still rough, but that's the Wyvern Orbital Hotel."

"Hold on a second," said Chance. "You're sending video from the tethers? All that extra data from orbit in addition to the telemetry . . . What are you going to do if it's exposed?"

"It'll be fine." With the tablet on his lap, Shiraishi grabbed his right arm in his left hand. With all his strength, he squeezed the Tsiolkovsky rocket equation tattooed on his arm through his jacket sleeve. "I wanted to see it! I wanted to see the Earth!"

Hearing Shiraishi speak in this tone for the first time, Chance looked closely at him. In his expression at that moment, absorbed with sparkling eyes as he was in the video of the Earth, the disdainful sneer he always wore was gone.

"Isn't the view marvelous?" he said.

Tue, 15 Dec 2020, 01:56 -0700 (2020-12-15T08:56 GMT)
Buffalo Café, Colorado Springs

"To the stratosphere! Cheers!" shouted Ricky, feeling strange to be making such an odd toast, and tipped back his mug of India pale ale. Apparently, it was a local beer brewed in the back of the bar, and the piercing bitterness was like nothing else. Second Lieutenant Madu Abbot, who piloted the F-22 Raptor that would serve alongside Ricky as an observation aircraft in Operation Seed Pod, was at the counter with him taking a shot of tequila.

They had come to the Buffalo Café to celebrate their transfer to USNORTHCOM, and although it was the middle of the night the place was full of life.

"We'll be seeing stars during the daytime," said Ricky. "Isn't that incredible?"

"You can see the same thing without going all the way to the stratosphere if the atmospheric conditions are right," said Madu, with just as much cheek as she showed when sober, and took another shot. Ricky had been planning to drink her under the table, but that wasn't looking likely at this point.

"I told you already! Quit getting so hung up on the details," said Ricky. "Instead, let's celebrate our transfer and the new record we're going to set."

The mission had been placed in the hands of Major Sylvester Fernandez, and USNORTHCOM was now fully aware of Ricky's plan to try for a new altitude record. Ricky's new superior was Colonel Daniel Waabboy, and when Ricky went to report his transfer to the colonel, the first thing Waabboy had said to him was, "Going to top seventy thousand feet, are you? Best of luck, Captain!"

Waabboy had also been informed that Ricky wasn't the only one aiming to break an in-mission record: Madu would try for the same with the F-22 Raptor. Since this jet was no longer being procured, if she managed to rise into the stratosphere as planned, it would probably be a long while before anyone topped her. Nonetheless, while Madu listened to Waabboy's advice and instructions, Ricky had watched as she shrugged her shoulders in annoyance.

"You can have the record all to yourself," said Madu. "I'll be sticking to my observations."

"Show at least a bit of excitement," said Ricky. "Your name is going to go down in history."

The F-15 Eagle was in the process of being decommissioned and would never set a new record after this. Such military records would undoubtedly appear on the websites of fans of the Eagle and most likely on Wikipedia as well. This meant that the name of Captain Ricky McGillis would survive forever beside that of the twentieth century's strongest fighter jet.

"So, Madu. Want to know the Eagle's kill ratio? It's one hundred to nothing," said Ricky, unable to contain himself in his excitement. "How about the Raptor's?"

"It shot down a number of Anjians in the Middle East," she replied. "You didn't hear about that?"

"You idiot! Don't try to put drones on the same level. Anjians are just tools for killing farmers, right? That's not what I mean. I'm talking about kills on fighter planes flown by pilots trying to kill one of us— Hey! What are you looking at?"

"You! Drunkard!" Madu shouted to someone in back of the counter. "Don't change the channel!"

"What's the matter?" asked Ricky.

"It's game time," said Madu. "They've made their move."

Ricky followed Madu's gaze to the television above the counter. On the screen appeared the white room that had been all over the media the past few days. Inside, two people were hovering just above the floor: the two Smarks. In the top right was a "Live" icon and in the bottom-right corner a video of what appeared to be a studio.

When Ricky read the caption at the bottom of the screen, he clenched his fists. "Rod from God? Mysterious Orbital Weapon in Range of Wyvern Orbital Hotel!" *Damn terrorist nation!* he thought. *So that's their plan!* Ricky had never suspected that he would come to learn the Rod from God's movements off base. On the program, the Smarks were about to be interviewed now that they were targets in orbit, and Ricky was determined not to miss a single moment of it.

"A report has come in from an amateur astronomer that a mysterious object is closing in on the orbital hotel where you two are staying," said the voice of the interviewer. "Were you aware of the situation?"

"We had no idea," said Ronnie with a shrug. "Can you please provide the details?"

As the station's narration explained, an object thought to be a Rod from God was about to enter a rendezvous orbit with the orbital hotel. Ronnie and Judy nodded with apparent fascination as they listened, and Ricky found the way their bodies shook with the motion intriguing. At the same time, he deplored the fact that the report had come from amateurs. What had happened to NORAD?

"There's also a rumor that the object approaching your hotel is an orbital weapon referred to as the Rod from God. What are your thoughts on the situation?"

Ronnie gave the stubble covering his cheeks a stroke with his hand and his handsome, round eyes twinkled like those of a mischievous child.

Isn't he scared? wondered Ricky, gripping his stool and adjusting his position on it. Suddenly a nightmare came back to him. A warning sound rang continuously in the cockpit as he flew through the skies above Kosovo in 1999. The scope of the Tactical Electronic Warfare System displayed a radar source in a location so close it almost overlapped with his aircraft and warned him that a gun had sighted him. *I'm going to be killed!* Ricky had thought. It was the first time he had felt the intent to kill directed at him, and he was so afraid that he wet his pilot suit. The alarm turned out to be nothing more than a phantom produced by a glitch in the TEWS. But even assuming that a real MiG-29 had locked on to him, there was still a chance, however small, that he could have survived. The Smarks appearing on the television at that moment were in a far worse predicament. How could Ronnie be smiling like that?

"It's not that I have nothing to say, but we've brought our PR person all the way from Earth, so I'd rather she spoke on our behalf. Over to you, Judy," said Ronnie with a wink.

He pushed Judy, who was still attached to the floor or the wall or whatever it was, gently on the back, and she was sent floating off to the side of the screen by the recoil. They were in a place free from the reign of gravity. Outside the wall that Ronnie clung to, there was no atmosphere. If even a tiny hole opened up in it, their lives would likely be over. There was no way they could be unaware of this fact, and yet they took it all in stride. After Ronnie had pushed her, Judy had straightened up as she approached the camera, and Ricky thought he saw her lips tremble for a moment, but she maintained an expression of grim composure. He had heard that the two Smarks had lived together up until she was ten, but clearly a remarkable woman such as her could only be the daughter of Ronnie Smark.

The hubbub at the Buffalo Café had settled into quiet. All of the patrons were gathered around the bar waiting to hear what Judy had to say. With their glasses on the tables, they all faced the TV.

"We aren't going to let unconfirmed reports disturb us," said Judy. "Project Wyvern will continue to facilitate our orbital stay according to schedule. The day after tomorrow, we expect to rendezvous and dock with the ISS."

"Good for you!" Over Judy's subdued voice, the patrons at the bar began to call out their praise for her.

On the screen, Judy took a breath and was about to continue when Ronnie shouted, "Cut!" and crossed his arms into an *X* in the corner of the screen. "Judy, say it in your own words! This is a live broadcast, after all. This sort of thing just won't get across unless you speak from the gut."

Apparently this had not been part of their preplanned script because Judy went wide-eyed and said, "Quit joking around, Dad," with a dismissive wave of her hand before turning back toward the camera. Her eyes were sparkling as the tension slipped from her face. As Ricky watched Ronnie nod to his daughter in approval, he suddenly realized something: Ronnie was trying to show the world watching them that they were just a father and daughter in orbit and that this was no big deal at all.

Judy spread her hands out in front of her chest and took another breath. No longer was she just someone handling PR but a human being standing there in the air before them with the trust of her father.

"Beyond this one foot of wall is the vacuum of space. If even the smallest hole were to open up, we would be in big trouble. So to be perfectly honest, having some unknown object approaching us is . . . scary. But let me tell you something."

Silence fell on the bar again and only the voice of Judy could be heard as if she were right there with them. Slowly, Judy raised her index finger to point it at the camera.

"I don't know who or what is behind this ridiculous scheme, but stop it. Let the world know who you are. Drop that metal piece of trash out of orbit immediately. If there's an accident because of this, you'll make all of humankind your enemy."

Judy's body began to glow from around her feet as a bright light shone into the room straight from her right side. Immediately it illuminated her from head to toe. The sun beaming in through the hotel window. Not even squinting in the glare, Judy reached her hand out toward the camera and said, "Did you really think such despicable intimidation would make us compromise our ambition? Did you really think we'd come down from orbit just like that? That we'd say 'Space is no place for civilians, please forgive us for trying' and just give up in tears? As if! I'll never forgive you for spreading terror through space!"

Ricky squeezed his fist resting on the counter with all his might. Heat rose up inside him, a feeling surging up from the pit of his stomach that was fundamentally different from what he felt when he was ordered into combat.

Judy raised her quivering middle finger and thrust it toward the camera. "If you've got a problem with us," she said, "then bring it on!"

The bar was enveloped in cheers, and glasses were raised high all around. Ricky stood up with the crowd and dove into the pandemonium with mug in hand. *She's right,* he thought. *We can't let these people off the hook. So hold on, Judy and Ronnie. Ricky's coming to take that thing out for you.*

Tue, 15 Dec 01:14 -0800 (2020-12-15T09:14 GMT)
Western Days Hotel

Despite the lateness of the hour, the suite filled with the sound of Chris, Daryl, Kazumi, and Akari clapping. Chris was impressed with Judy Smark's courage. It was an incredibly rare sort of person who could speak out so defiantly when in the line of fire, especially in the vacuum of space where staying alive was a tightrope walk to begin with. Chris felt certain that the many viewers who'd tuned in to the live broadcast from around the world had found it as moving as she had.

"Judy's incredible," said Chris. "But she's just putting on a strong face, which I guess you've all noticed already."

Kazumi, Akari, and Daryl nodded.

If they could prove Kazumi's tethercraft hypothesis, the two orbital hotel guests would inevitably learn that the Rod from God weapon was a feint, a phantom that didn't actually exist. Chris wished that clearing up this confusion for the Smarks might bring them relief, but she and her team were certain that this would not be the case.

"Chris," said Daryl, "you don't seriously think that Seed Pod—"

"Let's talk about that later," said Chris.

Today, the second stage of SAFIR 3 had entered a rendezvous orbit with the orbital hotel, meaning that Operation Seed Pod would move into action. Chris didn't want the team to know about this, as the operation was based on assumptions that were directly contrary to their hypothesis. Seeing it implemented could have an impact on their motivation. Instead, she thought it was crucial that the team stay out of Seed Pod altogether. Their job was to figure out what the swarm of space tethers' next move would be once it had kicked the SAFIR 3 along in orbit and brought it into rendezvous position.

"Kazumi," said Chris. "If the tethers were to attack the orbital hotel directly, what do you think would happen?"

"They would rip it to shreds," Kazumi replied after a short pause. He explained that the terminal apparatuses were moving many times faster than a bullet from a rifle and could easily pierce the outer shell of the hotel. "The same thing would happen to the ISS or Tiangong-2."

"If we wanted to stop them . . . where would be the best place to start?"

Chris pointed to the whiteboard. After their three-hour-long meeting earlier, it was covered in a list of various tasks. In addition to items proposed by Kazumi such as "Investigate potential of space tethers," "Examine Prof. Jahanshah's paper," and "Observe actual space tethers," the list also included a mission proposed by Akari: "Seek identity of terrorists."

"Is it really okay for me to decide?" asked Kazumi.

"Just say what you think," said Daryl, patting Kazumi on the shoulder. "Then we'll decide after that. Let's be grateful we have a boss to take care of us now." Daryl pointed at Chris with his thumb.

Chris found herself smiling wryly. Daryl wasn't exactly showing the disciplined attitude of a soldier, but he was helping to lighten the mood.

Kazumi laughed and pointed to a section of the whiteboard. "Understood," he said. "In that case, I think we should start by making observations."

"I agree with Kazumi," said Daryl with a nod. "However, we haven't succeeded in making observations with NORAD's radar."

"But Mr. Cunningham was able to observe them at his observatory, right?" said Kazumi.

Daryl leaned forward. "Yes," he said. "That's exactly what I don't understand. Why can't we see those guys? In case you didn't know, NORAD's radars are used to observe debris as well. It's a solid network."

"Hmm . . ." said Kazumi.

"Would it help to know what equipment Ozzy Cunningham uses?" asked Chris. She jerked her chin toward her desk. "Akari, can you connect my computer to the projector?"

Akari stood up and connected a palm-sized substrate to Chris's laptop. Immediately, her screen was projected onto the whiteboard. If Chris remembered correctly, the tiny device was a single-function computer kit called a Raspberry Pi. During their meeting, Akari had finished configuring several of the many that she had purchased so that they would function as display repeaters. Chris wondered where she'd acquired such astounding engineering proficiency.

"We haven't signed an official contract," said Chris, "but please don't disclose anything you learn during this operation. If you leak anything, you could serve up to twenty-five years in prison."

Chris opened a list of the Desnoeufs Island observational equipment extracted from the emails of Ozzy and his equipment suppliers. She caught Akari muttering "PRISM" and said, "This is just a taste," with a wink. In order to read Ozzy's emails, Chris was fairly certain that the PRISM information-gathering project leaked by Edward Snowden was being used. Not even Chris knew the full extent of the national surveillance network created by the CIA and NSA, however.

Daryl glanced at the screen and cried, "A Sampson-5!" kicking his chair as he got to his feet. "That's no radio telescope. It's a military-spec air defense radar!"

"Cunningham is a major investor in the manufacturer," said Chris. "He even received one of their test models."

"This isn't the sort of thing that civilians should have in their possession," said Daryl. "I hope he knows how to use it correctly. If you make a mistake, it has enough output to burn someone to death."

Chris explained that on the island of Desnoeufs that Ozzy owned, he was deploying a Sampson-5 multifunction active phased array radar on a flat surface. Though often mounted on Aegis-equipped ships and ground radar sites, Ozzy used it to track orbital objects.

"This is supposed to be for his hobby?" said Daryl when he'd heard all this, resting his head in his hands. "Unbelievable . . ."

"A man named Johansson Ashleigh is in charge of operating the radar. Cunningham calls him 'Friday.' Another amateur."

"Mr. Cunningham didn't specify a threshold, huh?" said Kazumi.

"For what?" asked Chris.

"Size," Kazumi replied. "NORAD's debris-monitoring radars use noise reduction, right?"

". . . So that's it!" said Daryl. "Good point. They're configured them not to detect anything 10 cm in length or less in low Earth orbit. With the Sampson-5 set to its performance limit, it can track objects as short as 2 cm from 2,000 km away. Usually it's not operated like that, because it would just get cluttered with noise."

"Is it possible to turn off the noise reduction on the NORAD radars?" asked Kazumi.

"Not right away," said Daryl with a shake of his head. "That would interfere with management of air traffic control and air defense networks."

Now is the time to show them what the CIA can do, thought Chris and, putting on an air of nonchalance, raised her hand. "In that case, what if we borrow Mr. Cunningham's radar?"

"We could do that?" asked Daryl.

"I'll ask nicely. So when should we get going on our observations?"

"Fantastic! Still, processing observational data filled with noise will take time."

Akari raised her hand. "Leave that to me," she said. "If we're talking about Cunningham's data, I can process it in real time. I thought we might need parallel processing, so I bought lots of the higher-powered Raspberry Pis, the FPGA model. I can track any number of those things in the tens of thousands."

"Great," Daryl muttered, and returned to his seat where he woke up his desktop.

Already, Akari had connected up a virtual private network with NORAD. Chris could sense sure signs that the team had begun to work organically.

"The observation date and time—" Daryl was just about to input some numbers, but suddenly his hands stopped and he looked in the direction of Kazumi. "Did you say something?"

Kazumi was holding his index finger out in front of his body and swaying it. With his eyes half-closed, murmurings of Japanese leaked from between his barely open lips. Like Daryl, Chris found herself unable to peel her eyes away from this odd behavior.

"The orbital hotel . . . To make the inclination thirty-four degrees . . . Before, wrong. No tether has such propulsion . . ."

Noticing their puzzled looks, Akari whispered, "He's doing calculations."

Kazumi opened his eyes wide and put his finger on Daryl's display. "Tomorrow, starting at twelve o'clock our time, 1600 GMT,
SAFIR 3 will pass over Cunningham's island. It should be surrounded
by space tethers."

Still staring at Kazumi, Daryl managed to squeeze out the words,
"What's that?"

"SAFIR 3 will rise from west-northwest in pursuit of the hotel.
Let's have Ozzy make an observation there."

"Can I just confirm that?" said Daryl. When he right-clicked on
a globe and input the time, two overlapping lines revolved around
the Earth, cutting across the Indian Ocean from diagonally above.
". . . His guess is right on. The orbital hotel will indeed cross the
Indian Ocean tomorrow afternoon."

"Great," said Kazumi, leaning back against his seat.

Taking note of Kazumi's reaction, Daryl swiveled his chair and
looked at Chris. "Chris, please allow me to be Kazumi's assistant. He
can fly orbital objects in his head. I've never met anyone who can do
anything like this. If we're going to follow this unknown spacecraft,
we're going to need Kazumi's ability. I'll do my best to utilize it to its
fullest potential."

"Okay, Daryl," said Chris. "You're his assistant now."

Flashing a white smile, Daryl patted Kazumi on the shoulder
and gripped his hand. "Kazumi, from now on all you need to do are
approximate calculations. I'll take care of checking them over and
dealing with other technological considerations. Just leave it to me!"

We're truly blessed, thought Chris. She was stunned by Kazumi's ability to do orbital calculus in his head, but more than that she was glad of his rare personality, which allowed him to earn Daryl's trust even though they had only just met that day.

Watching Kazumi and Daryl shake hands, Akari turned to Chris and said, "The CIA's power is amazing. I mean, you can just borrow someone's telescope like that."

"I'm relying on Kazumi and you to persuade him. Of course, I'll step in if he gives us any trouble."

"I see. In that case, can you help me with my 'observation' too?"

"What's that, dear?" said Chris, and immediately regretted responding in a tone of voice one might use for a child. She blamed it on Akari's boyish, shaved-head look and awkward English. But Chris knew she shouldn't let appearances throw her off. Akari was a full-grown woman and a master engineer.

Akari did some maneuvers on her keyboard and sent a message to Chris's laptop containing a phone number, an IP address, and a MAC address for a network card.

"This is the phone number and other information used by the terrorists. I acquired it in Tokyo," explained Akari. "I figured out that they're using China Mobility roaming SIM cards and a Fu Wen portable Wi-Fi hotspot. My guess is that they throw away the SIMs when they're done with them." Behind her display glasses, Akari's eyes sparkled keenly.

Akari could see right into the criminal agents' way of life. SIM cards and devices used under contract with cell phone companies such as AT&T were easy enough to track down. A smart method to avoid that risk was to use roaming cards sold by foreign cell phone companies and dispose of them periodically.

"I want the geographic data showing where those signals were sent," said Akari. "I wonder if the CIA would have access to that."

"Suppose you had that information," said Chris. "What would you do with it?"

"Start a war."

"A war?"

"I'm very sorry. Vocabulary—words, I didn't use enough of them. I want to perform wardriving. I'll lay honeypots in the city. Seattle is too big. I want to narrow it down."

Akari's strategy rendered Chris speechless. Wardriving. A hacking method where you roamed the streets scouting out wireless networks. The goal was to seek out portable Wi-Fi hotspots with specific network names. Now Chris saw why Akari had bought the bicycle: to cruise around the city. And Chris agreed that it would be more efficient to focus the search around the location where the phone was used.

"Kazumi will be looking for the space tethers, right?" said Akari. "I am going to expose the terrorists."

Here was the second blessing. Akari was even more of a find than Chris had imagined. When Bruce arrived from Los Angeles tomorrow, Chris decided, she would make him Akari's assistant.

"Okay. I'll have CIA headquarters look into it. Akari, you have free reign to do as you will."

Unbelievable that these two, Kazumi and Akari, have been reduced to doing contract web design, thought Chris. *What's happened to Japan?*

2020-12-15T10:00 GMT

Project Wyvern

```
Today I had my first shower in three days. Incred-
ibly, in this hotel we can even have hot showers.
The Wyvern Orbital Hotel has been fitted up with
```

thousands of unprecedented bells and whistles, but
this is the one that I like best.

In free fall (is it okay to say "without gravity"?),
water becomes a very strange sort of animal. If you
let it out slowly, it gloms around the showerhead
due to its surface tension. If you turn up the tap,
droplets remain floating in the air. Anyone who
entered such a room would drown.

Thankfully, the Project Wyvern engineers came up
with a method to solve this problem. Introducing
the "Showerpot"! Get inside a pot like a steel drum
with your head sticking out and wash your body with
the hot water that comes shooting out inside. Then,
when it's over, use pressurized air to blow away the
water and a hairdryer to dry off. Finis.

After waiting three whole days, it was the greatest
shower I'd ever had. I'm looking forward to using
the "Shampoopot" tomorrow.

What I'm getting at here is that a stay on the
Wyvern Orbital Hotel is very natural. Compared to
the astronauts working away on other space stations, this is an environment of true luxury.

Yes, luxury indeed. I'm fully aware of the implications.

Take measures to combat global warming, or medicine, or agriculture, for instance. I wonder how many people in need could have been helped with the money used to bring me here. Even I had my doubts about the project when I heard that the Showerpot, whose sole purpose is to provide comfort during our stay, cost $200,000 to develop (wow, is that all?) and $450 each time we use it. In the end, though, my heart was swayed by Ronnie's vision of spending time in space just as we normally do on Earth—of showing the world that this is possible—so I decided to set out on this trip with him, even though we hadn't spoken in fifteen years.

Did the Apollo program prevent famine? Did a shuttle? Maybe not directly.

But the portrait of the Earth, *Earthrise*, that we imagine when we think about our planet was a photograph taken by *Apollo 8* as they made their way to the moon. In the Cold War era, when we were at each other's throats with nuclear weapons, that frail image of our home in the solar system floating in the blackness of space had the power to bring us all together.

Earthrise was taken by a soldier. The privilege of conveying the beauty of the Earth floating in emptiness was reserved for an astronaut who had taken many years of special training. If many more

regular people came to see the Earth with their own
eyes, then think how much easier it might be for us
to consider the good of all.

Everyone, come to space!

I feel much better after writing this. Though I kind
of regret giving the finger during that television
broadcast.

Just when I thought everyone was beginning to forget me as a slobbering zombie during the launch, I
did an image search for "Judy Smark" just a moment
ago, and all I got were pictures of me with my middle finger up. Ronnie liked it so much he had them
stick it on the top page of Project Wyvern's site.

To everyone writing articles, you can download an
official press kit from this blog.

Judy Smark, sophisticated lady despite appearances

9 Great Leap

The bluing glow of the sky outside colored the room, except for a single table lit up with dazzling brightness by a pendant light overhead. On the table was an array of plates, and on the plates was food so hot the steam still rose from it. Glancing at the clock on the wall to confirm that it was evening, Ozzy twirled a generous ball of spaghetti and sauce onto his fork and brought it to his lips. The tart taste of tomato filled his mouth. At long last, Friday had made him some pasta.

"Excellent!"

Pure-white teeth danced before him. Friday sat at the opposite end of the table, naked to the waist, hands clasped together into a two-handed fist.

"What?" asked Ozzy finally.

"That is fish, Mr. Cunningham."

Ozzy lowered his gaze to his plate. There, immersed in the pasta sauce, was a familiar-looking red fish—and that white tentacle beside it was squid.

"What the hell are you feeding me?!" Ozzy threw his fork away.

"Glad to see you back to your old self. You had me worried, just lying around for so long."

Friday pointed at the television on the wall. Ozzy noticed the date on the news. "The fifteenth?!" he exclaimed in surprise.

"Yes, two days since that phone call."

"Two whole days . . . ?"

After being questioned via video call by the two CIA agents calling themselves Bruce and Chris, Ozzy had taken to his bed. He then seemed to have spent two days lying there listlessly. The fear that all of his actions were under surveillance had been too much for him.

"Did you know Bruce called me once more after that? 'Tell Mr. Cunningham the truth,' he said. Apparently they don't want liars mixed up with this. They know everything at the CIA, eh?"

"The truth?"

"Do you remember that I am from Somalia?"

"Now that you mention it . . ."

Friday told Ozzy his story. Arriving in France as a refugee from the endless Somali Civil War, he had entered university and graduated with a degree in astronomy but had been unable to find work. Upon his dejected return to his home country, his education saw him raised to a position of authority within his incessantly warring tribe. He had been searching for a way to escape this illegal lifestyle when he found a billionaire who planned to live alone on a remote island: Ozzy.

"Somalia . . . ? Were you a pirate or something?"

"Something along those lines. But please believe me: I chose to work here because you offered me free use of the telescope. Anyway, I'm glad to see you back to your old self. It must have been the fish."

"I don't want any damn fish. I hate fish! Tentacles too!"

Ozzy rose to his feet and headed for the large freezer in one corner of the kitchen. Two months' worth of hot dogs were stored inside. His intricately planned dining schedule could not be left to the capricious likes of Friday.

"Oh, that's right," Friday said. "As you instructed, I have continued to track the Rod from God. Since yesterday it has been moving somewhat mysteriously. Shall I put it up on the tele—"

"Forget it!" Ozzy spun around from the open freezer, silver-colored package in one hand. "Just forget it. Forget that damn Rod from God ever existed!"

"Are you sure?"

"Why should I care about that thing? It's the reason I'm under CIA surveillance."

"What about your friends?"

"My friends?"

"Ronnie and Judy Smark," Friday explained, a look of concern on his face. "They are your friends, no? They are the target of the Rod from God."

"What?!" An icy tingle ran down Ozzy's spine, and it wasn't just the cold air from the freezer. No way. That was ridiculous. The Rod from God was a bald-faced lie and Ozzy knew it; he had been the one who'd made it up.

"It's been on the news all day. Would you like to see a recording?"

Friday pressed a button on the remote control and Ozzy heard a familiar voice from his past come from the television on the wall. Ozzy spun to look at the screen. There was Ronnie floating in midair.

He pushed Judy forward and was sent flying backwards into the wall by the reaction. That unshaven chin, those glaring eyes, brought back memories. And how about Judy, staring at the camera without any sign of fear? Ozzy hadn't seen her since she was a little girl.

"Very impressive, isn't it?" said Friday. "One wouldn't expect anything less from Ronnie Smark, of course."

Ozzy grunted noncommittally. On the screen, he noticed Ronnie's left eye trembling as he tried to wink. Ozzy remembered that tic. He had seen it back when Ronnie was still based in Ozzy's warehouse, his settlement service just starting to take off. It was the day he had deleted all the accounts the Mafia used to deal drugs. Fearing reprisals, his staff had convinced Ronnie to have Ozzy put him up in Ozzy's top-floor apartment. Ronnie had offered the same wink as today as he apologized cheerfully for the imposition. But the things he groaned in his sleep kept Ozzy awake all night.

Ozzy shivered as the cold air crawled up his arms. He realized that he had sat down at some point. His hands were on the floor, a package of hot dogs squashed under one palm.

"Mr. Cunningham, you'll hurt your knee. Oof!"

Feeling Friday's strong, warm shoulder pushing into his armpit, Ozzy struggled to his feet, still swaying. The sandals had slipped off his feet. He stepped on the hot dog package, sending a spurt of thawed ketchup across the floor.

If the Rod from God hit the orbital hotel, would Ronnie's blood spread like that? Or would it be more like a freeze-dried red mist? No. Nothing of the sort was going to happen. The Rod from God was a fantasy.

Ozzy looked up to see Judy giving him the finger, glaring defiantly from the television screen. He'd often played with her as a child when Ronnie was too busy. She'd had the same powerful gaze back then, too.

"Mr. Cunningham. Mr. Cunningham!" Friday sighed. "I must clean the floor. Could I ask you to move?"

Friday bore Ozzy up with his shoulder again and helped him to his desk. The Aeron chair creaked as Ozzy worked his behind into it.

Ozzy scowled at the list of notifications on his screen. He was receiving a video-call request at that very moment. Who could that be, at this time of night? Without thinking, he hit the key to open a new window.

He heard the sound of the connection being established. Visual noise flooded the screen and, when he recognized it, gave him goose bumps.

The CIA. They had to be using an encrypted line. Those bastards. Ozzy's terror turned to rage. They were listening to everything he said to the outside world, but they kept their own damn calls private.

"What do you want?" he demanded.

"Are we . . . are bothering you?" The voice that came from the speakers was unfamiliar, its English less than fluent.

The noise began to clear up. Ozzy saw a young Asian man, solicitous in both expression and bearing, sitting before a silvery wall.

"Mr. Cunningham, nice to, uh, video meet you. I am Kazumi, owner of Meteor News. Do you remember me?"

"Kazumi . . . How— Ah, forget it. The CIA, right? You got my details from them?"

"Yes. I'm using a CIA line to speak with you."

A woman with a shaved head sat to Kazumi's right, a dark-complexioned man with impressively bushy eyebrows to his left. All of them were staring directly at Ozzy through the camera. He was just thinking how young they all looked when a woman he recognized stepped into frame behind them.

"Haven't seen you for two days, Mr. Cunningham. It's Chris. Remember me?"

Ozzy glared at the camera. Bruce, the black guy, had been the one who had actually interrogated him. But this woman had been the one who had hinted that they knew about his estranged wife—that they were listening in on everything he said.

"No need to go on the defensive," Chris said. "Today we want to ask you a favor. Can we borrow your Sampson-5?"

Kazumi leaned closer to the camera. "Mr. Cunningham, we would truly appreciate it. Please lend us the radar you use for observations."

Ozzy tried to gather his thoughts. "What's this about?"

"We are tracking spacecraft called space tethers. We need your radar to make observations." Kazumi explained that these space tethers had been responsible for the unnatural motion of SAFIR 3's second stage that Ozzy had observed.

Most of what Kazumi said was beyond Ozzy's understanding, but the gist was clear enough: Kazumi wanted to prove that the Rod from God was nonsense, and to do that, he had to observe the space tethers in action.

"Sounds pretty crazy to me. Space tethers? Never heard of them."

"Of course not. I was the one who discovered them in your observational data."

"My what? Oh, you mean that data I posted to the blog. You read that?" The observational data from Sampson-5 was incomprehensible even to Ozzy. He had only included it to lend his news post some scientific gravitas.

"Please, Mr. Cunningham. Let us borrow your radar. Let us save Ronnie Smark and his daughter in that orbital hotel."

Kazumi's words caught in Ozzy's chest. Ozzy had been responsible for starting the wild rumors that had Ronnie scared. But now Kazumi was saying that there was a real threat too—something else, something unknown, something he wanted to pin down and reveal to the world.

Saving Ronnie. Ozzy had no objection to that. He was on the verge of agreeing to the request when Chris spoke, standing with her hand on Kazumi's shoulder.

"Do you understand the situation? You just need to let us log in to your control system, and we'll take it from there. We'll even pay you for the time we use. You don't need to be at the controls. Just take your hands off them for a while."

Ozzy looked down at his fat, round fingers. Sit there doing nothing? While Kazumi and the others were saving Ronnie? "You're saying I should just back off?"

"That's right. Just lend us the equipment. That's all we need."

"That's not gonna work for me."

"Cunningham! Do you realize what you're getting yourself into here? Lend us your damn radar, or I'll requisition it by force."

"I'd like to see you try. I'm in the middle of the Indian Ocean, half a world away."

Even through the video link, he saw Chris's eyes narrow.

Kazumi brushed Chris's hand off his shoulder.

"Chris, we cannot just ignore what Ozzy has to say," he said, then turned his eyes back to the camera. "We want to save Ronnie Smark, Mr. Cunningham. Are you opposed to that?"

"Don't be ridiculous. The jerk's my best friend. Of course I want to save him."

"Then let us do it together."

Ozzy took a deep breath.

"What do you want from us, Mr. Cunningham?" Kazumi continued. He moved closer to the camera, face looming larger on Ozzy's screen. "I am serious about unraveling the riddle of the space tether. I want to save the orbital hotel and the Smarks too." His jet-black eyes looked directly into Ozzy's own.

"What do I want from you? Well . . . uh . . ."

"Let me make you an offer, then. Part ownership of Meteor News."

Ozzy's eyes widened at this proposition, completely unexpected though not unlike others he had heard many times before. At the other end of the video link, the two people on either side of Kazumi looked at him with startled expressions as well.

Eyebrows on the left grabbed Kazumi by the arm and tried to pull him back into his seat. "Kazumi, what are you saying?" he said. "You don't need to do that."

"No, I want Mr. Cunningham involved too. And I do not have anything else to offer him."

A deep nostalgia welled up within Ozzy. Would-be entrepreneurs, going from door to door with stock in hand. Tickets to a shared adventure fanned out before him.

"All right. You're offering me stock? I'll take it. Forty-nine percent, okay?"

"Cunningham!" Eyebrows pounded the table.

"Don't misunderstand me. This is how I buy in to your mission. I'm a stakeholder now. As co-owner of Meteor News, it concerns me directly, right? So . . . call me Ozzy, already." He grabbed Friday by the arm and pulled him into the frame. "This is my radar operator, Fri—uh, Johansson. If you have any questions about the Sampson-5, he's your man. At your service whenever you need him, whatever you need him for."

"Thank you, Mr. Cunningham."

"I told you. Call me Ozzy."

Kazumi's face crumpled for a moment, then broke into a smile. That was it. Ozzy hadn't seen an expression like that in a long time. Now he just wanted to see that smile on Ronnie's face again.

"Thanks . . . Ozzy," said Kazumi.

Tue, 15 Dec 2020 08:25 -0800 (2020-12-15T16:25 GMT)
Western Days Hotel, Seattle

"Chris, sorry to keep you—whoa! What's all this about?"

The silvery gleam that filled the penthouse suite left Bruce lost for words as he stepped inside. Wrinkled silver picnic mats had been stapled all over the walls. On closer examination, he saw that each sheet had strands of Nichrome wire running across it. The effect was indescribably odd after walking through the chicly appointed lobby and elevator hall outside.

"Bruce! You're early," said Chris, just beside him. She was making use of the room's original furnishings, sitting at a mahogany desk in a leather president's chair as she worked on her laptop. Bruce frowned, noticing that her computer didn't have a LAN cable plugged into it.

"Chris, what are you doing? You know that's against regulations."

"You mean the Wi-Fi? It's fine. This room is now an anechoic chamber." Chris swept her arm grandly, indicating the silvered walls and ceiling.

"The picnic mats? That's what they're for?"

"I had Daryl check how good the shielding was. Apparently the mats and Nichrome wire together create a darkroom that's completely impenetrable to Wi-Fi and cell phone signals."

Their operations center used dozens of Wi-Fi devices, and the shielding was to conceal their presence, she explained. The idea had come from Akari, the engineer who'd come along with Kazumi.

"We've gone full Geek House, then." Bruce pulled his emergency BlackBerry from its belt case and checked the signal strength. "BlackBerry's getting a signal," he observed.

"Look more closely," Chris said, gesturing toward the window with her chin.

A cell phone base station antenna! Chris explained that Daryl had been sent out to buy it. The store they'd visited earlier had carried them, but such equipment was normally raised on a pole and used on farms. Laying it on the floor inside was not an idea a normal person would have come up with.

"Akari had him run a wire out to the terrace this morning."

"I see," Bruce said after a beat.

He looked around the room more closely. The silver mats covering the walls caught the eye first, but the objects piled up on the floor were not your usual office equipment either. In the middle of the room was an oval table with a screwed-on monitor arm put together from aluminized steel. A ring of office chairs around the table completed the setup. This was standard enough for a field operations center.

But what was that mountain of tiny integrated circuits that lay on the other side of the table, plugged into LAN cables as thick as arteries? He could see from the twinkling LEDs that it was operational, but if this had been a movie, some kind of computer monster would be leaping out of that tangle of chips and cables at any moment.

"That knot of silicon is analyzing the observational data from Cunningham's radar," Chris said. "Apparently the space tether cluster is over Desnoeufs as we speak."

"Raspberry Pis, huh? I'm always hearing how cheap and useful they are, but I've never seen an army of them at work like this."

A fat power cable snaked into the room through the silver-covered window that looked out on to the terrace. Bruce listened closely. They were on the seventh floor, so that nearby engine noise had to be . . .

"She brought a generator in too? Big believer in DIY, huh?"

"Well, she's in the US now. Land of the garage workshop. When in Rome."

"If the problem is money—" Bruce said, but stopped when he saw the warning in Chris's eyes. She glanced over toward a whiteboard. Bruce followed her gaze to see a slender arm reach up from behind it with an interior designer's stapler and begin attaching a silver mat to the ceiling.

Chris lowered her voice. "Who cares if it's homemade as long as it works? We don't want to demotivate her."

There was the sound of someone jumping off a stepladder. A moment later, a small woman with a buzz cut wearing some kind of high-tech eyewear popped out from behind the whiteboard.

"That's Akari," Chris said.

Bruce composed his features into a smile. "Akari!" he said, offering her his hand. "Name's Bruce. Wish I could show your work to some of my colleagues. You sure you're not overdoing it, though?"

"Overdoing it? No way. Anything we can do, they can do also. We need a sword and a shield both. Am I wrong?"

Her English was stiff, but her boyish face looked relaxed. If she could talk with so little reserve to people she'd just met, she'd be communicating fluently in no time.

"No, you're right," Bruce said. "Welcome to the team." He shook her delicate hand, noticing the special-ops keyboard strapped to her other wrist.

"Bruce, you'll be Akari's support," Chris said.

Bruce nodded. He had no objection. He'd received the same

orders last night, and watching a civilian hacker at work would be educational.

"You heard the lady, Akari," he said. "What do you need me to do first?"

"Go shopping," Akari replied. She spread her arms and twirled on the spot. "I didn't realize the room would be this . . . wide. There aren't enough picnic sheets."

It was true that only half of the ceiling had been covered, and expensive-looking fabric wallpaper could still be seen in places between the mats near the door. Bruce's eyes went wide when he realized what he was seeing. There was real embroidery on that wallpaper! It must have cost thirty dollars a square foot. And Akari was stapling picnic mats to it.

"Also, I want to put a security camera outside the door," Akari said. "Can you buy one of those too? A small one."

Chris patted Bruce's shoulder. "I've got a favor to ask, too," she said. "This, uh, redecorating—can you talk to the hotel about it, see what they want to let it pass? Just think of it as start-up costs for the team and it'll feel like a bargain."

"No problem. What about Daryl? I don't see Kazumi anywhere, either."

"They went off to war," said Chris. "Looks like rain tomorrow, so they want to get as far as they can today."

"War? Rain?" Bruce repeated, puzzled.

Akari put her hands on her hips and puffed out her cheeks in pouty indignation. "Chris, tell it to him properly!" she said. "I have told you many times, it is 'wardriving'!"

"Oh, war*driving*." Bruce nodded.

An old civilian hacker technique that amounted to driving around town looking for open Wi-Fi networks. The CIA had no need for such tactics anymore. These days they had preassembled databases of all the information you could hope for, just waiting to be searched.

"Sounds good," Bruce said, and gave Akari the thumbs-up.

Tue, 15 Dec 2020 09:01 -0800 (2020-12-15T17:01 GMT)
80 Pike Place, Seattle

Noting the red light ahead at the foot of the hill, Kazumi reached down with his left hand to lightly engage the rear brake. As he approached the intersection, the surface of the road changed from asphalt to cobblestones that muttered under the block-patterned tires of his mountain bike. Although powdery snow covered the street, he didn't feel the slightest danger of slipping with these tires.

After engaging the brake, he made a fist and held it behind him at waist level. This signaled to the cars behind him that he was stopped. Many cycling hand signals were common to the US and Japan, and Tokyo also required cyclists to ride on the road, so the only modification Kazumi had to make when riding in Seattle was to keep to the right instead of the left.

As he brought the bike to a halt at what looked like the correct line, the blue hood of a car with a white star printed on it slid up along his left. Daryl's Chevy.

The window on the passenger's side opened. "Kazumi," Daryl called. "Can you go down Pike Street? The marketplace is straight ahead."

"Got it." Kazumi exhaled, releasing a pure-white cloud that thinned out through the falling snow and then dissipated. To steady his breathing, he inhaled deeply, feeling his mucus membranes dry out as the cold air streamed through his nose.

The marketplace began directly in front of him and stretched off to the right for maybe two blocks.

"You okay, Kazumi? Not getting tired?"

"I am fine. I will rest when I walk through the market."

The two of them had been roaming Seattle's bayside district since early morning. Akari had analyzed some cell phone call records provided by Chris and realized that the locations where the China Mobility SIM cards first came into service were concentrated near the bay. If North Korean spies were throwing away roaming cards when they were finished with them, then the area the cards were *first* used had to be their home ground.

"Make a leisurely stroll of it," Daryl said. "Wardriving's an interesting way to spend a day, isn't it? I didn't expect to find three hundred open Wi-Fi hotspots in two blocks."

Warcycling in my case, thought Kazumi, as his breathing came under control. He hadn't expected to play hacker on his trip overseas.

The Raspberry Pi FPGAs in Kazumi's backpack and on Daryl's passenger-side seat were using reprogrammable chips carrying a real-time password-cracking program of Akari's own design. The three hundred hotspots Daryl had just mentioned were only those with security settings weak enough for the program to break into as they cruised past.

"I was not expecting it either," Kazumi said. "Maybe because there are so many cafés. Only four of them are the Fu Wen spots we're looking for, though."

Kazumi looked down at the smartphone taped to his handlebars. A wardriving/cycling app whipped up by Akari counted and mapped the networks that had been detected, those that had been cracked, and Fu Wen wireless hotspots used by the North Korean spies.

"Anyway, it is all thanks to the antenna booster you made," he said. "We can even reach into buildings with this."

Daryl waved his hand modestly, then pointed at Kazumi's back-pack. "Do you have enough honeypots?"

"Seven left."

The honeypots were Wi-Fi routers on Raspberry Pi hardware, able to impersonate free Wi-Fi hotspots accessed by the China Mobility roaming SIM cards. Daryl and Kazumi were placing them under trash cans and benches as they went.

"Okay. Put all seven somewhere on Pike Street, then. Once you're done, hop into the car and take a break." Daryl pointed behind Kazumi. "Could you also get me a latte? Wouldn't be right to come to Seattle and pass up the coffee."

Kazumi looked behind him to see a familiar white mermaid logo. He had never seen a brown-and-white Starbucks before. Could this be their original location?

"I wonder if the spies get their lattes here too," he said.

Daryl slapped the steering wheel and laughed.

"No doubt about it," he said. "And we have to know our enemy, right? Okay, I'm going to try that block of warehouses by the wharf. Meet you when I get back."

The Chevy turned off to the left in a cloud of white exhaust.

Tue, 15 Dec 2020, 10:02 -0800 (2020-12-15T18:02 GMT)
Pier 37 Warehouse, Seattle

In the warehouse, Shiraishi was working in his usual position. He sat on a bed with a sleeping bag on it and typed on the tablet in his lap.

"Coffee and breakfast is here," Chance said. "Are you packed?"

Without taking his eyes off the television, Shiraishi turned his head back over his shoulder.

"All on the bed," he said. "Listen, I'm sure I can smell gasoline. Can't you do something about it?"

"It's just your imagination."

Shiraishi snorted.

Chance placed her Boston bag on an open space on the bed. Shiraishi's luggage was apparently nothing but a neatly folded change of clothes, a laptop, some power cables, and a large black blueprint case. The cluster of computers that controlled the swarm of orbiting space tethers ran on virtual servers in a data center somewhere. From the way North Korea had talked about Shiraishi, Chance had expected a gadget fetishist. His minimalist approach to possessions was a pleasant surprise.

"I'm glad you're traveling light," she said. "What are we doing today?"

"Preparing to hand this project off," Shiraishi said. "I'm creating an interface that will allow even nontechies like you to control the Cloud freely." He pointed at the screen. Chance saw what looked like an online data-entry form.

"A web app?"

"Yep. Looks easy, right?"

The app was very simple, Shiraishi explained. The Formation Settings menu let you choose the shape of the Cloud, from a sphere to a long line. The Impact Settings menu offered five levels of force to apply when the Cloud collided with something, from Contact to Annihilate. Then there was a text field for entering the TLE of your target in orbit. That was all. The intricate orbital maneuvers actually carried out by the individual space tethers were all calculated by virtual servers scattered around the globe, including the worldwide Sleeping Gun network built by the Cyber Front for intelligence operations.

"You enter the TLE, and then, when the estimated time for the operation to commence is displayed, just select either 'Go' or 'No go.' The order is sent from six hundred thousand base stations at once—the entire global network."

Chance nodded. Shiraishi's ideas had been invaluable in setting up the network of base stations needed to control what was, after all, a cloud of space tethers spread out in low Earth orbit.

Perhaps because his work was going well, Shiraishi was in a talkative mood. "Let's say you want to take a Japanese Information Gathering Satellite offline. Choose 'Sphere: High-density' from the Formation Settings menu and set the impact to 'Contact.' Then you just enter the target TLE, and you're done. The Japanese government thinks the IGS orbits are a secret, but TLEs for them prepared by amateurs are easy enough to find."

Shiraishi was right about one thing: his app couldn't be easier. It was amazing how simple he'd made controlling forty thousand space-craft.

"I ran a simple test where I left twenty thousand space tethers around SAFIR 3 and split the rest into two subclouds of ten thousand each. All eight of Japan's Information Gathering Satellites, along with the Wyvern's reentry craft, will become inoperable as early as today."

The edge of Shiraishi's lip curled upwards. North Korean head-quarters had suggested this program for the initial use of force. As targets for accidents of unknown cause, the IGSs were perfect.

"There are low-level controllers, too. A technician who can use them could reach targets forty or even fifty times farther away." Shirai-shi tapped at his tablet and a complex table appeared on the television screen. This, he said, was the spreadsheet containing what amounted to an orchestral score for the entire Cloud, calculating the correct timing for the application of Lorentz force by each of the forty thousand individual space tethers. Shiraishi opened the Help menu to show Chance how macros and formulas could be used as well, though the details were indecipherable to her.

"Will engineers in the North be able to use this?" she asked.

"Who cares? I'm not their babysitter. Anyway, this interface is for me. You think I want just anyone to be able to use it? The web app will be plenty for them."

"Good. I'm relieved to see this in action at last."

Shiraishi looked at Chance as she finally rose to her feet beside him. "Relieved?"

"There were concerns that you'd try to monopolize the Cloud."

Shiraishi snorted, his breath coming out in a puff of white. "Morons," he said. "Where would the fun be in monopolizing an obstruction? My focus is the Great Leap."

"You've done good." Chance gave him a short round of applause totaling three claps. The latex covers on her fingers made a hard sound.

"Watch yourself. It was my idea."

The Cloud of space tethers would cause a gradually increasing number of accidents made to look like collisions with space debris, whittling away at the enthusiasm for space development in the nations currently operating satellites. The world's satellites had been launched into orbit at great expense; when they broke down, budget cuts were bound to follow.

If North Korea then announced that it was actually expanding its investment in space development, it would be able to attract the best scientists and engineers from around the world. The great powers that had lost their appetite for orbital engineering for fear of accidents would be left behind as North Korea and its allies, including Iran,

Pakistan, a few small African countries, and some movements not even recognized as nations yet, took the lead in space development. This was the Great Leap.

The first time Chance had heard this plan, she'd laughed at the idea that engineers would betray their home countries so easily. But learning that China had been able to poach dozens of Japanese engineers every year to work on the Tiangong-2 space station had changed her mind.

Chance packed Shiraishi's luggage into her Boston bag. It all fit except for the blueprint case.

"Will you be carrying this?" she asked, holding the case out to him. On it she saw white lettering that read GREAT LEAP FOR THE REST OF THE WORLD.

Shiraishi's arm shot out and seized the case from her hands. He then cradled it against his chest with arms folded.

"There's nothing in here you'd be able to understand," he said. "You'd have to be Dr. Jahanshah himself. When *are* you going to bring him to meet me?"

"Not until the Great Leap is under way."

"All right, all right. I'll get back to my work on the app."

Chance noticed Shiraishi's left hand, the arm that held the case, tightly gripping the tattoo of the Tsiolkovsky equation on his right arm.

Seshambe, 25 Azar 1399, 23:56 +0330 (2020-12-15T20:26 GMT)
Tehran Institute of Technology, Tehran

This one? No, this isn't it . . . That's the one. That one hanging over there.

Jamshed pushed a creaking chair out of the way and pulled a yellow sheet of paper illuminated by a naked lightbulb closer. The sheet of paper was clipped to a piece of string, which hung in turn from the ladder wiring that wound across the ceiling. Diagrams and equations were scrawled across the sheet of paper in marker. On his desk sat the scientific calculator with the printing on its buttons worn away.

Paper, pen, and calculator: the only computer he had. He was fortunate to have plenty of paper, at least. Alef had given Jamshed the posters from the Azadi Interanet campaign he was planning.

At night the lab felt deserted. Perhaps because the Internet had been completely blocked for two days now, he didn't even see any of the students who usually came in to use the computers at night. No doubt they would all be attending Alef's demonstration tomorrow.

Jamshed yanked the paper out of its clip, placed it on the table, and drew a coordinate system on it.

"Unbelievable . . . It really is my exact design."

The connected coordinates that made up the observational data for the unknown objects reported by Meteor News were a perfect match with the principles of propulsion at work in Jamshed's space tether design. The randomly moving ballast implemented to fight tidal forces had been Jamshed's own idea. The wobbles in the observational data followed the equations in Jamshed's paper precisely.

While making his calculations, Jamshed had discovered a few elementary mistakes in his paper. Presumably whoever had stolen the paper had noticed these and was using an amended model.

"So Hamed didn't even read it . . ." Jamshed sighed, recalling the sight of Professor Hamed, his advisor at the time, glancing at his paper with an obvious lack of interest. That jerk. He'd written in his name as lead author without even reading the thing properly. How stupid did you have to be to read about a spacecraft that could generate electricity and maintain its orbit without fuel and just dismiss it with a shrug?

Jamshed clipped the paper back onto the string and placed a new sheet of paper on his desk. He pulled the cap off his marker and tried to draw a line of moment, but the pen was dry.

"Already?" Jamshed threw the pen onto the floor. It wasn't pens that he needed. It was someone to talk to.

Kazumi from Meteor News. He'd reacted to the tether-propulsion system, even to the words "space tether." He'd be hundreds of times more useful than Hamed had been. Jamshed wondered what Kazumi had thought of the half of the paper that he had managed to send. He longed to talk to him about it.

Whoever it was who'd actually engineered the space tethers would do, too. Sure, they might have stolen his paper, but there was so much Jamshed wanted to ask them. How had they approached the problems of bringing his ideas to life? What had they used to get the devices into orbit? How were they stabilizing their rotation?

And then there was the problem of base stations, which Jamshed had ultimately been unable to overcome. Three hundred fifty kilometers sounded pretty high up, but compared to the size of the Earth, it was barely off the ground. A space tether in LEO was only visible from the surface within a circular area of about a two thousand–kilometer radius. To communicate with an orbiting space tether, you would need multiple bases all over the Earth. If a tether was passing over Tehran, only a few other nearby countries would have the necessary line of sight to communicate with it. To bases on the other side of the world in North Korea or the US, it would be invisible.

He had mentioned this in his paper as a future challenge. If you were going to build bases around the world to receive telemetry from the space tethers and send back new target orbits, ideally you would need at least a few dozen locations—and if you wanted real-time control, more like a few hundred . . . no, a few thousand. How had the mystery space tether engineer gotten around this problem?

"Maybe you don't really need that many bases."

Deciding to recalculate the necessary number of antennas, Jamshed stood up to borrow a pen from a student's desk. Then there was a noise in the corridor outside.

"What's that?"

He heard several voices in conversation and the sound of something heavy and metallic being dragged across the floor. Had the students come to collect some materials for their barricades?

"Don't you know what time it is?" Jamshed pulled open the door to see three people passing by, illuminated by the light that spilled from his laboratory. They looked at him, clearly surprised. All three had green scarves wrapped around the lower halves of their faces and Kalashnikovs slung casually from their shoulders.

"Sorry," the man at the head of the three apologized in thickly accented Persian. "We didn't think anyone was here."

They were dragging a metal case painted olive. The other two men apologized in turn, and then the three of them hoisted the heavy-looking case off the ground and disappeared into the darkness.

Members of your demonstration, Alef? With Kalashnikovs . . . ? No. Something was wrong here. That rectangular case, Jamshed realized, contained a surface-to-air missile launcher that had been provided to the institute to shoot down drones. But wasn't tomorrow supposed to be a nonviolent protest?

"Alef . . . What are you planning?"

Tue, 15 Dec 2020, 14:03 -700 (2020-12-15T21:03 GMT)
Peterson Air Force Base

After finishing his ground-run test, Captain Ricky McGillis waited for Second Lieutenant Madu Abbot to disembark from her F-22 Raptor before returning with her to the briefing room.

"This pressure suit feels pretty good," said Ricky.

"Make up your mind, would you?" said Madu. "I thought you were complaining that it smelled like rubber or something."

"It's the power of Gore-Tex, you know? Keeps you from getting all hot and sweaty. Wish we could have it in our regular pilot suits too." Ricky opened the door and let Madu into the locker room ahead of him. "That clear helmet is great too," he continued. "Nice to be able to move your head freely—whoops!"

Upon entering the room, Madu had stopped in place, taken a step to one side, and come to attention with her feet apart and her hands behind her back. Ricky hurried to adopt the same pose.

Colonel Daniel Waabboy, their commanding officer as of yesterday, was sitting on the bench. Beside him were two cream-colored cardboard folders full of papers. When Ricky saw the air force's eagle seal and the words OPERATION COMMAND printed in fat letters on the cover of one, he felt his fists tighten at the small of his back above his belt. Operation Seed Pod was about to begin at last.

Waabboy picked up the two folders and motioned to Ricky and Madu to sit down on the bench opposite him.

"Ground-run test?" he asked. "How'd it go?"

"No difficulties, sir."

"The same, sir."

Waabboy nodded. He was flipping through the papers in one of the folders. Ricky could make out some of the small text on the cover. No mistake: the colonel was holding the papers for Operation Seed Pod. Orders had come through at eight that morning. The decision must have been made based on Judy's broadcast the previous night. It wasn't often you saw a response that quick these days.

"Operation Seed Pod is currently scheduled to begin at 1700 hours tomorrow," Waabboy said. "There is a possibility that our target will move, though, so you will be on standby starting tonight. We've included a flight plan for breaking the altitude record. Make sure you're up to it."

"Yes, sir." Ricky thrust his chest out and pulled his chin in. This meant that he and Madu would be sleeping in the scramble waiting room next to the hangar tonight, along with the maintenance crew.

Waabboy clasped his hands together and leaned in closer to the two of them, lowering his voice. "I suppose you already know this, but Operation Seed Pod *is* in contravention of the COPUOS guidelines, to which the United States is a signatory." He gave them a meaningful look, as if to remind them that this was a top secret mission. Ricky nodded. After a beat, Waabboy returned to his original tone of voice. "Three ASM-140s have been prepared, but you're to get it right the first time."

Waabboy extracted a weather chart from the bundle of papers and handed it to Madu. Ricky caught sight of the pressure fronts and closely packed isobars and shivered. A blizzard. By tomorrow, the whole northern end of the western seaboard would be buried in snow.

"The operation will take place completely in US airspace," said Waabboy. "Actually, I'm not sure if we can call it 'airspace,' but above those clouds, at any rate. It's an operation that would not be possible without your all-weather F-15 and F-22 to launch the ASM-140 out of the stratosphere. If we were to repeat this two or three times on a clear day, even an amateur might notice. The CIA's efforts to get Russia and China to keep quiet would go to waste."

Waabboy took the weather map back from Madu and returned it to its folder, then handed one of the folders to each of them.

"Operation Seed Pod. Your formal orders. Make sure you read them." Waabboy's face was grim.

"Is something wrong, sir?" asked Ricky.

Waabboy shook his head. "We've never been asked to knock a satellite out of orbit before. Not this base, not the whole US armed forces. There's a lot I don't understand in these folders."

Flipping through the pages, Ricky came across the sheet about the ASM-140 antisat weapon his Eagle would carry. He gave it a quick once-over, but there were some figures he couldn't work out. Then he realized the problem: the units of measurement. "Sir . . . this sheet . . ."

Waabboy flapped his hand as he rose to his feet. "It's in metric, right? That's one of the things I don't understand. Go through and find everything that doesn't make sense to you. Colonel Lintz from NORAD will be providing a separate briefing about the ASM-140 later."

Waabboy left the locker room with a wave, pausing only to look back at them with a final warning: "No slacking off!"

Ricky and Madu rose to their feet and saluted as he left.

"Hey, Madu," Ricky said, once Waabboy was gone. "You use metric in India, right?"

"Don't look at me. I'm going to have my hands full operating the external photography pod. I told them the Raptor isn't a surveillance plane, but do they listen?" Madu frowned and paged through their orders. "A seventy-degree climb, side by side, to seventy thousand feet?"

Madu glared at Ricky. His F-15 was supposed to have been the only one challenging the altitude record. She wasn't happy about getting caught up in that initiative. It had been their former commander, Major Sylvester Fernandez, along with Waabboy himself, who had authored that part of the mission plans.

"Not *my* fault."

"I know, I know. Listen, I'm going to visit the simulator. See whether I can actually get that high with something on the side of the plane dragging me down." Madu started to tie her hair back. "Why don't you drop by too, Ricky? The ASM-140 fires automatically. You'd do well to learn how it behaves after release."

"What's that you say?"

Ricky pulled a nine-page flight plan from his copy of their orders. Target velocity: 7.7 kilometers per second . . . Shit! Even the parts that mattered were in metric.

Tue, 15 Dec 2020, 14:12 -0800 (2020-12-15T22:12 GMT)
Western Days Hotel, Seattle

Bruce chose the chair nearest Chris and pulled it toward him. This action brought the central display to life and displayed a list of accounts Bruce could use. A reader screwed into place under the table was detecting the name card Akari had made for him.

"Who built this setup?" Bruce asked.

"Daryl built the hardware, Akari the software," Chris said. "They put it together yesterday—only took them one evening. You can connect it to a CIA desktop too. Headquarters is going to fail their security audit for sure."

If you wanted to display your laptop's screen directly, you simply inserted it below the display and plugged in a few cables.

"Amazing," Bruce said. "Very different from headquarters. You practically have to show your health insurance just to buy a keyboard there."

"I have no interest in US national secrets," came another voice. "You are safe with this system."

"Huh?" Bruce said. "Oh, that's fine. I trust you."

The third speaker was Akari, currently on her hands and knees attaching Nichrome wire to the picnic mats Bruce had gone out and bought for her. Conversation with her wasn't always smooth, but he appreciated the effort she made to communicate. Anyone who could make themselves this useful after being chased to a foreign country was a cut above the rest.

Bruce logged in to his CIA remote desktop and inserted a flash drive into one of the ports lined up beneath the monitor. A frame from a high-res video immediately appeared on the display, showing a man with a tightly wound air pushing his silver-framed glasses up the bridge of his nose with his middle finger. This was the man who had convinced Jose Juarez to draw the illustration of the Rod from God. Kirilo Panchenko, a forty-one-year-old Ukrainian. He had actually existed once, but thirty-eight years ago, at the age of three, he had gone missing. The profile for Kirilo in the video chat system was presumably an example of what people in Bruce's line of work called a "legend": a false identity backed by real documents.

Bruce thought back on the videoconference between the man calling himself Kirilo and Jose that he'd pulled from the NSA archives. They had spoken in English, Kirilo with a phony-sounding Russian accent. Once Jose had accepted the proposal to draw the illustration, Kirilo had sent him the plans.

Bruce was sure of one thing. Whoever this liar was, he had been at the center of the effort to muddy the waters around the Rod from God. The image that had come through on the videoconference had been doctored, thwarting the automatic facial-recognition engine. Not bad work for North Korean cyber command. The agent who'd processed the video at the CIA had been just as surprised.

"Pretty good-looking guy. Looks a bit uptight, though." As he cropped the rest of the image out to send the face to headquarters, Bruce saw a human form reflected in his display. Turning, he found Akari staring at the screen in disbelief. "What's wrong, Akari? Friend of yours?"

Bruce followed this up with a friendly chuckle, but Akari didn't react. She just gaped at the screen, not even blinking.

"*Ageha Ojisan . . .* "A mumble in Japanese escaped her lips as her trembling hand reached toward the monitor.

Bruce felt his body tense. "Akari, do you know this man?"

Slowly, Akari nodded. Her fingertips made contact with the screen, tracing the frames of the man's glasses. Haltingly, she began to speak.

"Yes. He's my uncle. Ageha Shiraishi . . . He changed his glasses."

Bruce felt someone poke his shoulder and realized that Chris was now standing directly behind him. She put her finger to her lips and jerked her chin toward her own laptop to signal that she would send out the request for information on this Ageha Shiraishi.

Akari spoke in English, clearly and carefully, eyes glued to the monitor. "Where did you find him? This is cropped from a video frame, right? Can I see the video?"

Akari obviously had strong feelings for this man. How would she react if Bruce showed her the video of him gleefully deceiving the illustrator? With anger? Dismay?

"This still was all that headquarters sent," Bruce said. This was a lie. He had the whole video on his flash drive. "Was he an engineer too?"

"He was my mentor," Akari said.

Now Bruce understood how a regular civilian hacker had managed to figure out so much of what the North Korean spies were doing. Akari had been able to see through the SIM reuse, the translation-engine corruption, and the trip wire ads because she thought the same way as Ageha Shiraishi, the man behind it all.

Bruce's experience as an intelligence agent whispered to him: *You can use this.* If Akari stuck with them on the team, they'd have someone who knew how Shiraishi thought. Who could read him.

"It seems he's the man who gave the plans for the Rod from God to the illustrator," Bruce said. "He's mixed up in this somehow. Are you sure that's your uncle?"

"Yes . . . Maybe the North Koreans are putting him up to this."

"Maybe so." Bruce quietly pulled out the flash drive with the video on it.

2020-12-15T23:00 GMT

Project Wyvern

We've had an absolute flood of inquiries and information since yesterday.

Thank you so much, everyone.

I know much more about the Rod from God now.

If we could get a photo of it, we could try zooming in, but unfortunately it's not yet visible to the naked eye. According to the orbital hotel's debris-detection radar, it's following us quietly at a distance of ten kilometers. We're correcting our orbit as necessary to make the planned rendezvous with the ISS, but the Rod from God's speed relative to us has stayed at zero.

In other words, that object can move as freely as we can, not to mention observe us.

What does it want? If there's someone out there who's mastered such advanced technology, why don't they have anything better to do? It's a bigger waste than this hotel's Showerpots.

Because, really, there's so much that needs to be done.

"That's one small step for a man, one giant leap for mankind." Neil Armstrong's first words after stepping onto the moon, 380,000 kilometers from Earth, as you know. It's been fifty years now, and no one has made giant leap number two yet. No one has gone any farther out than he did.

In fact, these days we can barely make it four hundred measly kilometers up—so low there are still atmospheric effects. And only a handful of people at a time, too. Six in the ISS, three in Tiangong-2, and two here in Wyvern. A grand total of eleven human beings in orbit.

And now someone's launched something into that same
practically deserted orbit just to cause trouble.
How petty and pathetic can you get?

Ronnie's acting tough, saying, "Let the idiots do
what they want. We have our own work to do." But if
something doesn't change, we'll be leading that Rod
from God right to the ISS.

That would be no way to repay their hospitality.

Judy Smark

10 Riot

"It's been a long day, my *Right Stuff* crew," said Chris. "You're all doing great."

Kazumi stopped rubbing his eyes and hurriedly sat up in his chair. It was eight in the morning, Japan time.

"But please hang in there for another two hours. Then we'll have something to eat, and Kazumi and Akari can get some sleep. I imagine your sleepiness is peaking right now, but just hang in there a short while longer, please. A workout at the gym tomorrow morning will work wonders for your jet leg."

"These two aren't as, ahem, mature as you, Chris," said Bruce, who was sitting at the edge of the table. "They're still young. A quick shower should do the trick." He winked at Kazumi. This black CIA agent was already fitting into the team nicely.

"Who are you calling 'mature'?" said Chris with a laugh. She wrote a short list on the whiteboard.

1) Analysis of space tether observational information

2) Discussion/information exchange: space tether

3) Op. Seed Pod

4) North Korean spies

"What's Seed Pod?" Kazumi asked, before Chris had even finished writing.

"I'll explain later," said Chris. "Is the analysis of Cunningham's observational data complete?"

Akari nodded. Kazumi noticed that she had faint circles under her eyes, though they were difficult to spot behind her display glasses. It was no surprise she was tired. Being the only programmer on their team, she had put together everything by herself, from the observational data and wardriving system to the operations center structure.

"You want to see it now?" asked Akari. "This is the data captured from the observation point on Desnoeufs Island two hours ago."

When Akari tapped at the keyboard on her left arm, a projector lit up and an ocean horizon appeared on the whiteboard. A single streak of cloud floated in a sky that darkened from light green to dark blue, and near the center of the image was a white dot labeled SAFIR 3. Akari's planetarium had been modified since Kazumi had seen it in Tokyo. The sky now had gradations, and the ocean was covered in ripples. Daryl and Bruce both let out a sigh of admiration. The game engine Akari was using endowed the planetarium with a certain aesthetic appeal that Kazumi supposed was missing from the schematic representations space professionals were used to seeing.

"Akari, that's beautiful," said Bruce pointing to the whiteboard. "You even drew in the clouds."

"Clouds?"

"Yeah, the streaks overlaid on SAFIR 3."

"Those aren't clouds."

Akari stretched her arms out in front of her, lined up her index fingers, and spread out her arms, making the display zoom in on SAFIR 3. Kazumi noticed a strange camera attached above the whiteboard: a mounted motion sensor for gesture control. He supposed being able to enter commands without bringing any unnecessary devices into this already equipment-filled room was handy, but there was no denying that Akari was taking the opportunity to indulge her eccentric tastes to the hilt.

"That's a point cloud representing the space tethers," she explained.

"What?" cried Daryl, standing up to go around the table to examine the whiteboard.

SAFIR 3 had been enlarged on the screen. Around it were faint dots indicating space tethers that were concentrated within a diameter of five . . . no, a range of about ten kilometers. These were the ones being used to kick SAFIR 3 along.

"The hell . . ." said Daryl. "How many of those things are there?"

"Only counting the ones revolving around SAFIR 3's location," said Akari, "Twenty thousand tether pairs."

"Twenty thousand?!" Daryl exclaimed.

Kazumi gasped in surprise. When Akari had analyzed Ozzy's data in Tokyo, she'd estimated ten thousand, but now she was saying double that number. Pointing to the brain of their operations center piled by the window, the mountain of self-assembly Raspberry Pi computers, Akari explained that it was counting the number of objects that were revolving, as this was the distinctive behavior of the space tethers. The Pis performed this task using the observational data from the Sampson-5, which was noise filled and only able to record 1,024 objects at a time.

"Akari," said Kazumi. "Did you just say something weird like 'only counting the ones around SAFIR 3'?"

"Yes. There are others."

"So there's another group?"

"Two other groups of about ten thousand each. Should I superimpose them on the globe? I saved the orbital information from when they passed over Desneoufs Island."

With her index fingers sticking up, Akari brought her hands closer together and then pointed downwards, making the sky zoom out rapidly until it became a 3-D globe. She then rotated the Earth so that Europe was in the center. There appeared three cloud-like streaks, two running east-west and one tilted on a sharp angle. Kazumi couldn't take his eyes off it, now that he finally grasped the true scale of the space tether phenomenon.

"Forty thousand space tethers . . ." said Chris, shaking her head slowly from side to side. "It's like an orbital cloud."

Daryl and Bruce, who were frozen gazing at the projected globe, both echoed Chris: "Orbital cloud . . ."

Akari look toward Chris and said, "Does this count as proof that the tethercraft exists?"

"Almost there."

Kazumi tried to get up, but Daryl stopped him. "Kazumi," he said. "This is still just unofficial data. We need some observations made using government radars from at least one more location. Don't you think, Chris?"

Chris gave a wry smile and said, "To the United States, this team's conclusions are still just one opinion among many about what's going on up there. However, we've taken the first step toward credibility with Akari's analysis. So I'd like us to keep operating under the assumption that the tethercraft and the orbital cloud exist. Does that sound good, Daryl?"

"Yes. I'll make a request to Colonel Lintz to verify the existence of these Clouds using NORAD's air defense radar. It would be great if the CIA gave him a little nudge too."

"Okay. Will do."

Kazumi sunk into his chair and watched the Clouds float around the globe. It was inevitable, he thought, that the team would prove the existence of the tethercraft. Clearly those three Clouds were being operated for some distinct purpose.

"Akari, can you throw up some numbers? Like altitude and so on . . . Whatever you have." Sticking out his index finger, Kazumi imagined the movements of the Clouds, entering into his visualization ritual.

Cloud streak number one. Stretching in an east-westerly direction, it was kicking along the second stage of SAFIR 3, thought to be the Rod from God, to bring it into rendezvous with the Wyvern Orbital Hotel. The two Smarks and their associates probably felt like a weapon was at their throats. There was no guarantee that this diversion to hide the presence of the Clouds would not serve some other purpose as well.

Cloud streak number two. Raising its altitude as it headed in a north-southerly direction, it was trying to enter a sun-synchronous orbit passing vertically across the Earth. Countless Earth-observation satellites followed such orbits. Half-closing his eyes, Kazumi picked out several candidates from the TLEs in his memory and overlaid his visualization on the projected Earth and predicted path of the Clouds. If this streak continued to change its path as expected, it would rendezvous with a satellite Kazumi knew all too well.

The third orbit was vaguely familiar. Was it the ISS? No. An object he'd mentioned recently on Meteor News. Enveloped by the Clouds he imagined. That's it, he—

". . . umi? Kazumi?"

Hearing someone calling him, Kazumi opened his eyes. Chris was in front of him with her hands on his desk. "The two remaining Clouds," she said. "Have you figured out what they're headed for?"

Kazumi was about to reflexively preface his answer with "This could be wrong, but . . ." but stopped himself. If he held himself to such high standards of proof, they'd have to investigate thousands of orbital objects, which would make it impossible to keep up with the movements of the Clouds. Kazumi took a deep breath and opened his mouth. "Japan's Information Gathering Satellites and the Wyvern's return vehicle."

Bruce raised an eyebrow, smiled at Kazumi, and said, "Whoa. How thrilling. I'd better warn the ISS while we're—"

"Quiet a second," said Chris, interrupting Bruce's wisecracking. "Daryl, verification."

Daryl's hands went at his keyboard in a flurry of movement. Akari and Kazumi peered at the screen of his console.

"What's the matter, y'all?" said Bruce in a silly tone of voice, apparently confused by the sudden shift in the room. "Orbital calculations can't be that easy. Chris, remember when we asked those NASA guys where the Rod from God was going, and they kept us waiting for hours? There's no way his guess is going to hit the mark just like—"

Saying nothing, Daryl pulled up the globe on the screen. The predicted orbit of the Wyvern's return craft overlapped with the orbit of the third Cloud.

"Come on . . ." muttered Bruce, half-standing with his butt hovering above his seat. "How'd you guess that?"

"I'm really sorry," said Kazumi. "I just know."

"Kazumi. There's no need to apologize," said Chris, taking out her BlackBerry and dialing a number.

Chaharshanbe, 26 Azar 1399, 03:53 +0330 (2020-12-16T00:23 GMT)
Imam Khomeini International Airport, Tehran

"I'm going to pick up our bags. Just hold on a second."

Without a moment's hesitation, Sekiguchi rushed straight for the blue counter. Kurosaki could make neither heads nor tails of its bilingual Arabic and Persian sign, but Sekiguchi seemed to have deciphered it immediately.

Watching him arrive at the counter and begin to gesticulate energetically as he spoke to the attendant, Kurosaki thought how well the man blended in with the environment. Sekiguchi could speak Persian. Very well, apparently. The woman at the counter casually brushed off Sekiguchi's jokes. All in black, with a hijab covering her hair, the sight of her keenly reminded Kurosaki of the fact that he had arrived in a foreign country. He hadn't seen anyone like her at the Ataturk Airport in Istanbul that they had departed just three hours ago. Across the counter, Sekiguchi accepted luggage wrapped in white plastic.

Kurosaki noticed that an error message had appeared on all the liquid crystal displays placed here and there throughout the lounge. Though he couldn't read the words, he could tell what kind of error it was by the shape of the dialogue box: a SERVER COULD NOT BE FOUND notification. Apparently, Internet connections to foreign countries had been cut off, and Kurosaki supposed it had had an impact on domestic service as well. Sekiguchi had told him that foreigners could use the Internet as usual on their smartphones, but Kurosaki had lost all desire to even check his emails when he'd heard they were being censored.

"So this is Tehran." Kurosaki cast his gaze around and looked up at the ceiling supported by thin trusses curving gently like wings in profile, a design seen in airports around the world. Such massive spaces lit up with white LED lights said nothing of religion or country. Remembering the cramped hallways of Narita Airport, Kurosaki smiled bitterly. There was something so definitively Japanese about it.

"Sorry to keep you waiting," said Sekiguchi.

"What the heck is that?"

On the cart Sekiguchi was pushing was a pile of small duralumin cases so high it looked ready to topple. Scraps of the plastic sheet covering the cases dangled off the edges of the cart.

"These are Iridiums. I had twenty-one of them delivered."

"Satellite phones?"

"Yes. I also had them send data-transmission modules to connect to the Internet," Sekiguchi said, patting the cases with the flat of his hand. He explained that he would hand out Iridiums to students seeking unimpeded Internet access and give the campus network an uncensored connection to the Internet. Before leaving Japan, he'd arranged to have them sent from Singapore.

". . . We're not meeting Jahanshah?"

"That's the plan, but we might not be able to get into the campus."

"What's this?"

"There's a demonstration happening at the institute tomorrow."

Sekiguchi explained that his friend at the NSC had told him about it. The demonstration in support of azadi interanet, Internet freedom, was being organized mainly by students of the Tehran Institute of Technology.

"So you knew about the demonstration already?"

"Yes. Which is exactly why I decided to come to Tehran. Oh, the receipt—" Sekiguchi peeled a strip of paper with a red mark printed on it from the plastic sheet and tucked it in his pocket.

"Make sure not to lose it if you're going to keep it in there."

"Don't lump me in with you," said Sekiguchi, stroking his smooth, stubble-free chin with a laugh. Kurosaki was tongue-tied, having rummaged through his pockets numerous times in search of his ticket on the way here from Narita. He felt utterly outmatched by Sekiguchi, not just in terms of his language ability and initiative, but also with little things like the way he organized his belongings.

"Let's go," said Sekiguchi. "I've hired a car with a driver. Once we've had a nap, we're heading off to the institute."

Tue, 15 Dec 2020, 16:53 -0800 (2020-12-16T00:53 GMT)
Pike Place Market, Seattle

Sliding off the upper crust of the French bread, Chance smelled shellfish and potatoes as steam rose from inside the bread bowl. Though the clam chowder was technically Boston-style, it was a popular dish in Seattle as well.

Chance had brought Shiraishi here to Pike Street to eat out. Though nothing fancy, this soup was made with plenty of fresh ingredients and would give them more energy than the meals Chance had always brought to the warehouse—just "dead calories," as Shiraishi called them.

Watching snow blow against the window, she felt relieved that they had managed to get out of the warehouse. The weather report called for the snowfall to get heavier. Chance wondered if they would move from the warehouse control room to their hideout in the city during a blizzard. Disappearing under cover of snow would be perfect.

"A hit," said Shiraishi, extending his smartphone upside down to Chance.

"What?"

"I took out Information Gathering Satellite 2 of group 1. The recording's right here." Shiraishi pointed to the screen where a video on repeat showed a cylindrical satellite approaching rapidly before the screen blacked out. Chance guessed that this was the moment of impact recorded by a tether.

"That's another hard hit. You don't think there will be debris?"

"Don't worry. When the tether struck, it was moving at five hundred meters per second, about equivalent to a full swing from a metal bat. Now the satellite is just scrap metal."

The impact might have torn off a solar panel, but it had not added to the satellite's orbital velocity, so it would likely continue following the same orbit for some time, Shiraishi explained with a laugh. Now that the satellite had suddenly become inoperative, the team that managed it would likely be in a panic. Even if they were lucky enough to receive its telemetric data when its antenna pointed toward the base station, all they would record was senseless spinning. According to Shiraishi, the remaining six Information Gathering Satellites would be rendered useless as soon as that very day. Since the Japanese government had no backups, this would leave it blind.

"Our second objective, hitting the Wyvern's return craft, will be complete in two hours. This one I'm planning to strike at high velocity to open up a hole."

"You're sure no one will suspect the North in either case?"

"There's no way the Japanese government will publicly announce that there was an 'accident' with their military satellites. As long as the Supreme Leader doesn't let anything slip, no one will ever guess what caused it. That girl will probably blog about the Wyvern's return craft, but that won't cast any light on why it happened. All nine targets will become orbital debris, though, so we should probably change our method in future."

On the screen, a notification popped up that read TAKANORI HASHIMOTO: NAGATACHO.

"The head of the Satellite Intelligence Center has been summoned to Nagatacho," said Shiraishi, flicking the notification to the side to make it disappear. "Poor guy's been working his butt off since bright and early."

Shiraishi's expression showed none of his usual disdain. Chance wondered if he was feeling nostalgic about JAXA. She knew that his first post after entering JAXA was head of the Satellite Intelligence Center. Afterwards he'd been demoted to busywork for fouling up his duties, and in the end he'd decided to leave Japan.

Seeing the notification from the MDM system pop up, Chance remembered one of her concerns. Kazumi and the JAXA staff holed up in the Nippon Grand Hotel. "What's happening in Iidabashi?" she asked.

"Can't you remember anything? JAXA is in Ochanomizu, not Iidabashi. I bet they're having a fit. Their pride and joy, a bunch of spy satellites that eat up a third of their budget, are all dead!"

"That's not what I mean," said Chance, pointing to his smartphone. "I'm talking about the man under JAXA's protection, Kazumi Kimura. He hasn't gone anywhere yet? It's been two whole days since they went into hiding at the Nippon Grand."

Shiraishi was about to say something, but then he took a breath, took back his smartphone, and moved his fingers quickly over the screen.

". . . They haven't moved at all."

"You mean they're still hunkered down there?"

Glowering at the screen, Shiraishi pushed back his glasses as he raised his head. Then he looked down at the smartphone again and said in a pinched voice, "We've been had. That bastard Sekiguchi fooled us. His phone kept transmitting messages, so I thought he was contacting people, but the screen hasn't been unlocked once this whole time."

What was more, Shiraishi explained, none of the apps on Kurosaki's phone had been activated, the battery level hadn't changed, and there were no signs that he had checked his email or social media. Sekiguchi's smartphone had been equipped with a utility that made it appear to be constantly in use.

"They left their MDM-controlled devices behind at the Nippon Grand. So most likely . . . they're not there."

"Are you serious? You don't know where they went?"

"I'll track them down."

"So you don't know, then."

Shiraishi pounded the table with the hand holding the smartphone. "I told you! I'm going to track them down!" he shouted.

Chance felt regret well up in her chest. Entrusting intelligence to Shiraishi while his hands were already full operating the Clouds had been a mistake.

"I'll sic the Cyber Front on them. Give me all your accounts that can break into JAXA. I'm going to dig up information about Sekiguchi and Kurosaki."

"No. I'll take care of that. I'm the one who kept these accounts going, after all."

"Give them to me! I'm going to turn JAXA upside down and ransack it from top to bottom!" Chance snapped. She held out her hand toward him with the palm facing up.

With Shiraishi's accounts, she would use the globally dispersed Sleeping Gun computers to infiltrate JAXA's servers and dredge up all of its data. In the process, the JAXA IT system would take devastating damage. There was a good chance that everything would crash, from their websites to their office system. However incompetent JAXA might be, they would know immediately that Shiraishi's accounts left on the servers, whether out of kindness or negligence, had been used for the attack.

"There's no time. Give them to me now!"

With forty-eight hours, they could be anywhere on earth by now. Looking at her own palm as she held it in front of her, she felt the flesh of her ring finger and pinky that had been sanded off when she was tortured twitching along with the resinous cover around them. This was an indelible mark of her failure.

"Shiraishi. There's no place for you at JAXA anymore. You threw all that away." Chance was surprised at how cold her own voice sounded and immediately regretted it. Still, she couldn't think of any other way to deal with her irritation. "You'll never be on center stage again. You know that. So please give over the JAXA accounts."

Shiraishi pushed his tilted glasses back up into place and let out a deep sigh that disturbed the steam rising from his soup-filled bread.

Chance squeezed her outstretched hand until the resin covers rubbed together and made a creaking sound.

The steam settled, and Shiraishi raised his head. "Do whatever you like."

Tue, 15 Dec 2020, 21:29 -0800 (2020-12-16T05:29 GMT)
Western Days Hotel

Daryl ran the meeting, which was interrupted by several breaks and meals. Bruce had ordered a pizza, claiming it was Seattle's best, and Kazumi watched as it cooled and congealed before his eyes.

On the whiteboard was a diagram of a space tether. Illustrated there were the two terminating apparatuses, the cable that joined them, and the moving ballast in the middle that Dr. Jahanshah (Bruce had looked into it and confirmed that he had indeed earned his PhD) had conceived. It had been a simple diagram when Daryl had first sketched it that evening, but now, after three hours, it was scrawled all over with notes.

"Can I ask something?" said Bruce, pointing at the whiteboard. Throughout the meeting, he had assumed the role of questioner. "How long can the Clouds remain in orbit?"

"Unlike objects in LEO, those space tethers are not going to fall down naturally due to air resistance," said Daryl. "Even one of Dr. Jahanshah's rather primitive models can maintain its orbit with a thrust of 0.2 newtons per minute."

Without missing a beat, Bruce moved on to his next question. "Where does it get its energy from?"

"Inside a magnetic field—in other words, while in orbit, it can produce energy with its tether alone, which means it can remain up there indefinitely."

"I see."

"A perpetual motion machine?" chimed in Chris.

"It relies on the magnetic field of the Earth," said Daryl. "Also, the battery will eventually wear out."

"I hope we're not talking about atomic batteries or something here," said Bruce. "Those last for decades."

"Isn't the question of whether they could have gathered forty thousand tethers' worth of atomic fuels like plutonium or polonium a matter for the CIA?"

Kazumi grunted in admiration at Daryl's reply. *Even if I knew what atomic batteries were made of*, Kazumi thought, *there's no way I'd have the nerve to make such a deft retort.*

"That's enough about batteries," said Chris. "So, to summarize, these things won't fall out of orbit for years. Daryl, please add 'Cannot be left in orbit' to our list of actions."

Bruce threw his legs up on top of the table. The shiny toes of his shoes reflected the silver-sheet-covered interior of the room like a mirror.

"These space tether things are maddeningly well thought out," said Bruce. "All right, then, let's move on to their size."

"This is an estimate based on the fact that they were unobservable with defense radars," Daryl said immediately. "The longest dimension of the space tethers' terminal apparatuses is one to two inches if they have metal cases, and about four inches if they're plastic. These are the smallest sizes that Cunningham's radar can detect. If they were more than twice this size, NORAD's radar should have been able to pick them up."

"Smaller than I thought," said Bruce. "How long are the cables?"

Daryl looked to Kazumi as if to pass him a relay baton.

"About two kilometers," said Kazumi.

"The material?"

"I can't guess."

"What if it were Nichrome wire like this?" said Bruce, pointing at the ceiling.

"The centrifugal force would sever it."

"If we're talking a strong and light material, it could be carbon nanotubes," said Daryl, looking quizzical. "Its conductivity would make it perfect for the tethers."

"Impossible," said Chris immediately. "CNT is a strategic material.

If the technology to make something two kilometers long out of it had been developed, the CIA would definitely have heard of it."

Kazumi found the way that Chris and Bruce asked sharp questions one after the other stimulating. Quickly pointing out contradictions and raising concerns, they systematically built up their information about the space tethers. As the one in charge, Chris was maintaining a particularly strong grip on the team. When Daryl or Kazumi began to wander off into discussions of the future possibilities for this unprecedented spacecraft, she would gently guide them back on track and incorporate their thoughts into the task at hand: stopping the Clouds.

"It's difficult to say anything definitive about the material," said Daryl. "There's another carbon material called graphene that's been made into ribbons, though it doesn't compare to CNT in terms of strength. As far as the space tether itself, that's all I have at the moment."

When Daryl had finished writing notes on the whiteboard and put down his marker, Akari raised her hand. "Can we talk about signal transmission now?" she asked. "How do you think the tethers receive commands?"

"The tethers themselves can be used as antennas . . ." said Daryl. "That's what it said in Dr. Jahanshah's paper."

"That's not what I mean. Um . . ."

"Akari," cut in Bruce, seeing her at a loss for words. "Let us sort out the technological issues first. Kazumi, wouldn't the sensitivity of a single line, a dipole antenna, be too low?"

Kazumi nodded. Jamshed had touched on this problem in his paper. But Kazumi wasn't well versed in engineering and worried whether he could convey the ideas accurately. "In Jamshed's paper," Kazumi explained, "it said that if the tethers are flying as a swarm, there will be parallel tethers in the vicinity, which means they can be used as a device that reflects radio waves."

Bruce licked his lips and closed his eyes. Here was a CIA agent so highly capable, thought Kazumi, that he had a good grounding in electrical and electronic engineering in addition to everything else. He would never stop being amazed at the talent of the people he met in America.

"I see what you're getting at," said Bruce. "Antennas arranged in parallel. If you fiddled with the polarity of the tethers, they would become reflectors and might work together like a yagi antenna. This would allow transmissions with a decent amount of directionality. Most likely the signals could be exchanged with terrestrial base stations."

Chris looked concerned about what Bruce had said. "These base stations, where would they be?"

"Yeah," said Akari. "That's exactly what I was trying to ask." She walked over to the front of the whiteboard and drew a big arc beneath the diagram. This represented the Earth. Then she drew a symbol for an antenna on the surface of it and labeled it "Location?"

"Where on the Earth's surface are the base stations?" she asked. "The space tethers are exchanging signals with the ground, right?"

"Right!" said Daryl, slapping himself on the forehead. "Akari, that's exactly it!" Taking the marker from her, Daryl drew a small space tether on top of the arc and another line approaching it. "From an altitude of 350 km, the line of sight only extends a distance of 2,000 km. I have no idea what kind of radio wave they're sending, but base stations in only one or two locations would be insufficient."

"Oh, I see," said Kazumi. "The range that they can communicate is restricted." Kazumi finally understood the problem that Akari had raised. The Clouds could only be viewed from the Earth's surface in specific places at specific times. They didn't appear on NORAD's defense radars, but whoever was operating them had to have some sort of method for obtaining telemetric data, including present location, from each of the space tethers and sending them updated commands to transfer between orbits.

Daryl wrote a simple formula on the whiteboard. "Even if we ignore attenuation caused by the atmosphere and topography, forty locations would be required. That's just dividing the surface area of the Earth by the area of a circle with a radius of 2,000 km, though."

Akari tapped on her arm keyboard and said, "That's 42.5. The circles overlap. You need to fill it with hexagons."

"Good point," said Daryl with a nod. "You're exactly right. Depending on the type of signal and output strength, they might allow them a bit more distance, but without twice, no, three times as many base stations, I doubt that communications would work."

"Couldn't the tethers just have commands sent from some single location stored inside them?" asked Bruce.

"No, because the Clouds are controlled in real time," said Kazumi. "It would be impossible for them to kick along the SAFIR 3 while following after the self-propelled orbital hotel using a stored command." Kazumi explained that the space tethers would cross the sky over a base station in midlatitudes no more frequently than every ninety minutes. In some cases, they might have to wait as long as fifteen hours before returning. With such a large gap between velocity-adjustment commands from the ground, it would be impossible for the space tethers to catch up to the Wyvern Orbital Hotel with their weak thrusters as it steadily changed orbit. "There should be base stations for the Clouds all over the world."

"Bruce, add the task 'Investigate Cloud base stations,'" said Chris. "This is a matter for the CIA."

"Yes, ma'am," said Bruce in a low voice and turned toward Kazumi questioningly. "You're totally certain those things need multiple base stations, right? If you can tell me the format of the telemetric data they're transmitting, I can use ECHELON to extract the transmissions between the base stations. What do you think?"

"Impossible," said Akari, shaking her head. Daryl frowned. Without knowing the format of the data they were searching for, not even an organization like the CIA that intercepted all communications could find it.

Everyone gazed at Kazumi, seeking answers. He shook his head to indicate he didn't know. "I think Dr. Jahanshah could make a pretty good guess. In the table of contents for his paper, there was a section entitled 'Robust Transmission of Device Information.'"

"Ah, that guy from Iran," said Chris. "I'm currently arranging to acquire a copy of the paper he wrote. But it's going to take some time."

Research and development in fields related to national defense were strictly controlled. This, Chris explained, extended from biological engineering to astronautics, and of course included weapons development. She was urging CIA headquarters to hurry up but expected it to take several days before they would reach the list of references at the end.

"How did North Korea get its hands on such a highly classified paper?" asked Kazumi.

"Technological exchange," Bruce replied. "The two countries are allies, after all." Since North Korea and Iran had almost no interaction with developed countries, he explained, they often swapped human resources and technology in various fields. The central pillars of the program were astronautics and nuclear development, since these contributed directly to their deterrence capabilities. Every year, numerous scientists and technicians went back and forth between the two countries sharing information. It was most likely in this way that Jamshed's paper had made its way to North Korea. "The CIA eats up a huge amount of resources just analyzing all the communications it collects. The reality is that we often don't get around to dealing with actual people and paper. Hey, why don't we try a random guess? We could try searching with whatever telemetric format Kazumi hits on."

Kazumi shook his head again. Most likely the transmissions were only made up of a few different kinds of data, but the combinations were endless if you considered all the different standards for numerals and ordering.

"You really think the professor would know?" asked Akari, who had been quietly scanning text on her display glasses. "We might be able to have a videoconference with him soon. I just got a message from Kurosaki and Sekiguchi that they'll be heading for the Tehran Institute of Technology."

"*Eh? Sekiguchi-san ha naikaku no dareka ni tanomu tte ittena-katta?*" Kazumi asked in Japanese without thinking, and everyone stared at him. Flustered, he immediately repeated himself in English. "Didn't Sekiguchi say he'd ask someone in the cabinet to take care of that?"

"From Tehran?" Bruce asked Akari, peering at her in apparent perplexity. "Kurosaki and Sekiguchi? Who are they?"

"Two JAXA staff," said Kazumi. "The ones who helped us escape, though I have no idea what they're doing in Tehran either."

"I got an email from them," Akari cut in. "About how they got there." Akari projected the email from Sekiguchi onto the whiteboard and lined up a machine-translated English version beside it.

"Wha . . ." Bruce grunted. "Is this for real?"

According to the email, Sekiguchi had failed to get the NSC moving and so had gone to the Tehran Institute of Technology himself, taking Kurosaki with him. There, they planned to give Iridiums to Jamshed and have him connect them to the Internet. Apparently, they had received the phones and transmission modules at the airport.

"Bruce!" Chris called out sharply. "Look into the JAXA employee named Sekiguchi and the situation in Tehran. Pronto!"

Bruce straightened his posture, pulled up the CIA workspace on his desktop display, and began typing.

Watching Bruce, Chris muttered as though speaking to herself. "Amazing that they brought telecommunication devices that can bypass Iran's censorship. That would be difficult to arrange even for the CIA. They picked them up at the airport, did they? Hardly an amateur move."

Kazumi was rendered speechless by the sudden transformation in Chris and Bruce. Their cheerfulness had vanished, and they now began to converse faster in English than Kazumi had ever heard. Here, the true character of these two CIA agents was on full display, and he suddenly realized how much effort they had been making to keep up the team's spirits.

"Akari, when did this email arrive?" asked Bruce, paling somewhat with concern. "And when was it written?"

"Most likely just now."

"So the 'today' in the text is *today* today . . . Why does the timing have to work out like this? Akari, please pull up my screen."

Akari manipulated her keyboard, and Bruce's desktop appeared on the screen in place of the email. It showed a simple one-page report with the title "Possibility of Civilian Death and Injury: Riot at Tehran Institute of Technology."

"The source for this report is an email exchange between Al Jazeera staff on the ground. The probability as verified by Viper is class A. Iran's regular forces are going to dispatch a unit of armed troops in front of Tehran IT. Also drones, two attack aircraft, and one spotter plane. What the heck is going on here?" Realizing that Akari and Kazumi were staring at them, Bruce returned his voice to a more relaxed tone and said, "Does this guy Sekiguchi know that Tehran is going to be a battlefield?"

Chaharshambe, 26 Azar 1399, 11:28 +0430 (2020-12-16T07:58 GMT)
Student Center, Tehran Institute of Technology

This is going to be a day to remember, thought Alef. *No—I'll make it one.*

Having sent his student supporters out of the hall, Alef was inside his office cubicle set up along the wall reading over a printout of a paper with the title "Azadi Interanet: A Lecture on Internet Freedom," by Alef Kadiba. He'd rehearsed his speech many times and was looking it over one last time, awaiting his moment.

"'Thank you to all my brethren assembled here. And thank you to Allah for this land, Iran.' Pretty good, I'd say. Sounds good too."

We just want to use the Internet without hindrance, he thought. *That's not so much to ask.*

It was a moderate request that the government should have been able to accept easily. He had carefully removed all passages and phrases that suggested democratization or seemed critical of the president. It wasn't as if they were rejecting censorship or demanding unrestricted access to foreign social networks. They fully understood that Iran faced difficult challenges concerning security. They just wanted permission to use inside the country even half of the information that Western nations like America soaked up like warm sunlight. Foreign companies operating in Iran had a certain degree of access, and Iranians deserved the same. True freedom would follow. In the meantime, they had to avoid bringing about in Tehran that state of anarchy called the "Arab Spring" that the sudden rush onto the Internet and social networks had wrought.

Alef put the sheet of paper down and imagined the streams of thousands of students that were set to gather that day. In front of the main gate, they would erect a stage approximately 30 cm tall. After Alef climbed up there and seized the gaze of the students, he would make a fist, look to the sky, and say, " 'Thank you to all my brethren assembled he—' "

Hearing a rattling sound, Alef swept his gaze around.

"Nice pose, Leader," said a man peeking his head out from the top of the cubicle wall. Wearing a green scarf that covered his mouth, he spoke Persian fluently but with a terrible accent. On his shoulder he carried a Kalashnikov rifle.

". . . Who are you?"

When the man shook his head, two other men dressed identically slipped in through the gaps in the cubicle. The first to enter pointed his Kalashnikov at Alef and jerked the barrel of the gun to indicate that Alef was to approach the wall. The man who came in next took the paper from Alef's hand and passed it to a man standing outside the partition.

"Mr. Kadiba. I'm relieved to see that you're even more handsome than in photographs. However, we cannot tolerate your speech." The man who spoke twisted himself into the gap that Alef had retreated to, pulled down his scarf, and brought his scarred face close. "You're going to begin your speech with *Allahu Akbar*. God is great."

"This country is one of the nations of Islam too, so saying this is fitting, don't you think?" The man continued, narrowing his eyes and repeating a prayer quickly three times. His accent was hard to follow, but no Muslim could fail to recognize that this was the *adhan*, the call to worship. This man's adhan had an unfamiliar tone to it, and Alef noticed that "*Ḥayya 'ala khayr al 'amal*. The time for the best of deeds has come!" had been omitted. This was a sign that this man's adhan was not that of Iran's national religion, Shia.

". . . What are you Sunnis doing?"

"I'm just chanting it in its original form. It's no big deal."

Alef sat down hard on the floor. The demonstration, thousands of students strong, was being surveilled by the government authorities, so at the very least, the police would come to prevent the demonstration from spreading. If he said the Sunni adhan, it would be seen as a proclamation from Alef and all the students that they were antinationalists.

"Afterwards, read this to them." The man bent his arm to reach into an inner pocket from the side of his cape. Seeing this awkward motion, Alef realized that the men were encumbered with body armor. These were armed activists. Members of Hamas who'd entered the country—no, more likely they were from God's Warriors, a group that had been gaining influence recently. A piece of torn-out notepaper was raised in front of Alef, reading, "Dissolve the cabinet. Islamic law demands freedom."

"N-no way. If I do that—"

"Have you memorized it?" asked the man, seeming oblivious to his reaction, and withdrew the paper. "The rest you can make up as you go long. Demand Internet access as you planned or whatever you like. The arrival of another Arab Spring in Tehran is desirable for us too."

The man reached out his hand to Alef and said, "All right, let's go, shall we? A crowd of ten thousand is assembled outside. There are no television cameras with them, but we'll make sure that everyone knows the name of the man who gave his life to advocate a noble cause, the great Alef Kadiba."

Alef pulled his arms away, but the man grabbed him by his shirt around the chest, stood him up, and kicked over the cubicle wall. From beyond the open doors of the front entrance came a chill draft along with the voices of the crowd. It was just as the man had said. There were far more than the one thousand or so people Alef had been expecting. The brick road that ran from the student center to the main gate was thronged with people. Men with black faces who didn't look like students were waving their dusty hands toward the student center.

The man pulled out a handgun from his waist, stuck it to Alef's back, and urged him toward the entrance. "There's another welcome party for you outside the gate. Can you see them? It's the Iranian army."

Alef was forced to stand on the roof of a red Peugeot parked in front of the main gate. Behind him stood the scarf-masked man holding a handgun to his back.

In the rotary in front of the main gate, the crowd jostled. Wrapped in dust-covered capes, these were laborers with their families. One of Alef's student comrades looked up at him with concern, but when Alef turned to meet his gaze, he faded into the crowd. On the far side of the rotary, a unit of maybe one hundred soldiers were lined up in formation behind a barricade. A man standing in the center of the unit raised his right hand. Immediately, the soldiers removed the cartridges from their guns, checked that there were bullets inside, and reinserted them, sending the sound of metal against metal across the rotary. The soldiers carried the same weapon as the man behind Alef—Kalashnikovs. They were not equipped for riot control. The bullets were real.

"Kadiba, can you see them?" asked the man standing behind Alef as he pointed over his shoulder at the sky. In the clear blue above there were two—no, three—sparkling dots. "A few drones have joined the fun. Anjians and—how unusual. They've even brought along Fengren observation drones."

It was at this moment that Alef realized that the Azadi Interanet demonstration he had planned was being co-opted not only by anti-government groups but by the government as well. The government knew that insurgents had mixed themselves in with the protesters in order to mobilize Tehran's malcontents and cause a disturbance and was planning to wipe them out along with all the students. Alef could sense no signs that the man holding him hostage was dismayed by any of this. Most likely he and his fellows were hoping that today's unrest would only spark more.

The crowd swayed with Alef's slightest movement. Everyone was waiting for his opening words.

"You couldn't hope for a better place to speak. So let's get on with it. Starting with the adhan. *Allahu Akbar.* God is grea—hey! What's . . ." The barrel on Alef's back shook, and the man holding it said in Arabic, "*Mahiza?*" What the?

Standing between the crowd and the soldiers aiming their guns to the sky were two men wearing suits. One was middle-aged and had a cart stacked with dully gleaming metal cases. The other had a youthful face with smooth, healthy skin. Beneath the wintry sky, they were spreading out a piece of white fabric.

"A white flag?" said the man behind Alef.

"The Red Cro—no, it's the flag of a country," said another.

When the two suited men stepped away from each other holding the upper corners of the cloth, an unmistakable flag unfurled, with a bright-red disk dyed straight through: the flag of Japan. Silence fell on the whole rotary as all eyes focused on these two men. The Anjians and Fengrens stood out clearly in the light brownish-gray sky, and the faintest sound of their engines could be heard. The two men began to walk toward Alef with long, slow strides as they held the sun disc between them. The young one took a megaphone from where it hung around his neck and put it to his mouth. Howling feedback echoed through the rotary. *What in the name of God are they doing?* Alef wondered.

"I'd like to express my gratitude to all my brethren who have assembled here today." Fluent Persian came pouring from the speaker. Alef was astounded to find that this one sentence was almost identical to the manuscript he had planned to use for his speech.

Kurosaki pushed along the cart fully loaded with Iridiums and glanced at Sekiguchi striding forward on the other side of the Japanese flag. Shaking the flag vigorously, he spoke in Persian with a dignified air. Though Kurosaki couldn't understand the words, he could hear Sekiguchi's megaphoned voice reverberating sonorously through the rotary. Not once did he falter or repeat himself.

Their objective was the red Peugeot and the man standing atop it.

When he and Sekiguchi were still standing in the narrow alley outside the rotary waiting for the right moment, Sekiguchi had identified him as Alef Kadiba. The dangerous-looking man standing behind him was either a member of Hamas or an extremist group connected to them. Remembering when Sekiguchi had said, "They're definitely armed," Kurosaki shuddered.

They continued to take slow steps toward the Peugeot straight ahead. Their frustratingly drawn-out pace reminded Kurosaki of the stabbing cold, but they couldn't allow themselves to move too fast and get apprehended by the soldiers behind them. At the same time, they'd be in even worse trouble if the man behind Alef clued into Sekiguchi's intentions and sparked up a riot. If that happened, the soldiers behind them and the drones overhead would surely transform the demonstration into a massacre without hesitation. So, as quickly as they could, but not so rushed as to raise anyone's guard, they continued forward.

From behind, Kurosaki could sense a stir among the soldiers and heard more metallic clacks. Most likely they were struggling to decide what to do with these two out-of-place men holding aloft the flag of a country that had diplomatic relations with Iran. Rotating his body from side to side, Sekiguchi continued speaking to the people gathered in the rotary. Kurosaki just shook his hand holding the flag and forced himself to smile. Everything they did was to appear incongruous and ensure that they could make contact with Alef. Kurosaki noticed that mixed in with the crowd around them were those who gave off the same vibe as the man behind Alef. They all had sturdy builds, had wrapped green scarves around their faces, and glowered at the two of them. Were they going to succeed?

Kurosaki's eyes met with those of an old man with a bent back.

In his whitish, clouded pupils appeared the clear signs of confusion. Kurosaki forced his tense cheeks into the shape of a smile and moved his head around, looking from face to face in the crowd. A scrawny youth wrapped in a dusty cloth. A man who looked like a laborer, gap-toothed mouth agape. An old woman carrying a grandchild. All of them squinted as they stared at Kurosaki and Sekiguchi.

"*Ooyomidouni* Amazon."

Finally Sekiguchi said something that Kurosaki could catch: Amazon. This was the part where he lectured them on how Internet shopping had transformed daily life. The manuscript for the speech that Sekiguchi was giving had been written as if they were an NPO from Japan come to support Alef's demo. By the way the crowd breathed, Kurosaki could tell that Sekiguchi's Persian was getting through to them as words. But there seemed little chance that these people would understand the convenience of the Internet, struggling as they were to maintain basic necessities. In all likelihood, they had never even seen a credit card, and Kurosaki could only wonder how this foreigner in a tidy suit speaking empty words might appear to them.

Looking straight ahead again, Kurosaki was surprised to see the Peugeot already almost right in front of them. The two of them had crossed the rotary before he'd even realized it. Surrounding them, a group of people were gathered who seemed somehow different from those before. Young people wearing modern clothes, their faces blushing in the hot air: students. Their eyes sparkled with excitement at the words of support that had come to them from a distant country.

Sekiguchi stopped and turned around as he spread out his arms, gestured for them to approach. Kurosaki imitated him, looking all around as he held the flag. Cutting through a wall of exhausted-looking laborer types, the students charged over. Alef, still standing on top of the car, broke into a smile. The man who had been standing behind him was suddenly nowhere to be seen. Sekiguchi raised his arm holding the megaphone and pointed it to the sky.

"Azadi interanet!"

"Azadi interanet!" Alef echoed, projecting his voice as he raised his fist toward the heavens.

Then he reached his arms out toward the students thronging around the Peugeot, beckoning for them to join in.

"Azadi interanet!" Countless fists went to the sky, as yellow confetti rained down.

Sekiguchi and Kurosaki edged over to the Peugeot through the pandemonium. Hopping down from the roof, Alef gave Sekiguchi a hug. Sekiguchi brought his lips near to Alef's ear and said in English, "Mr. Alef Kadiba, I presume? I'm glad you're safe."

Alef nodded again and again, shaking his trim mustache.

Sekiguchi grabbed Alef's shoulders and pulled him even closer. "I'm giving you these twenty Internet access modules and satellite phones. Please connect the access kit's local area network to the campus network. This will enable uncensored access to the network."

"Who are you two? Why . . ."

Sekiguchi yanked Alef in so close that their cheeks touched. "Mr. Kadiba. I have one condition," he said. "We're hoping that all of the students of this institute of technology will have free access to the Internet. Please connect all of the campus networks, including those in the dorms, to the Internet. I would really appreciate it."

"That's all you need from me?"

Sekiguchi nodded. "I've given you a voice that can reach the world. Only you can decide how to use it."

Yellow confetti was cast about from atop the gate. Kurosaki brushed pieces of the paper off him and looked through the gate to what was beyond it. Somewhere inside one of those dusty buildings was the scientist who had first conceived of the tethercraft, Dr. Jamshed Jahanshah.

One of the students who took the Iridium cases from Kurosaki shouted, "Free Internet!" and dashed into the campus.

2020-12-16T08:00 GMT

Project Wyvern

People of Earth, good morning! Our current orbital altitude is 370 km. The orbital hotel is operating as usual. There seems to have been a slight problem with the Wyvern return vehicle that was to serve as our backup spacecraft to go back to Earth, and we're currently investigating the cause. It's just one thing after another. Still, I'm not worried because our plan was to return from the ISS on the Soyuz to begin with. I'm sooo grateful for all your support!

There's something I've wanted to write about for a while but couldn't get to because of all the commotion about the Rod from God, so heere we go: food. I bet you're all curious to know what sorts of dishes are on offer in the microgravity environment of the orbital hotel. And since the first stage of the space tour is $50,000 for eight days, I'm sure everyone will want to be eating proper meals.

So I was preparing several drafts . . . But here's the problem. We have as much food as we could want, and it tastes delicious! I think most of you have seen the video of me and Ronnie having a meal, but the truth is, we had no trouble at all behind the scenes.

All we had to do was pull a tray out of one of the pantries embedded in the wall and put it in the microwave. The salad comes out fresh, the sushi rice comes out at body temperature, the soup and pasta come out at sixty-eight degrees Celsius, and the grilled fish comes out sizzling, all in their individual little bowls.

This is a triumph of molecular gastronomy. The hotel doesn't carry frozen dishes that have been preprepared, but dishes that are designed to come out of the microwave just perfect. I'm telling you, it's simply amazing.

The Project Wyvern chefs are stunningly talented.

I guess the only difference from Earth is the precautions taken to ensure that the food doesn't come apart and scatter about. Drinks would be a real hassle if they did that too, so they're kept in plastic containers. That's about the worst you have to put up with. I don't even want to think what it would be like to have raw hot pepper come flying into your nostrils while you were sleeping. Ronnie,

I can put up with your energetic nibbling, but please pay attention when you're eating!

Let's not forget the part everyone looks forward to: dessert. Today, it's . . . wait for it . . . "magnetoberry kiwitron wrap"! Don't get it? Neither do I! That's because this dessert doesn't exist on Earth. The slightly sour juice of berries is sealed inside a red, gelatinous nugget and wrapped in kiwi-flavored dough, kind of like pasta. Made with a pure molecular-synthesis recipe, there's no dish like it anywhere. Totally, utterly original.

Every day, Ronnie and I get to sample one of these creations.

On Earth, as we all know, many people are unable to eat as much as they need. Every day when we fly even ten degrees over Africa, there's no ignoring the parched, reddish-brown ground that we see. I hate to remember that the fish in the filet we're eating polluted the environment when it was farmed in Lake Victoria. When I see a clear pattern on the surface of vast plains, I'm aware that those are agricultural fields, and when we pass on to the night side of the Earth, I can sometimes see the glow of squid farms.

People have eaten up the Earth.

I wonder what kind of food we'll survive on when
we leave Earth. We hope to make molecular-synthesis
recipes the first step.

But, Head Chef Casper, please let me say just one
thing. I've had more than enough of your magnetoberry kiwitron wrap!

Guinea Pig Smark

11 Unity

Chaharshambe, 26 Azar 1399, 12:43 +0330
(2020-12-16T09:13 GMT)
Tehran Institute of Technology

Tumbling into a van, Kurosaki rolled up the flag and stuffed it in his bag. Alef had said earlier that he wanted to keep the flag as a symbol of their friendship, but they couldn't leave any evidence and were planning instead, with much reluctance, to cut up their talisman from a moment earlier and toss it.

Once Sekiguchi had given some kind of instructions to the driver, the engine started and the car began to roll over the rough pavement. Kurosaki felt the rumble of the pebbles scattered all over the road coming up through the creaking suspension.

"What a day," said Sekiguchi, passing Kurosaki a quilted field coat from the back of the van.

Putting his arms through the sleeves, Kurosaki felt the blood run to his fingertips and an itchy sensation climbing his skin. Considering the low temperature outside, they should have been dressed this warmly to begin with. But Kurosaki believed they had made the right move in deciding to wear only their suits, as this had allowed them to pose as out-of-place NPO members unfamiliar with the environment. Still, the tension moments earlier had made Kurosaki sweat heavily, draining his body completely of heat.

Every time the two men breathed, the windows fogged up white inside. Wiping the one closest to him, Kurosaki saw the parking circle in front of the institute rush by in the spaces between buildings. For just a moment, he glimpsed soldiers pointing their automatic rifles to the sky. Remembering how his back had been exposed to those barrels, Kurosaki felt a tremor rise from the base of his spine and reflexively hugged himself tight.

". . . Sorry. I seem to be tired."

"Of course, Kurosaki-san."

Sekiguchi flipped up the collar of his suit to cover his throat and began to zip up the coat he was wearing over it. His fingers moved supplely as he went on to button up the flap that covered the zipper, from bottom to top. Tracking Sekiguchi's motions with his eyes, Kurosaki arrived at his face and saw that his expression was just like always. Even though he had been in the line of fire just as Kurosaki had . . .

Questions welled up in Kurosaki's mind one after the other. Over the past few days, Sekiguchi's actions had gone far beyond what might be called simply "capable." He had clued in to the North Korean agents at Fool's Launchpad, slipped into the Nippon Grand Hotel used by Chinese spies, and even chartered a helicopter. Then, when he'd learned that JAXA's MDM had been hacked, he had turned this against the hackers by leaving behind his JAXA-issued device, activating a rather fishy app that sent blank messages. Everything up to that point could be put up to his inborn intelligence and the fact that he had a colleague in the NSC.

But the Iridiums were a different story. Though he claimed to have had them sent from Singapore, there was no way that importing equipment capable of bypassing the government's Internet barriers and censorship could be as easy as he had made it seem. How could he have gotten them through customs? Then there was the information about the demonstration. After meeting Alef and the students in person, Kurosaki was surprised to learn how small their movement was. Their demonstration wasn't exactly going to shake the nation the way the Arab Spring had. He hated to put it so harshly, but it was more like a game played by students with an inferiority complex toward the English-speaking world. If it hadn't been co-opted by the rebel groups, it never would have been so well attended that it was difficult to even enter the campus, and Kurosaki doubted that the intelligence agencies of Japan, which had fallen sorely behind the times, would have known who the organizer of such an insignificant protest was.

And when exactly did Sekiguchi come up with the strategy of securing their network access indirectly by giving the students Iridiums? The army had been called in because Hamas had tried to co-opt the demo, but somehow Sekiguchi had known about both the rebel involvement and the army's mobilization before they had even left Japan . . .

"Let's toast our success," said Sekiguchi, raising a pink plastic bag in his hand. "I had the driver go buy this for us. Just some water."

Sekiguchi scrunched the two plastic bottles together in one hand, opened the caps, and proffered one to Kurosaki.

"Thanks," said Kurosaki. "This time you—"

"Cheers," Sekiguchi interrupted, and lifted his bottle to take a gulp. "It was pretty cold out there, but only because we were sweating. The air is dry too. Go ahead, Kurosaki-san."

Urged on by Sekiguchi, Kurosaki took a sip. It felt good to have this liquid soak into the pasty membranes throughout his mouth.

Once again he tipped back the bottle and gulped down more refreshment.

"How about a smoke to go with that? I had him pick up some cigarettes too," said Sekiguchi, opening the seal on the pack adroitly and offering one to Kurosaki. "I bet you're dying to try shisha, though, since we're in Iran and all."

"You've done that before."

"Huh?"

"The cigarette. You don't smoke, right? The way you passed it over was pretty slick."

"That's because I was working for an organization with connections to China until last year. Members of the Communist Party still smoke like chimneys in their seats at conferences."

When Kurosaki lit the cigarette and took a puff, the heavy smoke clung to his freshly lubricated throat and he broke out coughing.

". . . This stuff is kind of harsh. I'm going to smoke the cigarettes I brought. So you were in China?"

Sekiguchi shrugged and thrust the pack of cigarettes he'd been playing around with into his coat pocket. "Yes, another country with no free access to the Internet."

"Were there demonstrations like this over there?"

"Sporadically, yes. But, boy, am I jealous." Sekiguchi put his lips to his bottle.

"Of what?"

"Of Kadiba and those students. They're incredibly unruly, but see how they're willing to risk their lives? Printing posters, searching the student body for people who believe in their cause, giving speeches. I doubt they expect things to change immediately, but I envy the fact that they're dedicating themselves to something. All I do is complain all the time."

Sekiguchi wiped the window with the sleeve of his coat.

At some point, the disturbance around the rotary had faded behind them, and office buildings came into view. Electric bikes began to fill the spaces between rows of cars as traffic thickened. The signs written only in Persian had disappeared, and Kurosaki could now see the logos of international corporations everywhere.

"The situation is the same in China," said Sekiguchi, "except here foreign companies that come hunting for oil have special permission to access the Internet without restrictions. So when people see this, of course they would—Kurosaki-san, are you okay?"

Listening to Sekiguchi, Kurosaki had suddenly been overcome with sleepiness. "Sorry," he said.

"Hang in there. Looks like a traffic jam is on its way. The hotel—is thirty minutes—away."

Sekiguchi's voice began to break up. Kurosaki struggled to keep his eyes open. Something rubbing against the back of his coat. Feeling tipsy. He closed his eyes slowly.

"Please take a nice, long rest. But before that—"

Kurosaki felt a cool hand on his cheek and then a thumb on the nape of his neck. When he opened his eyes, he realized that he was lying on his side across the backseat. Sekiguchi's face warped as it peered down from over him.

"Have you heard the phrase 'Great Leap'?"

". . . What the? No— Wait, the commander of the moon landing . . . but that was 'giant leap.'"

"I see you've never heard of it. Then can I ask you the next question?"

Kurosaki found himself nodding.

"How about the Hashimoto-san who works at the Satellite Intelligence Center?"

"Good guy. I think he—smoked Larks . . ."

Hashimoto had applied to JAXA, after being impressed by their CubeSat miniaturized satellites. But they were forcing him to babysit the Information Gathering Satellites—

Sekiguchi was nodding. Vaguely gazing at him, Kurosaki continued to talk about Hashimoto. Before Kurosaki realized it, Sekiguchi was asking him about something else: his colleague who had abandoned Japan, Shiraishi. As he tried to pull together the memories of his friend, Shiraishi's face, which he hadn't recalled in years, flashed in his mind's eye.

"Kurosaki-san, please take a nice, long rest."

The hand came away from his cheek, and Sekiguchi's face receded. Kurosaki heard the sound of a car door opening, and air began to blow in from outside. Looking in the direction of the sound, he saw Sekiguchi get out with an Iridium case.

Wed, 16 Dec 2020, 18:52 +0900 (2020-12-16T09:52 GMT)
Diet Members' Office Building, Tokyo

Takanori Hashimoto stared at the threadbare carpet in the Diet Members' Office Building and tried to think how he could get the reprimand he had been undergoing for a full thirty minutes now to stop. The minister of space policy standing over him and berating him had already exhausted his repertoire of abusive language and was beginning to repeat himself.

"Hashimoto-kun, you do realize the gravity of the situation! If we can't get in touch with JAXA at a time like this, we're screwed!"

If anyone was screwed, it was Hashimoto. While commuting to the Cabinet Satellite Intelligence Center in Shinjuku, he had received a report that communications with the Optical 7 Information Gathering

Satellite had been cut off, and had been called to the Diet Members' Office Building, where they had shut him up in this room. Almost immediately after, a report had come in that IGS-Radar 5 and 6 had gone silent. Then he'd watched as his laptop suddenly shut down. Following a notification of a forced logout, his computer had restarted and now would only display a pitch-black screen. He had tried toggling the power button, but this had been useless. His computer was now effectively a paperweight, doing nothing but occasionally spinning its fan.

Hashimoto later realized that his JAXA-issued smartphone and tablet had stopped working at the same moment as well. Their power had still been on, but the screens had remained black, and they had continued to give off heat as though processing something until their batteries had died about an hour ago.

Borrowing a phone from one of the secretaries, Hashimoto had contacted the JAXA help desk but was transferred to a busy reception number. He tried calling all the phone numbers that he could remember, but the result was the same in each case. JAXA's IT system had completely blacked out.

"Hashimoto-kun! Forty billion yen. You know what that is?"

This was the third time the minister had asked him this in the last thirty minutes.

"JAXA's budget for the entire IGS project."

Given the present circumstances, Hashimoto was wise enough to refrain from adding "five years ago." This year's budget actually exceeded ¥60 billion, an amount so large it was set to reach one-third of JAXA's annually shrinking total budget.

"So you do know, huh? That's exactly right. The problem is your failure to grasp how you've betrayed the Japanese people by causing a system crash in spite of their generosity."

That funding was used exclusively for IGS launches. JAXA was able to use it to improve the HIIA that conducted orbital insertion, but the rest of their budget, the money they could use for their original organizational goals of space development and operations, was shrinking every year.

"Your salary comes out of that too, dammit!"

"Yes, sir. I understand that, sir." Hashimoto had raised his head slowly so the minster wouldn't notice, but now he lowered it several centimeters. He couldn't go on groveling like this forever.

"If you have enough time to make a PowerPoint that says nothing but 'don't know,' 'cause unclear,' 'we'll investigate,' then how about you go run over to JAXA yourself and come back and tell us what's going on?! What do you expect us to do if North Korea launches a Taepodong?"

In preparation for that risk, Japan has one of the world's best missile-defense systems. You didn't know that? Hashimoto wanted to say, but held his tongue. The system was operated by the Ministry of Defense and worked independently of the IGS program. Hashimoto had already advised the minister that in a situation where every minute and second counted, satellites like the IGS units that only passed over the Korean Peninsula four or five times a day were completely useless. But Hashimoto had given up on his efforts to provide accurate information to this minister, who couldn't even visualize a sun-synchronous orbit no matter how many times he explained it.

"In your report, you claim that you lost communication with three groups consisting of five satellites—but according to the information we've received here, four groups consisting of eight satellites, which makes up the entire IGS fleet. And they've all fallen into the same condition. How the hell do you explain this?!"

The last time Hashimoto had managed to contact the Satellite

Intelligence Center in Shinjuku was at five in the evening, and he was now cut off from all sources of information. Since then, the situation had worsened, and, pathetically, the minister was now in possession of fresher news than he was.

"Eight satellites went down at the same damn time, so this must be JAXA's fault, no?!"

Hashimoto wasn't sure how that conclusion followed but found himself bowing his head automatically.

"I've been studying up on this too, you know. The hardware of the satellites may be outsourced to private manufacturers, but JAXA is surely involved with the software, operation, and control."

Wrong. That's what had been written in the original proposal ten years ago. In actuality, operation of the IGS was conducted exclusively by the Cabinet Satellite Intelligence Center. JAXA was only in charge of launches and operational observation, nothing more than what Hashimoto was doing right then. His position had been created in the first place because of how terrible communications were between the center, commanded by a man straight out of the Self-Defense Forces, and the manufacturers, who constantly waved about their technical jargon.

From what Hashimoto had heard, the man named Shiraishi who'd originally had his job had been demoted for an explosive rant directed at the previous minister of space policy. Later, he'd abandoned Japan after being headhunted by a Chinese space-development company—and he wasn't the only one. All the technicians who had been taken off astronautics for whatever reason—whether due to budget cuts, project cancellation, or transfer to an ailing project—had chosen a similar path.

Hashimoto was in his fourth year since being appointed as liaison for the IGS, and attractive offers had been coming his way too.

A space-development venture with its head office in the Cayman Islands wanted him to serve as manager for a small-scale satellite project revolving around something called the "Great Leap." Recently, he'd heard about a headhunter inside JAXA as well, and there was talk of a space-development venture in Hong Kong gathering personnel. While such overseas contracts might offer poor job security, many of Hashimoto's colleagues had chosen them anyway, rather than serve as specialists who had to bow down to laymen all the time.

"What's that look on your face about?"

Hashimoto forced down both his head and the discontent that rose all the way up to his throat as he stared at the carpet again. "My actions are inexcusable, sir," he said. "I'll look into the connection with JAXA as well. I'm going to visit headquarters in Ochanomizu and the Satellite Intelligence Center in Shinjuku. By first thing in the morning, I expect there should be some devel—"

"Yes! Tomorrow morning! Here at eight o'clock sharp! Washio, keep my schedule open!"

"Certainly, sir," said the minister's secretary, interrupting her typing of the meeting minutes long enough to move her mouse and click audibly several times.

Suddenly, Hashimoto felt the attraction of his two offers, Hong Kong and the Great Leap in the Caymans, surge in his chest.

Wed, 16 Dec 2020, 02:12 -0800 (2020-12-16T10:12 GMT)
Western Days Hotel

"Kazumi, wake up."

Along with someone calling out to him in English, Kazumi felt the slap of a soft palm on his cheek. Raising his sleep-glued eyelids, he saw dragon-patterned embroidery leap front and center into his field of vision. In gold thread that bulged from red linen, it was lit up from the base and appeared to stand before him in three dimensions.

Turning his head to look around, he saw a broad ceiling and then a man with thick eyebrows—NORAD serviceman Daryl Freeman. At last he remembered where he was and what was happening. He was in the bedroom of a hotel in Seattle, Western Days. Light came pouring from the adjacent lounge they were using as an operations center. Kazumi had been consigned to the bedroom, where he'd hurriedly changed and crawled into bed.

"It's 2 a.m.," said Daryl. "I'm sorry to disturb you when you've just gone to bed, but there's a call for you."

He pointed toward the open door, through which Kazumi could see walls covered haphazardly in silver sheets. Since Chris had wrapped up the meeting just before midnight, Kazumi calculated, he had been asleep for about two hours.

"Okay. I'll be right there." Kazumi sat up and put on the jeans and sweater he'd rolled up on the bedside table. Sitting on the edge of the bed to put on his shoes, he was reminded again that he wasn't in Japan, where wearing shoes indoors like this was unimaginable. He stepped into the gleaming silver operations center and looked back at the wall where the adjacent bedrooms were.

"Time to wake up, Kazumi," said Bruce. "I know it's a bit early, but we have a videoconference and we can't start without you."

"Akari is already in her seat," said Chris from somewhere behind him.

Looking back, Kazumi saw Daryl and Akari sitting at the table, an empty seat between them. Bruce sat off to one side, pointing at the whiteboard he was using in place of his display. There, Kazumi saw a face he hadn't seen in what felt like a long while: Jamshed. In a room filled with filaments of sunlight, the Iranian scientist reached out his hand and adjusted the angle of the camera. The sunbeams behind him wavered, blocked here and there by countless strips of yellow paper hanging from the ceiling.

Jamshed retracted his hand from the camera, raised it, and said in somewhat stiff English, "Hey, Kazumi. I introduced myself to be Jay. I am Jamshed Jahanshah." Jamshed scratched his cheek, flashed a white smile from beneath his mustache, and added, "Technically, I have my doctorate now. I am happy we can speak again immediately."

"It has been—" Kazumi recalled the day Jamshed had contacted him for the videoconference with the poor connection. They had spoken while Kazumi was watching the launch for Loki 9, which had been on Sunday. "Three days. I am in Seattle now."

Kazumi was grateful that his limited English ability had prevented him from coming up with the phrase "three *whole* days." For Jamshed, it had been *only* three days. But Kazumi felt as though he had been in Seattle for a week even though they had just arrived the evening before last.

"Bruce told me already. Seattle is a city at America. And seems the NORAD and even CIA were waiting for me." Jamshed put a hand to his breast and laughed. "Is like I am the important person. Make me nervous."

Chris raised her hand, and she became enlarged in the preview window for the video they were sending to Jamshed. "Dr. Jahanshah, you are without a doubt an important person. I am honored to be able to invite you, a genius scientist who conceived an incredibly unique spacecraft all by yourself, on to our team." Chris spoke even more slowly, with longer pauses between words, than when she was talking to Kazumi and Akari. "The CIA would like to hire you as a consultant on the space tethers. Please provide us with an estimate of the compensation you would like to receive."

"Compensation . . . I had not thought of that. Is not much I could use it for at Tehran." Jamshed touched his mustache and relaxed his cheeks.

"It doesn't necessarily have to be money. If your wish is to come to America, then please just let us know."

Hearing Chris's words, Kazumi's breath stopped. America. The country that had given birth to Ronnie Smark. Where passionate and talented individuals like Daryl went so far as to join the army there just for a chance to build up their careers. This remarkable place was where Chris was inviting Jamshed. When Kazumi saw the wide-eyed expression on the doctor's face, he asked himself for the first time: *If I were to leave Japan, would I have what it takes to succeed?*

"Wonderful . . . That is attractive proposal. Please let me think about it."

"Just let us know," said Chris and wrote QUESTION in big block letters on the whiteboard. "I'm sorry to have to write this for you by hand. Can you read it?"

"It is fine," said Jamshed. "English of these level is no problem. Screen is easy to see too."

A separate camera dedicated to displaying the whiteboard was sending its feed to Jamshed using a different account. Akari had set this up for them before Kazumi had even noticed.

"I wasn't expecting to be able to speak with you so quickly, Dr. Jahanshah, so we haven't prepared our questions yet," said Chris. "Over there right now . . . I guess it's shortly after noon. I'm very sorry to say this after you went through all the trouble of connecting us, but it's two in the morning here. Do you mind if we finish this up within about an hour? I'll arrange for us to have another meeting right away."

"Excuse me. I am thinking Kazumi is in Tokyo. How about we is have our next meeting at seven hours? Time difference is eleven and the half hours. When is night here is morning there."

"Well, you space people sure are good with time zones. Even CIA agents like us who are active around the world can't hold a candle," said Chris, and without any hesitation wrote *Scheduled Conference: 09:00 (Tehran 20:30)* on the whiteboard.

"How shall we begin?" Chris looked around at the members in their seats, and Akari immediately raised her hand.

"I'd like to know the communication format," she said. "If you were to design the space tethers yourself, Doctor, how would you design the application transfer interface? Also, what would be a good choice for the physical layer?" Akari began to enumerate the redundancies that would eliminate bit loss so as to secure a robust signal in a poor environment. "Once we have this information in hand, the CIA can root out the nodes transmitting and receiving the data."

Jamshed's eyes swam. ". . . Sorry, but I do not understand meaning. Application's layer?"

"That was just computer jargon," said Daryl, waving his hand with a laugh. "What she wants to ask you about is the communications protocol and so on for the space tethers. In particular, the method for transmitting telemetric data to base stations on Earth, the radio frequency and the data that signal carries. How would you standardize this?"

"So that is what she means. I guess everything is about computers over there."

"Not entirely. Kazumi uses a special sense to fly space tethers in his head."

"Then he might be kind of like me." Jamshed stretched his arm out behind him and pulled one of the sheets of hanging paper toward himself. It was covered in scribbled lines, numbers, Persian letters, and in a few places some English. "My computer is this and calculator. Anyways, about communication method and content. That is all on my paper."

"You must mean the section 'Robust Communication.' I saw it in the table of contents. Only part of the body of your essay has reached us."

"After our meeting I will send it once more. Space tethers do not need complicated information for their telemetry. That is one of advantages of space tether. According to my paper, all you is need is serial numbers, spatial coordinates guided by GPS, and motion vectors for terminal apparatuses."

"Can you read it?" asked Jamshed, writing the three figures on a piece of paper and holding it up beside his face. "To command a particular space tether to transfer from one orbit to another, all you have to do is send TLEs that will serve as their destination. With approximately three thousand steps of computational logic if you use Fortran, you can derive timing for activate Lorentz force required to shift from present position to that of destination TLEs."

Akari frowned faintly. Most likely she saw the programming language Fortran as a relic of the previous century. Kazumi felt the same way. Though he could follow Jamshed's line of thinking, it struck him as terribly out-of-date. At the same time, he found the simplicity of his system beautiful.

All you have to do is send TLEs that will serve as their destination. Kazumi ruminated on Jamshed's words. His space tethers had been equipped with the essentially unstable element of ballast that moved along the wire, and this allowed them to use their thrust in any direction. Based on feedback regarding whether they were approaching their target or not, the space tethers themselves could calculate the correct timing to accelerate and fire electrons from the electron guns in their terminal apparatuses in order to transfer to the correct orbit. It was a straightforward and robust system.

"Of course, this only applies at time I wrote paper," Jamshed continued, now looking toward Daryl. "But I imagine the type of programming language, processor, and sensors being used are more advanced than what I am familiar with. I have no way of knowing because I cannot connect to the Internet."

"How about when you send commands to multiple space tethers?" asked Daryl.

"All you do is send serial numbers followed by TLEs. If you vary slightly each command, then they will fly in mass formation."

"Dr. Jahanshah," said Kazumi, deciding to ask the question on his mind. "It doesn't seem to me that the space tethers kicking the SAFIR 3 along in orbit are being controlled by the method you just described. They appear to be moving according to a faster, more refined program."

"The TLEs are not absolutely necessary. Is possible to send timing to activate the Lorentz force as something like musical note. In that case, they would move more efficiently. Theoretically, their thrust would be multiplied four or five times."

"Would you be able to carry out such operations, Doctor?"

"No. I said 'theoretically,' didn't I?"

Jamshed turned around again and drew another piece of paper toward himself. On it was a diagrammatic map of the world with numerous arrows and numbers scrawled here and there all over it. Lined up densely at the bottom were different times alongside a zero and a one. Kazumi supposed that the arrows represented the "footholds" of the space tethers, namely geomagnetism, while the zeros and ones represented on/off states for the Lorentz force.

Jamshed compared the angle of the revolving space tethers to the direction of Earth's magnetic field and calculated the timing to activate the Lorentz force. None of the calculations were particularly difficult on their own, but their large quantity taken together presented a serious challenge—and here he was doing it all on paper.

"You have to think about space tethers' rotation, direction of geomagnetism, and the intensity all together. Since space tethers rotate in high velocity, their clocks would need to be accurate to millisecond, and their geomagnetism database would need to be in arc seconds."

Jamshed patted the paper with the back of his hand and puffed out his chest proudly. Being able to do such calculations by hand was indeed impressive, and Kazumi thought that Jamshed must have cultivated the same sense that he used when conducting his "ritual."

"However, I am only speaking theoretically. I can show you calculations, but I am not think is possible to realize these in practice."

Kazumi noticed Bruce and Daryl fidgeting uncomfortably. They seem to be wavering about whether to tell Jamshed that the practical problems he saw could be solved easily. The coordination of the clocks, the geomagnetism database, and the massive amount of calculations he had mentioned would not be problematic at all. The times sent by GPS satellites were so precise they needed relativistic corrections. For the geomagnetism database, they could also consult a map through NASA a hundred times more accurate than the one Jamshed wanted. And as for the size of the calculations, well, that would just be a matter of—

"Let me just try to put it together," Akari muttered in Japanese, and began to tap at the keyboard on her left wrist with her arms still crossed.

Wed, 16 Dec 2020, 02:25 -0800 (2020-12-16T10:25 GMT)
Pier 37 Warehouse, Seattle

Typing on the keyboard on his lap, Shiraishi listened to the sound of the increasingly heavy snowfall tapping the metal-framed window. A blizzard was approaching.

Facing the window as she spoke on the phone, Chance said something in Korean and hung up.

"It's done," she said. "Leaving it up to the Cyber Front was the right choice. They may have gone a bit overboard, but they found Kurosaki and Sekiguchi."

Shiraishi took one final look at the code he was in the middle of writing and put the screen of his tablet to sleep. The Cyber Front agents had used Shiraishi's account to access JAXA from all over the world, completely trashing their whole system. They had failed to break into the computers related to JAXA's development arm but had got their hands on all of the data contained in the regular office servers, computers, and smartphones, along with other mobile devices.

"They finally deleted your account."

". . . Oh." Shiraishi pushed his glasses up onto his nose and exhaled a long breath into the shelter of his palm, fogging up his visual field.

The last thing that had connected him to JAXA and Japan was now gone. The thirty-two-letter password and eight-letter ID that he could not bring himself to completely forget, even after abandoning the organization and his own country, were now just a string of meaningless characters. All he had brought with him from Japan was his body and a pair of bent glasses.

It seemed to him as though he were floating above the floor. What emotion was this? The same sense of loss he'd experienced when he'd realized that the satellite he'd designed for the China National Space Administration in Shanghai had been a mere reproduction of a project already realized by America and the EU? Or when the scout from North Korea had brought him to Pyongyang and they had shredded his Japanese passport? No. It was different. He had merely gained another kind of freedom.

His fogged-up glasses cleared. Beyond his sinewy hand, he could see Chance staring at her smartphone.

"So where did those two go, then?"

"Kurosaki and Sekiguchi are in Tehran. According to an application to travel abroad that we pulled from a photocopier cache, they departed the day before yesterday. To meet with Dr. Jahanshah." Chance explained that they had most likely gone to pick up the remainder of Jamshed's paper, and Shiraishi nodded.

"Do you think Kazumi and his team can find a way to stop the space tethers?" asked Chance.

"Even if they figure out how they work, stopping them is impossible."

Since the space tethers consisted of little more than tiny terminal apparatuses, removing them from orbit would be an incredible challenge. They would only appear as something like debris on radar, making it difficult to pinpoint their precise locations, and even if a device capable of deorbiting them could make a successful rendezvous, the tethers would come flying in at three kilometers per second. There was simply no safe way to stop them.

Blocking their communication pathways to the base stations would also fail to solve the problem because the tethers had what Jamshed described in his paper as a "survival instinct." In other words, they were installed with a program that autonomously alternated between maintaining their orbits and generating their energy, so even if communications with the ground were cut off, they would in all likelihood remain in the same orbit for some time.

"I can't even think of a way to remove them from orbit myself," said Shiraishi.

"So you're saying you've put things up there that can't be cleaned up later. Headquarters will have a fit when they hear that."

"That's why I'm developing a web application that even those guys can use. When the Cloud completes its job, all they have to do is use the app to increase their altitude." Shiraishi tapped his tablet with the back of his hand.

"When will you give it to us?"

"If I can work on it tomorrow, I'll give it to you by nighttime . . ."

"We're moving tomorrow. Can you have it ready the day after that? I want you to hurry on this. The more approaches we have to work with, the better. Maybe there's nothing that you and Kazumi can do about it, but NORAD and NASA might still find a way to stop us."

"NORAD?"

"When we were rummaging through the JAXA servers, we found an email that Kurosaki sent to NORAD's Colonel Lintz. The body was encrypted with PGP, but we were able to read the subject. 'Urgent: Unusual SAFIR 3 Orbit Caused by North Korea.' "

"When?"

"The day before yesterday. This means that the American government, in the form of NORAD, has been in touch with Kazumi, who's read Dr. Jahanshah's paper."

". . . I see." Shiraishi looked up at the ceiling. He'd never thought that they could keep their scheme secret forever, but things were developing much faster than he'd anticipated. Clearly, Kazumi had gathered some highly accurate information if he had succeeded in getting these usually plodding bureaucracies to move with such speed.

"We've been . . . found out. They know about the Cloud and the space tethers too."

"That's not necessarily true. However, I'm going to report to headquarters in the North about the *possibility* they've been exposed, so let me know if there's anything you'd like me to add."

"Don't be naive, Chance! The Orbital Cloud is out in the open now! Put that in your report!" Shiraishi closed his eyes and filled his lungs with the dusty warehouse air. The time had come at last. "Tell the Supreme Leader we're proceeding to a stage in which we can spread even greater terror. We're going to change the situation before Kazumi Kimura's voice becomes influential."

Chance's body tensed up, and she raised her index finger to her forehead. She was preparing to make a mental map of Shiraishi's explanation.

"You don't need to do that," said Shiraishi. "It's easy to remember. First of all, the orbital hotel. While the majority still believes that the second stage of SAFIR 3 is the Rod from God, we'll bring it even closer. So close that the Smarks can see it with their naked eyes."

"Good idea. That should buy us some time."

"Exactly. For a while, anyway."

Chance opened her eyes wide as though she'd suddenly sensed something. "If we lay on that much pressure," she said, "the American military will probably try to intercept the Rod from God immediately."

Shiraishi felt his lips curling up into a sneer. "But their target is just an empty rocket body. They'll fall right into our trap. The American army will be a laughingstock. And right in in front of the eyes of those panicking fools—" Shiraishi stared with intensity into Chance's eyes. "We'll conduct a massacre in low Earth orbit. I was planning to take my time and make it look like an accident, but the situation has changed. We can't give them time to think up a countermeasure. Instead, we'll send in all forty thousand of the space tethers and simultaneously knock all of the two thousand satellites in LEO down to Earth!"

"Wait. That's . . ." Mouth gaping, Chance's pale eyes quivered.

Yes, that's the face, thought Shiraishi. *That's the expression I'm going to stamp on all humankind.*

"Are you afraid, Chance?" Shiraishi curled the edge of his mouth up even farther. His dry lips split open, and the pain amped up his tension. "We're going to start a war."

Shiraishi imagined the hordes of tethers that composed the Cloud scattering in different directions and swarming on the satellites. The satellites would be struck by the terminal apparatuses of the space tethers at low relative velocity and cease to function or even spin out of control, dragging a tail of plasma with them as they fell into the atmosphere. Space stations, telescopes, GPS, communications satellites, weather observation satellites, reconnaissance satellites. All of the orbital infrastructure that humankind had come to depend on would be obliterated in an instant, and radioactive-material-filled satellites would cause widespread chaos when they rained down on the Earth. So be it.

Humankind would just have to start over. Enterprises involved with orbit had grown bloated, vulnerable to the slightest mistake, and the efforts of the have-nots had been frustrated by more than seventy years of space domination by the world powers. Better to start again from scratch than to try to fix such a system, with all its high-altitude satellites, space stations, accumulated debris, and complex tangle of rights and interests.

"There's no need to declare war. All of a sudden, one day, all of the satellites will just disappear. In the wake of the terror this will cause, the nations carrying out the Great Leap will be able to monopolize space development for the first time!"

". . . But if we do that, low Earth orbit will become an ocean of debris. You can hardly call that a Great Leap."

"I'm not going to sully the springboard for the Great Leap. I'm going to carefully knock each man-made object one by one into the atmosphere." Shiraishi stepped close to Chance as she stood by the window. "Contact them immediately!"

"North Korea doesn't have the courage for that."

"You sure about that?" Shiraishi moved in so close to Chance that his forehead pressed against hers. "What if we make someone a scapegoat and blame them for everything?"

Chance frowned. *You don't get it?* thought Shiraishi. There's only one person who could knock down every low-orbit object in a flash and show the way toward a new future. Someone who would never again stand on center stage—

"Me."

Wed, 16 Dec 2020, 03:21 -0800 (2020-12-16T11:21 GMT)
Western Days Hotel

The discussion with Jamshed shifted to how they might remove the space tethers from orbit. Kazumi and Daryl would shower Jamshed with questions, Jamshed would answer, and Akari would jump in with an observation from time to time.

Bruce followed what the four of them were saying and took notes. These he planned to send to the George Bush Center for Intelligence in Langley once the discussion was finished, so that the CIA could evaluate and substantiate their information before their next meeting first thing in the morning. This approach had been decided on by Chris, as she didn't want to burden the team with such chores.

"I am devoted one chapter of my paper to what I called the space tethers' 'survival instinct.' Space tethers can autonomously alternate between generating energy and using their thrust while waiting in orbit for a new destination. I am also proposed Fortran program for this that could be realized in approximately two thousand steps."

"Do you think the space tethers flying up there right now are equipped with this survival instinct?" asked Kazumi.

"I do not know. I cannot tell how carefully North Korean engineer is following my paper," said Jamshed in a joking voice. "My paper is poorly put together. My academic advisor would not read it, so there are some calculation errors and other problems."

Bruce thought it would probably be better to ask the protégé of the suspected mastermind. "What do you think, Akari?" he said.

"You mean about this so-called instinct? If it were me, I'd install it. The term 'autonomous' is attractive in itself, and if I were presented with the code to make it work I can't see why I wouldn't use it."

Chris clapped her hands together. "I'm going to make the call," she said. "It has this survival instinct. Continue to investigate under that assumption."

"That's just my opinion," said Akari, looking surprised. "Are you sure?"

"Yes. We have to decide either one way or the other. What do you think, Doctor?"

"If your objective is to make them inoperative, I think that is good way."

Something about what Jamshed said gave Bruce pause. He listened closely to what Jamshed said next.

"I am talking about method of stopping them. Most effective way would be seizing base stations operated by North Korea or seize transmission themselves and take control of tethers."

Daryl sunk into his chair. "I guess our only option is to search for the base stations after all," he said.

A similar supposition had been offered once before, but now that they'd heard the tangible idea of the survival instinct from Jamshed's lips, it was settled.

"Doctor, can you tell me the communication formula one more time?" Akari cut in. "The 'upstream' and 'downstream' from the satellite—how would you order the transmissions?"

Jamshed smiled and picked up a pen and one of the yellow sheets of paper. He was now able to understand because Akari had stopped filling her sentences with jargon. Running the pen over the paper, he jotted down the parameters.

"The information going up is the space tether's ID and TLEs, or its ID and the time to activate Lorentz force. Information coming down is its ID, its coordinates obtained from GPS, and vectors of the terminal apparatuses, in that order. If there is information from this observational devices, it would probably be tagged on afterwards."

"So you can use GPS in space too?" asked Akari, nodding her head and typing on her keyboard.

"In low orbits, yes," said Daryl drawing a picture of a GPS satellite on the diagram and connecting it to the space tether.

"What about the radio waves used for the transmission?"

"At my experiments, I am used AM waves. That was only kind of radio I could get my hands on. Since it only went up fifty kilometers, I was able to ignore reflection from ionosphere." Jamshed told them about his experiments with balloons. He had used them to drop his prototype loaded with an AM transmitter that sent its coordinates and vectors as a beeping sound from the stratosphere and verified the occurrence of the Lorentz force. He then recorded this with a tape recorder and transcribed it to paper by hand. "Of course, AM attenuates and reflects in ionosphere, so I am proposed VHF wave on my paper. Was tough work. Counting my fingers in time to beep, beep. And I used 8 bits including check digit, so I had to use both hands. Might have been more efficient if had used 5 bits though."

Jamshed showed them the back of his hands and extended the pinky of his left hand and the thumb, index finger, and ring finger of his right hand, smiling.

"Forty-three," said Akari, reading aloud the number of bits his fingers indicated.

"You can read it too?!" said Jamshed, clapping his hands together with a laugh.

"You are very passionate about this," said Kazumi, looking as excited as the others.

"Is disappointing for me that I could not bring this space tether to fruition with my own hands. I would love to meet North Korean engineer who realized it for me. I wonder what he did about this problem I could not solve. I am incredibly interested to know."

Something about what Jamshed said gave Bruce pause again. What was going on in orbit right then was no test run, and—

"I've put together the code to search for the base stations," said Akari, interrupting Bruce's thoughts. "We can make our query with both SQL and Hadoop. Can I have you search all global communications?"

Bruce turned to look at Chris. Chris looked back and gave him the thumbs-up as Akari's message arrived. It was a go.

"Sure," said Bruce. "You're really fast."

First he checked to make sure that Akari's email was formatted as a letter of request and forwarded it to headquarters. Within a few hours, the search query created by Akari, a mere civilian hacker, would run through the full CIA database that steadily accumulated nearly all global communications. This included the communications of Africa, Southeast Asia, most countries in the EU, the nations of the Pacific Rim, America, and so on, but it excluded the regular members of the UN Security Council who were exempt from surveillance by international agreement. While Bruce was doing this, Kazumi and Daryl were never short on questions, and the discussion shifted to how the space tethers were made.

"I am guessing you can use substrate of smartphone as this central processing unit for miniature space tether. But on this case you must be knowing better than me. Do most current smartphones have motion sensors attached?"

"Of course," said Daryl. "Some are equipped with atomic clock chips and compasses."

"That is incredible! I am simply astounded on the progress of technology. Not just GPS, but compass, motion vector sensor, and atomic clock . . . You are not going to tell me that some have radios even?"

"They most certainly do."

"If that is true, you could make space tether with just smartphone and electron gun. All you have to do is decide the material for the tether. Several years ago, I heard that Japanese audio manufacturer had succeeded in fabricating graphene rolls—"

"He looks so happy," Chris whispered in Bruce's ear.

"He sure does. I bet he had no one to talk to."

Jamshed had gone on theorizing all alone in a backwater, persisting with his research while cut off from information and without even getting proper attention from his academic advisor. Now he had the opportunity to talk with people like Akari and Daryl, who would gladly teach him about the technology of the future. Of course he was happy.

Bruce's smartphone began to vibrate in his pocket. Under the table, unseen by the cameras in the room, he unlocked his screen and read the notification. He had to confirm whether it was something he could tell Jamshed, and maybe also Akari and Kazumi. Fortunately, the notification was related to the space tethers. Finding a gap in the lively discussion, Bruce cut in.

"Excuse me," he said. "I have some news. Kazumi's guess was correct. Japan's IGS are down. The Wyvern return vehicle has also been hit. Apparently, a severe pressure leak was discovered. What the hell is this?"

The Project Wyvern blog had reported a "slight problem" with its return vehicle, but several hours ago, it had entered into an unplanned rotation. Gathering the intermittent transmissions, terrestrial bases had verified that the pressure inside the craft had reached zero moments earlier. NASA had just been informed.

"The space tethers," muttered Akari.

Bruce chewed his lip. He had been warning NASA through the CIA, but the view that space tethers were the problem had not yet gained wide acceptance. Despite the fact that the team had known what was happening, they had been unable to do anything about it.

"The entire IGS fleet?" asked Daryl.

"Four groups, eight units, all down."

"I'm going to check NORAD's observational data. Dr. Jahanshah, please excuse me for a moment." Daryl called up his NORAD device on his table display and entered IGS, bringing up a chart with rows of numbers. "The orbits of the IGS fleet have not changed at all since yesterday. However, the waves they reflect have gone random. This tells me the satellites are spinning. Communication with them has been cut off because their antennas are no longer pointing toward the base stations."

Daryl checked up on the Wyvern return vehicle in the same way and confirmed that it was also spinning. However, he explained, NORAD's observational data could not tell them whether or not holes had opened up in any of the objects.

"What's the matter?" said Jamshed with a quizzical look.

After receiving permission from Chris, Daryl explained the situation to Jamshed.

"I see. The space tethers nudged them," said Jamshed, when he learned that no debris was being dispersed and that Daryl had guessed that the satellites were spinning based on the reflected waves.

"Rotation velocity of space tethers can be controlled at will," he explained. "Once certain velocity is reached, tether cable will never get tangled up. Terminal apparatuses can be configured freely to any velocity, from that of punch, or, depending on the material, to ten times that of the rifle bullet, ten kilometers per second. They have struck this IGS lightly and smashed Wyvern spacecraft at high velocity. What fascinating idea this engineer has come up with. Amazing that he could drive satellites into shutdown with such simple method."

"It is a disappointment," said Kazumi. "Space tethers could do so much more than that."

"Maybe so. But even a space tether without any unnecessary equipment can work simply by being in orbit."

Bruce felt like Jamshed and Kazumi were having two conversations that didn't quite match up. Though he suspected that part of this was because neither of them were native English speakers, he also sensed that there was something more fundamental about their differences. But before he could get any further than this, Chris looked up at the clock and clapped her hands.

"I'm sorry, but can we wind this up for today? Thank you, Dr. Jahanshah. It's only the third day for you, Kazumi, since you first encountered the space tethers, so I bet your head is just bursting with information. Let's go off to sleep and be ready for our meeting tomorrow."

"Kazumi, you are not tether-propulsion-system specialist?" asked Jamshed, with a look of surprise.

"Unfortunately, no. I'm not." Scratching his head, Kazumi explained that he was an amateur and that his only connection to space was through Meteor News. "Even though I've had three whole days since we rushed off from Japan, we've been busy with all kinds of things, and I haven't had a chance to properly read your paper. I'm very sorry."

"An amateur . . . incredible. You are actually telling me that you have come to these level of understanding on only three days?"

"Two days," said Daryl. "Keep in mind that Kazumi was on the move and caught up in all sorts of trouble. I've been on this for only one day, and my head is jam-packed. The time I've spent on this has been truly stimulating. Thank you for joining us today, Doctor."

"You too . . . Well, I better not let myself fall behind. I will take a look at data you have all gathered. Let us meet again in five hours," said Jamshed, and with that the conference was over.

"Bedtime, kids," Chris called out, and Kazumi and Akari made their way to their bedrooms, Daryl to the bathroom.

"You think the professor's all right?" said Bruce, facing Chris.

"Take care with him," said Chris with a frown. "We'll be in trouble if he gets discouraged."

Bruce nodded. Jamshed had spent years developing this technology. This was his first time meeting engineers who could wield it as smoothly as if it were their own arms and legs. At the moment, he had to be merely surprised, but if the situation continued, he would probably begin to feel that he himself was outdated. They couldn't let that happen. If he could learn to use contemporary tools with the same natural ease as the others, he would likely be able to produce even better results and overcome his disadvantaged position due to being born in a have-not country.

"I think the professor will realize this too if he keeps up his contact with Kazumi and Akari. So I'm going to hold these meetings regular—oh, what's wrong, Daryl?"

Daryl had been in the bathroom for a while and had just come out. "Permission to speak, ma'am?"

"Go ahead."

"I noticed a moment ago when I looked at my NORAD device that SAFIR 3 has started to move."

"What? How come you didn't tell us before?"

"Because this involves Seed Pod, which we have yet to explain to Kazumi and Akari. If SAFIR 3 continues to accelerate at this rate, it'll enter a one-kilometer-radius range this evening. When is Seed Pod going to be run? Operations command set it for 1700 hours if I remember correctly."

Chris looked at the doors of the bedrooms Akari and Kazumi were in. "It's been bumped up to 1300."

"So . . . They're actually going to do it. Have the Smarks been informed?"

"Orders have been sent to the orbital hotel to accelerate randomly. When Seed Pod is implemented, we'll also have them shut down the power because it could be affected by the ASM-140's Blackout."

"Why didn't you stop them?" said Daryl, putting his hands on the table in apparent indignation. "You must know it's pointless. They're just trying to distract us from the space tethers."

"We've reported it," said Bruce, looking up at Daryl. "But you must understand that this operation isn't something that'll get called off just like that. No one has taken responsibility for knocking out the IGS and Wyvern return vehicle. They'll be treated as accidents. Not a single organization anywhere currently sees the space tethers as a threat."

Daryl's hand clenched into a fist on the table.

"I'm frustrated about this too," said Bruce. "I expect Seed Pod to be a total waste. But try putting yourself in the Smarks' shoes. From their perspective, the Wyvern return vehicle has been put out of commission by an accident with no clear cause. They have no choice but to go to the ISS, and all the while they're being haunted by some mysterious spacecraft. Given the situation, do you have any idea how stressful it would be if they were told that organizations on Earth were doing nothing at all about it?"

Daryl hung his head.

"Our main tasks right now are to find the base stations that are communicating with the space tethers and uncover the spies using the honeypots we've placed all over the city. We'll take care of sending in a thorough report on the space tethers."

"Daryl," said Chris. "Leave it up to Bruce today, and please get some sleep. We're going to be even busier at daybreak. A mountain of information about the tether communications will arrive from the CIA. The snow's going to get heavier too, so we'll be working here the whole time."

"Yes, ma'am. You two please get some rest too. We need you in good shape for tomorrow." Daryl headed for the bathroom again.

Chris put her hand on her shoulder and rotated her neck. Taking a cue from Chris, Bruce sunk into his seat and thought back on what they'd promised Daryl. For him and Chris, the real work began now.

"I'm sure I don't need to say this," Chris said, "but please hurry up with the report. If we don't satisfy their desire for recognition, the team's energy will drop."

Bruce rolled his shoulders and opened the report he'd started writing. He completely agreed with Chris. No matter how much motivation united the team now, it would quickly fade if their efforts weren't recognized. In fact, the higher the motivation, the greater the risk of despair.

"I wanted to ask your opinion about the mastermind, but it's this guy, right?" Bruce opened Ageha Shiraishi's file. Serving as profile pics were images from his JAXA days and one extracted from his videoconference with Jose Juarez. Perhaps because Shiraishi wore the same glasses in the extracted picture, he didn't seem to have changed much. The file contained information about how he had quit JAXA, given up being Japanese, gone over to China, and fallen off the map five years ago, as well as documents created by several CIA departments. In the introduction to his psychological analysis, it said "Pretend genius odd-job man." *Harsh as always*, thought Bruce.

"Ah. So I see the profiling is complete," said Chris.

"Yeah. There's hardly any information from recent years, but there's a fascinating analysis of his connection to North Korea."

The section that Bruce indicated pointed out that the activity of North Korea's Cyber Front had shifted to high-level operations ever since Shiraishi had disappeared from China. Until then, they had never succeeded at anything more than large-scale denial-of-service attacks, but around 2015 they had assembled a large number of enslaved computers code-named "Sleeping Gun" and had since succeeded in hacking into remote data centers and social media networks. The fact that they exploited security holes discovered by Shiraishi when he was in Japan had apparently caught the attention of the CIA analyst. These activities could then be seen as precursors to the advertisement deception and translation-engine contamination subterfuges in the current case.

"They really did their homework," said Chris.

"Well, that's their job. Oh yeah, we also got something about his connection to the space tether."

Bruce opened the report from the psychological profiler. It hypothesized that the trigger for Shiraishi's leaving Japan had been "the collapse of JAXA's inductive-tether program, in which he had an emotional investment." When Shiraishi went to North Korea and saw Jamshed's paper, he must have decided to take another stab at realizing the failed dream from his Japan days.

The analysis went on to discuss his connection with North Korean astronautics as well. A few years after Shiraishi disappeared, there had been a spike in projects inserting satellites into low orbits, though most of the satellites had apparently fallen into the atmosphere. Now Bruce could see why. They had been diligently launching space tethers. There was no need to use the third stage of a rocket to insert them into a precise orbit because they could transfer between orbits using their own energy. All the North Koreans had to do was pack the high-payload second stage with them and then scatter them randomly into space. The tethers could hide out in orbit for years, until their day arrived.

Akari Numata and Shiraishi's relationship had been that of uncle and niece, and did not seem to have developed beyond that of computer-engineering teacher and protégé, just as Akari had claimed. This came as a relief to both Chris and Bruce.

"How should we tell this to Akari?" asked Bruce. "She seems to want to believe that he was forced into it by North Korea."

". . . Hmm. Let's let her believe that for now. We can discuss how to broach it again later."

"Understood. Wha—another email . . . Oh, man."

"What's the matter?"

"The base station search result has come back from headquarters. Along with lots of wonderful complaints."

Bruce showed his laptop screen to Chris, pointing to digits reading two hundred thousand to six hundred thousand. "This is the number of PCs sending and receiving signals that meet Akari's specifications."

The investigator had commented that desktop computers all over the world seemed to be serving as transmitters. At the cyber center in Langley, it was 6:30 in the morning and the investigator, who felt he'd wasted his time conducting a pointless search at this early hour, had sarcastically concluded, "Could you narrow it down a bit?"

"If one or two of them turns out to be what we're looking for," said Bruce, "you think we'll still get any credit?"

Just downloading the search results would take two hours. They would have to consult with Akari about it.

2020-12-16T12:00 GMT
Project Wyvern

Today is Space Experiment Day.

I had Ronnie lift me up in the center of the room and gently let go, leaving me floating there with nothing to support me. What do you think would happen in a situation like this?

No matter how much you paddle the air, you won't move forward. You can try kicking and stretching, but all you'll do is keep spinning round and round in place around the center of gravity in your stomach. If you ever stay at the Wyvern, this is one thing I'd love for you to try!

There's only one way to move when you're in this state. Strip off your shirt or pants and hurl it at something. This will send your body moving in the opposite direction. It is a wonderful moment.

This is the principle by which spacecraft propel themselves.

I didn't think I'd be writing any formulas on this blog, but let me include just one:

$$\Delta v = v_e \ln {}^{m_0}/_{m_f}$$

This is called the Tsiolkovsky rocket equation.
It's a rule for rockets that was set down in 1903,
more than a century ago. It describes a law that all
rockets using propellant follow. Want to know how
much speed you can get if you shoot out propellant
at a particular speed from a spacecraft of a particular weight? Weighing 58 kg, if I were to throw
my 500 g pants at 3 m/s, I would reach a velocity of
0.2 m/s. So pathetic I might as well be stationary.

By expelling propellant at a higher velocity than
this and accelerating in a horizontal direction, the
hotel moves in the high orbit of the ISS (be careful
to remember that it doesn't accelerate upwards!).

The important point here is that in order to move
an object with a lot of mass, you need a lot more
propellant, or, to put it in simple terms, fuel.
Once you use up all your propellant, you will continue orbiting at the same velocity. Just like me
when I was left unsupported in space, you'll become
very lonesome.

Several spacecraft that don't use such fuel have been
conceived: a solar cell ship that propels itself by
catching light, a magsail that uses the electromagnetic force of the sun, and the tether-propulsion
system. All of them generate only a small amount
of power, but they're all indispensable. At Project

Wyvern, we're currently accepting applications from engineers who can make such technologies a reality.

Calling all people with exciting ideas!

To conclude, I have some news. The Wyvern return vehicle that carried up this orbital hotel will be dropped into the atmosphere. I'll let you know when the schedule for reentry has been decided. I think there's going to be a big shooting star. Look forward to it!

Little Rocket Smark

12 Seed Pod

"Our weapon for this operation is the ASM-140, a piece of equipment none of you have used before. Colonel Claude Lintz, chief of Orbital Surveillance at NORAD, where the R&D for this weapon was carried out, has agreed to be here today."

The voice of Operation Seed Pod's operational commander, Colonel Waabboy, reverberated throughout the briefing room where the team members were assembled, seated neatly in rows. Lintz raised one hand briefly and then turned his eyes to the map of North America that hung from the ceiling. Frowning, he noticed that the words "Rod from God" were written beside the line drawn from west to east that designated their target. He had pushed for the name "SAFIR 3 R/B," but apparently he had been unsuccessful.

"The air force's knowledge of space is limited," Waabboy said. "So please listen closely. Colonel, if you please." He retreated to the other side of the whiteboard.

Lintz was hoping for a quick escape from this performance.

Whether the team understood how the ASM-140 worked or not was irrelevant: it launched automatically, and once it had approached its target, it operated automatically.

"Let me put our objective in simple terms," Lintz said, tapping the map with his baton. "Our target will follow this route into sector 26 of the North Pacific Air Defense Zone. Its altitude is 390 kilometers, and current observations suggest that its velocity upon entry will be 7.6 kilometers per sec—yes?"

Captain Ricky McGillis had his hand raised. McGillis, Lintz knew, was the F-15 pilot who'd actually have the ASM-140 on board.

"Pardon me, sir," McGillis said, "but could we have those figures in feet? Mach numbers for velocities would also be helpful, sir."

The woman sitting beside McGillis—Second Lieutenant Madu Abbot, who was to pilot the accompanying F-22 Raptor carrying the observational equipment—looked at him sideways. "You haven't read the briefing material yet?" she hissed.

"Sure, I read it," McGillis said, then turned back to Lintz. "I just want to make sure we all share the same mental image, sir."

A few members of the maintenance team were nodding as well. Lintz smiled thinly. They'd asked for it.

"It seems we have some attendees who don't know the speed of sound," he said. "Fine. I'll start again from the beginning."

Sighs filled the briefing room. "Take it back, Ricky," someone muttered. Lintz ignored them and held the tip of the baton in his other hand like a teacher.

"Is everyone here at least aware that the speed of sound varies depending on air pressure and humidity? In fact, what we call the speed of sound is a figure defined by the physical properties of the medium we call the atmosphere—yes, Captain McGillis?"

"I apologize, sir. Metric units are fine."

"Oh, it's no trouble for me. There appear to be quite a few team members who find them hard to visualize. It can't hurt to do the conversion." Lintz wrote two figures on the whiteboard beside the map. "The altitude is 1,280,000 feet, entry velocity is Mach 23."

The room erupted with chatter. "Did he say *million*?" "Mach 23? Really?"

"Colonel, if I may?" Waabboy said, taking up a position before the whiteboard. "Surprised?" he barked at the assembled members. "The figures are correct. This mission involves shooting down the fastest target, at the highest altitude, the US Air Force has ever engaged. It contravenes COPUOS guidelines and as such is being conducted in secret. But eventually—maybe ten years from now, maybe thirty— the details will be made public. And by that time, we will most likely have entered an age of competition for hegemony over space."

Waabboy fell silent and raised his clenched fist to his breast.

"When that day comes, your successful interception and neutralization of the Rod from God during Operation Seed Pod will be revealed as the shining milestone it was. Wherever, whenever, whatever the objective, the US Air Force defeats its enemies. I am certain you will have no trouble demonstrating this. Understood?"

"Yes, sir!" said the team in unison, sitting up straight. Ricky McGillis's face had lost its smirk and was sober and tense.

"Please continue, Colonel," Waabboy said, returning the reins to Lintz.

Referring to the orders posted on one side of the whiteboard as he went, Lintz explained the dimensions and other physical characteristics of the ASM-140. The team members flipped hurriedly through their copies of the orders, nodding and taking notes.

"The ASM-140 has two armaments designed to minimize the chances of creating debris," Lintz said, pointing at the diagram of the ASM-140 with his baton. "The first is known as 'Blackout.' The second is extremely small-caliber ammunition."

"Sir," said one of the attendees. "Captain Gehner, serving as chief of maintenance. I have a question. Blackout is said to be effective only against civilian electrical equipment. Will it work on the Rod from God?"

"Good question. Satellites are usually built to be as light as possible, so most are not adequately hardened against attacks of this sort. The CPU might be safely behind a shield, but if the exposed sensors can be killed, that will do the trick. Clear enough?"

"Yes, sir."

"Blackout's range is five kilometers. Sixteen thousand feet." Lintz drew a point on the whiteboard, then, careful not to let his bitterness show, wrote "Rod from God" beside it. As he drew a circle indicating Blackout's range, he was struck by a sense of déjà vu. Hadn't he recently seen this same diagram before? That attachment from Freeman?

"Colonel Lintz?" Waabboy called to Lintz, who had paused to rack his brains.

"My apologies. Armament number two: slugs, just three millimeters in diameter. The basic principle is similar to that of a shotgun . . ."

Lintz continued his explanation, but all he could think about was that email from Freeman. What had it said—a large number of space tethers floating around SAFIR 3? The ASM-140 warhead would have to pass through that dense crowd of space tethers. But what would happen if it hit one?

"The ammunition seems too small to do much damage," said Gehner. "Will it really get through the Rod from God's shielding?"

"Nothing to be concerned about. The ammunition has a two-layer structure. When the outer layer strikes the shielding, both are vaporized together, and the core flies in. Same principle as an antitank missile."

"Is the core tungsten or DU?"

"DU."

Lintz sensed the tension rise slightly among the team members. The armed forces denied that the radiation from depleted uranium could have health effects. Even if such effects did exist, they were negligible. This common sense had penetrated the surface-bound members of the army and navy but not yet the air force.

"There's no need to worry about special handling precautions," Lintz said. "The rounds are completely shielded. If the shotgun mechanism functions normally, they'll sink into the atmosphere and burn up a few weeks later."

"Thank you, sir. That is very reassuring."

As the team members visibly relaxed, Lintz's sense of foreboding continued to swell within him. It was that email. He had to read the report from Freeman as soon as he could.

Noticing Lintz glance at the clock on the wall, Waabboy rose to his feet. "Any further questions?" he asked.

Only the sound of paper being folded came from the audience.

"I'll take that as a no. This concludes the briefing. Thank you, Colonel Lintz. Attention!"

The attendees rose to their feet and prepared to salute.

Lintz sat in the passenger seat of Fernandez's Ford, open laptop wedged in the narrow space between his belly and the dashboard. Fernandez glanced at the screen from the driver's seat.

"Daryl's report?" he asked.

Lintz grunted in the affirmative. "You read it?"

"Sorry. It was way over my head. Space tethers, right? Crazy stuff. Hard for me to follow."

"I see . . ."

The email from Daryl, sent from his new base of operations provided by the CIA, was full of surprises. An engineer from Japan named Kazumi Kimura had used a radar system borrowed from a Seychelles billionaire to observe the space tethers. Now Daryl was requesting that NORAD replicate the observations.

Opening the attached diagram again, Lintz saw that his sense of déjà vu before had been warranted. SAFIR 3 was densely surrounded by the mass of space tethers known as the Cloud. Apparently there were twenty thousand pairs—far more than he had imagined.

These space tethers were already past the hypothesis stage. They were a real and pressing threat.

"I should have read this before the briefing," he muttered. "Operation Seed Pod is pointless."

At best, Lintz thought, but kept it to himself. He thought of the two civilians who would be in the area when Operation Seed Pod went into action.

Fernandez shrugged. "No stopping it now," he said.

Lintz groaned and closed his laptop, stowing it in the map pocket on the passenger's side. "How many staff do we have not involved with Seed Pod who we can use to make orbital observations?" he asked.

"Twelve," Fernandez said. "They're scheduled for video-call training for NORAD Tracks Santa. Which is next week, by the way."

"Cancel the training," Lintz said. "I'm redirecting all resources to support Daryl—the Seattle team. Gather everyone in my office. We need to be prepared for a video call from Seattle at any time."

"An emergency, then. Understood, sir."

Fernandez stepped on the gas. The Ford accelerated quickly to forty miles per hour, the on-base speed limit.

Wed, 16 Dec 2020, 09:14 -0800 (2020-12-16T17:14 GMT)
Western Days Hotel

Bruce watched Akari's shoulders sink as she stood miserably in front of him.

"All right," she said at last. "But I'd like to see it for myself. Can I have the data?"

The results of the search he had asked the CIA to perform last night had been nothing like what Akari had expected. Scanning *all* communications for messages containing three numbers indicating ID, time, and two three-dimensional decimal vectors indicating coordinates and heading had smoked out a vast number of computers. Between two and six hundred thousand devices had been sending data in that format—four orders of magnitude more than the few dozen space tether base stations they had expected. What was more, the data was extremely unwieldy. Most of the search results also included an enormous binary attachment. "These are not the sort of messages that one expects to be transmitted from orbit," the CIA search team had observed drily in an attachment of their own.

"It's nothing to worry about, Akari," Bruce said. "As long as you can find the needle you're looking for somewhere in that haystack."

Akari silently opened the data and expanded the window, filling three whole monitors with rows of figures.

Jamshed's voice came somewhat hesitantly from the display that had been set aside for video calls.

"What has happened?" he asked. "Is that the communications with the base stations? May I read it too?"

Still silent, Akari projected the figures on the whiteboard so that Jamshed could see them. On-screen, he stroked his chin and pulled one of the pieces of paper that dangled behind him closer.

"Doctor Jahanshah," Bruce said. "You can wait until we've narrowed it down to the likely candidates before you begin your analysis, if you like. Let's leave this part to Akari. Right, Kazumi . . . Kazumi?"

Kazumi was standing before the figure-filled whiteboard. He had his index finger up and his eyes half-closed as his lips moved silently, trying to use that mysterious power of his to perceive objects in orbit. Daryl, too, was sitting before a computer, waiting for Kazumi to open his mouth.

So that's how it is, thought Bruce. *The whole team's bonkers except for me.* Whatever Kazumi's forecasting methods were, they were completely impenetrable to Bruce. The CIA agent watched as Kazumi slowly lowered his index finger to one side, his entire body leaning as he did so. "Look out!" he said.

Kazumi took a half-step forward, regaining his balance. Daryl turned around to see what was happening.

"Overlay it on a globe," Kazumi said. "This data is longitude, latitude, altitude, in that order. Latitude is reversed north-south. Altitude is a floating-point number with the Earth's surface at 1.0."

Jamshed held up a yellow piece of paper. "Kazumi is right," he said. "This is the order I used on my paper too. Location indicated by first line of data is—"

"First line of data is—" Kazumi said, speaking at the same time.

"Edge of Washington state, directly overhead," Jamshed continued.

"Seattle airspace," Kazumi finished.

"Roger," said Daryl. "Putting it on-screen now." He tapped at his keyboard, and a single dot appeared on the globe projected on the whiteboard. The dot was at the western edge of North America, right near the border with Canada. Seattle. The city they were in right now.

"Adding the data," Daryl continued, and clattered at his keyboard again. One dot after another appeared on the whiteboard. Their locations matched the predictions Kazumi had made based on the Cloud observed by Ozzy.

"Wait a minute," Bruce said, waving his hand and stepping in front of the whiteboard. "You're joking, right? There are two to six *hundred* thousand PCs worldwide acting as base stations? That's imposs—"

"I've figured out what the attachments are," Akari interrupted. "JPEGs." She placed a new portable projector on her table. A blue and white gradient appeared overlaid on the globe.

"Photos?"

"Yes," Akari said curtly, and began to open more of the images, all of the same sort, one after another. Blue and white stripes. Sometimes a fade from blue to black, or a stripy pattern of green and blue. Daryl and Kazumi cocked their heads in confusion. Bruce, of course, had no idea what he was seeing. Only Akari seemed on top of the situation as she opened image after image.

"These photos don't mean anything on their own," she said. "I'll write a program to stitch them together. Just let me check to see if anyone's already coded some bits and pieces I could use in it."

The crowdsourcing site MegaHands appeared. Akari entered a few search keywords and brought up a list of parts and libraries for image-processing programs. Bruce looked closely at the "Ordered by" field. The same name appeared in every line: Kirilo Panchenko. The pseudonym Shiraishi had used. Bruce wasn't sure what Shiraishi had been up to, but once again Akari had managed to follow her uncle's thinking perfectly. He glanced at Chris, who nodded with apparent satisfaction.

Akari scanned through the project results, clicking the Buy button on item after item. "Looks like someone commissioned a similar program but split the task up," she said. "Most . . . no, almost all of the parts we need are here. Surprising. The design is a little old-fashioned, but I know how to use nearly everything without modifications. Even the naming conventions are familiar."

Akari opened the source code she had downloaded and began to combine it into a single program. A sphere popped up on the whiteboard. A blurred photograph appeared pasted to it on an angle and then disappeared.

"Well, I'm done," said Akari. "All I did was join the libraries together, mind you."

She tapped one final key on her keyboard. A small window containing "Building project . . ." appeared, and then the whiteboard was awash in blue. A rainbow-colored balloon spun on the screen as the image began to divide into four, then eight, gradually taking recognizable form.

"Whoa!" Bruce said before he could stop himself.

In two blinks, the whiteboard was displaying a high-resolution image of the Earth. They could see the breathtakingly beautiful pattern of the oceans and the billowing swirls of storm cloud on the horizons. And a single small but brightly shining white spot in space. Then another white spot appeared beside it. To judge from their location, the bright spot was probably SAFIR 3, while the one beside it was the orbital hotel.

Daryl peered at Akari's hands. "A light field," he said. "Photographs overlaid to create a 3-D space."

"Yes," Akari said. "I joined together the eighty thousand digital cameras inside the space tethers' terminal apparatuses. This image might have been taken by the largest camera in history."

The image grew more vivid even as they spoke, revealing the Earth in finer detail than they had ever seen. The swirls of clouds bathed in morning sunlight looked like they might move at any moment—no, they *were* moving, turning slowly in the sun's rays.

"This is a *feed*?" Bruce asked, astonished.

"From a few hours ago," Akari said. She pointed at the whiteboard. "Our point of view is above the Pacific Ocean. The camera is pointed toward Seattle."

Chris stood up from her boss's seat and gazed at the whiteboard from beside the table. "So that swirl is the blizzard we're in right now?" she asked. "Does the camera move, Akari?"

"Of course. It's a 3-D light field. I set it up so that you can stand here and move both your hands to rotate the Earth."

Chris waved her hands. The Earth lurched. The feeling of actually being in orbit looking down at the Earth was so strong that Bruce gasped.

"Akari, is this only for looking?" he asked. "No two-way interaction?"

"Right."

"How, and why, is this kind of data being sent back? It makes the transmissions bulky. Must eat up the batteries, too. And wouldn't it also increase the risk that the messages would be detected?"

"It's obvious *why* they're doing it," Akari said. "They want to see Earth."

That was it? Bruce was about to raise an objection when a husky voice spoke from the monitor. "What am I looking at? You say this image was taken from space tethers? Overlaying individual photos to create three-dimensional Earth? This is possible in theory. I know that, but . . ."

Jamshed's eyes were wide open, face in close-up after he had brought it right up to the camera. The knuckled fingers raised before his face were trembling. This was bad. Akari had stepped into a domain Jamshed was not prepared to understand.

"The space tethers can be used this way too, then, Doctor Jahanshah?" Bruce asked.

There was a pause. "I did not realize this," Jahanshah said finally. "It never occurred to me."

"Please, come to America. You'll find it a very inspiring place for ideas," Bruce said.

"You think so?"

"Of course," Chris said. "Environment is everything." Despite her efforts to smooth things over, the shock had not left Jamshed's features. They needed a topic where he was a crucial player, and fast, or he would start to feel worthless.

"Next I will identify the transmitting stations," Akari said, determination in her voice. "Chris, can I show the base station locations to Professor Jahanshah? The data has geographical information from the CIA's Internet positioning system attached."

After a moment's hesitation, Chris granted her permission. Yellow dots appeared all over the projected globe.

"Six hundred thousand transmission stations," Akari said.

"These are the base stations?!" Bruce exclaimed. It made no sense. North America, Japan, South America, Africa . . . Yellow dots shone almost everywhere there was human habitation. How could North Korea possibly have built a worldwide transmission network like this—in secret?

"Bruce, you saw the live feed earlier," Kazumi said. "That video could only have been shot from the space tethers. There is no mistake. There are this many computers exchanging data with the space tethers."

"All right, fine," Bruce said after a pause. "But where *are* they?"

"Why don't we take a look?" Akari waved her arms and spun the Earth to center on Seattle. Hovering over it were billowing storm clouds and a dense field of hundreds of dots. She zoomed in on the swirl of the blizzard. It filled the screen, and then the familiar Google 3-D map appeared.

"Functionality from the original game engine," Kazumi explained to the surprised team members.

Near the Seattle landmark that was the Space Needle, a single point was displayed. Akari increased the zoom ratio.

"Hey!" said Bruce. "That's our hotel!"

Akari moved the mouse on the table until the arrow was directly over the Western Days. An IP address and port number appeared.

"I see that the router's IP masquerade table is already decoded," she said. Benefits of working with the CIA. "The original address is 10.0.0.2. That's the lobby." Akari crammed a Raspberry Pi that had been lying out on the table into her pocket and stood up. "I'm going to go find it," she said.

"Akari!" Kazumi tried to follow her out of the room, but Chris stood in his way.

"Kazumi, you stay here," she said. "Bruce!"

But Bruce was already dashing out of the room in pursuit. The elevator had left the floor. Bruce pushed open the fire doors that led to the emergency staircase.

"Who are these people?" he muttered as he began to descend. "It's only day two!"

Wed, 16 Dec 2020, 10:32 -0700 (2020-12-16T17:32 GMT)
Peterson Air Force Base

"Lookin' good, flyboy," said Madu, pounding Ricky on the shoulder.

Unfortunately, as he was just then being lowered by crane into his aircraft while strapped into an ejector seat, this caused him to swing and spin like a pendulum, stretching the writing on the pre-flight checklist stuck to his thighs.

"Hey, no jostling," he said. "I've still got some checks left."

Madu waved over her shoulder and disappeared behind the F-15 Eagle in the direction of her own ride, the latest F-22 Raptor. A gigantic reconnaissance pod hung from the belly of the fighter. Definitely not standard issue.

"Ricky, we all like to play Tarzan, but try to stay focused here."

Gehner, the maintenance crew chief, stopped Ricky's wild spinning. Looking down, he called "Clear!" and pulled out two ribbons. There hadn't been enough space in the cockpit for the compressor that pumped oxygen into the pressure suit, so they'd had to bolt it to the base of the ejector seat.

Ricky raised his head. The runway extended out from the hangar's entrance, and in the distance beyond that rose Pikes Peak, pure white with snow. The sprawling mass below it was Cheyenne Mountain, where NORAD had once been headquartered. Though inhabited now only by mice, during the Cold War the underground complex had been filled day and night with hundreds of operators, all monitoring the Soviets.

Ricky's beloved F-15, greatest fighter plane of the twentieth century, his orange pressure suit, and the original form of the ASM-140 now loaded into the F-15 were also products of that era. They had all been developed in an age of intense competition to soar higher, move faster, hit harder than the other side.

Anything, anywhere, anytime: the fundamental attitude of the US Air Force was the same even today in the twenty-first century, when there was no one left to compete with. But how it operated in practice had changed profoundly. Today it was all about stealth fighters like the F-22, drones, and cyberwar. Once Operation Seed Pod was over, even this spectacular F-15 would be restored to its standard equipment profile and added to the wait list for retirement from service, just like Ricky himself.

Ricky dropped his gaze to his thighs and began filling in the checklist, picking up where Madu had interrupted him. He was just considering the possibility that this would be his last real mission when Gehner called out to him.

"Check it out!"

Ricky raised his head and saw a few crew members stenciling something onto the F-15's nose cone with spray paint.

"Clear breach of regulations, but they insisted."

One of the crew members brandishing a template waved in Rick's direction. The letters now painted on the nose cone in gray paint were sharp and clear: SHOOTING STAR.

"Once Seed Pod is finished, we'll add a big star and take a photo together," Gehner said. "This is the first time a plane has ever taken down a satellite. I want a picture of me alongside the pilot who shot down the highest, farthest target ever."

Ricky stretched his back. The smooth material, so different from that of his usual pilot suit, caressed his entire body. Their target today was the North Korean Rod from God. He would go up there for the sake of Judy Smark and her angry upraised finger, for her father, and indeed to restore the freedom of space itself.

"All right, let's go. If the visor's ultraviolet shield gets in the way, just pull it off." Gehner placed the transparent helmet over Ricky's head and locked it into place at his shoulders. "All clear. Take him up!"

The winch groaned and the seat was hoisted into the air, Ricky and all. He saw the F-15's main wing spread out below him. So large it was known as the "tennis court," it smoothly merged with the fuselage to create one unified winged form, giving the fighter a balance of power and agility. Enjoying the rare view, Ricky clenched his gloved first tight.

A monstrous orbital weapon: another idea from the Cold War. Fitting that he was flying out to meet it in the greatest fighter of the Cold War era, if not the entire twentieth century. He was going to take his F-15 up there and annihilate this Rod from God completely. The F-15 deserved no less for its final send-off.

Wed, 16 Dec 2020, 10:15 -0800 (2020-12-16T18:15 GMT)
Western Days Hotel

Hearing a knock at the door of their suite, Chris rose to her feet, checked the image from the security camera, and opened the door to allow Bruce in. He was pushing a luggage cart with a computer on it.

"Kazumi," said Bruce, "can you have a word with your girlfriend? She's out of control."

Akari slunk in after him.

"What happened?" asked Chris. "Isn't that the computer from down in the lobby?"

"You should have seen her down there," Bruce said, pushing the cart up against the table with a wry smile.

He had arrived at the ground floor, he said, to find Akari already clinging to the front desk engaged in a shouting match with the clerk.

While he was explaining things to the clerk and peeling Akari off the desk, she had knocked over a hundred thousand–dollar white speaker, had moved the sofa, and was pulling up the carpet in the lobby.

To calm the uproar from the guests and staff members who didn't understand the situation, Bruce had said "Metropolitan police investigation!" and flashed the fake badge he'd used to apprehend the illustrator Jose Juarez in Los Angeles.

"Unbelievable," Bruce finished. "Good thing none of the guests realized it was an LA police badge."

"And did Akari find the base station?" Chris asked.

"If she hadn't, I'd be kicking her out into the blizzard right now," Bruce said, flashing his dazzling smile. He pointed at the computer on the luggage cart. "They were using this to control the audio in the lobby. Akari left them a replacement she made with her Raspberry Pi."

"The audio?" Chris said.

"We know what the base stations look like," Akari said.

Bruce lifted a thickly insulated USB cable from the cart. Just under an inch in diameter, the cable had a D-Fi logo printed on it. When Bruce drew the cable through his hand to smooth out the twists, Chris got a whiff of the same rosy fragrance she had smelled in the lobby.

"A USB cable?" Chris said.

"Yes, the best audiophile USB cable money can buy," Bruce said. "Sold by a Japanese company called Sound Technica. The technology they use was developed by a Portland audio research lab called D-Fi based on analysis of sound data from around the world. It uses audio profile information to open up the high-frequency range. A two-foot cable costs $300. They were discontinued recently, but they've been popular for a long time. Maybe a million sold in all?"

"You're oddly knowledgeable about all this," said Chris.

Akari laughed. "He told me he owns one," she said, pointing at Bruce.

"You believe that audiophile woo?" Daryl laughed.

"Oh, so you're on her side too? Yeah, you got me—I fell for it. But I just called my housekeeper and had her pull the cable out."

Bruce scratched his head and put the D-Fi cable on the table. Then he produced a pocketknife and cut into the cable's insulation to pull out not only the vinyl-covered USB cable itself but also a long copper wire that came with it.

"This is the antenna," Bruce said. Then he cut into the USB terminal itself. He twisted the tip of the knife, and a tiny chip tumbled out. It was a black resin package with a European chip maker's logo printed on it. "And this is a VHF transceiver. That settles it. This cable itself is the antenna, and the transmitter-receiver circuitry is built into the USB terminal."

Akari placed the computer on her desk. "When you plug this USB cable into a computer, D-Fi's audio drivers are automatically installed," she said.

"Plug and play, eh?" said Daryl.

"Except what gets installed is the space tether base station software."

As Akari explained, once resident in the system, the D-Fi drivers sent the space tether telemetry received via the USB cable antenna to servers scattered around the world. When they received orbital-maneuver commands in fragmentary form from those same servers, they transmitted them back into orbit. Genuine drivers from approved manufacturers ran on PCs with administrative privileges, so security software did nothing to stop this.

Bruce went to the kitchen and started making some coffee.

"Akari's explanation came as a surprise," he said. "They manufactured their own hit product just to install a Trojan . . . That's something the CIA should put in their textbooks. We ought to have Akari come lecture on it, too."

He returned with several cups of espresso and lined them up on the table. "Let's take a breather," he said. "Not much point in being in Seattle if we're going to drink coffee from a machine, but once this is all over we can go out to celebrate at the original Starbucks at First and Pike."

"I saw that yesterday," Kazumi said. "With the brown logo, right?"

"Nope," Bruce said. "The real one's farther in. Tastes the same, though," he added with a wink.

"Bruce, you have work to do," said Chris. "Raise a research request for information related to this D-Fi place."

"Already done," Bruce said. "Fast service back at headquarters, day or night." He took his seat and touched his mustache to his espresso cup. "These cables were made by an assembly company in Singapore called Falang. Three years ago, it started buying up smartphone boards by the thousand. Tens of thousands in all. And do you think they ever shipped a single handset?"

Daryl took a break from his work and sat down at the table, coffee in hand. "So they were actually making space tethers," he said. "Do you think they knew that?"

"You'd have to ask them," Bruce said. "Seems they were also buying up a lot of graphene, which Dr. Jahanshah said would work for the tether component. You have to admire whoever thought that strategy up. Building orbital weapons right out in the open in a civilian facility. Manufacturing costs were probably about a hundred bucks a tether, given five-digit production volumes."

Bruce took a sip of his espresso, looking more than satisfied with the taste.

"One more fun fact," Bruce said. "The address D-Fi give for their research lab in Portland is a dummy, but they did rent a warehouse on Pier 37 in Seattle. And according to our sources, it's still piled high with containers returned from Sound Technica."

Chris picked up a coffee cup. The resinous scent typical of capsule coffee machines mingled with the fragrance of roses. She took a deep breath. "Did you say that these cables cost $300?" she asked.

"Please, don't ask," Bruce said. "I *thought* it improved the sound. But it was just a regular USB cable inside. I was imagining it."

"I doubt that's all there was to it."

"But the data comes through exactly the same."

"That's right," Akari pouted. "Only data in standard USB audio formats comes through."

Chris picked up the cable and squeezed it in one hand. The scent of roses grew stronger.

"Perfume," she said. "Probably essential oils in microcapsules designed to melt slowly from the heat. Our sense of hearing is surprisingly malleable. If a gullible audiophile comes home bursting with expectation after spending $300 on one of these, they aren't going to hear the same thing as the day before. A little perfume helps make an impression. I'm not surprised these things were popular."

Chris tossed the cable aside and reached for her coffee cup again.

Presumably the perfume idea had been Shiraishi's, just like the strategy of making a hit product to spread the Trojan. Neither would occur to the average thinker. But by weaving together scraps of information, this team would uncover all of his schemes. This was intelligence work in its ideal form.

Perhaps taking a cue from the report Bruce had sent in, head-quarters had dubbed them "Team Seattle" and recognized them as an official CIA base of operations. They had even arranged to have all of the communications between the space tethers and the base stations bounced to Akari's cluster of Raspberry Pis. The movement of the space tethers would now be communicated to Team Seattle in real time. And they knew where the base stations were, too.

They could win this. Chris was full of confidence. All they had to do now was find that man whose twisted ideas had given the CIA the runaround.

"Just you wait, Ageha Shiraishi . . ."

"Uncle Ageha?" Akari stared at Chris, returning the espresso cup she was holding to the table. She frowned, and her lips quivered.

Chris realized her mistake. She had revealed too much.

Akari gritted her teeth and glared at Chris. "Hey," she said. "Do you think Uncle Ageha did all this?"

Bruce was glaring at Chris too. Just then, a notification appeared on a monitor.

China Mobility Wi-Fi activation.
Washington - Seattle - Pier 37

A smartphone using a China Mobility SIM card had connected to one of the honeypots Kazumi and Daryl had planted the previous day. The location matched D-Fi's warehouse.

"You're wrong!" Akari shouted. "There's no way that's true!" She dashed out of the room.

After a moment of surprise, Kazumi ran after her. "Akari!" he cried.

He was closely followed by Daryl, who said, "Meet you at the car!"

Once they were out in the hall, Chris heard Kazumi shout "The stairs!" over the heavy sound of the fire doors opening.

"I blew it," Chris said, left alone in the room with Bruce.

"Save it for later, would you?" Bruce said. "I'm going after her too. She'll be on a bike at best—I can cut her off." He pulled his Walther PPS from his ankle holster and checked the loaded chamber indicator on the slide before wedging the weapon into his belt at the small of his back. "I'll need more than this peashooter. Better make a stop along the way."

"Where?"

"The coast guard just beyond Pier 37. We need M4s and ammunition. I'll also be borrowing someone with on-the-ground army experience, so please make the necessary preparations."

Wed, 16 Dec 2020, 11:02 -0800 (2020-12-11T19:02 GMT)
Pier 37 Warehouse, Seattle

Chance snapped the SIM card free of its credit card–sized plastic frame and handed it to Shiraishi.

"Change yours, too," she said.

"It's only Wednesday," Shiraishi replied.

"Lot of network access last week. Today's the move, too—perfect timing. We'll burn the old one here."

Chance pointed at the zinc box in the corner of the room, a so-called incineration box. It contained a powdered mixture of iron oxide and aluminum along with some thermite, designed to burn at a high temperature. They would use gasoline on the warehouse itself, but anything they wanted to eliminate completely would go into the box.

Shiraishi changed his SIM card and entered the numbers Chance read out. As the SIM activated, the "No service" message was replaced by a 4G signal indicator and a Wi-Fi connection was established.

"Huh?" he said.

Wi-Fi? Shiraishi checked the log in the notifications center. The device was connected to a hotspot run by "China Mobility Services."

"Hey, show me your phone," he said.

Chance's smartphone was connected to the same hotspot as his. Shiraishi pulled the torn-up card out of the incineration box and turned it over. "China Mobility Services" was on the list of free Wi-Fi spots that the card would connect to automatically. But why would China Mobility offer Wi-Fi service in Seattle?

Shiraishi brought up a UNIX terminal and checked the network they were connected to. It was running from a Raspberry Pi device, a seventy-dollar kit computer. No one would offer commercial service through something like that.

They'd been set up.

"Turn off Wi-Fi," he said.

"What's wrong?" Chance said

"Someone set a trap for us. They know we're here now."

Chance looked up from her smartphone, frowning.

Shiraishi explained that one of the services their roaming cards were designed to connect to upon activation was being spoofed.

"NORAD . . . ? No, they couldn't pull off something like this. The CIA?"

"I don't know. Although I wouldn't expect the CIA to use a cheap gadget like a Raspberry Pi."

Chance opened her right hand and gazed down at it. "Can the mission still be salvaged, I wonder?"

She took hold of her little finger and wrenched the resin cover off. Then she repeated the operation for her ring finger. In the places where her flesh had been ground away, the bones of her fingers showed palely through the thin layer of skin that clung to them.

"Let me just say this," she said, producing an oddly shaped pistol from her handbag. Her bone-thin fingers fit snugly into the custom-molded resin grip. A quick motion of her other hand saw the magazine slide partway out. Chance checked it, pushed it back into place, and then pulled the slide. The first round was in the chamber. A bright-red beam of light stretched from underneath the barrel into the room. Chance shone the laser sight onto Shiraishi's chest.

"I will protect you right down to the wire," she said. "But if you are about to fall into the hands of the US government, I will not hesitate."

Chance crammed the smooth pistol, now merged with her right hand, into her coat pocket. "You follow my orders."

Shiraishi nodded.

Chance reached into her bag again and pulled out a few passports, then tossed the bag into the incineration box. She turned as if remembering something. "Did you finish preparing for the Cloud handover?"

"Not yet. I need until tomorrow."

Give up control of the Cloud in a situation like this? If he did that, this woman would kill him without blinking, long before he was "about to fall into the hands of the US government." Right now, his only choice was to do exactly what she told him to.

Wed, 16 Dec 2020, 13:03 -0700 (2020-12-16T20:03 GMT)
Rocky Mountain Airspace

The roar that rattled Ricky's transparent helmet came in through the headset that was supposed to be soundproofed and hit his ears like thunder. Orders from Control came thick and fast.

"Shooting Star, go to maximum thrust."

"Roger," Ricky said.

Carefully but promptly, Ricky pushed the throttle forward. Through the thick gloves of his pressure suit, he felt the faint click that told him where to stop. Pushing the throttle farther than this would engage the afterburner and leave him short of fuel before the mission was over. The trembling F-15 didn't move an inch. It was still bound to the runway by its own brakes and wires.

"Maximum thrust confirmed," Ricky said.

"Go!"

A slight jolt. The wires had been cut with incendiary charges. The thrust of the F-15 slammed Ricky's back against the ejector seat. In anticipation of recoil throwing him forward, Ricky tried to push back with his feet planted firmly on the floor, but the seat just kept on pressing into his back.

The view from the canopy flew past with terrifying speed. Passing the four hundred–foot marker, Ricky pulled lightly at the control stick. The vibration transmitted up from the ground vanished. He was airborne. But he could not raise the fighter's nose. He had to pass Mach 0.6 horizontally first. That was the liftoff protocol for challenging the altitude record.

The headrest pressed against his head. His eyeballs wouldn't stay in place. Ricky let out an internal whoop of joy. The power of the F-15!

The custom airspeed indicator recorded Mach 0.65. A green LED lit up.

Ricky slowly pulled the control stick toward him. The plan was for him to perform half an inside loop at 2.5 G and then go straight up to thirty thousand feet. The mountain range at the edge of his vision shrank suddenly, and he saw the sky ahead of him. "Above" and "below" swapped places in an instant.

He saw the ground above his head. Returning the control stick to the center, he slowly pushed it to the left to roll once, completing an irregular Immelmann turn. He was gradually getting used to the feel of the pressure suit's gloves.

"Altitude thirty thousand feet, heading west," Ricky said, using pedal and control stick to turn the fighter's nose westward. He saw a pitch-black shadow to the right of the fighter. It was Madu's F-22. She was maintaining her relative position precisely, the underside of her plane with its observation pod visible.

"Mission leader, do you copy?" came her voice over the radio. "Looked pretty good there, Ricky."

"This is Control," crackled the radio next. "Thanks to Madu, we'll be putting our feet up and watching the show from here on out. Go for it."

Ricky turned his head from side to side, taking in the white-capped Rockies at the foot of the blue sky. The transparent helmet offered a fantastic panorama. But he wasn't entirely happy with his high-altitude pressure suit.

"Control, I'm freezing up here!" he yelled into the mic. "My fingers are going numb." The suit's heater wasn't switching on. The AC unit had been removed from the cockpit, too. He didn't want to think what the temperature must be.

"This is Gehner. The heater is active. Go ahead and adjust its output. Over."

"I can do that? Where?"

"Behind your head. Oh, you can't reach?"

Ricky groaned. What idiot had designed this suit? Now that the pressure in the cockpit had dropped, the suit was so overinflated he could hardly bend his arms.

"AC malfunction? Sounds rough." Madu's cool tones came through clearly.

"Can it. Hey, what am I supposed to do?"

"We value your feedback," Control said drily. "Expect improvements in future."

Sure—they weren't the ones getting flash frozen. Confirming that the autopilot was on, Ricky pulled his digits in from the fingers of his inflated glove. He made a fist to let the blood flow through them. Okay. That should do it.

"Mission Leader, do you see the ISS straight ahead?" asked Control.

"The space station? Hold on. I see something like a dot . . ." Ricky squinted. There, in the dark-blue sky, was a sharp point of shining light. "That's it! Visible to the naked eye, huh?"

According to what he'd picked up at the briefing, the ISS's orbital altitude was 1.3 million feet. That made it the farthest man-made object Ricky had ever seen unaided. Even at the F-15's operational altitude, the horizon was only 150 miles—a million feet—away, and you couldn't see an aircraft at that distance with the naked eye anyway. The atmosphere was too thick; it misted up the view.

"You didn't know?" Control said. "In the evening you can even see it from the ground. There's six people on that thing. As we get higher, the orbital hotel will enter our field of view. Judy and Ronnie Smark are on board that one."

Ricky squinted at the ISS. He knew that it should have two great solar panels spread wide, but it was so far away that all he could see was a dot. He was finally getting an intuitive grasp of their mission.

"Ten seconds left till seventy-degree climb," came the voice from Control. "Ready afterburner."

"Good luck," came Madu's cool voice again. She needed no such words of encouragement herself. She was flying the latest fighter model, with supercruise capabilities that let it break the sound barrier without any afterburner at all.

"Readying afterburner," Ricky said. With his left hand, he pulled the throttle back half an inch, then carefully began to push it forward again. He was waiting to feel the click through the pressure suit's thick glove that signaled military power, maximum thrust without afterburner. This would be his second ignition, the first one coming when he had broken the sound barrier. From here they would climb straight up to an altitude of seventy thousand feet.

"How much colder is it gonna get?" Ricky felt the faint click from the throttle. His hand stopped.

"You're a mammal," said Control. "Generate your own heat. And—go!"

"Engaging afterburner," Ricky said. He pushed the throttle forward as far as it would go. An instant later, the fighter shook violently. Jet fuel was injected into the nozzles burning at high temperature.

"Acceleration as expected," said Control. "Don't black out now. Begin climb."

Ricky put his warmed-up fingers back into the fingers of his glove, switched autopilot off, and pulled the control stick toward him. In a more contemporary aircraft like the F-22 flying alongside him, the tail assembly vibrating like a bee's wings would cancel out the shaking of his hand, but this model from the nineties was sensitivity itself.

Pitch-black sky spread out before his eyes. There was hardly any atmosphere above him. This was space.

"Target coming from below, twelve o'clock. Mission Leader, you see the stars?"

"Nope. The target's below?"

Ricky carefully moved his head to the side and peered down through the gap in the instrument panel. Right about where pitch-black became tinged with blue, he saw two white dots that looked the same as the ISS. The objective.

"I see them. The hotel and the Rod from God. Both moving pretty fast, aren't they?" The two dots rose higher as he watched.

And then Ricky saw something impossible. He put his finger under a corner of the ultraviolet visor and peeled off the film. There in the pitch-black sky, which had been clear just a moment ago, was a faint strand of cloud.

"Hey," he said. "What's that? Control, do you copy?"

"What is it?

"The Rod from God's wrapped up in a cloud."

"Clouds don't drift out of the atmosphere, Mission Leader."

"I see it too," came Madu's voice. "Really does look like a cloud."

"Observation craft, can you get it on camera?"

Were they crazy? The two of them were climbing at Mach 2. The observation pod on the belly of the F-22 could only film what was under the fighter.

"I'll give it a try."

What was she doing? This was the stratosphere. She'd lose velocity. But before Ricky could object, the black shadow beside him began to move. Madu's F-22 had pulled up farther and was losing airspeed rapidly. Twisting his head to see behind him, Ricky caught a glimpse of the F-22 with its belly pointed in the direction they were traveling. The woman was executing a Cobra, on a real mission, at this incredible altitude.

Ricky focused his nerves on his control stick and maintained his course straight ahead. At some point the altimeter had reached 75,000 feet. This was the highest altitude a standard F-15 had ever reached. But the number didn't even register for Ricky. The faint cloud of light around the Rod from God was connected all the way to the Wyvern Orbital Hotel in a tattered string of glittering fragments. What the heck was it?

"This is Control. Madu, we see it. A cloud. An orbital cloud!"

"Watch this!" Ricky shouted into the mic. "Launching!"

There was a faint jolt as something kicked into Ricky's back. Unburdening itself of the ASM-140's weight had allowed the F-15 to accelerate farther. A moment later, the F-15 was illuminated from straight below by a brilliant flash of light.

Ignition.

The newly independent ASM-140 flew off through the pitch-black sky in a straight line, trailing smoke behind it.

Ricky watched the smoke stretch out like a living thing. At the edge of his field of vision, the altimeter showed eighty thousand feet.

Wed, 16 Dec 2020, 12:08 -0800 (2020-12-16T20:08 GMT)
Western Days Hotel

Alone in the room, Chris watched the video projected on the whiteboard, sent direct from the Operation Seed Pod control center at NORAD's Oregon site. The ASM-140's first stage had just disengaged, and the second stage was beginning its acceleration.

In geographical terms, the two pilots had flown over the Rockies and were now directly above the West Coast region and its swirling blizzard. Chris craned her neck and cast a glance at the display on the table, which showed two dots moving on a map of Seattle. One was Daryl and Kazumi, while the other was Bruce, who was trying to cut Akari off. Would they catch her? Alaskan Way, the road that ran along the waterfront directly to the piers, was closed due to the blizzard, but that was the route Akari would probably take on her mountain bike.

Who had activated the new China Mobility SIM card in Pier 37—Shiraishi himself, or another operative based in Seattle? If Shiraishi was there in person, he had to have some kind of observer or guard with him. They would be armed. And there was no guarantee that their weapons would be limited to what the law permitted.

"Talk about bad timing." Chris moved her chair so that she could see the map and the Oregon operations center together. There was movement in the image on the whiteboard.

"Second stage disengaged. Visual contact made with objective."

The Oregon staff cheered, and a new image source was added. It was the feed from the ASM-140's warhead camera, currently showing two dots in a pitch-black field. SAFIR 3 and the Wyvern Orbital Hotel. The space between the two dots widened. The dot at the center of the screen gradually grew larger. As it became visible as a three-dimensional body, an uncertain voice came from the Oregon video.

"Hey . . . is that right? A satellite? Looks like a wreck to me." The screen showed a battered metallic mass.

Chris breathed a sigh of relief at the knowledge that Team Seattle's prediction had been correct. This was no Rod from God. It was just the wreck of a rocket, kicked across the sky by a swarm of space tethers. Operation Seed Pod was a failure. An overgrown bottle rocket, come all this way just to bathe a hunk of scrap iron in electromagnetic rays and ventilate it with a barrage of depleted uranium pellets.

The voice of Colonel Daniel Waabboy, operational commander at Peterson Air Force Base, came over the video. "Stop grumbling," he said. "Mission proceeds."

Chris thought back on the Operation Seed Pod orders. The ASM-140's armaments all fired automatically. All that could be done from the surface was to stop them. Once the warhead was within five kilometers, it first used its electronic armament Blackout to burn out the electrical equipment on board the target satellite with powerful microwaves. It was only expected to be effective against civilian equipment, but it should work just fine on any sensors, cameras, or antenna protruding from a satellite. Just to be safe, the nearby orbital hotel had been asked to temporarily shut down all its electrical equipment.

"Roger. Blackout firing . . . What was that?"

The image from the camera was just a white screen. Chris blinked. The image flashed between white and black. For a moment, she saw a blue surface at an angle.

"Commander! The ASM warhead is revolving!"

At that moment, in the image being sent by the warhead camera, a number of bright-red lines raced across the black screen. Sounds of chaos rose from the ASM's Oregon control center.

Chris gritted her teeth. She needed Kazumi and Daryl here. The video was being recorded. She would have to ask their thoughts on the revolving and the red lines later.

"The orbital hotel . . . Oh no!"

"What happened? Make your report!"

"The microwaves from the spinning Blackout have passed through the orbital hotel."

"What did you say?!"

Chris felt as if the blood were draining from her body. The orbital hotel, with Ronnie and Judy Smark aboard, had received a dose of microwave radiation strong enough to fry sensors. They didn't know yet if any damage had been done. But it couldn't have escaped unscathed. The orbital hotel was a civilian structure with no reason to be shielded against electromagnetic warfare.

The vacuum of space . . . On the orbital hotel, life support was left entirely to the computers. Even a small amount of damage could have serious implications for the people on board.

Chris heard Waabboy's voice again. "Abort! Stop all armaments! What's the meaning of this? Why is the damn warhead spinning?"

Suddenly, Chris realized what was behind the spin. One of the space tethers clustered densely around SAFIR 3 had given the ASM-140 warhead a kick. Chris recalled Shiraishi's sneering photograph.

"He's a demon," she muttered, glaring at the video from the ASM-140 warhead. It was still flashing black and white. She had expected Operation Seed Pod to be a waste of time but had never imagined that it might actually damage the orbital hotel. One way or another, they had to stop this. Should she tell Oregon, or perhaps Waabboy, why Operation Seed Pod had failed? No, that would be pointless. Giving them the background at this stage wouldn't improve the situation.

Chris shook off her uncertainty and reviewed the cards in her hand. They had confirmed the existence of space tethers floating like a cloud in orbit. All transmissions to and from the base stations were being sent to the mountain of handmade computers Akari had thrown together. And they had located the mastermind behind it all.

Not too bad!

With the superior brains and bottomless motivation this team had, they were sure to come up with a way to stop the space tethers. Yet another reason why she absolutely needed Akari, Bruce, and Daryl to return safely.

Chris glanced at the map. Daryl's Chevy was stopped in the middle of the market. The snow. The dot indicating Bruce's Mustang was tearing down Alaskan Way at breakneck speed.

2020-12-16T21:00 GMT

Project Wyvern

It wasn't on the schedule, but today we had a disaster-preparedness drill. Let me tell you all about it.

The Wyvern Orbital Hotel is designed so that your routine is as close to an earthbound one as possible, but there's one thing that's completely different: the types of disasters that might happen here.

There'll never be an earthquake in orbit, or lightning, or torrential rains, or a hurricane or cyclone. What there is instead is equipment failure, collisions with debris, and bursts of solar wind. (Equipment failure could happen on Earth too, but in orbit it could be fatal.)

Today, we turned off almost all the power in the Wyvern to perform a blackout test. Broadly speaking, the Wyvern has seven electrical systems. Power is generated by two fuel cells and a solar panel array, and stored in five separate batteries.

Today's test cut everything but the light support battery, simulating what would happen in case of an equipment malfunction

Judy stopped typing on the laptop held to her lap by Velcro and pressed her palm to the display. Her skin, illuminated only by earth-light through the oval window, looked like a sculpture trapped in solid ice. The light was slightly dappled from the condensation on the cupola window.

Judy closed her laptop and peeled it off her lap. Once the ripping sound had faded away, the only noise was her father, Ronnie Smark, grunting one side of a conversation into his headset. He was floating free and ramrod straight in the middle of the room. During the forty-five minute "night" when the sun was blocked by the Earth, the water in their walls quickly chilled. Floating in midair like that was the best way to stay warm.

Ronnie raised his hand to his ear and switched the headset off. He arched his back like a cat and waved his arms to turn his body toward her, still clinging to the window frame.

"It's always something," he said. "We're just lucky there aren't guests on board yet."

His breath came out in puffs of white. The temperature was just above freezing. Information from the CIA suggested that their air conditioning had stopped as a result of an accident during a USNORTHCOM operation called Operation Seed Pod. Countless other electrical devices had died too, including every one exposed on the exterior of the hotel and half the solar batteries. All that had survived had been the orbital maneuvering system, powerfully shielded against the possibility of solar bursts, and the core life-support functionality.

"More bad news?" asked Judy.

Ronnie bent forward and attached the strap that extended from his belt to a hook on the wall. This was the spider monkey technique, one of the many methods for relaxing in the hotel's microgravity that they had been testing.

"Nothing serious," Ronnie said. "Just our life expectancy. As things stand, apparently we have two weeks."

Judy clenched her fists.

"One more thing," Ronnie added. "Apparently some dangerous craft are flying around in low orbit. Let's change into our space suits, just in case."

Ronnie glanced at a container in the corner of the room and winked. "Hopefully we won't have to ruin our first space walk experiments," he said.

"I wouldn't mind. At least it'd slim me down," Judy said.

One of the hidden innovations of Project Wyvern was a pressure suit that didn't use air pressure. Instead, the person inside was wrapped in countless belts containing tubes of water, the result adding up to one standard atmosphere of pressure. This "strap suit" had been tested countless times in chambers on Earth but had never actually been used in space. Either way, if there was an accident in orbit causing a hull breach, they would die from lack of oxygen before help arrived. The strap suit, designed for emergency evacuation, was nothing more than a temporary comfort.

"A space walk would be exciting, too."

"Spare me the bravado," Ronnie said. "Faking good cheer makes you hungry. Losing our microwave ovens—that hurt. Our molecular gastronomy packs aren't any good if they thaw out on their own. What are we going to do?"

A ringtone that sounded like a pigeon's coo came from Ronnie's thigh. Judy remembered that ringtone. Whenever Ronnie heard it, he would throw whatever he was doing aside and tear out of the house, headed for his warehouse office. That had been fifteen years ago, when Ronne had been just another entrepreneur.

"Hotmail?" Judy asked. "You still have that account?"

"It's a handy way for old friends to reach me," Ronnie said.

He reached into the thigh pocket of his overalls, reciting names from his start-up days: Ethan, Farrell, Mike . . . Judy remembered the faces of at least half of them.

"Unbelievable. Can't you think of a better way to keep in touch?"

"For some reason, it's hard to give it up," Ronnie said. "Hey, it's Ozzy. Remember him?"

"Mr. Cunningham, the landlord? Based in Seychelles now, right?"

Ronnie stroked his smartphone. "He's living like a hermit on an uninhabited island he converted to an observation base," Ronnie said. "Huh, so he was the one who made up this Rod from God thing. Well, he would."

Ronnie laughed, no doubt picturing the world in a panic over Ozzy's tall tale.

"And what does he have to say now?"

"Hold on. The guy's not known for his brevity," Ronnie said, attaching the strap that extended from the wall to a loop on his belt and floating lightly in the air. He curled up and stared at his smartphone. Apparently what Ozzy had to say was of great interest. After a while, he finally looked up.

"You'll like this, Judy," he said. "Go ahead and read it."

He pushed his smartphone with his finger and sent it sailing toward Judy's chest without any spin. After getting comfortable in microgravity, the two of them had spent the past two days competing to see who could handle the center of gravity in small objects more accurately.

Judy allowed the smartphone's mass to come to rest against her gently yielding index finger, then spun it around and pressed it against her palm. One set of phrases leaped out at her immediately from the avalanche of text.

Tether-propulsion system. Space tether. Really?

"Like father, like daughter," Ronnie said.

"What do you mean?" Judy asked.

"You're smiling," Ronnie said. "Just after being told you have two weeks to live."

"But isn't this amazing? A tether-propulsion system. Really in use. Who should we go to to talk about it? This Kazumi guy? Let's invest in it!"

"I knew you'd say that. But apparently he doesn't have a company for tether propulsion."

"We can figure something out, can't we? I thought you were Ronnie Smark!"

Ronnie doubled over with laughter. "You're right," he said. "Let's get right on it."

"It'll be a development company, so we'll start up as an LLC. Okay? Next we have to decide on a DBA and business address so that we can obtain an EIN . . ."

"It takes two weeks to register an EIN."

"Let's ask Ozzy to take care of the rest. He may be fat, but he's a start-up pro, right?"

"He's in Seychelles now."

"Who cares where he is?"

Judy kicked the wall and flew across to the oval window that faced up toward Earth. She wiped off the condensation. "We can still get people working on things," she said. "If this becomes the next big step for space exploration, how great would that be? Can I call a board meeting to get approval for investment from Project Wyvern?"

"Why would we want to do that when I can just invest from my personal funds?"

PART THREE
Orbital Cloud

13 Pier 37

Wed, 16 Dec 2020, 12:15 -0800 (2020-12-16T20:15 GMT)
Alaskan Way, Seattle

A mass of snow flew at Akari's face. She ducked and tried to dodge but lost her balance. The rear wheel of her mountain bike skidded out of control. She squeezed both brakes frantically but finally went down, leaving two long tracks in the surface of the road.

Alaskan Way was covered in snow. This was Akari's third fall since speeding past the sign declaring the highway closed. Snow filled the pockets of her cargo pants. She pushed herself up from the ground, burying her hands in white to her wrists. Her fingers were as cold as ice.

Akari checked the map on the smartphone attached to her handlebars.

"Just five hundred more meters."

She was almost at the warehouse . . . but then what? Akari wasn't sure herself. Hearing the CIA agents accuse her uncle of being some sort of terrorist mastermind had enraged her so much that she had simply run out of the room, with no particular long-term plan.

Straightening up, Akari yelled into the snow that beat at her face.

"It's impossible!"

She knew this wasn't true, of course. She didn't even believe what she was shouting. The CIA's deduction that Shiraishi had master-minded the Cloud fit perfectly with what she knew.

The technique for corrupting the online translation engine. The shadow-ware hidden in advertisements. The rose-scented D-Fi audio cables. The SIM card switching. And the program specifically written to view the Earth . . . She had not found these things by accident. She was chasing her uncle's shadow.

He was enjoying running the Cloud. He wouldn't be using up his bag of tricks on it otherwise. Asking herself what her uncle would do had always led her to the answer before. Even back when he had happily taught her how to program.

By the time he had left Japan, Shiraishi had changed. He allowed his irritation with companies who refused to take his security warnings seriously to show clearly, speaking with undisguised contempt. His geyser of ideas, once so abundant, dried up. "No one cares what an engineer has to say," he would say bitterly. Akari had distanced herself from him after he became like that. Even hearing that he had left Japan had meant little to her.

Not wanting to end up like him was the main reason she had come to Fool's Launchpad after finishing school. People there let her make full use of the skills she had cultivated. Especially Kazumi. Even minor refinements and tricks delighted him. She felt that this helped her stay focused on what lay ahead, even though her skills far exceeded her experience.

Akari forced herself to her feet. She heard the snow that had fallen on her head slide onto her shoulders. To the right, through the gaps in the line of trees by the side of the road, she could dimly see the cluster of snow-covered warehouses at Pier 37. Shiraishi had long sought a role that would recognize his talents, and he had found it in the field. He had to be in one of those warehouses.

She heard a metallic squeal behind her and saw a black Mustang stop on the rails under the Alaskan Way Viaduct. The passenger-side window opened.

"Akari! Get in!" called Bruce.

"I'm going to see Uncle Ageha!"

Bruce leaned across the passenger's seat and opened the door. "Yeah, I know!" he said. "Me too, so get in!"

Akari shook her head and righted the mountain bike, swinging her leg over the seat.

She was almost there. She didn't know what the CIA planned to do with Shiraishi, but she had some questions she wanted to ask him herself. Why had he abandoned Japan? Why was he involved in some North Korean scheme that amounted to terrorism?

Bruce spun the wheel to steer the Mustang off the tracks and into the street. Its once-shiny bumpers were cracked now, covered in snow and scratches.

"Just tell me one thing," he said. "If that's really Shiraishi in that warehouse, will he have realized that we've found him?"

Akari nodded. Her uncle would have noticed as soon as his new SIM card connected to the fake China Mobility hotspot, quickly ascertaining that the hotspot was actually a honeypot running on a Raspberry Pi.

"Better hurry, then," Bruce muttered to himself, then leaned toward her again. "I'm going to drop by the coast guard on the way to the warehouse," he said. "If you find Shiraishi, don't try anything. Just sit tight and wait."

The Mustang tore down Alaskan Way, half-skidding rear wheels kicking up flurries of snow in its wake.

Wed, 16 Dec 2020, 12:17 -0800 (2020-12-16T20:17 GMT)
Pier 37 Warehouse, Seattle

Shiraishi stepped out onto the external staircase on the north side of the building only to be forced back behind the door by Chance, who had gone ahead of him to check their surroundings. A black Mustang was tearing down Alaskan Way toward them, clouds of snow in its wake.

"The driver looked at me," she said.

"Sure you didn't imagine it?" he replied.

"No, he turned his head. Look how fast he's going. No one would take their eyes off the road in weather like this without a good reason. He knows we're here and he's coming for us."

"You worry too much."

Chance pointed to the stairs. "Move," she said. The snow had been falling since the night before and was now ankle-deep. Shiraishi held his blueprint case in one hand and gripped the railing with the other.

"Wait!" Chance said, then changed her mind. "No, hurry! A bike's coming."

Shiraishi craned his neck. Through the line of trees swaying as one in the blizzard, by the side of the road he saw a green mountain bike approaching. The woman riding it had Asian features and a shaved head, and didn't appear to be wearing anything warmer than a long-sleeved shirt.

"Shiraishi," Chance said. "Down."

Chance's arm emerged from her coat pocket. Shiraishi saw a red dot appear on the step below him. The laser scope on the gun that was now fused with her hand.

"Think of it as encouragement," Chance said, noticing Shiraishi's nervous reaction.

The mountain bike attempted to make it over the planter at the rear of the warehouse and failed spectacularly, throwing its rider into a snowdrift. The woman got to her feet immediately and brushed the snow off her face. The red dot slipped off the staircase and darted across the ground toward her, crimson flickers appearing here and there in the falling snow. Finally reaching her, it drew a line across her path.

The woman froze for an instant, then began to run again.

"Uncle Ageha!" she called.

Akari?

Shiraishi tried to rise from his crouch, but Chance held his head down.

"The laser scope's not scaring her off," she said. "Japanese, I presume? Who is she?"

What was Akari doing in a place like this? As he watched her approach, Shiraishi suddenly realized why Meteor News had been so overengineered—and why he had been tracked down so quickly. He had been up against a former coconspirator, a hacker he himself had shown the ropes to.

"Akari! Stay out of this!" Ageha called.

The red dot moved from Akari's feet to her thighs.

"Don't shoot her," he said to Chance. "Please."

Shiraishi reached above his head to grip Chance's arm. For a moment, his vision blurred white, and he felt a series of blows to his back. His ankle made an awful sound as it caught on one of the stairs.

He turned his head to look at Chance, now upside-down from his perspective. She had kicked him down the stairs. Without lowering her gun, she descended the snow-thick stairs after him, surprisingly agile for a woman in heels.

Shiraishi saw the blueprint case lying nearby and pulled it toward him. He raised his head. Akari was already close enough for him to read her face clearly.

The gun rang out: a small, dry sound. Chance had fired it into the warehouse wall. A large piece of the snow-caked exterior fell away, sending up a plume of sparks and snow right before Akari's eyes.

Surprised, Akari came to a halt. The red dot moved to her chest.

"Freeze!"

Chance grabbed Shiraishi by the collar and dragged him to his feet. Shiraishi cried out in pain as his ankle twisted.

"An associate of yours, I gather," Chance said. "If she doesn't get in our way, I won't have to kill her. Consider this the last favor I grant you." Chance glanced down at Shiraishi's twisted ankle. "Can't run?"

Shiraishi shook his head.

Chance tsked. Seeing Akari approach, she shouted, "Don't move!" and fired into the ground at Akari's feet before opening the warehouse door. The stink of gasoline came from within.

"Wait until the service entrance at the far end opens," she said to Ageha. "Then come out that way. I'll bring the car around. Meanwhile, no open flames of any kind inside the warehouse. The sprinkler system is full of gasoline, and I'm going to activate it just before I open the shutters at the service entrance. A moment after that, I'll be lighting it up. If you'd rather not burn to a cinder, wait inside the container."

Chance turned her gaze to the blueprint case under Shiraishi's arm.

"I'd appreciate it if you could arrange for that case to be lost in the fire, too," she said.

Shiraishi clung to the case tightly. Losing it would leave him with no other reason to keep running.

Chance wrapped her arm around his head and pulled him toward her. Her strength was startling. He smelled the familiar scent of her perfume blended with sweat.

"If Akari's lucky, she'll survive. Understood?"

Shiraishi nodded.

He turned and hobbled back inside the warehouse, dragging his injured foot. Chance closed the door behind him. The warehouse was illuminated only by what little sunlight fell through the skylight. Shiraishi headed for the container located in the middle of the echoing space.

If Akari was here, that meant that Kazumi had informed NORAD, too. No doubt the CIA would soon be along as well. If Shiraishi was captured, the space tether technology he had brought into being would be picked apart and then put to some practical use by the US—or, worse yet, by some US corporation. People like Ronnie Smark would adopt the new technology greedily. His daughter's blog had made that much clear just the other day.

The rest of the world would be forgotten, left to fall even further behind.

Shiraishi crawled into the windowless container as Chance had ordered and sat on a D-Fi package with his sketch case on his lap. The slogan written in white marker leaped out at him as his eyes adjusted to the dark:

GREAT LEAP FOR THE REST OF THE WORLD

He *had* to succeed.

"If even someone like me can reach out and touch space, anything's possible."

He needed to prepare the way for someone else to take control of the Cloud. Just in case.

Shiraishi searched his memory for a certain email address and began to compose a message.

Chahar-shambeh, 26 Azar 1399, 23:52 +0330
(2020-12-16T20:22 GMT)
Esperanto Hotel, Tehran

There was a muffled buzzing and a faint but familiar melody. An angular xylophone tune. The ringtone heard around the world.

Kurosaki felt his unshaven cheek scrape the pillow as he moved his head. He frowned and forced open his gummed-shut eyes. He saw raised embroidery on the wallpaper, which looked unnaturally thick in the warm light of the floor lamp. He tried to open his mouth, but his lips were stuck together as well. By his bedside he saw a glass of water. That was something to be grateful for.

Kurosaki reached for the glass and drank the water down in one gulp. That was when he noticed the neatly handwritten note:

UNBOILED WATER TO KEEP AIR FROM DRYING OUT—DO NOT DRINK!

The handwriting was Sekiguchi's.

"Idiot . . . Of course I was going to drink it. Use mineral water next time, would you?"

Kurosaki's head still felt fuzzy. He needed more sleep. What had woken him up this time?

"Oh, right. The phone."

The ringtone just now had been his.

Kurosaki sat up and looked around the room again. The wallpaper was covered in ethnic embroidery, but it was a perfectly modern hotel room. Beside the desk he saw Sekiguchi's suit and the field coat he had worn in the van yesterday. Both hung from clothes hangers, looking like servants standing at attention.

At some point Kurosaki himself had been changed into some kind of hotel nightgown. His skin was clean. Someone must have given him a sponge bath and put him to bed. In the bed alongside his own he saw Sekiguchi, lying with his face to the wall.

Kurosaki had fallen asleep while talking to Sekiguchi in the van after folding the flag and putting it in a bag. He could still feel how rough those Iranian cigarettes had been on his throat—uh-oh. Now he desperately wanted one. There was an ashtray on the desk. Must be a smoking room. Didn't see many of those in Japan these days.

"Pay you back later, Sekiguchi," Kurosaki muttered. As he recalled, those Iranian cigarettes had gone back into Sekiguchi's pocket. He slid his feet into a pair of soft leather slippers complete with heels and padded over to Sekiguchi's suit.

Reaching into the pocket, his fingertips brushed a scrap of thin paper. The cigarettes must be in the field coat.

For no reason in particular, he snagged the scrap of paper with his fingers and pulled it out. What he saw made him draw in his breath sharply.

中华人民共和国外交行李票

They were somewhat different from the Chinese characters used in Japan but were similar enough to be legible:

People's Republic of China - Baggage Tag

A red rectangle with yellow stars was printed in the top-right corner—the national flag of China. This must be what Sekiguchi had torn off the duralumin cases and stuffed into his pocket after picking up the Iridiums at the airport.

"Diplomatic privilege," Kurosaki murmured. "So that's how you got them into Iran."

The way Sekiguchi had detected and outsmarted the spy at Fool's Launchpad. The suite at the Nippon Grand. The chartered helicopter, the fluent Persian, the advance knowledge of an attempted takeover by antigovernment groups of a student demonstration in Tehran . . . It was just too much to accept as the work of a mere bureaucrat, no matter how elite.

Sekiguchi was a Chinese spy.

He heard the xylophone tune again. His phone.

Sekiguchi sat up. "Good morning. Did you sleep well? Ah—your phone's ringing. It's in the pocket of your suit, in the closet."

"Forget the phone," Kurosaki said. "You—you're . . ." He unfolded the baggage tag again and held it up.

"Busted!" Sekiguchi said, slapping his forehead and falling back onto the bed. "You've got me. I was planning to tell you on the way home. Anyway, go ahead and take that call. It's probably urgent."

"We'll be having a long talk about this later," Kurosaki said. He opened the black lacquered doors of the closet to reveal his wrinkled suit. Rummaging through the pockets, he produced his cigarettes and lighter first, then his phone, which had already stopped ringing. He unlocked the screen and checked the call history. Two calls from Kazumi in Seattle.

"Kazumi," he said. "Want to hear the voice message?"

Sekiguchi nodded. Kurosaki set the phone to speaker and played back the message from Kazumi.

"Kurosaki-san! I'm looking at Shiraishi right now. You have to help persuade him to cut his ties with North Korea. Please call me back on video."

Kurosaki stared at the screen. With Shiraishi? Wasn't he supposed to be in China?

He was about to tap the button to call Kazumi back when Sekiguchi leaped to his feet.

"Not a voice call!" Sekiguchi said. "It has to be video, or we won't be able to see what's going on over there."

Kurosaki tapped the video-call button instead. After the whistle announcing the connection, the screen showed a mass of white. Snow.

"Shirashi-san!" they heard Kazumi yell in Japanese. "Open the door!"

"Step aside, Kazumi." A man's voice they didn't recognize, speaking in English. "I'll break us in."

There was a sharp, metallic report, and after some confusion a dim room appeared on-screen. A woman in cargo pants with a shaved head—Akari—ran across their field of view.

"Uncle Ageha!"

"Please come out, Shiraishi-san. We just want to talk."

The picture shook again. They saw a carelessly stacked pile of boxes. Containers, a crane. Kazumi was in a warehouse.

"Looks like things are heating up there," Sekiguchi said. He stripped off his own hotel nightgown and grabbed his coat from the hanger rack. "Let's put it up on the TV. I'll turn the lights on."

Sekiguchi picked up Kurosaki's smartphone and connected it to the television with a cable he pulled from his suitcase. He then carefully set the phone at the right angle for the two of them to appear in the video call.

Kurosaki watched impatiently. "We don't have time for—"

"It won't do any good to get excited," Sekiguchi said. "Our job right now is to stay calm and back Kazumi up." He zipped up his coat and dragged the sofa over in front of the television. "Unlike them, we aren't in any danger of getting shot. So let's stay calm."

"Shot?"

"We don't know if Shiraishi has a gun or not. Either way, though, there's bound to be someone with a gun watching over him. You'd better get dressed. There's probably time for a cigarette too."

Sekiguchi took another coat from the hanger rack and tossed it to Kurosaki.

"The battlefield's over there now."

Wed, 16 Dec 2020, 12:23 -0800 (2020-12-16T20:23 GMT)
Pier 37 Warehouse, Seattle

Chance raised her collar to protect her eyes from the pelting snow and crouched behind the planter. She looked back and forth between the service entrance Shiraishi was supposed to emerge from and the parking lot in front of the building that she had just circled back around. The falling snow began accumulating on her right side almost immediately.

The Porsche Cayenne they would use to make their escape was parked beyond the two trucks in front of the service entrance. Shifting her position, Chance noticed an air force–blue Chevy wagon stopped next to the Cayenne. Tsk. It must have rolled up just moments before. There was no snow covering the white star painted on its hood yet. NORAD, then.

That woman who had arrived by bicycle—Akari—was no longer the sole obstacle to their escape. Chance searched her memory map for Akari's full name. There it was: Akari Numata. Quite a coincidence. How unlucky could one man be? Chased down in a foreign country by someone who knew him personally!

Not that Chance was doing much better in the luck department. If a man was in the picture as well now, he might be able to break the door to the warehouse she'd stowed Shiraishi in.

Chance went over the escape plan in her head once more. She would use the smartphone in her left hand to activate the service entrance shutter and the ignition inside the warehouse. When the building caught fire and Shiraishi came hobbling out on his bad leg, she would pull him to the Cayenne by his left arm. Akari and whoever was here from NORAD would be sure to give chase. If she used her gun to keep them at bay, she would run out of free hands. That meant that she needed to unlock the Cayenne now, while she still could.

As Chance rummaged in her pocket for the remote control, another problem occurred to her: that black man who had been flying down Alaskan Way at ridiculous speeds in his Mustang. There was no question that he had looked directly at her. He must have been headed for the coast guard base between this pier and the next one.

Chance rose slightly and turned her head from side to side. She was just in time to see two figures running toward the warehouse from Alaskan Way. Both were carrying M4 carbines.

The black man was in the lead, still wearing the same inappropriate suit but with a helmet on now too. Probably a CIA agent, Chance surmised, but she did note that the brisk pace he kept up through the snow in his combat boots suggested some experience under fire.

The other man followed closely behind. He was wearing body armor and a fluorescent harness. This was the coast guard, then. He was just as sure on his feet as the other. The two of them exchanged hand signals and dropped into crouches, advancing in alternation toward the warehouse a few yards at a time to minimize the amount of time each of them was exposed.

"Just great," Chance murmured.

Both men were armed professionals. Even one of them would have posed a threat to Chance, who was carrying only a pistol.

Squinting against the snow, Chance watched their route and hand signals closely. The CIA agent pointed at the trucks in front of the warehouse's service entrance and raised two fingers. They would split up and go around the vehicles separately.

The trucks were ten meters away. If Chance ran, she would get there first. If she could put one of them out of action, her escape would be certain. Both, and she could take Shiraishi with her.

Chance waited for the exact moment that the two men disappeared behind the trucks, then leaped out from behind the planter.

Her target was the coast guard sailor bringing up the rear. She opened the front of her coat and tore open her shirt, letting the buttons pop off. Snowflakes fell on her chest.

"Help!" she cried.

Carefully timing her move, Chance ran around the corner and threw herself on the coast guard sailor's chest. She quickly read his name tag: A. NASH.

"Nash, look! Over there!"

Nash was so taken aback that he turned unthinkingly to look where Chance was pointing.

Chance darted around behind him as if cowering from some enemy. As she clung to him with her left arm, she searched the nape of his neck, his shoulders, and his lower back for seams in his body armor.

Nash tilted his head back, still looking where she'd pointed, and asked, "What am I looking at?"

"Inside the shutters! Look!"

Nash looked at the service entrance again. Chance jammed her pistol into his side and pulled the trigger.

There was a muffled crack, and Nash's whole body shook. The reduced-powder hollow-point .45 round had made mincemeat of his insides, then hit his body armor and stopped, just as Chance had planned. On a snowy battlefield, a spurt of enemy blood could be the giveaway that ended your own life. She didn't want the CIA agent in the suit to realize that his companion from the coast guard was dead. When pressed directly against a human target, her SIG with its resinous modifications was even quieter than it would have been with a silencer. Out in the open during a snowstorm, the noise was unlikely to have carried to the far side of the trucks.

She reached from behind to grasp Nash's neck warmer and pulled it up to cover the bloody foam coming from his mouth. Then she lowered his body to the ground and leaned him against one of the truck's tires, carefully arranging him on one knee to look as though he were still providing covering fire. Finally, she hid behind him and waited.

No sooner had she concealed herself than the CIA agent appeared at the other end of the truck. He flattened his back against the wall of the warehouse and gestured: *Come.* Chance carefully took hold of Nash's sleeve and raised his arm. This was the army hand signal for *Understood.* The snow was falling thick and fierce in front of the warehouse where the agent stood; at a glance, he would not notice her lurking behind his companion.

Chance shook Nash's body, stabilizing him in his kneeling stance.

Nash was carrying only the equipment ready at hand. He didn't even have a radio. The agent must have been requisitioned in a hurry, just moments earlier. So it would not be unusual for the two of them to miscommunicate occasionally.

The agent kicked the snow in apparent frustration, then crawled through the gap in the shutters into the warehouse. That suit of his probably meant that he was more of an investigator than a soldier. He would be no match for her in a game of cat and mouse.

She would have preferred to kill him while he was still outside the warehouse, but if she missed and he fired back, a round from his M4 would go right through Nash's body and into hers. Going up against his rifle with only a pistol would be foolish.

Chance produced her smartphone and pressed a white app icon that read simply "Fire."

The app came up on the screen. Inside the warehouse, if all had gone well, a lightbulb hanging just beside the fire alarm had just lit up. The surface of the bulb had been scored with a file in a cross-hatch pattern and covered in tar. Within minutes, the tar would start to vaporize from the heat. The fire alarm would interpret the smoking tar as a fire and trigger the sprinkler system, the tanks of which had been emptied of water and filled with gasoline instead. After the sprinklers had had a chance to spray the warehouse full of gasoline, the lightbulb would break and its exposed filament would set the whole thing alight.

That moment would be Shiraishi's only chance to escape.

After watching to make sure that the CIA agent wasn't coming back out of the warehouse, Chance took Nash's M4. She knelt, using the slowly stiffening body as a shooting bench to aim the rifle at the service entrance.

She licked the resin cover on her left index finger and touched it to the trigger. A red dot flickered on the shutters of the service entrance. Using the laser scope, even firing with her left hand she should have no trouble hitting whatever came out of the door.

When the fire alarm went off, the shutters would rise. If she could shoot everyone except Shiraishi then, the two of them could escape. As long as that CIA agent didn't try to shield him . . .

"Better make your way out," she muttered. "I'd rather not have to kill you."

She let her index finger move off the trigger and dug her knees into the snow, stabilizing the gun's barrel. Her back caught the worst of the pelting snow, inadvertently sheltering Nash's body below her.

Wed, 16 Dec 2020, 12:24 -0800 (2020-12-16T20:24 GMT)
Pier 37 Warehouse, Seattle

Stepping inside the warehouse with Daryl following closely behind, Kazumi covered his face against the pungent smell. The smell of gasoline, blended with the rose perfume of the D-Fi cables, filled the air. A container sat square in the middle of the dim warehouse, with a bed, a television, and other furnishings piled up beside it. The far wall had what looked like a service entrance set in it, with external shutters that were currently raised just enough to allow the wind and snow into the room.

"Why did you leave Japan, Uncle Ageha?" Akari screamed, shaking the snow off her clothes.

"Go home, Akari. You're going to get yourself killed this time."

The voice carried surprisingly well from inside the container.

Daryl tapped Kazumi on the shoulder and pointed with his hatchet at the right side of the container, suggesting that they split up and approach the container from both sides at once.

Kazumi waved at Akari and pointed at Daryl's back. If something went wrong, the soldier would be the one they looked to for help. Akari nodded and stepped behind Daryl.

"Shiraishi-san, please hand over control of the space tethers," Kazumi said in Japanese.

Daryl glanced his way. He probably would have preferred that Kazumi use English. But Shiraishi was Japanese, as were Akari and Kurosaki. Daryl and the CIA agents would just have to watch a recording of the video call later to catch up.

Kazumi slowly walked toward the left side of the container.

"I've got Kurosaki-san on a video call," he said. "You can talk to him. We've been watching those space tethers you have up there, Shiraishi-san. We know . . ." He caught himself before he said "almost." There was no need to underplay their hand here. "We know everything about them."

Akari turned toward Kazumi, wide-eyed.

"No one's been harmed in orbit yet," Kazumi continued. "It's not too late. Come out of hiding. Join Dr. Jahanshah and make the space tether system public."

Daryl and Akari disappeared around the side of the container.

"The picture of the Earth you took from orbit gave me chills, Shiraishi-san. An eighty thousand–camera light-field image of our planet—one look at that is all the proof anyone would need that the space tethers are going to change everything. Spacecraft that can orbit forever without even needing any fuel! The whole world will have ideas about how to use them."

Kazumi paused. There was no sign of movement.

"Please, Shiraishi-san—"

There was a rustle from inside the container and then a man's voice said, "That's far enough. Stop where you are."

Kazumi froze in place.

A man wearing a coat emerged from the container carrying a black blueprint case. He pushed his glasses up the bridge of his nose with his middle finger.

"Kazumi, was it? Not bad. Only a couple of days and you got as far as the light field?"

"Yes. We're eavesdropping on all of the telemetry the tethercraft send back. Akari stitched the images together."

"Eavesdropping? So the CIA is working with you? Maybe the NSA? Not bad at all!"

Shiraishi put his hand in his pocket. Kazumi suddenly realized how vulnerable he was. Did Shiraishi have a gun?

As if sensing Kazumi's unease, Shiraishi took a step toward him. "This isn't the sort of party you should come to empty-handed," he said.

"I came here to talk," said Kazumi. "That's all. Stop the tethercraft and come out of the shadows."

"I'll pass on that one," said Shiraishi. "I took out the Wyvern's reentry vessel and Japan's entire IGS fleet. I'm a wanted man."

"Kazumi, let me talk to him," came Sekiguchi's voice. Kazumi held his phone up. "Shiraishi-san, can you hear me?" Sekiguchi said. "This is Sekiguchi from JAXA. Please do as Kazumi says. It's not too late. Seek asylum in America. The Japanese government won't go after you there."

"And then?"

"The space tether plus some intelligence on the North Koreans should be enough to get you a place on the Witness Protection Program."

"I'm not talking about me. If I give up now, what happens to the people cut off from space altogether?" Shiraishi took another step forward. He held up the black case he was holding, showing the white lettering: GREAT LEAP FOR THE REST OF THE WORLD. "Can you read

that, Sekiguchi? As I recall, JAXA was just a stepping-stone for you—
you're really more the international type. You should know as well as
anyone how fortunate Japan is."

Lips curling into a sneer, Shiraishi pointed his finger at the phone.

"Is that Kurosaki there with you? You've put on a few, Kurosaki.
But if you leave Japan and its wealth behind, you start to notice things.
The rocket men in North Korea know that whatever they manage to
put into orbit will be labeled a weapon or a missile, but they keep
clawing for the stars anyway. What little pay they do receive all goes
to bribes to keep them on the space program. But do they give up? "

Shiraishi's finger began to tremble.

"There's a man out there doing cutting-edge research without
even an Internet connection. Kazumi, you know him too, right? I'm
talking about Jamshed. He'd do anything to get his spacecraft off the
ground. It's my job to make that happen."

Kurosaki coughed. "You haven't changed a bit, Shiraishi," he
said. "Can't bear to see a technician in trouble."

"That's not what this is about."

"But you can't sacrifice yourself for their sake. It starts to go to
your head. Are you serious about what's written on that case?"

Shiraishi glanced down at the lettering on his black blueprint case.

"Neil Armstrong meets Apple," Kurosaki continued. "I like it.
You always did have a way with words. Almost enough to take me in
as well."

Shiraishi turned the case around and hugged it to his chest.

"Shiraishi-san," Kurosaki said. "Please. Stop doing this to yourself. There are people here right now who need your help. Give Kazumi
what he wants. He's got a knack for this stuff. He can help you."

There was a brief pause.

"No," said Shiraishi finally. "I don't need anyone's help. I mobilized a nation all by myself to get those forty thousand tethers up there. No one else could have done that."

"You're wrong, Shiraishi," said Kazumi, stamping his foot. "Your Cloud is just a bunch of debris boosted into low Earth orbit."

"You think that's what the Cloud's for too? Don't move!" Shiraishi glared at where Daryl and Akari were standing beyond the container, then turned back to Kazumi. "The Cloud is the first step in freeing all the countries denied access to space. Developed countries will be forced to withdraw their satellites from orbit, and launching new ones will be pointless. With tens of thousands of tethers up there, we'll be able to knock their satellites down as fast as they can send them up."

"You want to close off orbit altogether?" Kazumi said.

"That's right. Not forever. A few years should do it. That'll be enough time for North Korea, Iran, Pakistan, and the countries of Africa to advance their space-development programs. Engineers will flock to them from all over the world. Orbit doesn't belong to America and Europe. We're going to clear the decks and start again. That's the Great Leap."

A slightly overdramatic sigh came from Sekiguchi over the speaker. "Is *that* what the Great Leap was all about?" he asked.

"You'd heard of it already?"

"Only the name. I didn't know the details until now. Sounds pretty stupid, to be honest."

"What did you say?"

"He said it was stupid!" shouted Akari from behind the container. "Uncle Ageha, what's happened to you? You always hated enclosure and monopolies. The greater the flow of information, the better, you said. What are you going to achieve by shutting out the people making the most effort?"

"Space development isn't like the IT industry," Shiraishi said.

"You think someone like Ronnie Smark could come out of Ethiopia or Iran?"

"That's not what I mean! No one's saying that where Ronnie was born or where he grew up doesn't mean anything. You know this, Uncle Ageha!"

"Shiraishi-san, I can tell you exactly what the Great Leap will achieve," Sekiguchi said coldly. "Most of the new projects will just be poor imitations of what the developed countries are already doing. The engineers you'll 'save' will be stuck reinventing the wheel with fewer resources and worse technology."

"You're wrong," Shiraishi snarled. "I'll feed them fresh ideas, better ones. The space tether is just the beginning."

"Come out of hiding and do it, then!" Kazumi cried. "The space tether is enough to excite anybody. It's a dream come true. It deserves to be used for more than orbital terrorism." He reached out to Shiraishi with one hand. "Shiraishi-san, come with me. I want the whole world to learn what you can do."

"Please, Uncle Ageha," said Akari. "It's not too late."

Shiraishi knocked Kazumi's hand back and turned away from them.

There was a screech as the shutters across the warehouse began to move. Shiraishi smiled.

"I always enjoy catching up with old friends," he said. "But I'm afraid my ride is here."

"Isn't there anything I can say to convince you, Uncle Ageha?" pleaded Akari.

Shiraishi glanced up at the roof with a look of concern but continued to retreat toward the service entrance. "Take care of yourself, Akari," he said. "Don't try to follow me. The woman I'm seeing wouldn't like that very much."

Turning toward the exit, Shiraishi froze. A figure was crouching before him.

Bruce was down on one knee with his M4 at the ready.

"So you're Shiraishi," Bruce said. "CIA. Take that hand out of your pocket and put both hands above your head."

Shiraishi withdrew one hand from his pocket, still gripping his phone. He raised both hands high, holding his phone in one and his blueprint case in the other.

"Where's your minder?" asked Bruce.

Shiraishi shook his head. Bruce rose to his feet, drew a pistol with his left hand, and slid it across the ground to Daryl.

Akari pointed at the service entrance. "A woman just ran past there," she said.

"So she's circling around to the front," Bruce said.

That was where Nash was. Bruce wished he'd joined them in the warehouse, but at least this way the front was secure. They should be able to capture Shiraishi safely.

"I didn't catch everything you said in Japanese, but I advise you to take Kazumi up on his offer," Bruce said. "Tell us what you know and seek asylum in the States. I'll get you into Witness Protection. You can continue your research—just not in public. Daryl, search him."

Daryl jogged over to Shiraishi and patted him down. He was as unarmed as he looked.

"Think about it," Bruce said. "You say no, we'll still get the information out of you one way or another. The only difference is whether or not you go to prison. Now slowly crouch down and put what you're holding on the floor."

"*You* think about it," Shiraishi sneered. "If you shoot me, your only hope of stopping the space tethers vanishes too."

Bruce slammed the stock of his M4 into Shiraishi's abdomen.

"Bruce, stop it!" cried Akari.

Shiraishi's glasses went flying. He fell to his knees.

Bruce grabbed a fistful of Shiraishi's hair and forced his head down to the floor before pinning him down with one knee in his back.

"Don't get cocky," Bruce said. "Kazumi will take care of the space tethers for us. What's that?"

The warehouse was suddenly bathed in flashing red light. The fire alarm. Bruce looked around but saw no sign of smoke or flames.

"So this is it," Shiraishi groaned under Bruce's knee. "About time, Chance."

"What are you talking about?"

"Run, you idiot," Shiraishi said. "Unless you'd rather burn."

There was a hollow thunk and the groan of a motor. The sprinkler system sprang into life, spraying the warehouse with a foul-smelling liquid.

"Gasoline! Everybody out. Daryl, open the shutters."

"They're opening on their own!"

Daryl was right. The shutters were rising, letting in ever more of the howling wind and snow.

"It's a trap! Run toward the service entrance and stick to the wall close by. Scatter!"

Bruce dragged Shiraishi to one side of the entrance, Kazumi following closely behind. Looking back, Bruce saw Akari still standing in the middle of the warehouse, apparently dazed.

"Daryl! Get Akari down!"

A bright-red dot had appeared on Akari's lower back. An M4's laser scope. Nash?

Looking out through the service entrance, Bruce thrust out his open palm, the signal for *Stop*. Next he raised his head and brought his hand to his throat: *Civilian/Hostage*. Outside he could see Nash still leaning against the tire, his hands dangling at his sides. The red gleam of the laser scope was coming from just above his shoulder.

Not Nash. Someone behind him.

"Wai—"

Shiraishi shoved Bruce aside midword, running past him. "Chance!" he screamed. "Don't shoot!"

He had just passed Akari when there was a sudden cloud of red mist.

Bruce leveled his M4 at Nash and fired a hail of bullets in that direction. A figure holding an M4 slipped out from behind the jerking corpse and ran for cover behind the truck.

Kazumi tried to push past Bruce. "Shiraishi!" he cried.

Bruce caught Kazumi by the belt and pulled him back. Shiraishi was lying on the floor, neck bent at an impossible angle and blood pouring from a throat wound.

They heard a burst of gunfire. Sparks fell on the container.

"Daryl! Three shots out through the door!"

Bruce moved his M4's selector to BURST. Daryl fell back, supporting Akari as he fired his pistol. Three, two, one. Now it was Bruce's turn. He leaned out and checked for any sign of another person behind Nash. Nothing. Whoever it was didn't even seem to be behind the truck.

Bruce burst out of the service entrance and dropped to his stomach to survey the parking lot from between the wheels of the truck.

A woman in high heels was running through the snow.

Bruce fired a controlled burst of three rounds at her. She stumbled in a spray of snow and red mist. He caught one glimpse of her bright-red lips in the white flurry as she glanced his way before rising to her feet again and firing a burst into the tires of Daryl's Chevy. Then she leaped into a Porsche Cayenne, gunned the engine, and sped away.

". . . Ageha. Uncle Ageha! Somebody, stop the bleeding!"

Bruce turned his head at the sound of Akari screaming and saw heat haze rising from the haphazard pile of D-Fi boxes in the container. Gasoline—sparks—

"Everybody out!" Bruce yelled. "Away from the warehouse!"

Akari clung to Shiraishi's neck, pressing at the wound with her hand.

"Daryl!" Bruce called. "Pull Akari away! We have to run—this place is gonna blow!"

With Kazumi's help, Daryl peeled Akari off Shiraishi as Bruce ran toward them.

"No!" Akari cried. "We can't just leave him!"

Bruce swung the struggling Akari over one shoulder and began running toward the pier.

"Uncle Ageha!" she cried. "Bruce, let me go!"

Bruce kept running. When that explosion came, he planned to be as far away as possible. Akari stopped struggling and went limp over his shoulder. The case in her hand bounced against his lower back as they ran.

"Why?" she wailed. "Why would they shoot him? Was what he did so wrong? He could still have called it off . . ."

Bruce was beginning to wish that he'd never learned Japanese. Then a brilliant light shone behind them, followed by a wave of unnatural warmth that washed past them a moment later. The explosion. Thermite?

Bruce tossed Akari into a drift of snow and flung himself to the ground. Looking back he saw the warehouse engulfed in flames, rocked by the occasional smaller blast here and there. Buffeted by the blast wind, Nash's still-kneeling body swayed before slowly toppling over.

Sorry, Nash. You answered my call for help, and this is how I repaid you.

Kazumi and Daryl caught up with them.

"Are you two okay?" Bruce asked. "No burns? If you got any gas on your skin, rub it off with snow. You'll get a rash otherwise. Akari—"

Akari was still on her knees, watching the warehouse burn to the ground. Shaking, she hugged Shiraishi's case to her chest with arms that were still red with blood. She was in shock. She might understand that Shiraishi was dead, but it was unlikely that she had processed everything else that had happened that night.

Shiraishi, dead. All at once, Bruce felt the weight of the loss.

A man who had realized one unique idea after another, culminating in a scheme that turned a far-fetched concept for a new type of spacecraft into a reality orbiting the planet right now. And all he had left behind was the case in Akari's arms—which, Bruce knew from the way it had bounced against his back, contained nothing but paper.

Shiraishi had schemed on a scale that approached the absurd. But he had kept it all in his head and taken it with him when he died.

Bruce threw his helmet into the snow and pulled his smartphone from his pocket.

How was he going to report this to Chris?

Wed, 16 Dec 2020, 13:02 -0800 (2020-12-16T21:02 GMT)
Western Days Hotel

The glass screen of the phone Chris held to her cheek had warmed above body temperature. She seldom received reports this long by phone.

"Ah," she said. "I see. I'll get on that right away."

"What happened?" came Jamshed's composed voice from the video-call speaker.

"Sorry to keep you waiting at this time of night," Chris said.

"It is no problem. I have too much data analysis to finish for sleep anyway. Is something wrong?"

Chris had placed a video call to Jamshed to check whether he had made up his mind about their offer of refuge, only to be interrupted by a phone call from Bruce.

She debated for a moment whether she could tell Jamshed what Bruce had reported. But the demonstration today of the damage that hiding things could do was too fresh in her mind. If everyone had been sharing the same information, Shiraishi and Nash might both still be alive. In any case, it would all be public knowledge soon.

"Shiraishi is dead," she said.

Jamshed was silent for a moment. "I see," he said. "This is unfortunate. Did the CIA kill him?"

"No. It seems that he was shot by his North Korean handler."

"Nations . . . I am not sure how to say this. They are . . . a problematic framework. I see. It was because he died, then."

"What was?"

"I received a message. From Shiraishi."

"Will you tell me what it said?"

Chris double-checked that the conversation was being recorded.

"Was very simple," Jamshed said. "His goals for swarm of space tethers, which he calls a Cloud. His plans for the future. Also, controller and account for space tethers. He was perhaps expecting that he is killed or captured one day."

Chris felt a wave of relief. Now they could learn what the North Koreans planned to do with the Cloud and also seize control of it. The final pieces of the puzzle had come together.

"So you can stop the space tethers now?"

"Yes, that would be possible." Jamshed's gaze did not meet the camera as he spoke. He was looking at another screen. He stroked his beard and rocked his head slowly from side to side. "This control panel is very interesting. Everything I proposed in my paper is realized perfectly. It seems Shiraishi understood my space tethers completely. I wish we could have talked just once."

Through the speakers, Chris heard the sound of Jamshed's mouse clicking.

"So Shiraishi was a compatriot of Kazumi's. A wonderful country, Japan. It reminds me of when I was first learning about tether propulsion with Lorentz force from an illustration by Japanese space agency. Spacecraft that use only electricity—no need to make engines. Iran could research this, develop it. So I thought."

"And you were right. Your paper was the starting point for those space tethers flying around up there right now."

"Thank you, Chris. But for real development I needed an environment with interest in technology and engineering. Tehran is not such an environment. I had no way to share these ideas." Jamshed was still looking at the other screen. "Hmm. This is quite brilliant too." His mouse clicked. "I will read from Shiraishi's notes, yes? He planned to use the space tethers to cause accidents of unknown origin in low Earth orbit. Many times, hundreds of times more accidents than orbital-debris density suggests, sparking uncertainty and fear of space. This creates opportunity for countries that know of space tethers and where they are to attract workers from all through the world and take the lead in space development. He calls this plan the 'Great Leap for the Rest of the World.' Very well named."

"He planned to . . . to close orbit off entirely, then," Chris said. "But the space tethers have been discovered. Even if there are accidents, they won't be mysterious."

"This is true. Kazumi saw through to the truth. Brilliant work. With someone like that, you may even think of a way to stop the space tethers."

"I'm sure we will. But he'll need your help too."

Jamshed's hand stopped moving. His gaze returned to the camera, meeting Chris's eyes across the connection.

"He does not need someone like me."

"That isn't true. Kazumi's an amateur."

"An amateur who is more than a match for me, Chris." Jamshed laughed, giving Chris goose bumps. "It is I who am 'the rest of the world,' as Shiraishi says. I am the left behind. So I shall see that the Great Leap becomes reality. Even if space tethers are known to exist, there is a way to break the will of developed country to go into space. This is Shiraishi's final message to me."

"What is?" Chris demanded. "Tell me what you're going to do!"

"Kazumi might know. Ask him. I must be going. My workload has just increased significantly."

The video call was disconnected. Chris tried to reconnect but received only a "User unknown" message. Jamshed had deleted his account.

Chris's goose bumps had spread across her entire body.

They had lost Jamshed.

Shiraishi was gone, but his forty thousand space tethers were still up there in orbit. The threat had not been reduced at all. On the contrary—it had grown. Jamshed would surely take measures more extreme than anything Shiraishi had done.

Chris glanced at her watch.

She had to get the team back on track and start working on countermeasures. And she had to do it before Jamshed made his own move.

14 Team Seattle

Panjshambe, 27 Azar 1399, 03:22 +0330 (2020-12-16T23:52 GMT)
Tehran Institute of Technology

Inside the dim laboratory, Jamshed reached for one of the yellow pieces of paper hanging from the roof and pulled it toward him. He copied the blurred numbers on the cathode tube onto it, then went through a few calculations to obtain a set of coordinates which he circled and numbered: #343.

He was still less than one hundredth of the way through the work he needed to do.

Letting go of the paper, Jamshed folded his arms above his head and slumped in his chair. Clearly, tracking and controlling each of the forty thousand space tethers individually was not going to work. He looked at the swaying slips of paper, checking the coordinates one by one.

Shiraishi's Cloud had been divided into three separate clusters, moving independently, but Jamshed could see no order in their spin, velocity, or formation. This meant that the calculations had been done using computers, not by hand.

"I'll just have to reunite the Cloud," he murmured to himself.

He would gather the whole group of forty thousand space tethers in one place. That much would be easy. If he directed them all at the same destination, before long they would all arrive. By adding a few tiny variations to the orbital elements he sent, he could shape the swarm into a dense spherical cloud.

That was more in line with his goals, too. He had neither the technique nor the time to destroy satellites with the sort of finesse Shiraishi had exhibited. Over in Seattle, Kazumi was desperately searching for a way to knock the space tethers out of orbit. Jamshed had to sweep low Earth orbit clear of satellites before that happened.

Jamshed Jahanshah, genius spacecraft inventor, was now flying the flag of the Great Leap, entrusted to him by Shiraishi at the moment of his death.

Jamshed gathered up all the yellow posters lying on the floor with nothing written on the back yet and carried them to his desk. Pen in hand, he visualized the three subclouds that Shiraishi had left behind and began working out an orbit that all three could easily converge on.

After a few minutes of experimental calculations, a suitable orbit began to emerge from the figures. If he had the space tethers move at top speed, the Cloud could be reassembled in four hours. Now he needed a TLE with that moment as the epoch. Inclination 43 degrees, right ascension of ascending node 120 degrees . . . Velocity expressed as mean motion, 15.1 revolutions per day.

"This will do nicely."

There was, it occurred to him, another celestial body with a similar TLE. The Project Wyvern orbital hotel. Let that be the first object the reformed Cloud devoured, then. If he set the space tethers to their maximum rotational speed, their terminal apparatuses would move at ten kilometers per second. Whatever sort of spacecraft the orbital hotel might be, this would surely tear it to shreds. The two civilians aboard would become symbols of the LEO massacre.

"And after that, Tiangong-2. I'll just need to raise the orbit a little."

After cleaning up his target TLE and adding a small margin of error, he entered it into the controller he had inherited from Shiraishi and hit Submit.

The controller transmitted the instructions to the sixty thousand base stations scattered around the world, which sent them on VHF waves to the orbiting space tethers. Receiving their new orders, the tethercraft used the feedback program Jamshed had devised to skew their motion toward the target orbit.

Jamshed checked the mass of coordinates flowing down the screen and confirmed that things were in motion. He was master of the space tethers once more.

"Marvelous."

Shiraishi's design embodied Jamshed's theories perfectly. From the use of spin and randomly moving ballast for stabilization to the flocking flight pattern and trial-and-error feedback mechanism for attaining the target orbit, Shiraishi had understood and given form to all of the possibilities Jamshed had hinted at.

What kind of man had this Shiraishi been? A Japanese engineer who had built the space tethers with North Korean resources. A man who could achieve an impossible task like that would surely have had no difficulty finding employment away from the shadows if he had so desired.

Jamshed closed his eyes. As he did, he heard the door open.

"Who's there?!"

An Asian man with thinning hair in a mousy suit stood at the entrance with a flashlight in his hand. The flashlight's beam reflected from the floor to illuminate his face from below, lending an eerie cast to his already tired and unhealthy-looking features.

"Professor Ryu," Jamshed said. "What brings you here at this time of night?"

Jamshed had met Ryu before. He was here on the technological exchange program between Iran and North Korea. Iran had sent Jamshed's old advisor Hamed to North Korea in exchange, apparently with Jamshed's space tether paper in his suitcase. About Ryu's personal life Jamshed knew nothing, although rumor had it that he had been sent to Iran as punishment for his role in the failure of Taepodong-2.

"My apologies for disturbing you at this hour," said Ryu. "May I have a few minutes of your time?"

He turned out the flashlight and walked toward Jamshed.

"According to one of our agents in the US, Professor Jahanshah, you have stolen a weapon belonging to my country."

"Weapon?"

"Something called a 'space tether.'"

Jamshed leaped to his feet. The paper piled on his knees tumbled to the floor.

"You are the ones who stole it!"

Ryu shrank from the outburst. "Wait," he said, backing away with one palm upraised.

Jamshed kicked a folding chair out of the way and closed the distance between the two of them, treading on the fallen paper without a second thought. "The space tether was mine," he snarled, "until North Korea stole it from me!" He seized the smaller man's collar in his fist.

"I can't breathe!" Ryu said. "Let me go!"

His flashlight fell to the floor and broke, sending shards of plastic flying.

"Listen!" gasped Ryu. "The space tether is yours. We have decided to give it to you—no, *return* it to you. We only ask one favor. Do not carry out the plan the previous mission leader conveyed to you. There must be no LEO massacre."

"What?" Jamshed loosened his grip. Had the plan to destroy all satellites in low Earth orbit been against North Korea's wishes? "We clean out low Earth orbit so that North Korea, Iran, and Pakistan can begin space development together—the Great Leap. That was the plan. Surely you aren't getting cold feet now?"

Ryu looked down at his stretched-out collar. "I am only a messenger," he said.

Jamshed's fist clenched again. "That does not answer my question," he said. "Tell me."

There was a pause. Finally, Ryu said, "Yes. Apparently Shiraishi was acting on his own initiative. When the mission to move the Iranian rocket was played up as a 'Rod from God' and our leader delivered his speech, we thought the Great Leap would succeed. But only because there was no evidence tying the orbital phenomena to our country."

Ryu revealed that he himself had been sent to Tehran as a scout for the Great Leap. However, the existence of the space tethers, supposed to be kept top secret, had been exposed by a Japanese meddler. The CIA had seen through Shiraishi's carefully arranged diversion. The leader had lost his nerve.

Nevertheless, the leader and the intelligence community had both continued to place their trust in the always-resourceful Shiraishi. It seemed that right up until his final moment, they had hoped that he would figure out some new direction for the Great Leap to head in.

"But Shiraishi is dead," Ryu said, shaking his head weakly.

"Yes," Jamshed said. "As I heard it, it was his North Korean minder who killed him."

"I haven't been told the details," Ryu said after a brief pause. "But his death leaves a hole at the heart of the Great Leap."

"So you refuse to go through with it?"

"The leader and his associates have finally realized what a serious thing orbital sabotage is. How strong the international reaction would be."

"And this is all fine with you, Professor Ryu?"

"Wh—"

As Ryu looked up, Jamshed slammed him into the wall again.

"When Shiraishi told me about the Great Leap, my heart sang," Jamshed said. "To reach out and touch space, even from a place like this! What did you feel, Professor Ryu? My space tethers will put orbit beyond the grasp of developed countries. Researchers and engineers will flock to the rest of world—to us. Real space development with real professionals, right here in this country! You are prepared to give this up?"

Ryu closed his eyes and turned away.

Jamshed loosened his grip and jabbed Ryu in the chest. Ryu's legs had gotten crossed in the tussle, and he fell back and sagged against the wall.

"Get out," Jamshed said, pointing at the door. "I see that Shiraishi's death was in vain. You are right about one thing: the Great Leap could never work with cowards like you at the reins. I will do what is necessary myself."

Ryu straightened his collar and picked up his flashlight before turning back to Jamshed. His knees were shaking.

"You have something else to say?" demanded Jamshed.

"I beg you, at least rethink the LEO massacre," Ryu said. "And I have one more message for you. Will you come to Korea? We want you to develop the next generation of space tethers in Shiraishi's place. No one else understands how they work."

"To a country controlled by incompetent cowards?"

"Professor Jahanshah, do you not want to share your research? Was the space tether not an amazing development? You cannot go on working alone like this. Please think it over once your temper has cooled."

Ryu produced a phone and a charging cable from the pocket of his suit and placed them on the floor.

"I will leave this phone here," he said. "The line is safe. Use it to contact me whenever you like."

The door closed and the sound of Ryu's defeated footsteps receded down the corridor.

Jamshed sighed and surveyed his dim laboratory with its hanging forest of paper.

Ryu was right about one thing. There was nothing he could do here. But should he follow Ryu to Korea, or should he contact the Chinese man in the suit who had brought him the Iridium?

He glanced at the Iridium on his desk. No, China was no good. He would be out of his element in so desirable a country. There must be somewhere where a researcher left behind by the times could feel at home. And weren't such countries exactly the ones that Shiraishi had hoped the Great Leap would help to transform?

The Chinese man had known about the space tethers. If Jamshed took down Tiangong-2, no doubt the Iridium service would be cut off. In any case, the Iridium satellites were in low Earth orbit too and would not survive the massacre.

Jamshed picked up the phone Ryu had left by the door. The other end of the charging cable had a port for connection to a computer.

"A safe line . . ."

Could he connect to the network this way?

Wed, 16 Dec 2020, 16:03 -0800 (2020-12-17T00:03 GMT)
Western Days Hotel

Chris gazed at Daryl as he stood in front of the whiteboard. He had redrawn the diagram of the space tether and was now explaining it to the camera, writing notes and drawing lines as he went. This was part of a pre-countermeasure orientation for the benefit of those at the other end of the video call: NASA, the CIA, and NORAD.

The picture of the Orbital Cloud that Second Lieutenant Abbot had taken from the stratosphere during Operation Seed Pod had finally been accepted as reliable proof of Team Seattle's claims, and a Space Tether Response Team had been hastily assembled. Daryl was currently bringing those new to the crisis up to speed.

"I think that about covers it," he said finally. "If you have any questions, please send them over chat."

The monitor displaying the chat room quickly filled with questions from the members of the NASA team who had been watching. Most of the questions were about the space tethers themselves and the principles of the tether-propulsion system.

Is that sort of drive really feasible? asked one of the messages. Chris felt a flash of anger. "Feasible?" There were forty thousand of them in orbit already! She was just wondering if it might not be better to cut NASA out of the loop when she heard keyboard noise over the speakers and superbly crafted answers began to appear from Colonel Lintz's Orbital Surveillance team at NORAD. Clearly he didn't want Team Seattle to have to spend their time teaching Space Tethers 101 to NASA either.

"Hey, Kazumi," Daryl said, returning to the table.

Kazumi didn't even look up from the papers laid out on the table before him—the contents of the blueprint case that Akari had brought back from Shiraishi's hideout. He was physically present, but his thoughts were far away.

Kazumi had clearly not been prepared for the role he would have to play now that Jamshed had cut ties with them, Chris mused. Was studying these documents his way of escaping? Or had Shiraishi's death right in front of him made everything seem less real somehow?

Akari was in a corner of the room silently adding calculation nodes to her Raspberry Pi cluster. Chris doubted that she had fully processed seeing her uncle killed right in front of her. It was Chris who had brought Akari into contact with Shiraishi without adequate preparation, and ultimately it was Chris who had caused Shiraishi's death. Akari's engineering skills had supported the team thus far, but it would be unreasonable to expect her to function on the same level now.

Bruce finished checking the camera and projector. "Chris," he said. "Let's get started."

A 3-D globe indicating the Cloud's current location glowed on the whiteboard. The video-call screen showed that the NORAD Orbital Surveillance team was ready and waiting, as were Kurosaki and Sekiguchi, standing in their suits in a dimly lit room. The NASA and CIA teams, who had just finished their orientation, would just be observers for this one. If they had something to say, they would have to say it in the text-only chat window.

"Let's," Chris agreed. She stood behind Daryl and Kazumi in their seats and took a deep breath.

Kazumi put Shiraishi's papers down and turned to face the

camera. Chris had to keep him sharp and motivated. The veterans at NORAD and NASA couldn't be allowed to lord their professional status over him. She also nursed the hope that this meeting would bring Akari back to her old self.

Chris turned away from the sight of Lintz's troubled gaze on the whiteboard and looked directly into the camera. Ensuring that your gaze met your listeners' was the ironclad rule for maintaining control in a videoconference. You could not fall into the trap of looking at the screen where their faces were. You had to keep your eyes on the camera and put everything you had into ensuring that the meeting met the goals you had set for it.

Chris extended her awareness to her entire body.

"Colonel Lintz and everyone at NORAD, Mr. Kurosaki, Mr. Sekiguchi," she said. "Welcome to Team Seattle."

She spread her arms in a well-practiced gesture.

"Can you all see the whiteboard? Our objective is to bring the forty thousand space tethers in orbit down into the atmosphere. I look forward to a vigorous exchange of opinion."

Kazumi raised his hand.

"Kazumi Kimura," he said. He glanced at Bruce standing by the whiteboard. "Bruce, would you mind writing this up for me? I am going to explain the most rational countermeasure I can think of in our current situation: seizing control."

Kazumi raised his index finger. Bruce obediently wrote *1* on the whiteboard.

"First, we cut off Dr. Jahanshah's Internet connection. Next, we update the drivers for the D-Fi cables that make up the base station network—change them to give us control. Finally, we drop the Cloud into the atmosphere."

Bruce kept pace on the whiteboard.

1. *Cut connection*
2. *Update base station drivers*
3. *Control space tethers*

Sekiguchi raised his hand. "Step one is finished," he said.

"Huh?" Kazumi said.

"We suspended network service to the twenty Iridiums we provided to the students at Tehran U as well as the one we gave the professor personally. With luck, we've stayed Professor Jahanshah's hand until the Iranian government restores Internet service—perhaps two weeks from now."

"Well, that was easy," said Chris, folding her arms with a look of satisfaction.

"It's all done through the Iridium customer website," said Sekiguchi.

"Thank you, Sekiguchi-san," said Kazumi. "That gives us some breathing room. The next step is updating the drivers, then."

"I've got people at the company working on reverse engineering them right now," Bruce said. "Rothko, you listening? Hurry it up."

Okay, appeared from the CIA in the chat window. *Should finish in . . .*

As Kazumi and the others stared at the screen, waiting for the ETD to appear, Akari spoke in Japanese from the corner of the room.

"Dr. Jahanshah's connection hasn't been cut," she said.

Kazumi and Bruce turned their eyes to the base station

communication console projected on one corner of the whiteboard. Bruce relayed the news to the non-Japanese speakers.

Kazumi couldn't believe his eyes. "She's right . . ." he said. New TLEs were being sent to the space tethers at a brisk pace.

"I just reconfirmed that none of the Iridiums are operational," Sekiguchi reported.

"Then who's doing this?" said Bruce. "The North Koreans?"

Something nagged at Kazumi about the TLEs that were scrolling past. They were different in some fundamental way than the ones Team Seattle had begun receiving from the CIA that morning. But how?

"Those TLEs have been calculated by hand," Akari muttered in Japanese again. "They're too neat."

"Thanks, Akari," said Kazumi. He had Daryl take a screenshot of some of the data and approached the whiteboard to look at it more closely. "Dr. Jahanshah must have written these TLEs himself," he murmured. "Look at this. The epoch shift is exactly a hundredth of a second." He pointed out some other parameters that were too neat. "If he did this with a computer, there'd be more digits after the decimal points. They wouldn't all cut off after just two."

"So he has another way to transmit directions to the Cloud," Sekiguchi said.

Kazumi put his elbows on the table. The team had gotten stuck already. They had no way to stop Jamshed.

"Well, this is a problem," said Daryl. "Now he can do whatever he wants with them."

"Can we tell what satellite he's aiming for?" Chris asked.

"Leave that to us," said Lintz from the NORAD screen. "We just need to check what crosses paths with the orbits in these TLEs, right?

Hey, Harold! Get half the team working on this. Just start from the top and work your way down."

That would take more time than they had. Kazumi half-closed his eyes.

He held up his index finger, overlaying it in his vision with the globe projected on the whiteboard, then visualized the TLEs being sent to the space tethers. The orbits they described were circular and simple in the extreme. He allowed the slight variations added by hand to give him a sense of what form the finished Cloud would take. Jamshed's manual calculations made the results easy to follow. He moved the Cloud in his mind's eye, searching for an orbital object in his memory . . .

"The target is Project Wyvern's orbital hotel," he said.

"What?"

Kazumi ignored Lintz. He had to stay in the zone.

"Then it will raise its altitude and intersect with Tiangong-2. Next, Hubble and the spy satellite KH-12. The Cloud's shape will be a flattened spheroid fifty kilometers in diameter on the orbital plane and twenty kilometers thick."

"Listen, this is no time for fortune-telling!" shouted the man sitting next to Lintz on NORAD's screen. He was red with indignation, pointing his finger at the camera.

But this was no worse a reaction than Kazumi had expected. He calmly advanced the hands of the clock in his vision.

"Rendezvous in approximately four hours over the Atlantic—no, the west coast of Africa, where the Cloud will engulf the orbital hotel as it gathers," Kazumi said. He opened his eyes again and turned to the camera. "Please double-check that projection before you do anything," he said.

"Listen, uh—Kazumi, was it?" said one of the NORAD team members. "We're chasing an entirely unknown tether-propulsion system here. There's no way you could predict its movements so easily."

"Drop it, Harold," said someone else at NORAD.

"But it makes no sense," protested the first man. "Isn't this guy just some amateur?"

"Bruce," Chris said. "Cut the camera."

Bruce reached for the button, but Kazumi stopped him. "That will not be necessary. Daryl, please show the orbital hotel's position four hours from now."

"You got it," said Daryl. "Check it out, folks: Kazumi's sixth sense."

Daryl's fingers danced across his keyboard. The globe on the whiteboard spun forward four hours. The icon indicating the orbital hotel was over the west coast of Africa, just as Kazumi had predicted. There were cries of surprise.

"You see that? He got the orbital hotel's location right. Now I'll overlay the TLEs sent up to the space tethers. You won't believe your eyes."

Daryl hit the Enter key and a single point appeared over the orbital hotel. He hit Enter again, and again. Each time he did, a dot appeared in a slightly different position. Gradually the orbital hotel was obscured by a flattened spheroid of dots accumulating around it: the Cloud, right in line with Kazumi's predictions.

"That's impossible," said Lintz, his gaze fixed on the screen. The red-faced man next to him, who had risen to his feet, froze with his index finger still raised.

Kazumi pointed at the screen. "These are the instructions Dr. Jahanshah sent," he said. "About four hours from now, the Cloud will rendezvous with the orbital hotel. However, my method cannot give an exact time. So please start working on some more exact calculations."

"How does he—"

"Later," Chris said, cutting Lintz off. "Kazumi, if your prediction is correct, what then?"

"The orbital hotel will be torn apart by terminal apparatuses moving at ten kilometers per second. Two hours after that, the Cloud will reach Tiangong-2, which will meet the same fate."

There was a burst of conversation on the NORAD side: "Ten kilometers per second?" "That's unbelievable." "We'd better tell China." Questions from the CIA and NASA popped up at a furious pace in the chat window.

"Four hours . . . Daryl, if we sent an evacuation order now, would that be enough time?"

"Not for the orbital hotel," Daryl said. "They don't have a return vehicle anymore. And they aren't capable of much in the way of orbital maneuvers after all the damage they took."

"What about Tiangong-2?"

"Six hours till impact. Probably enough time to evacuate."

"Find the meeting attendee who can get a message to the Chinese the fastest. Report back to me in ten minutes."

"Chris," Sekiguchi said, raising his hand on the JAXA screen. "I sent a message to Director Huang at the China National Space Administration about Tiangong-2 earlier. Please just focus your efforts on sending a formal recommendation through diplomatic channels."

By the time he had finished speaking, all eyes were on the JAXA screen.

"You, uh . . ." Chris was lost for words. "Without even asking . . . ? But how did you know?"

"Unfortunately, we don't know much about orbital mechanics, so we can't help with the countermeasures," Sekiguchi continued, ignoring her. "But we *are* in Tehran. We'll try to convince Professor Jahanshah to call off the Cloud."

Chris found herself swept along by Sekiguchi's smooth patter.

"If he won't agree to our request, well . . ." Sekiguchi smiled and drew a leisurely thumb across his neck.

Kurosaki put his hand on Sekiguchi's arm. "None of that, Sekiguchi," he said.

Sekiguchi shrugged, apparently not bothered either way. "Fine," he said. "We'll just try to convince him with our debate skills, then. Can we offer him asylum in the US as a bargaining chip?"

"But there's no US embassy in Tehran," Kurosaki said.

"I know that. But there's a Canadian one. And Mexican, Japanese . . . Plenty of windows the CIA could reach through if they wanted to. Chris, could you please lay the groundwork?"

Chris thought for a moment. "All right," she said. "If he finds his way into the Canadian embassy by the end of tomorrow, I'll see to it that he gets asylum in the US. Bruce, make it happen."

"Your wish is my command," Bruce said. "But, Sekiguchi, I wouldn't recommend going to visit him. There are still drones—Anjians—in the air around Tehran IT. It's not the sort of place a tourist can just stroll around."

Sekiguchi reached out and grabbed the camera trained on the two JAXA members, then adjusted its angle to show the phone he was holding up in his other hand. He pointed at an icon on the screen.

"It'll be fine," he said. "I'm carrying my amulet against Anjian strikes."

Chris's eyes went wide.

"You . . ."

"Yes," Sekiguchi said lightly. "I'm a Chinese spy. That's how I was able to contact Director Huang. But the only orders I've received about this matter are to gather information. Things are moving so fast that headquarters is on the back foot. Anyway, the drones won't be firing at me. This app deactivates the fire control system on every Anjian within twenty kilometers."

Bruce opened his mouth in amazement. "A back door . . . I'd heard rumors, but I never imagined it'd be a smartphone app. Does it really work?"

"I'll let you know when I get back."

"Hamas or someone like them are out there too," Bruce warned. "The Anjians aren't the only danger. Don't take on more than you can handle."

With a smile, Sekiguchi rose to his feet and pulled on his field coat.

"Hold on," said Kurosaki, stubbing out his cigarette. "I'm coming too."

"As long as you don't cramp my style," Sekiguchi said.

"Things might get physical."

"What are you talking about? We're just going to talk to him. "

The banter between the two JAXA members in Tehran echoed through the quiet operations center. Chris studied Sekiguchi's smooth face more closely.

"Sekiguchi," she asked. "Why are you doing this?"

Sekiguchi rubbed his face and smiled. "I don't want any more Shiraishis," he said. "My mission is to put people where they can do their best work. I headhunt engineers. I'm the one who gave the professor his Iridium. I'll admit that I did it because I was hoping to recruit him, but . . ."

"And what about you? What will you do after this?"

Sekiguchi's smile was warm and genuine. "Good question," he said. "Headquarters isn't going to let me walk around free now that I'm known to the CIA. I suppose I'll go into hiding."

"No!" said Kazumi, waving his arms as he stood in front of the camera. "It would not be good for you. Shiraishi did the same thing, went off on his own—and look what he ended up involved in. Do not get yourself in trouble. Please be sure to come back."

Sekiguchi paused as if thinking. Kurosaki put an arm around his shoulders.

"I'll be sure to bring him back, Kazumi," he said. "Don't worry. Any messages for the professor?"

Kazumi grabbed a few of the documents from Shiraishi's case and held them up to the camera.

"Tell him I want to work with him on using space tethers to change the world," he said. "Tell him we can work together to realize the plans Shiraishi left behind."

Space tether technology would redefine space development forever. Shiraishi's light-field image of the Earth alone would change attitudes toward the whole enterprise. Kazumi fervently described a few of the plans he had come up with based on Shiraishi's work.

"Please, Kurosaki. I need Dr. Jahanshah."

"Understood," Kurosaki said. "I'll be sure to tell him. As for Shiraishi . . . Well, he never was the type to be straightforward about his feelings, but I'm sure he'd want you to see these plans to completion too."

With a final farewell, Kurosaki and Sekiguchi left the videoconference.

"Kazumi," said Chris from behind him. "You'd make a good boss, you know that?"

Panjshambeh, 27 Azar 1399, 03:45 +0330
(2020-12-17T00:15 GMT)
Esperanto Hotel, Tehran

Kurosaki picked up the phone that they had connected to the television. "You were kidding about that drone repellant thing, right?" he asked.

Sekiguchi shook his head, phone pressed to his ear. "Why so suspicious? It's all true—excuse me, let's pick this up later. *Salam!*"

He began a conversation in fluent Persian. Kurosaki caught Jamshed's name a couple of times, but apart from that all he could tell was that whoever Sekiguchi was calling, they weren't from China or Japan.

After noticing the word *interanet* a few times, he finally realized who was at the other end of the call—the man who had been standing on the Peugeot the other day leading the student demonstration. Alef Kadiba.

Sekiguchi ended the call and gave Kurosaki the thumbs-up. "I've hired us a guide."

"The guy leading that demonstration?"

"Yup. He's also a friend of Dr. Jahanshah's. Says he'll show us the way to his lab. I went there yesterday, but I'm glad we won't be going there alone at night."

"I'm surprised he agreed."

"He's worried about his friend. That, and I told him that if we managed to persuade Dr. Jahanshah to rejoin our side, I'd have service restored to the Iridiums. "

"That makes sense."

Kadiba and the students must have been crushed when the Internet cut out so soon after they'd received the phones yesterday. Sekiguchi explained that he at least wanted them to be able to use the

Iridiums until Iran restored its connection on a national level. Kurosaki had no disagreement.

"Did he say anything about Jahanshah?" asked Kurosaki.

"Apparently he's been acting strangely for the past few days. Now, we have fifteen minutes until our guide arrives. Let's make sure we're ready to leave."

Sekiguchi placed a duralumin case on his bed. It was the last of the cases he'd brought in through diplomatic channels. He opened it up, pulled out a few handfuls of passports, banknotes, credit cards, and SIM cards, and distributed the items among the pockets of his suit.

Kurosaki craned his neck to see the paraphernalia still left in the case. A hypodermic needle wrapped in a plastic bag. Drugs. Some kind of white powder. He didn't even want to think what it might all be for.

"The tools of the trade, huh? The SIM cards are a modern touch."

"I had them add the SIMs after we talked to Akari."

Sekiguchi peeled back part of the case's lining and produced a pistol small enough to hide in his palm.

"Of course, some things never go out of style," he said.

"You could put someone's eye out with that. Let me hold on to it for you."

"Absolutely not."

Kurosaki caught Sekiguchi by the arm and snatched the gun from him.

"You don't even know how to use a gun," complained Sekiguchi. He had made only a token attempt to prevent Kurosaki from taking the weapon. No doubt he didn't really want to use it either.

"Carrying the gun yourself will just make you want to use it," Kurosaki said. "Remember, we're going to persuade him."

"There are taikonauts on Tiangong-2 as well. I can't let them die."

"Enough with the 'I can't let them die' and 'I have to do it.' You sound like Shiraishi. And you saw how he ended up."

Recalling the procedure from a movie he'd seen, Kurosaki pressed a button on the side of the pistol's grip. A resin magazine slid out, exposing the small bullets through a hole in the side. The weapon was loaded. Kurosaki pulled the slide and saw the empty cavity. So the first round wasn't chambered yet. He pushed the magazine back in and pulled the slide again. In that moment, the machine in his hand had became a deadly weapon. The awareness gave Kurosaki shivers.

"You always think of the worst-case scenario," Kurosaki said. "Think about what you're going to do if everything goes well. Hey, where's the safety?"

Sekiguchi silently pointed at the lever beneath the slide. Kurosaki lowered the lever and confirmed that the trigger no longer moved.

"If we kill the professor, your only choice will be to go to ground. I wish I could tell you to do whatever you like, but I promised Kazumi. To give Jahanshah his message and to bring you home."

"What will you do if the professor won't listen?"

"Knock him out and carry him back?"

"Knock him—" The tension in Sekiguchi's face dissolved into his familiar indulgent smile. "What's the difference between that and shooting him?"

"Are you kidding me? They're completely different."

Kurosaki decided to stow the gun in a large coat pocket. If Jahanshah was alone, the two of them—no, counting Kadiba, the three of them—could bring him back to the hotel and wait for the Canadian embassy to open in the morning.

"Might need these later," Sekiguchi muttered, scooping up the drugs and needles and dumping them back into the case. Whatever Sekiguchi had used on Kurosaki after the demonstration must have been in that jumble. Truth serum?

Come to think of it, he still hadn't talked about that with Sekiguchi, though he surely knew that Kurosaki realized. Should he bring it up now? As Kurosaki hesitated, the phone in their room rang. Sekiguchi picked up the receiver, spoke briefly, then announced that Kadiba had arrived.

"That was fast."

"No traffic this time of night. He said he's waiting in the lobby with his car outside. Whoops—these don't autolock."

Kurosaki followed Sekiguchi out of their room into the pitch-black corridor. The single light of the elevator hall was visible at the far end. Kurosaki patted his pockets as they went: phone, wallet, passport. Couldn't find his lighter. No cigarettes.

"I have to go back," he said.

"Here's the key," Sekiguchi replied. "I'll carry your coat. Smoke a cigarette or two if you like—I'll be talking to Kadiba."

Sekiguchi took Kurosaki's coat, waved, and headed off to the elevator hall.

"Thanks," called Kurosaki.

Back in the room he found his cigarettes right away. They were in front of the television. He pulled one out and lit up. His first cigarette break alone since that suite at the Nippon Grand. Now that he thought about it, he'd hardly gotten any rest at all since meeting Kazumi on Monday.

Blowing a column of smoke into the air, Kurosaki looked around the room. Perhaps because he knew what was inside, the duralumin case on the bed looked particularly sinister to him.

"A spy, huh?"

Thu, 17 Dec 2020, 04:27 +0400 (2020-12-17T00:27 GMT)
Desnoeufs Island

Johansson watched Ozzy's jiggling belly go. Headset over his ears, Ozzy waved both his arms as he walked around. The video call with Kazumi and the others yesterday had reinvigorated him. He had spent his time since then writing long emails and making some calls of his own.

"No, listen," he said into the phone. "Tether propulsion. Doesn't need any fuel. Hey— Dammit! He hung up."

"No good?"

"Useless. How about over there?"

Johansson checked Ozzy's screen and reported that there was no new email.

"Morons! 'Is it profitable?' they say. It's never been seen before! Who the hell knows if it'll be profitable or not? Building an ecosystem and *making* it profitable is the fun part! What are these people even investors for? If it's money they want, they should switch to FX trading or speculation or something." Ozzy pulled a Coke out of the refrigerator and opened it. "Looks like Ronnie and Judy are the only ones we can count on."

"I wonder how they are doing," Johansson said. He turned his gaze to the sky. There was a hint of blue in the darkness now as dawn approached. The Smarks were four hundred kilometers above the Earth, still at the center of a dangerous maelstrom even as they approached the ISS. Ozzy had told them about the space tethers, so they at least understood what was happening—but they remained powerless to do anything about it.

"Ronnie? He dumped it in my lap. Told me to found a company for Kazumi to do his space tether thing. The jerk's acting like he's about to die. You know what I told him?" Ozzy slammed the Coke bottle down on the table. "I told him to get back here and do it himself!"

Johansson nodded. He had heard this story four times today.

"Mr. Cunningham, about the Cloud . . ." he began.

Ozzy looked away. It was no surprise that he should not wish to discuss the matter that was threatening Ronnie's life. But today's observational data could not be dismissed.

"It is now visible through the optical telescope," Johansson said.

"Huh?" Ozzy turned to face him again.

Johansson brought up the photograph showing a dim, smoky form on the wall monitor, explaining that it had been spotted passing over Desnoeufs by a program designed to scan the whole sky for unknown satellites.

"It appears to be more densely grouped than, er, Kazumi, was it?—than Kazumi suggested," he said. "Under the right conditions, it might even be visible to the naked eye."

"It's . . . it's enormous."

Ozzy's shoulders shook. Johansson did not think of the space tethers as anything other than directed debris, but tens of thousands of objects so close together was a threat in itself, able to destroy satellites simply by allowing them to pass through.

The Cloud and the space tether propulsion system had yet to appear in any news source. As Johansson understood from Ozzy, the true situation in the orbital hotel was the exact opposite of what Judy's cheerful blog suggested.

"Has Kazumi gotten in touch with us?" Ozzy asked. "It's still evening in Seattle, right?"

Johansson shrugged. "We only started sharing radar data the evening before last. They may still be reading through it, no?"

"No," Ozzy said. "Kazumi would already be at the next stage."

"Oh, come now . . ."

Johansson felt a deep sympathy for the young man he had seen on the video call. No doubt he was hearing the same demand from everyone these days: find a way to neutralize this orbiting swarm. Worse, it was now a matter of life and death. He could hardly imagine the pressure Kazumi must be under.

"Let's wait for him to contact us," he said. "I will make breakfast. Will you be needing some?"

Ozzy took a packaged hot dog from the freezer.

Johansson shrugged and turned to gaze out of the enormous window, with its unobstructed view of the ocean below and the cloudless sky above.

Wed, 16 Dec 2020, 16:54 -0800 (2020-12-17T00:54 GMT)
Western Days Hotel

Under the watchful gaze of the NORAD team, Kazumi was engrossed in the video from Operation Seed Pod.

Chris stood behind him with her hand on the back of his seat. There was, she had said, one part she particularly wanted him to see. Second Lieutenant Harold Fisher of NORAD provided commentary on how to read the simultaneous telemetry from the ASM-140's warhead.

"The bottom left shows the warhead's pitch. Right now it's moments from impact. Will this do, Chris?"

"Perfectly, thank you," said Chris. "Pause it for a second."

Kazumi realized that his coffee cup was empty and reached for the pot.

"Have a doughnut too," said Bruce.

"Maybe later," Kazumi said. "They are a bit sweet."

"You skipped lunch too. You have to eat something."

Bruce, however, hadn't taken a doughnut either.

"Sorry to keep you waiting," Lieutenant Fisher said. "I'm going to play it in slow motion, starting just before Blackout fired."

"There! Right there!" Chris pointed at the screen from over Kazumi's shoulder. A number of red lines were crossing the screen. "Do you see that, Kazumi? The red streaks."

"I see them. What is Blackout?"

"Think of it as a microwave oven on steroids," Fisher said. "It uses microwave radiation to burn out electronics."

"In this case, including the orbital hotel's computers," Chris said. "Their life support will be operational for just two more weeks." She managed to keep her voice under control until the end of the sentence.

The room fell silent.

There were only three hours left before the Cloud would rip the orbital hotel to shreds. Everyone knew it, but presumably Chris was worried that speaking it aloud would put too much pressure on Kazumi. The crease of concern on her brow spoke volumes.

Daryl pointed at the screen. "Hey, Kazumi," he said. "I wonder if these red lines are the actual tethers."

"I think they are," Kazumi said. "And they were burned through."

The tethers did not form a circuit and were not grounded. Even when free electrons within them were excited by the strong burst of microwave radiation at close range, those electrons remained trapped with nowhere to go. As they collided into each other, their kinetic energy was converted to heat. The principle was the same as the one behind the miniature fire that Mary had started in the Fool's Launchpad microwave oven.

"So we can burn them out with strong EM radiation," Lieutenant Fisher said excitedly.

"Yes. It had not occurred to me."

"EM radiation," Colonel Lintz said from the NORAD screen, audibly relieved. "So there's a way to get at them physically. That's a major advance. And we learned it from Operation Seed Pod. I wish the orbital hotel hadn't gotten caught up in things, but I suppose you never know where things will go right."

"Could we use nuclear weapons, Kazumi?" asked Lieutenant Fisher. "That'd give us a strong EM pulse."

"No, Harold," Colonel Lintz said immediately.

Chris stepped into the camera's field of view. "No nuclear weapons," she said. "We're already playing fast and loose with the COPUOS guidelines. We can't tear up the Outer Space Treaty too."

"But the Smarks—"

"Harold," Kazumi cut in. "If we use nuclear weapons, we will ruin orbit for good."

"What do you mean?"

"The terminal apparatuses are rotating in pairs at ten kilometers per second. If we cut all those links, they will be completely scattered. Eighty thousand new pieces of debris in orbit."

"He's right," said Daryl, who had been running a simulation. "If we burn them all out at once, forty thousand pairs—eighty thousand individual chunks—will spread out in all directions. Orbit will become a junkyard—completely impassable. Nuclear weapons are out."

Murmured acknowledgments came from NORAD as the people on-screen took notes.

"Conclusion," Chris said, clapping her hands to get everyone's attention. "No one needs to investigate nukes. Agreed? However, just in case, I'd like NORAD to perform some preparatory calculations for launching an ICBM into low Earth orbit, and select a facility that could carry this out."

"Yes, ma'am," said someone on the NORAD side.

"Next—excuse me. Headquarters." Chris produced a headset from her pocket and slipped it over her ears. Bruce stood to take over the meeting, but Chris shook her head to stop him. "Everyone, please stop what you're doing for a moment. I have a video call."

"From whom?" asked Bruce.

"Ronnie Smark. He's calling from orbit."

"What?!" Daryl spilled his coffee. "Ronnie Smark?"

"Why's he calling us?" asked Bruce.

"Ozzy Cunningham. Looks like he told Ronnie about the space tethers and our operation. Apparently he's already started working on some space tether–related investments."

"That idiot!" Bruce clutched his head. "What is he thinking? What happened to 'top secret'?"

"We'll let it go this time. It might be the last business Ronnie ever does, after all."

Bruce sighed and rose to his feet to clear away the doughnuts and empty coffee cups from the table.

"Kazumi, Daryl," he said. "The Smarks have CIA clearance. You can tell them anything. They only have three hours until the Cloud engulfs their hotel. The position they're in is unbearable. But don't try to comfort them. I'll take care of that."

"Here's the call request from Ronnie," Chris said, tapping at her laptop's keyboard. "Putting him through."

The familiar flutes whistled, and the whiteboard brightened. Bruce hurried to take a seat at the end of the table.

For a moment, Kazumi wasn't sure what he was looking at. Skin the picture of health. Deep blue eyes, pink lips. A smile so big it seemed about to burst, filling the screen.

"Hi there, everybody in Seattle! This is Judy Smark, astronaut. Call me Judy."

"There are two Smarks at our end, so go ahead and use our first names." Judy gave an exaggerated wink for the camera. She needed her best smile.

Judy let go of the camera arm and swung her upper body back, neatly extending her folded legs with the confidence that comes from repeated practice. The camera drifted away from her face and her body floated into the air.

After she had traveled three meters, flying on her back through the empty room, her father caught her arm with strength that belied his age. Right, like that—

"You're heavy," he whispered into her ear, pushing her shoulder to the ceiling and pulling her legs toward the floor.

"Shut up! They'll hear you." Judy hooked her feet into a pair of straps on the floor.

"Whoops," said Ronnie, noticing the white cloud of his breath. He waved his arm, dispersing the condensation. The room was minus ten degrees Celsius. The heaters in their space suits kept them from feeling the cold, but they couldn't control what their breath looked like.

Judy turned her eyes to the monitor on the wall. Three men and a middle-aged woman were staring at her with surprise on their faces. The room they were in had silvery walls and was dimly lit, even though it was supposed to be daytime there. The exact opposite of the stark white room in the orbital hotel, which was illuminated to the farthest corner by the light that shone in through the oval window.

The woman spread her arms. "I'm Chris," she said. "CIA. Judy and Ronnie, thank you for getting in touch. This is Team Seattle, working on countermeasures for the space tethers as we speak. From the left, we have Daryl Freeman from NORAD, then—as you know—Kazumi Kimura, discoverer of the space tethers, and then Bruce Carpenter, also from the CIA."

Chris looked back at the shaven-headed woman standing behind Kazumi. "This is Akari Numata, another trusted partner," she said. She finished by explaining about the JAXA employees on their mission to Tehran.

"Wow, it's like a spy movie down there," Judy said.

"You look very cold," Kazumi said, concern in his voice.

"It's not a problem," Ronnie said, shrugging casually. Judy smiled. Only Ronnie would put in the hour of practice it had taken to learn to shrug in zero gravity.

Ronnie stroked the straps around his thighs. "Pretty slick, right? We were keeping them a secret, but these are strap space suits developed by Project Wyvern. Heater and all mod cons, of course. I could put a helmet on right now and step outside for up to twenty-four hours."

"Twenty-four hours?" repeated Kazumi.

"Yep. Just in case of accident, to allow for pickup by the backup, Loki 9. Twenty-four hours is enough to save a customer in orbit. Amazing, right? This goes well beyond the Apollo series or the Space Shuttle."

The strap space suit required no time for low-pressure adaptation,

Ronnie boasted. Rescue staff could bring customers directly inside the Wyvern return vehicle.

"If not for those space tethers, we'd be out there calling for pickup right now," Ronnie laughed. The faces at the Team Seattle end turned grim. "Oh, don't worry about us. I hear there's still three hours until the space tethers rendezvous with our hotel, right?"

Ronnie held up one of the straps, woven with high-tensile carbon. A light but strong lifeline for extravehicular excursions.

"Judy and I will connect ourselves with this, put on our helmets, and curl up. Even if the hotel gets torn apart, with luck my daughter and I will have another twenty-four hours together."

Ronnie's knees shook at the lie. If anything hit the hotel at ten kilometers per second, the Mach 30 shock wave transmitted through the walls would flatten the both of them. The space suits would be completely useless.

"Oh, that reminds me," said Judy. "We have something interesting to show you. That's why we're calling, actually." She raised her index finger beside her face and forced a smile. "The space tether dance! We hope you like it."

"A dance?" asked Kazumi.

The five people at the other end of the call stared, their mouths agape.

That's right, a dance, Judy thought. *We're betting on that sixth sense of Kazumi's that we heard about from Ozzy and NASA. Maybe this'll give him the idea he needs to get us home in one piece.*

Ronnie pushed off and soared to one corner of the room, then tossed one end of the strap to Judy, just as they'd practiced. The neatly rolled strap flew true, unrolling as it went. Catching the ring at the end of the strap, Judy clipped it onto the fastener at her belt and then moved to the wall opposite Ronnie.

"Kazumi," she said. "We want you to watch this most of all. You've never seen a real space tether, right? Well, we're going to show you what they look like, choreographed by yours truly, Judy Smark. I hope this is worth the bruises we got practicing!"

Judy confirmed that the strap was pulled tight. Next, the two of them each gripped a foothold on the floor with one hand and let their bodies rise into the air. They stretched out straight at opposite ends of the room, parallel to the floor but with their heads facing in opposite directions.

"Three, two, one!"

Judy gave the foothold a sharp push with her fingers. She began to move in the opposite direction, soaring headfirst through the air, and then Ronnie's mass tugged at her belt and changed her path. She stiffened, keeping her body ramrod straight. Linked together, the two of them began to describe a circular path centered on the middle of the room.

"Ah . . ."

Judy heard Kazumi's voice through the speakers. *That's right. Watch closely. This is how the space tethers move. Give you any ideas? Spark that sixth sense of yours?*

She felt the flush on one side of her body as her blood began to collect there. The skin on her face was being pulled toward the outside of the circle. A flaked-off piece of foundation bounced off her face and spun off into the room. She raised her head. It was a strange sensation. Inertia was pulling her body straight ahead, the strap was pulling it to the left. How many rotations had they done now?

"Look out!" said Kazumi.

The strap connecting her to Ronnie went slack, and Judy's trajectory became a straight line. Bouncing off the soft wall, she dragged her hand on the ground to catch a foothold. At the other end of the room, Ronnie was clinging upside-down to the wall.

The strap had come loose from his belt.

"Oh, come on!" snapped Judy.

"Sorry. I guess I didn't clip it on properly."

"All right, let's do it again. Are you watching, Kazumi? . . . Kazumi?"

On the screen, she saw that Kazumi had gotten to his feet.

"Judy, Ronnie," he said. "Thank you. I have thought of a way to eliminate the space tethers."

"Really?" Ronnie bounced off the wall.

"So quickly?" Judy heard Chris ask.

"I will have to look into the details," Kazumi said. "When and exactly how to do it, that I am not yet sure of."

"Underpromising as usual, I see," Ronnie said. "So you're saying that you aren't sure if you can get it done before our time runs out? Three hours, two weeks, whatever it turns out to be?"

Kazumi paused for a moment, conflicted, then nodded firmly.

Ronnie kicked the walls and floor a few times to propel him toward the camera.

"Okay, now we're being honest," he said. "Good. That's fine. Your mission isn't to save us. It's to clear the space tethers out and keep orbit open. You're saying that's theoretically possible now."

"Yes. It is possible."

"Fantastic. Then the flame of space exploration won't be snuffed out."

Ronnie reached for an arm attached to the wall and moved his face closer to the camera. His unhealthy skin tone was visible through the cracks in his foundation, as were the dark bags under his eyes.

"Whenever you try to make a theoretical possibility a reality, you're guaranteed to hit a wall at some point," he said. "If private space development taught me anything, it's that. So let me give you one piece of advice."

Kazumi's face was pinched and nervous.

"Lucky you, Kazumi," said Judy. "He normally charges a thousand dollars a minute for lectures."

"Quiet, Judy," growled Ronnie. He turned back to the camera. Kazumi's expression had softened. Good. "Listen carefully," he said. "That theoretical possibility of yours is probably going to sound dumb to everyone else. Otherwise they'd have thought of it themselves."

"Yes," Kazumi said after a moment's thought. "Perhaps you are right."

A toothy grin spread across Ronnie's grizzled face.

"But that's the best part," he said. "You get to execute a plan that's crazy. Completely nuts! Don't let this chance get away."

"Huh?"

"Tell someone as soon as you can. Your team will understand. And then keep working to convince everyone else."

Kazumi's eyes wavered as they stared into the camera.

The hand Ronnie was gripping the wall arm with was beginning to go white. "Now," Ronnie said. "Do it now."

"Yes," Kazumi replied. "I will do it right away."

Ronnie raised one trembling index finger. "Just once," he said. "You only have to succeed once. Do it, Kazumi!"

Kazumi's face crumpled, his eyes gleaming.

"Understood," he said. "I will do it."

15 Meteors

Wed, 16 Dec 2020, 17:05 -0800 (2020-12-16T01:05 GMT)
Western Days Hotel

No sooner had the Smarks signed off than Lintz's face appeared in close-up on the NORAD monitor.

"Kazumi," he said. "I heard everything. You say you have an idea?"

Put on the spot like that, Kazumi started to feel nervous. Was he sure he hadn't missed anything?

"Don't hold back, Kazumi," Daryl said. "NORAD has rooms full of professionals ready to check your ideas. What they don't have is someone with your intuition." He kept his voice light, but his fingertips drummed tensely on the keyboard.

Kazumi made up his mind. As far as he could see, his idea was the only way to wipe out the space tethers quickly enough. Was it crazy? Maybe. But he had to propose it anyway.

"We burn through the tethers," he said, "with powerful, long-wavelength radiation."

Lintz gave him a quizzical look. "Didn't you say earlier that if we burned through the tethers the terminal apparatuses would fly off in all directions and make things worse?"

"I thought of a way to prevent that," Kazumi said. "The Smarks' space tether dance gave me the idea. If we do it my way, we can control exactly which way the two terminal apparatuses fly."

Everyone's eyes were on Kazumi now. He felt their stares acutely.

"This is what we do," Kazumi said. "We burn out the tethers while they are exactly perpendicular to their direction of overall motion."

"But that will just send the apparatuses flying from centrifugal force," Lintz said. "Forty thousand—no, eighty thousand high-speed objects in orbit. It won't change a thing."

"There is no danger of that," Kazumi said. "One of the terminal apparatuses will fly forward in the direction of the Cloud's motion. The other will fly back in exactly the opposite direction."

Lintz furrowed his brow. Voices began to come through from the NORAD feed, some siding with Kazumi, others still doubtful. It was the reaction Kazumi had expected.

Daryl looked up at the roof and twirled his fingers in front of him. "Centrifugal force . . ." he said. "I get it. It's a fictitious force."

"Exactly," Kazumi said. "Everyone, please recall when that strap came undone during the Smarks' space tether dance. Judy and Ronnie both went flying in the exact direction their heads were pointing. They didn't drift off to the side a bit. They flew at an exact tangent to the circle they were moving in."

"Like the hammer throw at the Olympics," Lintz said.

"Yes. The two terminal apparatuses of each space tether will fly precisely in opposite directions too. We just need to control the timing."

When a pair of apparatuses went flying as their tether was cut, Kazumi explained, each apparatus's rotational velocity of ten kilometers per second would be combined with the velocity of the Cloud as a whole, roughly seven kilometers per second. In the case of the apparatus that flew backwards, its final velocity would be the former minus the latter, and three kilometers per second was too slow to stay in orbit. It would fall into the atmosphere and burn up. On the other hand, the apparatus that flew forwards would have the Cloud's overall velocity added to its rotational velocity, and seventeen kilometers per second would kick it out of orbit entirely.

Daryl grinned. "Now those are some numbers, Kazumi!" he said. "Seventeen kilometers per second? That's faster than the third escape velocity. Those apparatuses won't just leave Earth—they'll shake off the sun's gravitational pull, too, and head into deep space!"

Kazumi smiled back at Daryl. Shiraishi had written about using rapidly spinning space tethers for orbital projection in the papers he had left behind. It was another possibility inherent in the technology.

"So we cut the tethers at just the right moment and all our problems are solved," Lintz said. "Understood. Next: how? Do you have a plan for cutting through only those tethers that happen to be lined up nicely?"

Kazumi studied Lintz's face on the screen. He would have to explain this part of the plan carefully.

"We must bombard the Cloud from the direction of its movement with radio waves a fraction shorter than the tethers themselves," Kazumi said. "The tethers will only receive enough radiation to be damaged when they are perfectly side-on. At all other times, the radio waves pass through harmlessly."

"How's that again?" Lintz frowned. "I don't follow you." Other members of the NORAD team could be heard voicing their doubts. But Kazumi knew he was right.

Leaving his inconspicuous post by the door, Bruce approached the table. "Kazumi, that's brilliant," he said. "You're saying we should treat the space tethers themselves as antennas. If they aren't facing the 'station,' they won't pick up the signal. So if we bombard them from directly ahead, they'll only get the full dose when they're perpendicular to the Cloud's direction of movement—just where we want them. Plus, a two-kilometer wavelength means a frequency of 157 kilohertz. That's ham radio range. We can do that."

Lintz shook his head. "No good," he said. "Waves that long will just bounce off the ionosphere. That's why ham radio works in the first place."

"Ah," said Kazumi. He had forgotten about the ionosphere.

And after Jamshed had mentioned it, too! The ionosphere had been why the AM radio signals Jamshed used for his balloon-borne prototypes wouldn't work on the space tethers, leading Shiraishi to use the D-Fi cables and VHF.

Kazumi had made a fundamental error. They couldn't burn through the space tethers this way after all.

He pounded the table, staring at the circle drawn on the whiteboard. Why had he told Ronnie and Judy that he could do it?

Bruce clapped a hand on Kazumi's shoulder. "Kazumi!" he said. "You should see your face! Team Seattle has transmission equipment strong enough to punch through the ionosphere, remember? Am I wrong, Daryl?"

"Huh?" Kazumi looked up. Daryl was giving him the thumbs-up.

"Yes, sir," Daryl said to Bruce. "We have pretty much everything." He tapped at his keyboard and displayed a page of background material on the whiteboard. "Colonel Lintz, we have access to Cunningham's Sampson-5 multipurpose active phased array radar."

"Cunningham?" Lintz said. "Don't think I'm familiar with that ship. Is that the captain's name?"

"No, sir, the Sampson-5's owner's name. Ozzy Cunningham, based on Desnoeufs Island in Seychelles. He's a stockholder in Kazumi's company. He'll give us whatever access we need."

"The *owner's* name?" repeated Lintz in amazement. "A private citizen? Does he know how powerful that thing is? It was designed for nuclear vessels! Could burn a human to a crisp. What on earth does he use it for?"

"Observing debris in low orbit, sir," said Daryl. "A hobby of his."

Lintz paused to take this in. "Who *is* this Cunningham?" he asked finally.

Kazumi's certainty had returned. This was how they would finish things. "Ozzy Cunningham is part of our team, Colonel," he said.

It was Ozzy's Rod from God hoax that had set everything in motion, sweeping a simple stargazer like Kazumi up into an international incident that had left two men dead and turned another into a terrorist. And now things had circled back to Ozzy again.

Now they knew where they would make their stand.

Kazumi's gaze met the camera, looking at the NORAD staff. "We burn through the space tethers by firing radio waves from Desnoeufs Island," he said.

On the NORAD video feed, Kazumi saw Harold Fisher whispering something in Lintz's ear before taking a seat in front of the camera.

"Kazumi," Fisher said. "In that case, there's another problem. I checked the orbits. The Cloud will hit the orbital hotel in just three hours, long before it passes over Seychelles again."

Lintz's face looked pained.

"In fact, it's not due to pass over Seychelles for three days," Fisher continued. "And that's assuming it doesn't change course. Jahanshah's going to have plenty of time to knock down satellites before the tethers are burned through."

"Kazumi," said Lintz. He was almost choking the words out. "Do we give up on the Smarks?"

"No," Kazumi replied. "We will save Ronnie and Judy. But we need the help of the United States to do it."

"What sort of help? Anything NORAD—hell, the whole air force—can do, we will."

Kazumi looked up at the ceiling, then back into the camera, then over at Chris and Bruce.

"Colonel Lintz," he said finally, "Chris. I have a request that must be asked of the highest-ranking person in the United States. I want the US to move the Earth."

The room fell silent. Even Akari looked up from her mountain of Raspberry Pis.

"Move Earth?!" she said. Then, after a pause: "Ah, I see!" She leaped lightly to her feet and approached the whiteboard. She touched the diagram of a space tether Daryl had drawn, then moved her finger to the network he had sketched out. The flow of information went from Jamshed in Tehran to the D-Fi base stations, then on VHF waves up to the tethers. Finally her finger came to rest on a picture of a satellite.

"These?" she asked.

"Correct," Kazumi said.

There was a short silence before Bruce whistled. "You two are on another level," he said. "That's perfect. Tell me, everyone, who do

I need to explain this stroke of genius to? Leave the coordination to me—I'll get the whole CIA on the case if I have to."

Daryl pulled two keyboards together and brought up a mass of data on the display atop the table.

"NORAD can run Ozzy's radar," Daryl said. "If the Oregon control center could handle Operation Seed Pod, they can handle this too. Correct?"

"Correct," said Fisher from the NORAD screen.

Lintz rose to his feet beside Fisher. His hands disappeared under his belly. "I'll call right now," he said. His hands reappeared holding a BlackBerry, so old that the color of the plastic was fading. Bruce glanced at the screen and whistled again. Chris let out a short cry of delight as well.

"This, Kazumi," said Lintz, "is a hotline to the president. It's supposed to be used by NORAD to report nuclear missiles headed for North America. I've had it fifteen years but haven't used it once. Never thought the time would come so close to retirement.

Angling the BlackBerry so that the camera could see, Lintz punched in eight zeros and hit the dial button. Then he raised the phone to his ear.

"Mister President," he said, standing to attention. "This is Colonel Claude Lintz, chief of Orbital Surveillance at NORAD." He gave a brief summary of the failure of Operation Seed Pod. "Yes, sir. We can save the Smarks. We're going to secure orbit for good. But to do it, NORAD needs control of some of America's global infrastructure for the next three hours. I'll take full responsibility for whatever happens."

Chris rose to her feet. She was about to clap for attention when Kazumi stopped her. This was something he had to say himself.

He stepped before the camera, back straight, chest out.

"Well, everybody," he said. "Let's get to work!"

Panjshambe, 27 Azar 1399, 04:38 +0330
(2020-12-17T01:08 GMT)
Tehran Institute of Technology

The corridor was dark, with only faint emergency lighting to guide them as they advanced.

Seeing the light coming from under the door ahead, Kurosaki tried to settle his nerves. He recalled the videos of a calmly chatting Jamshed that Chris had showed him.

He placed one hand over his coat pocket. He had no idea how to use the gun he had taken from Sekiguchi, but its heft gave him a feeling of security anyway.

Alef opened the door. Kurosaki started to follow Sekiguchi inside before instinctively drawing back from the strange space. Yellow walls? No, sheets of yellow paper hung from the ceiling. Too many to count. Seeing the notes scrawled on the sheets, Kurosaki realized what they were: Jamshed's handwritten calculation aids.

Through a gap between the papers and the wall, he saw a man rise to his feet and look in Sekiguchi's direction. He had seemed larger in the video calls.

"You," said Jamshed. "I just stopped using that Iridium you gave me. It will not connect anymore."

Behind Jamshed, Kurosaki saw a phone connected to a USB cable.

"Well, Professor," said Sekiguchi, "that's because you're trying to bring down the Wyvern Orbital Hotel and Tiangong-2."

Jamshed's eyes went wide. "How did you know my—ah. Kazumi. He has predicted this."

"Yes, and also your next two targets: the Hubble Space Telescope, and then KH-12."

"The Hubble?"

Jamshed frowned. He glanced at a yellow sheet of paper on the desk before him, then picked up a pen and scribbled out a few figures.

"Amazing," Jamshed said. "It is true. After Cloud eats Tiangong-2, I can simply nudge its orbit to put it on collision course with Hubble. And then KH-12 . . . This power of Kazumi's is most impressive." He shook his head, pen still in hand.

"We came to ask you to stop," Sekiguchi said.

"Stop? Stop what?"

"All of this," Sekiguchi said, pushing aside a swaying sheet of paper as he took a step forward. "This is not the way to realize the Great Leap. If you need a place to exercise your talents, I can arrange that. I've been authorized to offer you asylum in the US, if you want it. You haven't done any harm yet. You can still be Jamshed Jahanshah, brilliant rocket scientist."

Alef had closed the door behind him after entering. Now he stood behind Sekiguchi, listening to the conversation quietly.

"If you don't like the free market, you could start a venture in China," Sekiguchi continued. "There are regular flights to Tiangong-2. Couldn't you launch your space tethers from those? I can make it happen, Professor."

Jamshed picked up the smartphone behind him and tapped out a number before holding it to his ear. "How comfortable it must be in countries with functional economies," he said. "My envy knows no bounds. Professor Ryu, were you asleep? I have decided. Come down."

Sekiguchi's face hardened. "Ryu . . . a Korean?"

"Yes. Try your speech on him. You will see how effective it is on us have-nots. Me, I have decided to go to North Korea. That was where Shiraishi turned my research into reality. I will continue his work."

Sekiguchi was about to speak again when Kurosaki interrupted. "You can't fill Shiraishi's shoes, Professor," he said.

Jamshed looked at Kurosaki for the first time. "What?"

"I knew Shiraishi well," Kurosaki said. "We worked together."

Jamshed's brown eyes narrowed. There were dark bags under them from overwork, but the gleam of intelligence in his piercing gaze was undimmed.

"He could do anything," Kurosaki continued. "Good enough at hacking to join the intelligence services. Comfortable with both IT and engineering. Had business sense too, apparently, although I didn't know it at the time. He spent all his time using these abilities to help others. Always sticking his nose into other people's projects, just like the Great Leap—helping them, encouraging them, making announcements on their behalf . . ."

Hearing the door open behind him, Kurosaki fell silent and turned to see who it was. A man in a drab suit stood in the doorway, eyes wide.

"Professor Ryu," Jamshed explained. "Now, about Shiraishi? Continue."

Ryu began edging around to stand behind Jamshed, hugging the wall to keep as far from Kurosaki and the others as possible.

"Well, here's the truth," Kurosaki said, "And it hurts. The fact is, everything Shiraishi did was second-rate. Kazumi uncovered his space tethers. Akari detected his hacking. Orbital engineering was supposed to be his career, but his achievements don't even rival yours, Professor. He was a jack-of-all-trades, but a master of none. That's why he thrived in North Korea, where there's never enough of anything."

Jamshed was listening to Kurosaki with unblinking intensity.

"Can you do everything yourself, Professor?" asked Kurosaki. "Managing people, obtaining materials, even using computers—that's all outside your comfort zone, right? Not to mention the politics. Shiraishi took all of that on. He ran himself ragged doing everything for everyone. And then . . . he died."

Kurosaki turned his gaze to Ryu, who was trying to hide behind Jamshed.

"Let me ask you, Mr. Ryu," Kurosaki said. "Are you willing to hand over the entire space tether program to the professor here? Will he have a budget? Staff? Is North Korea really prepared to take space tethers seriously again after Shiraishi's failure?"

"Do not insult my homeland," Ryu said weakly, not meeting Kurosaki's eyes.

"Just look at him, Professor," said Kurosaki. "He can't offer anything you need."

Jamshed shrugged. "I know they are nothing but weaklings and cowards," he said.

"Then you must also know how draining it is to deal with people like that," Kurosaki said.

"Let me ask you a question," Jamshed said. "How much use would I be in America? As you say, I cannot even use a computer. I have no right to claim a place among you who can."

"You're wrong, Professor," Kurosaki said. "Kazumi gave me a message for you. He says the possibilities for the space tether drive are infinite. You saw the light field, that live video of the Earth, and that's just the beginning."

Kurosaki told Jamshed about the plans Kazumi had found in Shiraishi's papers. The space tethers weren't only usable in low orbit. Their ability to attain high orbital velocity without fuel made them ideal for all sorts of tasks. Even Kurosaki could understand the appeal.

"He wants to work on this with you, Professor," Kurosaki said. "He told me so. What do you think? Sounds to me like it'd be right up your alley."

Jamshed's mouth fell open. He blinked several times. "He . . . Kazumi told you all this?" he asked. "And you understand it?"

"Huh?" Kurosaki said.

"As for me, sadly, I understood less than half," Jamshed continued. "Kazumi learned of space tethers only three days ago but already has surpassed me." He closed his eyes and turned his face toward the ceiling.

Everyone in the room froze. Only the light cast by the computer monitor flickered as strings of coordinates scrolled past, proof that the space tethers above were slowly wending toward the orbital hotel.

Ryu moved suddenly, yanking a sheet of paper hung from the ceiling and throwing it to the floor. Jamshed opened his eyes again at the sound and slowly shook his head.

"Yes, it is clear to me now," Jamshed said. "I have no place beside Kazumi. I will go to North Korea."

"Professor—" Kurosaki began.

"Understood," Sekiguchi said, taking a step forward. "Though very unfortunate." He pulled a pistol from his coat pocket and pointed it at Jamshed.

"Sekiguchi!" Kurosaki said.

But wasn't he carrying the pistol himself? Kurosaki reached into his pocket and felt something rubbery. Pulling the heavy object out, he saw that it was a phone charger and cable, duct-taped into the shape of a pistol. Sekiguchi must have made the switch.

"What are you doing?" Alef cried, leaping at Sekiguchi.

Sekiguchi opened his stance and kicked Alef in the knee. Alef fell to the floor clutching his leg. Sekiguchi glanced at him, then took a step away and aimed the pistol at Jamshed again.

"Give us control of the Cloud, Professor," he said.

Jamshed shook his head. "Shiraishi gave it back to me. The space tether drive is mine."

"Don't, Sekiguchi, please!" groaned Alef from the floor, still holding his knee.

Ryu pointed at Sekiguchi from behind Jamshed. "Do . . . do you think a foreigner can get away with something like this?" he demanded.

Sekiguchi disengaged the safety with his thumb. "These things have a way of working out," he said. "Professor, I'll say it once more. Give us control of the space tethers."

Jamshed thrust out his chin, contempt in his face. "You are no different than agent from North who killed Shiraishi," he said.

Sekiguchi's index finger entered the trigger guard and came to rest on the trigger, trembling slightly.

"No, you idiot!" Kurosaki cried, striking Sekiguchi's hand from behind with the taped-up battery charger. He closed his eyes at the sound of the gun firing. The smell of blood filled the air.

Cautiously opening his eyes again, Kurosaki saw Sekiguchi down on his knees before him, gritting his teeth as he applied pressure to his thigh. A pool of dark blood was spreading beneath his feet.

Alef shoved Kurosaki aside, sending him staggering backwards into a desk. Jamshed pushed away the chairs nearby to make room for Sekiguchi to lie down.

Sekiguchi was shivering in shock as Alef eased him to the floor. Alef pushed Sekiguchi's hands away from the wound. Fresh blood bubbled through a hole in his already blood-soaked suit.

Without hesitating, Alef bore down hard on the area. "Get me something to cover it and something to bind it," he said to Kurosaki.

Kurosaki hurriedly unwrapped the tape from the battery charger and handed it over. Ryu threw them a handkerchief. Alef thanked them, folded the handkerchief into a makeshift bandage, and bound it tightly over the wound with the tape.

Alef slapped Sekiguchi's cheek to see if he was conscious. "First aid is now complete," he said to Kurosaki.

Sekiguchi was lucky that the bullet had been low caliber, Alef explained; the wound didn't look life threatening. He helped Sekiguchi to his feet.

"Looks like he can wait until hospital opens tomorrow morning," Jamshed said from behind them. "Leave now. Our talk is over."

Kurosaki turned to see that Jamshed had picked up the pistol. The professor reengaged the safety with practiced ease as he slipped the weapon into his pocket.

"I'm sorry he did that, Professor," Kurosaki. "But please call off the orbital sabotage. People's lives are at stake."

"Shiraishi already lost his," Jamshed said. "Is death in orbit any different from murder on Earth?"

"That's not the issue here," Kurosaki said. "I don't want anyone's hands to get dirty. I won't allow anyone to—"

He took a step forward. In a single, smooth motion, Jamshed reached into his pocket, produced the gun again, and aimed it at Kurosaki's chest. Kurosaki froze at the sound of the safety being disengaged. Jamshed then pointed the gun toward the computer under his desk.

"One more step," Jamshed said, "and I will destroy this computer. Space tethers have already been sent directions to orbital hotel.

You can do nothing to stop this. I will use Shiraishi's legacy to honor his wishes. Every satellite in low Earth orbit will be destroyed."

His brown eyes glared at them unwaveringly, but Kurosaki saw no hint of madness there.

"I can only hit them one by one, so perhaps it will take two—no, three—weeks," Jamshed continued. "Perhaps Shiraishi would have found a way to knock all satellites out of sky at once. But I will achieve same thing eventually."

"In two or three weeks, Kazumi and the others will have found a way to destroy the space tethers," Kurosaki said.

"I suppose so. Someone of Kazumi's abilities, eventually he will find some way. But until then, I will do what I must. Call it a race."

Jamshed gestured with the gun toward the door.

"Tell him and his friends I said so," he said.

Kurosaki realized that Jamshed was smiling for the first time.

"Farewell," Jamshed said. "And thank you for an enjoyable night."

"But . . ."

If you enjoyed it, come with us. There's still time. No one will compare you with anyone else. The things Kurosaki wanted to say whirled into his mind before vanishing again.

Jamshed had made his decision. There was nothing they could do. It was all up to Kazumi and his team now. All Kurosaki could do was fulfill the promise he had made.

"All right," Kurosaki said. "Goodbye, Professor. Take care of yourself."

Kurosaki spread his coat across the backseat of Alef's Citroën and pushed Sekiguchi in. Alef handed him a blanket and he wrapped it around the younger man, who had begun to shiver. Then he squeezed into what little room was left in the backseat himself.

"Why . . . why did you stop me?" Sekiguchi said.

"You be quiet," Kurosaki replied.

Alef closed the door and walked around to the driver's seat. "You should give him water," Alef said. "I'll turn on the heater. Hold on."

Alef offered a plastic bottle from the passenger's seat and Kurosaki accepted it. After a few coughing noises, the engine caught and warm air began to flow around their legs as the heater sprang to life.

"Drink some water, Sekiguchi," Kurosaki said. "It'll speed your recovery." He pulled down the blanket and held the bottle to Sekiguchi's mouth.

"You have to go back," Sekiguchi said. "You can't let him kill."

"Drink first," Kurosaki said. "We'll talk after that."

Sekiguchi gave up his protests and took a few noisy swigs from the bottle, holding Kurosaki's arm. "There," he said. "Is that enough? Now go back and stop him."

"No," Kurosaki said. "It ends here. You're going to the US in his place."

"The US? What are you talking about? I'm . . . I could . . . That's strange . . ."

It had started to kick in. Good.

Kurosaki pulled the medication bottle from his pocket and waved it before Sekiguchi's eyes. "Lights out," he said. "When you wake up, you'll be in America."

"That's . . ."

"Yep. I borrowed it. Potent stuff, isn't it?"

"What have you . . . But I won't be able to . . . to move . . ."

Sekiguchi's hand lost its grip on Kurosaki's arm and slipped off the seat. Kurosaki tucked it back inside the blanket.

"Everything's fine, Sekiguchi," Kurosaki said. "Sleep. Our work is done. Let's leave the rest to Kazumi and the gang."

He felt movement under the blanket, but it soon began to weaken.

"Kazumi . . . too much . . . Please . . . stop the professor . . ."

Kurosaki smoothed out the twisted blanket and put his arm around Sekiguchi's shoulders. "It's been fun, Sekiguchi, hasn't it?" he said.

"What?"

"Helping Kazumi these past few days. It looked like you were enjoying yourself. Am I wrong?"

Weakly but unmistakably, Sekiguchi shook his head. "It's been . . . fun . . ." he said.

"There you go. Isn't that enough?"

"Enough . . . ?" Sekiguchi chuckled faintly. Then his head drooped and his breath grew slow and regular. Kurosaki rubbed his thumb on Sekiguchi's cheek, still smooth and stubble-free despite all they'd been through, but there was no response. Sekiguchi had fallen into a deep sleep.

Kurosaki leaned his arm on the headrest of the passenger's seat. Alef turned to look at him.

"Alef, could you take us to the Canadian embassy?" Kurosaki said. "I'm going to seek asylum for him."

When Alef gave him a dubious look, Kurosaki explained that Sekiguchi was a Chinese spy. He could hardly return to Japan now.

"I see. Good fortune for you, then."

"What is?"

"Well, it seems that you have saved your friend," Alef said, closing his long-lashed eyes. "If only I had listened harder to mine."

Kurosaki thought again about Jamshed's circumstances. The best years of his life spent in intellectual solitude, no one to talk to about his research—and then to learn that it had been stolen from him.

"There might have been a better way," he admitted. "To tell you the truth, I lost a friend of my own as well."

"My sympathies," Alef said.

"And this guy'll live, but he's about to disappear forever," Kurosaki said, jerking his thumb at Sekiguchi.

Once Makoto Sekiguchi passed through the gates of the Canadian embassy, Kurosaki would never meet him again. He would be sent to the US, where he would trade information about the illegal activities he had performed in China's intelligence services for a place on the Witness Protection Program. A new name, even a new life, complete with its own history.

Kurosaki pulled the crumpled package of Iranian cigarettes Sekiguchi had bought him out of his field coat pocket.

"Mind if I smoke?" he asked.

"If I can have one too," said Alef.

Kurosaki lit up two cigarettes and passed one forward to Alef in the driver's seat.

The car filled with white smoke as it moved through the rising haze of morning.

Wed, 16 Dec 2020, 19:16 -0800 (2020-12-17T03:16 GMT)
Western Days Hotel

"So, the Earth moved, eh?" Chris said, taking a slice of the pizza that no one else had touched. She looked at the two globes projected on the whiteboard: one was the real Earth, and the other was based on the false signals currently being sent by GPS satellites.

Kazumi's plan was already in motion. All thirty-two of the US

Department of Defense's GPS satellites had been put under the control of NORAD's orbital surveillance team. The satellites visible to the Cloud—eight at most, at any given time—were sending clock and orbital information crafted to mislead the Cloud about its position.

These false signals were leading the forty thousand individual members of the Orbital Cloud to Desnoeufs airspace. Jamshed, having no way of observing the actual space tethers, would be relying on the location data they were sending back, which should still show them on their planned rendezvous route with the orbital hotel.

Chris looked with satisfaction over the mass of information spread out before her—steadily scrolling feeds cast by more than thirty microprojectors on eight whiteboards scrounged from the hotel conference room. A map of the world, a grid of numbers, a 3-D globe, the staff at the Oregon radar site . . . According to Akari, it was easier to just use spare Raspberry Pis to project everything at once than to try to write a program to integrate it all into a single display.

"Now this is an operations center," Chris said, and took a bite of the pizza.

The whiteboard in the middle was relaying video from Orbital Surveillance at NORAD. Lintz was issuing orders rapidly, exercising the leadership skills he had been trained to use in case of nuclear war. Chris doubted he had imagined using those skills for something like this.

On the left, video feeds of the teams carrying out Lintz's orders were scattered across an improvised triptych of three more whiteboards. AWACS aircraft took off one after the other as FA-35s soared from the decks of the Atlantic Fleet. Almost four thousand aircraft from the navy and air force were taking part, chasing the Cloud that flew overhead at Mach 23.

The AWACS aircraft with massive radar arrays on the top of

their fuselages flew above the Cloud in an unorthodox upside-down formation that gave them a clear view of the space tethers, allowing them to confirm that they were proceeding along the expected route. Meanwhile, the FA-35s were using their superior electronic-warfare capabilities to send the Cloud additional spoofed GPS signals. Both ideas had come from Daryl.

Akari watched the FA-35s taking off. "I hope the program I gave them is working all right," she said to Chris.

"I'm sure it is," Chris said. "No need to worry."

The spoofed GPS signals being sent to the Orbital Cloud by the aircraft were generated by a program Kazumi had designed and Akari had implemented in response to a request from NORAD, who had worried that faking the satellite signals alone wouldn't be enough.

"Remember," Chris said to Akari, "strategic responsibility now rests with those guys." She pointed at Lintz, who was currently having his brow mopped by Fisher so that he could keep up the unbroken stream of orders. Fernandez was there, too, rushing to and fro in the background. "We just sit here and wait."

The operation had already moved out of Team Seattle's hands. They were simply watching events unfold; the other teams no longer even asked their opinions.

The only ones still talking busily into their headsets were Daryl and Kazumi. They were dealing with a fire hose of questions about the space tether drive from the theorists at NASA and NORAD.

Chris checked the time stamps visible here and there on the whiteboards and realized that it was time to end the Q&A session. "Bruce, can you pull Daryl and Kazumi out of their meetings?" she asked.

Bruce nonchalantly rose from his post by the door and relieved Daryl of his headset.

"Sorry," Bruce said. "I know this is the fun part, but that's all for today."

He reached out with one long arm and tapped on the keyboard to end the videoconference, then tossed the headset onto the table.

"Showtime," Bruce said to the room. "Can we give this our full attention, everyone?"

Kazumi, whose conversation with NASA had also been ended, looked up at Bruce. "Already?" he asked.

"Yep," Bruce said. "Everything meet with your approval, Kazumi?"

Kazumi looked at the whiteboard, then half-closed his eyes and thought for a minute. He opened his eyes and read some more data, then half-closed his eyes to consider it with what NORAD was already calling his "sixth sense." After repeating this process a few times, he leaned back into his chair.

"Absolutely fine," he said. "Everything is going perfectly. The orbit is a little skewed, but the Cloud is heading for Ozzy's island."

Daryl reached toward the center of the table and turned on the speaker. "Call from Colonel Lintz," he said.

Lintz was beaming and waving from the central whiteboard. "Team Seattle!" came his voice over the speaker. "Just a moment of your time. Everything's A-OK here. We strike the Cloud in ten minutes."

"And we have ringside seats, everyone," Chris said, rising to her feet. She noticed another video feed in the corner of the whiteboard triptych, where someone was waving a sketchbook with LET US IN, TOO! written on it.

"Bruce, add Mr. Cunningham to the call," she said.

"Are you sure?" Bruce asked.

"We're using his radar. Let him in."

"If he doesn't behave, I'm cutting him off," Bruce said, then turned on the sound for Ozzy's feed.

"Talk about ungrateful!" Ozzy shouted, his face red with indignation. He was wearing a tank top. "It's my radar, remember? You know how much that thing costs to run?"

"Our apologies, Mr. Cunningham," said Chris. "We'll reimburse your costs. Is your equipment all in order?"

With a deep sigh, Ozzy fell back heavily into his chair. "It's fine," he said. "I just had Johansson polish the dish."

Daryl shook his head. "Unbelievable," he said. "Mr. Cunningham, if he'd mistimed that, he would have been burned to a crisp. Please be careful. That radar's not designed for civilian use."

"He's *fine*," Ozzy repeated. "How many years do you think we've been using that thing? More to the point, check this out. I treated myself to a new button for the occasion."

He dangled a brand-new tracking ball before the camera, pointing at the button with a fat round finger.

"Is he going to operate the radar?" Chris asked Daryl.

Daryl snorted. "Are you kidding? It's locked to a timer set by the NORAD site in Oregon. He just likes theatrics."

Ozzy was peering at his watch. "You said 7:32, right? Almost time. Let's start the countdown. Eight, seven, six . . ."

Chris cast a hurried glance at the times projected on the whiteboard. There were still almost ten seconds left. Ozzy hadn't synchronized his watch.

"Ozzy!" she said. "You're four seconds off. Three, two, one, go!"

They saw the room Ozzy was in dim for a moment. Johansson and Ozzy looked up at the ceiling.

"Team Seattle," came Lintz's voice through the speaker again. "Oregon reports that they have begun the attack. Our next step is to analyze the AWACS data from overhead and confirm its effect."

"Roger that," Chris said. "Looking forward to hearing from you."

Ozzy leaned in toward the camera. "Hey, Kazumi," he said. "Don't you have any way to see whether it's working or not?"

"We just have to wait for the observation data from NORAD," Kazumi said.

"We can see that from here, Mr. Cunningham," Johansson said. "Kazumi, I will send the video from the optical telescope. It captured the space tethers burning through."

"What?!" Lintz cried. "You can see them?"

A deep-blue gradient appeared on a whiteboard. Against the blue were a few shining horizontal threads.

The Sampson-5 on Desnoeufs Island had fired a full-power twenty-five-kilowatt burst of long-wave radiation, frequency 157 kilohertz and beam narrowed to just 0.2 arc seconds, which had punched through the atmosphere and burned the tethers out. These shining threads were the proof. The Orbital Cloud's fifty-kilometer radius meant that it should have taken seven seconds or so to pass through the target area, but the space tethers went through one full rotation every 0.6 seconds, burning each time they were directly in line with the radar.

In just a few moments, they had all been eliminated.

"We did it!" Daryl said. "We did it! They've all burned through at the same angle! We did it, Kazumi!" He kicked his chair away and jumped to his feet to give Kazumi a hug.

Akari stood too. Kazumi held out his hand to her. She produced a projector from her pocket and placed it on the table.

"We can confirm the interception right away," she said. "Ozzy's radar has switched to observation mode."

She turned on the projector, and a map with Desnoeufs Island at the center appeared on a whiteboard. Most of the map was ocean, but there were a few dots heading east-southeast and north-northwest on it. Akari read the figures that appeared in her lens display.

"The space tether terminal apparatuses were successfully severed," she said. "Those thrown off in the direction of the Cloud's movement are all at the predicted speed of 17.7 kilometers per second. This is cosmic velocity?"

"Yes," Kazumi said. "Yes, it is. That is faster than the third cosmic velocity."

His hand was still extended. Akari seized it and switched to Japanese. "Congratulations, Kazumi," she said. "It really worked."

Kazumi pulled her in for a hug.

Seeing this, Lintz tapped his forehead on-screen. "What's this?" came his voice through the speaker. "You've beaten us to the punch again?"

"Colonel Lintz, I . . ." began Kazumi, but couldn't think of how to continue.

"Oh, it doesn't bother me," Lintz said. "Our job is establishing proof, after all. Sylvester! Tell the AWACS pilots to hurry up. The amateurs are beating us again."

"Come on, Colonel," said Fernandez. "We can't compete with Team Seattle." He poked his head into a corner of the frame. "Looks like they didn't notice our present, though. Everyone gather round!"

"Present?" said Kazumi.

Lintz grinned and pushed his chair back. The NORAD team gathered around him. Kazumi recognized Fisher in the crowd too. Everyone had their hands behind their backs.

"Congratulations on a successful interception!" the group shouted together. They produced red-and-white Santa hats from behind their backs and put them on their heads.

"Merry Christmas!" said Lintz. "It's one week early, but we have a present for you, Team Seattle. We're sure you'll like it. Especially Kazumi. Well done—and make sure you use it for Meteor News."

"What are you talking about?" asked Kazumi.

"It'll be obvious soon enough," said Lintz. "Answer me this: Where will the terminal apparatuses that fall into the atmosphere go?"

"They will turn into shooting stars somewhere," Kazumi said. "Wait a minute . . ."

He looked at the map of Desnoeufs Island that Akari had projected. Then he closed his eyes halfway. The apparatuses that had lost orbital velocity would head back the way they had come—north-northwest—at three kilometers per second, losing altitude as they went. As they exited African airspace and passed over Europe, their altitude would be about 200 kilometers. They would graze Greenland's airspace at 150 kilometers. Then, on the map, their course would flip around to take them southwards, down over North America. Through Canadian airspace, and then . . .

They would be quite a bit farther north than the orbit he had worked out a few hours earlier.

"Over the Rocky Mountains," Kazumi said finally, "and then Seattle. Here."

Akari looked at him wide-eyed.

Lintz coughed. "This is NORAD's present to Team Seattle. The blizzard's cleared up, too. It'll be a once-in-a-century cosmic show."

"I never thought I would see such a thing," Kazumi said. "I must update Meteor News."

Daryl threw his hands up, balled into fists. "Awesome!" he cried.

Akari leaped to her feet, finally realizing what Kazumi was talking about. "Really?" she cried. "Really?!"

The room filled with the sounds of celebration. Chris hugged each of the three young people in turn.

"Report from AWACS in the field," said Fernandez from the
NORAD monitor. "Thirty-eight thousand pairs confirmed shot down."

The space tethers had been cleared from orbit. The video from
the various operations centers projected on the whiteboard showed
team members hugging and congratulating each other.

Bruce alone stood unmoved by the festive mood. He was watching a single surveillance feed projected onto one corner of the whiteboard. No one noticed him produce the pistol from his ankle holster.

She was too late.

The sounds of celebration coming from within the hotel room
she was standing outside were proof. She had failed. Her utility to her
employers had dropped to zero.

Her final mission had been to make contact with US authorities,
provide them with all the information she had about Shiraishi, and
launch a joint operation to clear the space tethers from orbit.

The Chinese government was behind this change in direction,
having brought pressure to bear on North Korea when they realized that Tiangong-2 was in the Cloud's sights. Call off your orbital
weapon, right now, or prepare to face the consequences—that had
been the gist. But losing Shiraishi had left North Korea without any
way to stop the space tethers.

And so Chance had received her new orders. She had doubted
that the US would be interested in the offer; it was a little too
convenient.

But it was all moot now.

Chance looked down at her hotel uniform, which bulged oddly
from the explosives she had strapped to her body. She wobbled off-
balance and felt a wetness at her ankle. Bruce's M5 had blown most

of her calf away at the pier. She had bound the wound with tape, but the bleeding hadn't stopped completely.

Enduring the pain, she had followed for a while the tracking device that she had previously attached to Shiraishi's blueprint case, but somewhere around the Space Needle the signal had dropped out. Unable to detect anything resembling the electromagnetic signature of an anti–space tether base of operations, she had finally identified and infiltrated the hotel only after spotting Akari's bicycle in its parking lot.

The tacky feel of the blood in her pumps crawled over her whole body. This was an illusion, she knew. Her senses were off-kilter from the combination of morphine and amphetamines she had self-administered to kill the pain without dulling her edge.

She shook the sensation off and listened closely to the cheerful voices from within the room. There was no question about it: The space tethers had been eliminated. It was time to leave.

Chance was just turning away when the door opened slightly.

She drew her pistol and tried to spin back toward the hotel room, but her wounded calf shrieked. Losing her balance again, she fell forward and hit the door with her right hand, still holding her weapon.

Hanging her head, she realized that a man down on one knee was looking through the crack at her with a Walther PPS aimed directly between her eyes.

"Freeze," he said.

Bruce surveyed the unnatural bulges under the woman's hotel uniform and tutted to himself. No doubt she'd rigged herself to blow if he shot her.

"Slowly put your weapon on the floor," he said. "Never forgetting that, personally, I'd rather just shoot you right now."

He watched her slowly sink into a crouch, favoring one leg. Yes, this was the woman who'd killed Shiraishi and Nash.

Bruce kept his gun trained between her eyes as she moved, noticing also the unusual outline of her pistol. It appeared to be a SIG, but it had been remodeled almost beyond recognition.

"Open your hands and put them above your head," Bruce said. "Step back slowly."

The woman complied, moving backwards until she was standing before the elevator doors.

"Fingers filed off, I see," Bruce said. "Was it the Syrian secret police?"

The woman shook her head with the minimum necessary movement. It didn't look like a denial, though, or a confirmation. Bruce recalled the gruesome torture that one of the CIA's agents had endured in Syria. This woman had been another victim.

"So you're a contractor," Bruce said. "Let me guess. You've come here to salvage the situation by offering information. Pressure from China, perhaps?"

"If you let me go," the woman said, "I'll give you the full logs of Shiraishi's communications from Seattle. Everything you need to know to make your own space tethers."

"Usually," Bruce said, "I'd point out that I could kill you and take them for myself if I wanted them, but I'd rather avoid an explosion today. So, you've got yourself a deal."

The woman asked for permission to reach inside her jacket, and Bruce granted it. She produced a large smartphone and placed it on the floor. Bruce heard a new round of cheers in the room behind him.

He approached the woman and, very carefully, reached out with one hand to call the elevator.

"Sounds like a party in there," the woman said.

"We had some surprise good news," Bruce said. "Make sure you watch the skies tonight."

The woman listened closely to the sounds of celebration, closing her eyes with a sigh.

"What is it?" Bruce asked.

"He didn't have anyone to celebrate with like that," the woman said.

"'He' . . . ? Ah, Shiraishi. I'm not surprised to hear that. But his legacy will live on. Akari recovered some materials about some Great Leap or something. Kazumi and the others are going to carry on his work."

"Really?"

The elevator doors opened with a ding. Bruce gestured with his gun, urging the woman inside. She slowly stepped backwards through the doors.

"Any messages?" Bruce asked. "Kazumi, Akari—I can pass something on to either of them."

"Just one, then," the woman replied. "Tell Akari I was starting to fall for Shiraishi."

Bruce's gun quivered.

"Idiot," he said. "You think Akari needs to hear that?" he said.

The elevator doors quietly closed.

Wed, 16 Dec 2020, 19:58 -0800 (2020-12-11T03:58 GMT)
Pike Street, Seattle

At his back, Kazumi felt the chill from the aluminum chair he had just wiped the snow from. Not even the down jacket Sekiguchi had bought him in Tokyo could keep this cold out completely. Huddled in a blanket beside him was Akari, holding Shiraishi's blueprint case close to her chest.

"Two lattes, right?" asked Bruce, appearing before them tightly wrapped in a supple leather coat holding two enormous cups. They were a seasonal red and green and looked like they held at least half a quart each.

"Surprised?" Bruce said. "Everything's big in America. Be careful you don't put on a few pounds yourself."

"Watch yourself, Bruce," said Chris, who was sitting on Akari's other side. "If Kazumi and Akari turn anti-American, I'll cite you for aiding and abetting the enemy." Under her letterman jacket, she wore a blue flower-print dress, and under that were tracksuit pants and sneakers—a casual look that Kazumi had not expected after all those suits she had worn running meetings for Team Seattle.

"Oh, come on," Bruce said. "I'm only telling them the truth."

"He's right, though," said Daryl, who was sitting beside Kazumi. He clapped his hands. "Even us soldiers put on weight if we aren't careful. Just look at Colonel Lintz."

"A toast," Bruce said, standing before the table with a cup in one hand and his arms spread wide. "To our first gathering at Starbucks store number one!"

Kazumi and Akari turned in their seats to look at the sign outside. It was the same green as any other Starbucks, but the logo was completely different: the STARBUCKS was in slightly awkward-looking block letters, and there was a picture of a mermaid that looked like a faded stamp. The history was palpable.

"It's quite a small place," Akari said, turning up the collar of her down jacket.

"Every business has to start somewhere," came Ozzy's voice

through the tablet on Daryl's table. They'd told him there was no way he'd be able to see the show through the tablet's camera, but he'd insisted on joining the viewing party anyway. "Could someone stand this thing up?" he said. "I can't see any of your faces."

With a rueful grin, Daryl opened the tablet's stand and set up the tablet in landscape orientation on the table. Morning light came through the tiny screen. Ozzy was still in his tank top, but he now had a corked bottle in each hand and was shaking both.

"That you, Daryl?" asked Ozzy. "A little to the right. Yeah, that's it."

"For heaven's sake!" they heard Johansson say off camera. "It is nighttime in Seattle. Try to keep your voice down."

"Ah, cram it," Ozzy said. "Hey, Kazumi, did you read Judy's blog?"

"Huh?" Kazumi said. "Has a new entry been posted?"

Akari handed him a phone with the blog already on-screen. Chris picked up her tablet too.

Bruce walked around the table to look over Chris's shoulder as she read. He whistled. "This is big," he said. "What kind of readership does this blog have?"

"The pageview count is probably a secret," Daryl said.

"Based on the advertising," Akari said, "I would estimate twenty million views per entry. It's been increasing since she left Earth."

Bruce grabbed Chris's tablet and jabbed at the lower half of the article with his finger. "Look at this," he said. "Right there in plain type. Kazumi, are the Meteor News servers ready for this? Millions of people are going to drop by. It'll be your very own miniature DOS attack."

"Do not underestimate Meteor News," Kazumi said, recalling the round-robin server system Akari had put in place before they had left Japan. "Our engineer is the best in the business."

Akari produced her lens display from her pocket and hit the switch. Text began to scroll across the orange glass. "Currently at four million visitors or so," she said. "No problem. Meteor News can handle pageviews in the billions."

"Very impressive," said Chris. "Bruce, give that back." She reached out to grab the tablet back from Bruce, revealing the Mariners logo embroidered on her sleeve. "It's almost time, everyone," she said. "Are you ready?" She folded her arms and looked up at the sky.

"Which direction will they come from, Kazumi?" asked Bruce.

"From behind . . . Let me check."

Kazumi half-closed his eyes and imagined the terminal apparatuses falling into the atmosphere. They wouldn't be bright enough at this stage to be visible to the naked eye. Moving at three kilometers per second, they would skip across the surface of the atmosphere like flat stones on a pond, slowing as they cleared the Rocky Mountains.

They would start to give off light just over the western seaboard: Seattle. NORAD had done an elegant job.

Kazumi held his index finger above his head and let it fall slightly to the right. "This way," he said.

"This is the life," said Bruce. "Watching a once-in-a-century cosmic light show with the world's leading expert on the topic. I'll treasure this memory till I die. Secretly, of course."

"No need for secrecy," Chris said, putting her reading glasses away. "Team Seattle's about to become public knowledge."

"What do you mean?"

"The whole world's going to know what Kazumi and the others did," Chris said. She counted the details off on her fingers. "An announcement from the CIA, dinner with the president, press conferences, television appearances . . . Kazumi and Akari won't be able to go back to Japan for at least a month."

Shiraishi's and Jamshed's personal information and Sekiguchi's illegal activities would be kept quiet, she explained, but the member of the coast guard whose involvement in the affair had ended in tragedy would receive the honor he deserved for his contribution.

"And all because of Ronnie," she concluded. "No—*thanks* to Ronnie. You should hear the things he was saying. 'We cannot start tether-based space development on a fair footing unless we acknowledge those who faced terrorism and orbital sabotage head-on.' He and Judy started lobbying for it yesterday, apparently."

"Yesterday? You mean before that videoconference?"

Kazumi finally realized just how serious Ronnie and Judy were about this. They had performed the space tether dance for him half-expecting to die in orbit anyway. But rather than despair, they had already begun their new investment in the future.

"I hear the two of them are going to found a space tether–related company," Chris said. "Fully funded by Ronnie personally."

"Wait, wait, wait, that's not right," Ozzy said. "I'm in for 50 percent myself. I can tell you one thing—Judy's obsessed with the idea. Won't shut up about it. I've been tasked with handling company registration and the rest, and she wants it all up and running by the end of the year."

"But that's less than two weeks away," Chris said. "Won't that be impossible?"

"Don't underestimate a free entrepreneur, you government bureaucrat," Ozzy said. "Hey, it went dark! Daryl! Check the camera, would you?"

"It's just the lights going off, Mr. Cunningham," said Daryl. He was right: the lights were going off all over town. Everyone who read Judy's blog was switching theirs off. Even the Starbucks baristas dimmed the lights and came outside too.

"Daryl," Ozzy said. "Or Kazumi. Whoever. Turn me to the right a bit. Yeah, that's it. Now hold that angle."

"Mr. Cunningham, I want to watch too," said Kazumi. "I am going to put you d—"

A flash of light streaked by in the corner of his eye.

He looked up.

The air was clean and crisp after the blizzard, and the sky was cloudless. Smeared across the stars, Kazumi saw a smoky meteor train: the lingering afterglow of a shooting star.

"I can't see!" Ozzy complained.

Kazumi turned the tablet's volume down.

The second shooting star cut through the starry night. The angle was just as Kazumi had predicted.

The terminal apparatuses were finally falling into the atmosphere, leaving long trails of plasma behind them. Perhaps because of the rare metals in their electronics, the shooting stars had a slight green tinge to them.

Three. Four. Ten. Within moments there were too many to count. Shooting stars filled the night sky.

"—mi. Kazumi! You don't have to answer now, but listen to me."

Ozzy's muffled voice cut into Kazumi's awareness.

"Will you come join the space tether company Ronnie and I are going to start? We want Akari and Daryl too. A new company needs a world-class team. We'll launch our own space tethers by this time next year. What do you say? You wanna come fly with us?"

Kazumi looked down at the tablet. At that moment a particularly large shooting star lit up the table, making the phrase written in marker on Shiraishi's case glow:

GREAT LEAP FOR THE REST OF THE WORLD

"Okay, Ozzy," Kazumi said. "Count me in."

"All right! There's one more thing we have to decide: the name of the company. We need to pick something right away."

"Call it 'Great Leap,'" said Kazumi. "Let's talk again later." He turned the tablet facedown.

There was no turning back now. The plans Shiraishi had left behind would become a reality.

"Good," Akari whispered in Japanese.

"What is?" Kazumi said.

"Just before he died, Uncle Ageha said something to me," Akari said, looking down. "I couldn't hear him properly, so I'm not quite sure . . ."

She took Kazumi's hand in her own. Her fingernails were orange once more, reflecting the shooting stars above in their silky sheen.

"But I think he said, 'Tell Kazumi I leave the future of the space tether drive in his hands,'" she finished.

Daryl clapped Kazumi on the back. "What are you doing, Kazumi?" he asked. "The meteor shower's almost over. Look at the sky!"

Kazumi raised his head and proudly watched the shooting stars fly by. There were more than anyone could keep track of now.

Shouts of joy echoed around the town. Every meteor that sliced through the sky was bright enough to cast shadows on the snow-covered streets of Seattle.

2020-12-17T04:30 GMT

Project Wyvern

Sorry to keep you waiting, everybody. Project Wyvern has received a report from NASA that all the problems faced by the orbital hotel during tour number zero have been resolved. We can finally make our way to the International Space Station.

Yesterday, we learned the truth about the Rod from God that had the whole world on edge. An overactive imagination and a few early missteps snowballed into a much bigger problem. It pains me to report that in the course of resolving it all, two people's lives were lost, while a third has gone into hiding—although not before providing some crucial information, for which they have our thanks.

Once I'm able to go into more detail about the incident, I assure you that I will. There were people Earthside who gave their all for our sake, and I feel a responsibility to introduce them to the world. It'll be my top priority once I'm back on solid ground—which sounds very appealing right now . . .

Ugh, formal writing is so lifeless, isn't it? I'm going to switch back to my normal mode.

So—surprise announcement!

People on the west coast of the US: please look up at the sky at 8:08 p.m. tonight. Turn off all your lights first, if you can. And spread the word. Just

go ahead and switch off your neighbors' lights—I
promise they'll thank you when 8:08 rolls around!

What you'll see is a meteor shower.

But not just any meteor shower. Tens of thousands of
shooting stars filling the night sky for ten whole
minutes. The sort of celestial show that comes once
in a century.

You can find the details on Meteor News, a shooting
star forecast site run by Mr. Kazumi Kimura from
Japan—the man who saved our lives. The site's a bit
technical, but just click on the link on the home
page that reads "18/12/2020: Meteor shower" and
you'll find what you need.

We'll be making a slight detour from our rendezvous
orbit with the ISS to watch the meteor shower too.
So when you're looking up at those shooting stars,
make sure you wave to us! We'll be in the sky with
them, looking down from 360 kilometers away.

Judy Smark, Shooting Star

EPILOGUE

December 25, 2022
Western Days Hotel, Seattle

The reception for the unveiling of the Great Leap project was being held in the main hall of the Western Days Hotel. The hubbub had settled for a moment. The unbridled flashing of cameras directed at the two life-size models of the exploration satellites headed for Jupiter and the sun that hung from the ceiling had ceased, the organizers had stopped milling about schmoozing, and everyone was watching the stage.

Judy Smark, wearing a maternity dress over her seven-month-pregnant belly, announced the appearance of Ronnie Smark to the stage. In response, Ronnie stepped up to the podium from front and center holding a champagne glass.

Backstage in the wings, Kazumi stared at Ronnie in his white tuxedo as Akari and Daryl whispered to each other about how poorly it suited him. Kazumi couldn't help but agree. Ronnie's facial hair, from his sideburns to his beard, was unkempt; an unruly bunch of hair sprung up at the back of his head.

Kazumi couldn't blame him for his less-than-sterling appearance. Until just yesterday, Ronnie had been with Kazumi and their team heading up the final adjustments to the probe that would be launched from the site at Cape Canaveral. The preparations and launch had taken three whole days, depriving all those involved of the time and focus required for personal grooming. Without thinking, Kazumi touched his own head.

"Thank you, everyone," said Ronnie. The flash of cameras diminished as quiet fell over the hall. "Allow me to introduce our latest spacecraft, launched from Loki 10 just yesterday."

Behind him a screen displayed the space tether blueprint that they had checked over ad nauseam. The sound of keyboards clicking away came from the press-section seats.

"This is the space tether, a spacecraft that can remain in orbit almost indefinitely without propellant. The concept of tether propulsion has been known for some time, but we've built space tethers that incorporate a variety of revolutionary new ideas."

Looking at the quizzical expressions on the faces of the journalists as they held out their recorders, Kazumi imagined the barrage of questions that would soon be directed at him and tried to think where he might hide.

"This space tether was conceived by—" Ronnie stopped, looked right to Kazumi waiting backstage, and met his gaze. Kazumi nodded. "An Iranian astronautical researcher. And the framework to realize this design was developed by a Japanese engineer. Unfortunately, neither of them are here. They are not employees of Great Leap."

The hand of a journalist went up. "Are you referring to the terrorists responsible for the Rod from God incident?"

Kazumi supposed that the journalist must have read *Challengers*, Judy's book about the incident two years earlier. She had written it after getting the American government to disclose the information it was based on with unusual speed. The book explained that an Iranian had created the original design for the space tether crafts that had attacked the orbital hotel, though it had been a Japanese man who had actually developed and operated them dangerously in orbit.

Only the Japanese government had suffered significant damage from the series of events that had followed and, shielding itself with state-secrets protection laws, had declined to make public the loss of the IGS. Perhaps discouraged by this concealment of publicly known facts, there was no Japanese translation of *Challengers*, despite the fact that it had sold over ten million copies worldwide. However, after the publication of Judy's book, CNN had conducted a follow-up investigation and revealed in a documentary that the Rod from God had been under the control of a former JAXA employee named Ageha Shiraishi.

Ronnie had been asked numerous times about the connection between all this and the spacecraft with the same name being developed by Great Leap but had so far refused to comment.

"That is correct," he said now. "The two men behind the space tethers that attacked us."

A stir moved through the hall. The individuals whose ideas had formed the basis for the project, it seemed, had not just been outside the project itself, but were now considered terrorists.

Grinning shamelessly, Ronnie waited for the commotion to settle. "It is for this reason that we have not patented the space tether. If other companies wish to use the same idea, we welcome the competition. To put it another way, 'bring it on!'"

Ronnie put up his middle finger. Judy put her face in her hands. Akari brought her glass up in front of Kazumi, and Daryl followed suit. Kazumi shifted slightly to make space for where Jamshed and Shiraishi ought to be standing.

Many engineers from North Korea were taking part in the Great

Leap, but no one had heard any news of Jamshed. Chris had spent the past two years headhunting astronautical engineers in countries such as Iran and North Korea at the request of Ronnie and the American government, and her best guess was that he was under house arrest in Pyongyang. The three of them tilted their glasses and raised a silent toast.

"Can I get in on that?" A fourth champagne glass flew in through the gap Kazumi had left open. A man with an easygoing smile on his smooth-skinned face had taken the spot intended for Shiraishi.

"Wang, you made it!" said Kazumi.

"And, boy, did I have a time hard time of it. Why didn't you put the company in Cape Canaveral? I had to cross the continent three times this week alone."

The three of them were already used to his new name, Wang Jinming. With his previously long hair trimmed short, his body built up two sizes bigger, and his nose subtly reshaped, Sekiguchi looked completely different. Under the Witness Protection Program, he had obtained a new identity as a Chinese American and passed the Great Leap's recruitment exam that selected from among the have-nots, despite Chris's opposition and fierce competition that saw only one candidate in hundreds accepted. He had also hooked up with Judy and was so active in the company that he was known internally as "Ronnie's Third Arm."

Wang gestured at the ceiling with his glass. "Those Ageha models are slick."

The other three looked up. Hanging there were life-size models of two spacecraft linked by thin tethers, the Jupiter probe *Ageha 1* and the solar probe *Ageha 2*.

Ronnie's talk began to touch on the Agehas. "At this time, the two Ageha probes waiting to depart at an orbital altitude of 500 km will be inserted into a Hohmann orbit using the space tether auto-swing-by projection system."

Ronnie pointed at the models on the ceiling and pantomimed a hammer throw as he began to explain the orbital insertion of planetary probes using space tethers.

"The tether that connects the two Agehas is 70 km long. It is most definitely the largest moving device humankind has ever made. The tethers complete one rotation in thirty seconds, making the Agehas attached to both ends revolve at a velocity of 7.3 km per second. Release them with the appropriate timing and you produce an acceleration inconceivable with any rocket to date. This auto-swing-by projection model was theorized by Kazumi Kimura, one of the Great Leap's executive officers. Another round of applause, please, for Kazumi."

Hearing his name called, Kazumi raised his glass in response to the applause and camera flashes.

"Kazumi will break down the details in a *very* clear presentation later, so look forward to that. For now I'd like to introduce our new space tether. Space industry professionals are already aware of this, but actually we already have ten thousand space tethers in orbit."

Another stir went through the audience at this previously unreported information.

"However, the images I'm about to show you have probably never been seen by anyone. Hit the display!"

Ronnie spread his arms. A high-definition real-time video feed of the Earth appeared on the screen behind him. Sunlight angling downwards lit up the clouds. The shadows they cast were changing from moment to moment. The reddish clouds turned purple as they ran toward the pitch-black night side of the Earth. There, they were lit by flashes of lightning. The thin veil of atmosphere wrapped around the planet changed from blue to red and then to purple. This was a video of the living Earth.

Enthusiastic applause came from the audience, their breath taken away.

"Until now," Ronnie said, "we were unable to view a real-time image of the Earth in such pronounced 3-D. This too was made possible by the low-cost space tether craft that are able to orbit indefinitely—what, Judy?"

With her cheeks puffed up indignantly, Judy was pointing at her wristwatch.

"Oh, right. I almost forgot. Time to release the Agehas."

Judy gave the signal and stage staff dashed out hurriedly and began to rearrange the room. A spotlight shone on the ceiling models. This all unfolded in front of the astonishingly vivid image of the Earth.

Akari came over to Kazumi. "This reminds me of the last time we were here."

"Yeah." Kazumi remembered watching the video of the Earth sent by the space tethers for the first time two years ago in the penthouse suite directly above the hall. Though he had seen it many times since, he still felt as though he might get sucked inside the image on the enormous screen. He thought of the man who had come up with it. "Shiraishi-san saw this too, right?"

"I checked the logs the agent from the North brought. Apparently, Uncle Ageha only watched this image once, for about two hours."

"Just once? What a waste."

"Yes. It's so beautiful—hey, is that them?"

In the dark sky, two dots approached, receded, then approached again. They were moving in a circle. Half-closing his eyes, Kazumi raised his champagne glass so that it overlapped with the Earth and calculated the location of the two celestial bodies. At the bottom he could see the continent of Africa. Moving in the direction of the equator, the camera was accurately— "There's no mistake. The one that just moved right is *Ageha 1*, and to the left is *Ageha 2*."

The two devices bearing Shiraishi's name were embarking on a long journey. *Ageha 2* would head for the sun and deploy another space tether sunwards of Mercury. Rotating along a precisely circular orbit corrected by Lorentz force–generated electrical power that would never run out, that tether would become Space Lighthouse Number One, transmitting a precise clock almost indefinitely.

Ageha 1 would deploy a massive one hundred kilometer–long tether near Jupiter, the largest planet in the solar system with a magnetic field twenty thousand times that of Earth. With powerful thrust derived from this mighty energy source, it would descend into the upper region of the atmosphere and extract helium-3. Four years later, it would detach from its tether and make a beeline for Earth. That was when the next Ageha helium-extraction craft would head for Jupiter. Signposts for these missions would be provided by *Ageha 2* and successor craft inserted later to serve as space lighthouses, together forming a solar positioning system. Essentially, they were creating a mill wheel that directly scooped up fuel from Jupiter for nuclear fusion: a foothold for the cosmos. The crafts would traverse space with the accurate positional information obtained from the space lighthouses and establish a space tether interplanetary rapid transit system to carry helium-3. This would provide an endless supply of energy, allowing humankind to reach new celestial bodies and secure a habitat in orbit. That had been Shiraishi's plan.

Ronnie called loudly from the stage for a toast. The sound of glasses striking each other spread through the event hall of the hotel like ripples on water.

The cable connecting the two Agehas detached. The two points flew away from each other at unbelievable speed. The spacecraft envisioned by the two men who had dreamt of space shook off Earth's gravity and flew into the void.

Listening to happy sounds of celebration, Kazumi and Akari watched the points receding from Earth.

About the Author

Taiyo Fujii was born on Amami Oshima Island—that is, between Kyushu and Okinawa. He worked in stage design, desktop publishing, exhibition graphic design, and software development.

In 2012, Fujii self-published *Gene Mapper* serially in a digital format of his own design. The novel was Amazon.co.jp's number one Kindle best seller of the year. The novel was revised and republished in both print and digital as *Gene Mapper–full build–* by Hayakawa Publishing in 2013 and was nominated for the Japan SF Award and Seiun Award. His second novel, *Orbital Cloud*, won the 2014 Nihon SF Taisho Award, the Seiun Award, and took first prize in the "Best SF of 2014" in *SF Magazine.* His recent works include *Underground Market* and *Bigdata Connect.*

GENE MAPPER

TAIYO FUJII

"The new face of Japanese sci-fi"—*The Japan Times*

"*Gene Mapper* is entertaining, thought-provoking, and funky"—*SF Signal*

In a future where reality has been augmented and biology itself has been hacked, the world's food supply is genetically modified, superior, and vulnerable. When gene mapper Hayashida discovers that his custom rice plant has experienced a dysgenic collapse, he suspects sabotage. Hayashida travels across Asia to find himself in Ho Chi Minh City with hired-gun hacker Yagodo at his side—and in mortal danger—as he pushes ever nearer to the heart of the mystery.

SRP:$14.99 USA / $16.99 CAN / £9.99 UK   ISBN:978-1-4215-8027-2

HAIKASORU
THE FUTURE IS JAPANESE

ROCKET GIRLS—HOUSUKE NOJIRI

Yukari Morita is a high school girl on a quest to find her missing father. While searching for him in the Solomon Islands, she receives the offer of a lifetime—she'll get the help she needs to find her father, and all she need do in return is become the world's youngest, lightest astronaut. Yukari and her sister Matsuri, both petite, are the perfect crew for the Solomon Space Association's launches, or will be once they complete their rigorous and sometimes dangerous training.

THE OUROBOROS WAVE—JYOUJI HAYASHI

Ninety years from now, a satellite detects a nearby black hole scientists dub Kali for the Hindu goddess of destruction. Humanity embarks on a generations-long project to tap the energy of the black hole and establish colonies on planets across the solar system. Earth and Mars and the moons Europa (Jupiter) and Titania (Uranus) develop radically different societies, with only Kali, that swirling vortex of destruction and creation, and the hated but crucial Artificial Accretion Disk Development association (AADD) in common.

SAIENSU FIKUSHON 2016—EDITED BY HAIKASORU

Three new stories from three of the best science fiction writers in Japan:

"Overdrive" by Toe EnJoe—How fast is the speed of thought?

"Sea Fingers" by TOBI Hirotaka—A small enclave survives after the Deep has consumed the world, but what does the Deep hunger for now?

"A Fair War" by Taiyo Fujii—The future of war, the age of drones, but what comes next?

Saiensu Fikushon is Haikasoru's new e-first mini anthology, dedicated to bringing you the narrative software of tomorrow, today. Now more than ever, the future is Japanese!

WWW.HAIKASORU.COM